INFERNO

INFERNO

DANTE ALIGHIERI

TRANSLATED INTO ENGLISH VERSE,
WITH NOTES AND AN INTRODUCTION BY

Elio Zappulla

ILLUSTRATED BY THE PAINTINGS OF

Gregory Gillespie

VINTAGE CLASSICS

VINTAGE BOOKS · A DIVISION OF RANDOM HOUSE, INC. · NEW YORK

FIRST VINTAGE CLASSICS EDITION, OCTOBER 1999

The Library of Congress has cataloged the Pantheon edition as follows:
Dante Alighieri, 1265–1321.
[Inferno. English]
Inferno / Dante Alighieri ; translated into English verse,
with notes and introduction by Elio Zappulla.
p.   cm.
Includes bibliographical references.
ISBN 0-679-44280-4
I. Zappulla, Elio.   II. Title.
PQ4315.2.Z37   1998
851′.1—dc21   97-37482
CIP

Vintage ISBN: 0-679-75708-2

www.vintagebooks.com

Book design by Suvi Asch

Printed in the United States of America
10 9 8 7 6 5 4

This translation is dedicated
to the memory of
my father,
Giuseppe Zappulla
(1901–1977)

E l'altro sonno aspetto: o fine o volo
che l'anima anela conduca
verso la luce.

—G. ZAPPULLA
(from "Stanchezza")

CONTENTS

PREFACE

ix

ACKNOWLEDGMENTS

xiii

INTRODUCTION

3

THE INFERNO OF DANTE ALIGHIERI

19

SELECT BIBLIOGRAPHY

309

LIST OF PAINTINGS

313

PREFACE

In view of the quantity of English translations of the *Inferno* already in existence, many will ask what possible excuse there can be for yet another. One answer, quite simply, is that, since no one who attempts to render the complex simplicity of Dante's Italian into English (or into any other language) will succeed in capturing much more than the atmosphere of the poem, though each translation will undoubtedly have its unique virtues, the challenge to create a version that pleases the palate and yet nourishes is ever present. Accepting the challenge, I have aimed at creating a clear, readable English version of Dante's epic that nevertheless retains some of the poetry of the original. Whether or not I have achieved my purpose will be for the reader to judge, of course. Another possible answer is more speculative: perhaps at the heart of the permanent, restless imperative to render Dante into accessible, contemporary speech is the impulse to recover for the present the fusion of the lyrical with the epic within an unforced vernacular that once can be said to have established Western literature's claims to authority and underwritten literature's assertion of a psychologically convincing universalist ethos. Every new translation, then, in effect registers the distance we have traveled from that fusion and measures it differently.

I have chosen to render the *Inferno* into blank verse—iambic pentameter unrhymed—the form that seems most congenial to poetry of a high order in the English language: Milton chose iambics for *Paradise Lost;* Wordsworth, for his *Prelude;* and Shakespeare, for nearly all his plays. Its long and distinguished tradition in our language, its broad and noble sweep, its approximate equivalency to Dante's hendecasyllabic line make it the logical choice.

A well-known Italian saw pithily pronounces: *Traduttore, traditore* ["Translator, traitor"]. The present version of *Inferno* may not be as loyal to the original as purists would prefer, but I hardly think it is traitorous, for my intention has been to remain faithful to the spirit of Dante's poem while eschewing an insipid and fatal literalness. That intention has sometimes led me to alter, insert, or (rarely) omit a word or phrase in order to clarify some obscure idea for modern readers or make some knotty point resonate more vibrantly with them, without committing *lèse-majesté*. My hope is that I will have done a small service to those readers who may find Dante more accessible in this version, its many failings notwithstanding.

By contrast with many other writers, whose works often present the reader with linguistic hurdles that must be cleared before comprehension can set in, Dante usually employs a language of striking limpidity and immediate comprehensibility. His style in the *Commedia* frequently approaches the conversational, as if he wishes to engage the reader in intimate dialogue. True, his vocabulary is wide-ranging: often we are greeted with some abstruse term from moral philosophy or theology; nevertheless, the vast majority of his words are common ones. His similes, for example, are usually grounded in easily understood language:

> *Like one who's rescued from the angry waves,*
> *Then, breathless, stands ashore to stare in awe*
> *And terror at the cruel sea, my soul,*
> *Still fugitive, turned back to scan the wood*
> *That none before had ever left alive.*
>
> (INFERNO I:22–26)

Or:

> *Like cranes who chant their cries across the sky*
> *In never-ending lines, so did they seem*
> *Who wailed in winds that bore them darkly on.*
>
> (INFERNO V:40–42)

Nor is he averse to using vulgar words with which everyone would be familiar (and which would have been less shocking to Dante's contemporaries than to later, more Puritanical, ears), *e.g., merda* ["shit"] or *puttana* ["whore"]. What difficulties do arise, for the modern Italian reader, involve changes that have occurred in the Italian language over the centuries. For his contemporaries, however, the meanings of Dante's words were, for the most part, readily grasped. To be sure, not all of the *Commedia* was intended for Everyman, but the bare narrative and the emotions it conveys, though perhaps not its theological, anagogical, or allegorical elements, were not difficult to follow. In an English version of Dante, therefore, it would seem wise to shun an excessively academic vocabulary—except here and there when doing so appears to be unavoidable—and to employ more ordinary words as often as possible if the reader is to have some sense of the impact of the *Commedia* on fourteenth-century readers. In my translation, therefore, I have tried to avoid the overuse of learned words, although there were more than a few instances, of course, when only a more learned or more scholarly word seemed the appropriate, if not the inevitable, choice.

The paintings by the contemporary artist Gregory Gillespie included in this translation powerfully complement Dante's words. They possess an analogous, unblinking, even shocking, intensity of attention to the observed world; at the same time, they record a profound, recognizably related, modern-day allegorical engagement with the visionary.

This translation has clearly benefited from the fine work of previous translators, each of whom undoubtedly journeyed through his or her own Purgatory in the struggle to squeeze the magnificent tercets of Dante into a pair of English shoes. Of particular help to me as I wrestled to pin down the right word were the poetic versions of John Ciardi and Dorothy L. Sayers; the very accurate prose translations by John Sinclair and Charles D. Singleton; the precise nineteenth-century iambic rendering by Henry Wadsworth Longfellow; and the indispensable century-old literal translation by William Warren Vernon. The fine notes in those editions were also very useful to my own attempt to annotate each canto. The very greatest assistance, both for the translation and the notes, was provided by the densely annotated editions of the *Commedia* prepared by Italian scholars: Enrico Bianchi, Ernesto Bignami, Natalino Sapegno, G. A. Scartazzini, Pietro Vetro, and others: anyone who seriously studies Dante cannot ignore the work of the Italians. Useful, too, though dated in so many ways, were the classic editions of Dante by Carlyle-Okey-Wicksteed and Charles H. Grandgent. The *Enciclopedia Dantesca* and Paget Toynbee's *Dictionary of Proper Names and Notable Matters in the Works of Dante* were indispensable. Other books were of significant assistance to me; at the end of this volume, I have listed a Select Bibliography of works that may be helpful to anyone wishing to delve more deeply into the life, the era, and the works of the great Florentine.

ELIO ZAPPULLA
Stony Brook, New York
March 1997

ACKNOWLEDGMENTS

Although I must live with the fear that I may inadvertently omit some names, I want to express my thanks to a number of people. First among them is Peter Dimock, my editor at Pantheon Books, who had faith in the translation from the very beginning. I shall not forget his unshakable confidence in me or his many excellent suggestions, welling up from an extraordinary intellect, for improving my original manuscript.

I am indebted to several colleagues at Dowling College who read portions of the early cantos and encouraged me from the very outset: Professors Miriam Baker, Andrew Karp, Stephen Lamia, Susan Rosenstreich, James O. Tate, and William Thierfelder. Dr. Frank Littlefield, an historian with an encyclopedic knowledge of history, read an early draft of my Introduction and made helpful suggestions for changes.

I owe a special debt to an extraordinary human being, my late colleague at Dowling, Aaron Kramer. One of our fine American poets, possessed of an infallible ear and exquisite taste, Aaron scrutinized two of my early cantos and, while always encouraging me, pointed out, ever so gently, a number of limping lines and infelicitous phrasings. I am profoundly grateful to him for sharpening my sometimes blurred vision and fine-tuning my occasionally dull ear. Like all who knew Aaron, I will miss, above all, his decency and his humanity.

I am obliged to Dowling's President Victor P. Meskill, to Provost Albert E. Donor, to Dean James E. Caraway, and to the members of the Committee on Long Range Planning and Development of Dowling for grants of released time to work on this project and for other assistance and encouragement. The library staff at Dowling were often helpful in obtaining materials for me.

To Wallace Fowlie, one of America's great teachers and an old friend and colleague with whom I have had many a good talk about Dante's language over the years, I am grateful for so many profoundly stimulating comments about Dante, to whom, as a noted writer on modern French literature, he brought an excitingly fresh perspective. Particularly useful to me at a few difficult moments was his *Readings on the Inferno,* a sparkling introduction to Dante. How very fortunate several generations of Duke University students have been to have studied the *Commedia* in translation in Professor Fowlie's legendary Dante course!

I am indebted to George Hoffman for his thoughtfulness: he sent me to the right person at the right time. Greg Hanscon's efforts did not go unrecognized. I want to thank David Frederickson, who copy-edited my book, and Grace McVeigh, production editor at Pantheon, for their good work.

My son David gave excellent suggestions for improving my manuscript; my daughter Eve helped generously with the typing; my son Robert lent much encouragement; Debbie and Stuart Hoffman gave frequent loving support; to all I am deeply thankful.

Mere words of thanks are completely inadequate, however, to express what I owe to my wife, Lynette, without whose love, patience, encouragement, and marvelously critical eye and ear this book would clearly never have been completed. She has been, in so many ways, and in every aspect of my life, my very own Beatrice.

Of course, I alone am responsible for whatever shortcomings this book contains.

I cannot conclude these acknowledgments without saying a word about my father, who was the greatest impetus for this translation. Giuseppe Zappulla was a gifted Italian poet and journalist, and an excellent translator from English into his native Italian. During World War II, he served the United States (where he had arrived in 1922 from Sicily as a poor, self-educated twenty-one-year-old immigrant) by writing Italian radio scripts for the U.S. Office of War Information and broadcasting them to Italy, helping Italians see the war—and America—from a non-Fascist perspective and encouraging resistance to the Fascist regime. There was something quite Dantean about my father: his fierce pride; his intolerance of mediocrity (especially in literature); his tremendous love both for his native land and his adopted country. It was his abiding interest in Dante, in literature and history, and in the study of languages that greatly influenced my own choice of career.

My one great regret is that I began this translation many years after my father's death. I only wish he could have been alive to see this book come to light; I like to imagine that it would have pleased him.

INFERNO

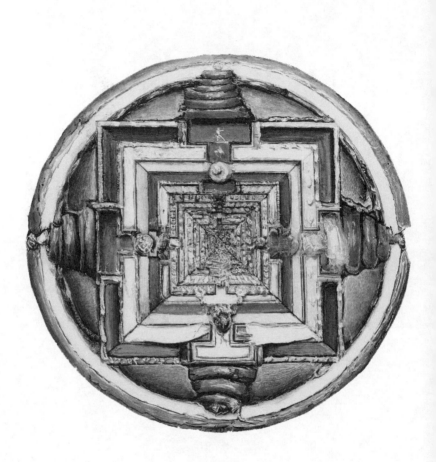

INTRODUCTION

"Reader, garner fruit / From what you read. . . ."
INFERNO XX.20–21

The *Inferno* is great poetry and great drama. Once we have read this tale of a journey through Hell, we can never forget the dark wood of sin and death; the horrible inscription over the gate of Hell; the murdered lovers, Paolo and Francesca; the wrath of Filippo Argenti; the gentle Brunetto Latini; the towering figure of Farinata, that striking emblem of scorn and arrogance; the ever-inquisitive, self-deceiving Ulysses; the pathetic Ugolino gnawing the head of an archbishop; the sinners bobbing up and down in rivers of excrement or rivers of blood, metamorphosed into trees, supine in a lake of ice, entwined by snakes, dazed and disemboweled; all naked, all in agony, all existing forever without a shred of hope; and the figure of Satan himself, half buried in ice, mindlessly beating his six enormous bat's wings and chewing in his horrible triple mouth the three men whom Dante believed to be the chief sinners of the human race.

It is an unforgettable work, a difficult work. Above all, it is a poem of the highest and deepest ethical value—yes, even for the sophisticated reader of our times. For the poem's highest purpose is to make us ask ourselves the age-old question: How shall I lead my life? To Dante the answer is clear: love God, shun evil, let every action originate not in self-interest but in the knowledge of what God has told us is right. It is an answer that we all know but that we often ignore. In his supreme achievement, Dante replies to the question vividly and memorably.

The Divine Comedy, of which the voyage through the Inferno is the first part, is a strange and unique epic, whose relatively simple language masks a deeply complex structure. It describes a journey through Hell,

Purgatory, and Heaven that the poet, Dante Alighieri, the protagonist of his own poem, tells us he took in the year 1300 A.D. The poem has achieved an international fame matched only by Homer's epics and the plays of Shakespeare, and its reputation continues to grow as the centuries roll on. Consider, as one barometer of the interest it still generates, the vast number of critical books and articles that have been written about it, especially in the twentieth century. And the flow of English translations alone shows no sign of diminishing; the Bible and Homer's poems may be the only other books that continue to be translated with such frequency into our language. These facts tell us something about the enduring power of this highly original poem that continues to haunt, to fascinate, to charm, even to instruct, for it is surely, after the Bible, one of the most significant moral works of literature in the Western canon.

It was during his years of exile, from 1302 until the end of his life, that Dante composed his masterwork. Called, in Italian, *La Divina Commedia*, and originally entitled simply *La Commedia* (the adjective *Divina* having been supplied by others more than two centuries after Dante's death), it is divided into three parts, called canticles (in Italian, *cantiche*): *Inferno, Purgatorio,* and *Paradiso;* these parts are sometimes published as separate books. Each canticle is divided into cantos, which vary in length, averaging about 145 lines each. *Inferno* has thirty-four cantos; *Purgatorio* and *Paradiso,* thirty-three each, for a total of one hundred.

The poem's meter is the immensely variable *hendecasyllable,* meaning "eleven syllables," each marked by anywhere from two to five stresses. The *Commedia*'s 14,000 lines have an intricate rhyme scheme called, in Italian, *terza rima: aba bcb cdc ded,* etc. Even to attempt to replicate such a scheme in English (it has been done) is an undertaking that commands admiration. Dorothy Sayers uses this rhyme scheme in her version, although with varying success (for English is a rhyme-poor language). Perhaps John Ciardi was wiser to have used a modified form of *terza rima* that gives at least the flavor of the original rhyme. Most translators (including me) have opted for blank verse, or unrhymed iambic pentameter, as being the form most suitable to the English language. It is, of course, the form that has been used for poetry of the highest order in English.

The word *Commedia* (stress on the *e*)—originally spelled *Comedia*, with the stress on the *i*), may be puzzling: after all, a reading of it (especially of *Inferno*) does not make one want to laugh. Clearly, by "comedy" is meant something other than a work designed to provoke amusement in the reader. What the word signified, according to Dante, was a work written in a less grand, more down-to-earth style than that which characterized poetry of a higher, more "tragic" order, though few now would view the *Commedia* as anything less than just that. (Furthermore, in order to reach the ears of all his countrymen, Dante wrote his poem in Italian: Latin was regarded as the language to be used for poetry of a high order, such as Virgil's *Aeneid*). Also, a comedy could be a work in which the hero, after suffering through adversity, achieves his goal and, perhaps, happiness. In Dante's poem, the hero, having witnessed the terrors of Hell and having undergone the painful, though far less terrifying, process of purgation of sins on the mountain of Purgatory, reaches Heaven and stands before the ineffable God, Creator of the universe. Such an ending is certainly happy: could any ending, in fact, be happier?

At the outset of the *Commedia*, Dante finds himself in a dark wood. He is subsequently escorted through the bowels of Hell and up the mountain of Purgatory by the spirit of the poet Virgil (whose works Dante deeply admired), and through part of Purgatory and all of Heaven by the soul of his beloved Beatrice, who had already been dead for many years when the poem was completed, until he looks into the face of God Himself in the last canto of *Paradiso*. Along the way, Dante sees thousands of souls and converses with, or listens to, many dozens of them: great sinners, ordinary people, great saints; the famous and the infamous; the mythical and the real. Many of the souls he encounters are Italians, especially Florentines, some of whom had recently died, some of whom he had known personally, and as they speak with Dante, the reader learns not only about their individual lives—especially their sinful or their virtuous deeds—but also about contemporary Italian politics and history.

The poem carries an immense cargo of philosophical and theological ideas, many derived from Saint Augustine, Thomas Aquinas, Aristotle. The reader who lacks some knowledge of these ideas is often at sea (hence the need for annotated editions of the poem), particularly in the *Paradiso,* but it is possible to read and enjoy the story *qua* story, especially the *Inferno,* without any firm grounding in philosophy or theology.

Inferno is the record of human sin. In his travels through the nine circles of Hell, each holding sinners of a particular sort, and many subdivided into further circles (such as Circle Eight, Malebolge, with its ten ditches), Dante encounters people who sinned in ways that seem hardly deserving of infernal punishment (such as not taking sides on moral issues) and those who committed sins that cry out for chastisement: bribery, theft, murder, treason. As he looks, listens, and converses, all the while guided by the sage Virgil, Dante comes to see sin in all its horror and perhaps sees himself in some of the people he meets. As a result of the fantastic journey, he comes to understand God's justice more clearly; perhaps, through having grasped the nature of sin, he may spend the remainder of his life learning to avoid it. By extension, the reader is enjoined to know what sin is, to shun it in all its forms, and to walk in the ways of God.

What kind of man was the author of this masterwork? Some knowledge of his life and the era in which he lived is essential if one is to have a deeper understanding of the *Inferno.* Thus, an initial overview of the great Florentine and his era will be useful as the reader accompanies Dante and Virgil in their spiraling descent into the sewer of Hell. (Also, in the present edition, a considerable amount of explanatory material will be found in the notes appended to each canto.)

Dante Alighieri, whom the world has come to refer to simply as Dante (short for Durante), was a citizen of the city of Florence (Firenze, in Italian), in north-central Italy. The city was to become very famous indeed a century or two after Dante's death, for it was here that the Renaissance was to begin its magnificent flowering before spreading to the rest of Europe. Today, most of us associate Florence principally with the Medici family, with Machiavelli, with Michelangelo, but these figures belong to a later time than Dante's: he was born in 1265 and so lived in Florence during the late medieval period, before the city was to achieve world renown as the cradle of that rebirth that Italians call the *Rinascimento*, better known to English speakers by its French name, the Renaissance.

Still, Florence in the thirteenth century was hardly an insignificant place. It had already begun to show its vitality in many ways, largely through its businesses and manufactures, but especially through its banking system and financial savvy. In Dante's time, for example, the coin of Florence, called the florin, was highly valued throughout Europe. It was because of its wealth and its financial dealings with so many other cities and countries that Florence became embroiled in international politics.

It must be understood that Italy at this time did not exist as a unified country. As late as the nineteenth century, Metternich could accurately (if sneeringly) maintain that the term "Italy" was only a "geographical expression." In truth, it is easy to forget that Italy did not become a nation until around the time of the American Civil War. Yet the term "Italy" was often used long before its many towns and cities joined together to form an actual nation just over a century and a quarter ago.

We must recall that the Italian peninsula had been the center of the Roman Republic and then of the Roman Empire. Beginning in the fifth century A.D., Roman civilization was severely disrupted by a long series of invasions from the so-called barbarians from the north. Italy itself was invaded in the fifth century by Ostrogoths, in the sixth, by Lombards, later, by Huns; the southern peninsula and Sicily were targets of the Normans. However, towards the end of the first millennium after the birth of Christ, the Italian boot (together with much of the rest of Europe) was well on the way to revival, both economic and cultural. The rediscovery of ancient Roman and Greek civilization began a process that was to accelerate dramatically during the Renaissance, some centuries down the road.

Italy began, in part, to recover from the invasions of the barbarians because of the French kings who swept down the peninsula with their armies in the eighth and ninth centuries, driving out many of the invaders and restoring territory to the popes (rather than to the "new" Roman emperors), thus clearing a path for the growth and dominion of the papal states in Italy, and of the Church in Europe, for centuries to come.

In the centuries after the death, in 814, of Charlemagne, who had been anointed as a new Roman emperor, a political arrangement had been established that made those who bore this title rulers of a number of lands, including Italy. But, after Charlemagne, the empire lost strength, and as it did so, the nobles of northern Italy enlarged their own spheres of influence; hence, a number of small Italian states, or communes, were created, each ruled over by the most powerful lord or lords in a given region. Because these lords did not usually live in the cities but in their country castles, the cities were not, during this time, the centers of power. However, about three centuries before the time of Dante, the focus of power began to shift to the cities, which had begun to oppose the extra-urban lords who were interfering with trade by their imposition of taxes, by their exaction of tolls, and by their bold-faced robbery of people passing through their lands.

The northern Italian cities, however, in declaring their liberation from the tyranny of the lords, had begun to tread, to some extent, on the territorial and political rights of the new Roman emperors, soon to be called the Holy Roman Emperors. Thus, in 1154, the emperor Frederick Barbarossa descended into the peninsula to reassert his supremacy. Banding together in the Lombard League and backed by the pope, the Italian cities were victorious against Frederick at the battle of Legnano in 1176. In 1183, he had no choice but to concede, in the Treaty of Constance, that the cities did indeed have rights that he could not abrogate. The distancing of the Italian cities of the north from the transalpine empire was inexorable from that moment on, and the pace did not slacken. As Muriel Grindrod, in her book *Italy*, succinctly puts it: "Indeed, some historians regard the Lombard League, Legnano, and the Treaty of Constance as the precursors of Italian nationalism."

Northern Italy was caught, however, between two forces engaged in a struggle for power that had already been raging for some time. As early as the eleventh century, a battle over turf had been going on between empire and papacy and was manifesting itself in dramatic fashion: in 1075 Pope Gregory VII excommunicated Emperor Henry IV because of a dispute over the question of who had the power to invest bishops. Two years later, the European world was treated to the spectacle of an emperor begging forgiveness from the pope.

This friction between Church and empire, or pope and emperor, was exacerbated during the reign of the Emperor Frederick II, a figure whom Dante mentions at key moments in his poem. Although a member of the same Hohenstaufen family as Frederick Barbarossa, Frederick II was passionately fond of Sicily, his southern kingdom, and lived there, establishing at Palermo an Arab-fertilized cultural center of considerable breadth and depth. A man of genius, ambition, and independence; an astute politician; a feared warrior; and a poet and scholar as well (his contemporaries called him Stupor Mundi, *i.e.*, "Wonder of the World"), Frederick could not fail to earn the enmity of a series of popes who viewed him, correctly, as a threat to papal ambition and Church hegemony. He, too, was excommunicated, twice, and his efforts to unite Italy were resisted and thwarted by papal forces. When he died in 1250, his ambitious plans died with him. The Church had won again.

Anxious to consolidate the Church's power in Italy after the defeat of Frederick, Pope Urban IV, a Frenchman, convinced Charles of Anjou, the brother of the King of France, to intervene in Italian politics. Charles came to Italy with his troops, winning the battle of Benevento in 1266 and so eliminating Manfred, the bastard son of Frederick. In 1268, at Tagliacozzo, Charles defeated and then executed Conradin, last scion of the Hohenstaufens, thus securing for himself the title of king of Sicily. (However, the Sicilians were violently opposed to this French dominance and rose up against them in 1282 in the bloody "Sicilian Vespers"; French soldiers were slaughtered everywhere in Sicily. Unfortunately for the Sicilians, the French yoke would all too soon be replaced by a Spanish one.)

Charles's intrusion into Italian affairs initiated a long era of French meddling in the peninsula. Furthermore, the Holy Roman Emperors were now losing their influence in northern Italy, whereas the Church was strengthening its claims to the papal states of central Italy. (In the *Inferno*, Dante repeatedly condemns the increasing temporal power of the Church.) But the Church paid a heavy price for having invited the French to Italy, for France soon gained considerable control over the papacy. In fact, from 1309 to 1377, the popes resided not at Rome but at Avignon in France; this period is known in Church history as the Babylonian Captivity.

During the thirteenth century, the contest between papacy and empire was keenly followed by, and had powerful effects upon, the northern Italian cities, where those who supported the pope were called Guelfs and those faithful to the emperor were called Ghibellines, names of German origin. During the rule of Frederick II, the Guelf–Ghibelline conflict in Italy was particularly intense, especially in Florence, and the struggle between these two factions was to have profound consequences for Dante. It intrudes itself repeatedly in the pages of his epic.

The nobles outside Florence, whose powers, for reasons noted above, had been severely reduced by the city, began moving into Florence itself. They allied themselves with the Ghibelline faction and thus with the emperor; the merchant class of Florence, fearful that the nobles might rise to positions of power, allied themselves with the Guelf party and thus with the papacy. After a time, the names Guelf and Ghibelline became simply party labels, both in Florence and in other cities of northern Italy. The two factions bitterly fought each other with word and sword.

After the death of Frederick, the Ghibellines of Florence attempted a *coup d'état* against the municipal government. For this offense, they were exiled and their homes destroyed. Rallying in nearby Siena, the expelled Ghibellines led by Farinata degli Uberti (whom we shall meet in the tenth canto of *Inferno*) assembled to fight against Florence and won the battle of Montaperti in 1260. Marching into Florence under Farinata's leadership, the victors threw out the Guelfs and would have destroyed the entire city had not Farinata prevented this barbarous act, an episode recalled by Dante in Canto X.

It was just a few years after these events that Charles of Anjou, as we have seen, came to Italy, defeating Manfred. Yielding to the superior French forces, the Ghibellines left Florence. They did not, however, disappear from the political scene in other cities. Slowly they gained power in nearby Arezzo and became rulers there in 1287, a development so deeply disturbing to Florence that it declared war on that city. At the battle of Campaldino in June 1289 the Aretine Ghibellines were defeated. In August, the Florentines, unwilling to lose the momentum of the war, attacked the Ghibellines of the city of Pisa at the same time as they were attacking Arezzo and, with their allies from Lucca, captured the Pisan fortress of Caprona. Dante, we note, was a soldier for Florence in both battles.

Having been born in Florence in 1265, Dante thus grew up in a city in which Guelf–Ghibelline strife was vividly remembered. During his lifetime the Ghibelline threat in Florence subsided, as we have seen; the Florence of his mature years was dominated by the Guelf party. The Guelfs, however, were soon to divide into two factions the Blacks and the Whites. The friction between them would affect Dante in a dramatic way. Before we examine Dante's own political involvements, which were to lead to exile from his beloved city in 1302, it is necessary to take a look at his early years.

Dante came of a noble, if undistinguished, family, although one illustrious ancestor on his paternal side, Cacciaguida, achieved fame during the Crusades. (He makes an appearance in Dante's *Paradiso*.) We know that Dante's father was a notary, a rather ordinary profession at the time. Of his mother, we know almost nothing. Both parents died before Dante grew to adulthood.

Dante seems to have been a "normal" boy, though perhaps more studious than most. He enjoyed games, had friends, got into scrapes. The greatest event of his youth seems to have been his meeting with a young girl, Beatrice Portinari, whom he barely knew yet who was to become the most important person in his life, if we are to believe what Dante tells us in the *Commedia* and elsewhere. Beatrice became for him the traditional beloved woman of courtly poetry, whom one admired from a distance and for whom and about whom one composed love poems; she was also a quasi-religious figure presented in *La Vita Nuova* (The New Life), a remarkable little book of prose and poetry. In the *Commedia,* she is a soul of ineffable spiritual grace and beauty who mixes with the most august personages of Paradise. Although her role in *Inferno* is small (she appears in only one canto there, in flashback, and does not interact with Dante), her spirit hovers in the background, for Beatrice is the divine protector of Dante during his subterranean journey. In the *Purgatorio,* she at last emerges from behind the scenes, until in the *Paradiso* she takes center stage, along with her faithful worshiper. The structure and concept of the *Commedia,* especially of the *Paradiso,* cannot be properly appreciated without a firm understanding of the centricity of Beatrice in Dante's mental and spiritual life. Readers of the *Inferno,* however, can survive without a detailed knowledge and understanding of her importance in Dante's thought, but, *caveat lector,* no one can hope to achieve a reasonably accurate comprehension of the intellectual underpinnings of the *Commedia* by reading only the *Inferno.*

Still, Dante's early attachment to her was curious by today's standards: he rarely spoke to her during her life, she married another man, and she died when she was quite young. Yet her influence upon him was profound, and unless we resort to the language of mysticism and religion, we are at a loss to explain the power of Beatrice over him.

Other important facts of Dante's early life can be briefly stated: his mother died when he was quite young; his father remarried but died before Dante was eighteen years old. The poet married a woman named Gemma Donati, whose family was influential in the city, but he never mentions her in his writings. They had four children. We have noted that he fought in at least two battles for his city. We are not certain about how he was educated, but it is clear from his literary output that he somehow learned a great deal as a youth, enough to become fully conversant with the literature, philosophy, theology, and science of his time, and with much of the learning of antiquity, especially the works of important

Latin authors: Virgil, Ovid, Statius, and Cicero. He may have studied with the Franciscans; possibly he went to Paris and studied at the Sorbonne. Some few (very few) people believe that he was at Oxford for a while. It is more likely that he was a student at the University of Bologna, the first university in Europe. He may also have studied in Florence with Brunetto Latini, a thinker and a politician who had written an encyclopedia of international renown. (Dante speaks fondly of him in Canto XV of *Inferno*.)

We know that Dante began to write poetry at some point in his formative years and that he wrote it very well. He gradually developed an original style through the influence of a number of contemporary poets and that of an older friend, Guido Cavalcanti, who, along with others, was developing a new form of poetry, known as the *dolce stil nuovo*, the "sweet new style," written in Italian instead of in Latin. These poets, in turn, had been strongly influenced by the troubadours of Provence in southern France and by the school of Sicilian poets of the court of Frederick II, themselves imitators of their Provençal predecessors. Many of these poets of Tuscany (the region around Florence), especially Dante, were only too conscious of the interesting parallels between the love for women that their poetry celebrated and their love for God. The love they spoke of and wrote about was a love reserved for the "gentle heart." When he composed *La Vita Nuova*, Dante had these poets in mind; in fact, the book is dedicated to Cavalcanti.

But his excursions into love and poetry were soon overshadowed by political events; to these Dante turned at a crucial time in Italian affairs. This entrance into the political turmoil of Florence "halfway along the journey of our life," was to determine his fate for the next twenty years. The Black–White conflict almost destroyed him.

As we have seen, the Guelfs had succeeded in wresting power from the Ghibellines, but they themselves split into two parties, the Whites and the Blacks, and the friction between them was to be almost as destructive as that of the earlier Guelf–Ghibelline feud. The Blacks and Whites originated in the city of Pistoia, a city that Dante excoriates in his poem, not far from Florence. A family of the name of Bianchi ("Whites") and their supporters, whose political ideas resembled those of the old Ghibellines (thus, very conservative), clashed with others in Pistoia who began to call themselves Neri ("Blacks") to distinguish themselves from the Bianchi.

In Florence, White and Black parties also sprang up: the Whites were headed by Vieri dei Cerchi and the Blacks by Corso Donati, one of Dante's relatives through marriage. Into this maelstrom stepped the new pope, Boniface VIII, whose name resonates like a darkly tolling bell throughout the *Inferno*. He was a man of powerful intellect and strong ambition who wished to increase papal power and influence over the northern Italian cities, especially Florence, at a time when the emperors were losing their grip over northern Italy. Boniface decided to back the Florentine Blacks. An excuse for direct intervention presented itself in May 1300 after a bloody Black–White clash in the city. Boniface threatened the Florentines with excommunication if they did not cease their open quarreling. The Blacks urged Boniface to do something he had already planned to do: intervene in Florentine affairs with the help of French troops led by Charles of Valois, the brother of the king of France, and thus help the Blacks take control. Many Florentines were quite aware, however, of Boniface's ambitions and knew Charles of Valois for what he really was: a cruel and untrustworthy scoundrel.

It was at this perilous time that Dante became involved in the ugly situation. Having noted his interest and ability in politics, the Florentines had demonstrated their trust in him by sending him on diplomatic missions to help cement their alliances with Guelf parties in other cities of Tuscany. Now, in 1300, he was elected prior, a ruling position that had a two-month term. Although he was not the sole ruling prior, those serving along with him were nondescript persons—designedly so, for Florence wished to give Dante a free hand in trying to bring order to the turbulent city.

Although his sympathies were with the Blacks (his wife's family, after all, was composed of leading Blacks), the agonized Dante nevertheless decided to support the Whites, for they were not in league with Pope Boniface's high-handed attempts to destroy Florence's political liberty. However, events got out of control. On June 23, 1300, there was another serious outbreak of violence between the two parties, as a result of which Dante made a fatal decision: he would punish both the White and the Black leaders. Many were fined; many exiled. Among those he ordered to leave was Dante's friend, Guido Cavalcanti, a White and a violent enemy of the Black Donati clan. No doubt Dante suffered much at having to send Cavalcanti away; that suffering would shortly become much more intense when, a few months later, the exiled Guido died of malaria.

The intrigues in Florence at this time were complex and Byzantine, and it is beyond the scope of this short essay to enter into great detail about ensuing events. (The notes at the end of each canto will inform readers, when necessary, about relevant historical events.) In brief, Dante was sent to Rome as an ambassador from Florence with instructions to ask the pope to prevent Charles from entering the city and to plead with him to deal honorably with the Florentines during these turbulent times. Boniface, however, was determined to bring Florence to heel. With one excuse or another, he kept Dante in Rome because he knew how influential the poet could be with his compatriots. Meanwhile, Charles entered Florence with his army, promising to establish peace and to be fair to all parties. As soon as the Florentines accepted Charles's conditions, however, the Frenchman quickly revealed that he was a firm supporter of the Blacks, permitted the exiled Black leader, Corso Donati, to come back into the city and looked aside while the Blacks murdered Whites and destroyed their property during a rampage that lasted several days. The absent Dante, along with the other priors who had ruled with him, was later falsely charged with the crime of barratry (or graft—barrators have their own special niche in the *Inferno*), without an iota of proof. Dante and others were exiled from their beloved city on January 27, 1302. He would never return.

He spent the remainder of his life as a wanderer among various cities of northern Italy. We do not have very much information about the details of that exile. We know that for a few years he tried to help the Whites from a distance, but that party soon lost all its power. He lived at the courts of some well known people: the Malaspina of Sarzana; Can Grande della Scala of Verona; Guido da Polenta of Ravenna (the nephew of Francesca da Rimini, whom Dante portrays so magnificently in Canto V), where Dante spent his last years. His brother Francesco spent some time with Dante, and some of his children were with him at the end of his life.

Dante continued to hope that Florence and Italy would be saved from the greed of popes and the ambition of men like Charles of Valois. For a while he pinned his hopes on the new Roman emperor, Henry VII of Luxembourg, in whom Dante saw a chance for a restoration of order and the establishment of Dante's ideal world government, for Dante believed that temporal matters were the exclusive domain of the emperor and spiritual matters the province of the pope; both leaders would be directly responsible to God. (Dante's treatise, *De Monarchia*, outlines his views on world government.) To Henry he wrote impassioned letters, urging him to come save Italy. To the Florentines he penned bitter words, calling on them to cast off their blindness and arrogance. But Henry died prematurely, and with his death Dante's dreams for the salvation of Florence and Italy dissolved.

In the verses of the *Inferno*, Dante poured out, perhaps exorcised, his pent-up bitterness, his hatred for the corruptness of the clergy, his detestation of the arrogance and moral blindness of so many of his townsmen. The work often reads like a Jeremiad: his words ring with moral outrage; his posture is that of a fiercely proud man who understands not only the evils that have overwhelmed his native city—the corruption of the clergy, the worldly ambition of Boniface, the intrigues of the French, the sinfulness of Florence, the inter-urban rivalries of Tuscany—but also the evils of which all of us, including Dante himself, are capable. For he was acutely aware that the will to sin and the rush to damnation were not the province alone of the Italians or Frenchmen of his time, but were the hallmarks of human beings everywhere and in every era.

In the *Purgatorio* and the *Paradiso*, the poem turns sweeter, and the thunder recedes; light begins to conquer darkness; reason, nearly extinct in Hell, revives. But in Hell, buried deep in the sunless earth, sin is king, the light of reason is all but extinguished, and Dante often indulges himself in the spectacle of the human will to damnation.

The *Inferno* is harsh. It has some of the ugliest moments in all litera-
ture; its protagonist is sometimes cruel; occasionally he assumes some of
the monstrous traits of the personalities he claims to despise. But always
we must remember that this first part is a preparation for the books to fol-
low. It shows us the soul taking its first steps on the path to salvation by
attempting to understand the roots of sin in human perversity and in the
ceaseless workings of the great Enemy of God. In this sense, the poem is
a supreme work of moral philosophy, calling upon each of us who has
lost the good of the intellect to confront the evil that men do in its mani-
fold and complex manifestations. Dante reminds us that, having come at
last to understand the nature of sin, we may begin the long process of
conquering it in ourselves, for only when we have arrived at such under-
standing will we be able to begin our journey along the twisting road that
will lead us out of the dark and savage wood of death so that we may
stand, at long last, beneath the stars.

THE

INFERNO

OF

DANTE ALIGHIERI

VOLUME I OF

The Divine Comedy

What was the manner of my coming there?
Impossible to say, for when I'd left
The one true way, my mind was drunk with sleep.

  (11–13)

CANTO I

Halfway along this journey of our life,
I woke in wonder in a sunless wood,
For I had wandered from the narrow way.

Oh how can I give voice to what it was,
That wild, that savage, and that stubborn wood.　　　　5
The very thought of it renews my fears,
For death itself can hardly be more harsh
Than is the memory of that monstrous place!
But let me sing of other things I saw,
For evil, in the end, gave rise to good.　　　　10

What was the manner of my coming there?
Impossible to say, for when I'd left
The one true way, my mind was drunk with sleep.
But, stumbling towards the bottom of a hill,
Just where the valley ended that had filled　　　　15
My heart with fear, I looked up, and I saw
Its shoulders mantled in the Planet's rays
That always leads men right on every road.
And so the fear, that in my poor heart's lake
I had lain that night so pitifully passed,　　　　20
Began to fade, for I had seen the sun!
Like one who's rescued from the angry waves,
Then breathless stands ashore to stare in awe

And terror at the cruel sea, my mind,
Still fugitive, turned back to scan the wood   25
That none before had ever left alive.

Dead with fatigue, I paused awhile to rest,
Then dragged my body up the barren slope,
My right foot always lower as I climbed.
No sooner had I started the ascent,   30
When suddenly there loomed ahead of me
A lithe, swift leopard with a dappled hide
Who would not move away but blocked the path
To bar my progress up the mountainside
And force me back into the wood of death.   35

The sky was growing lighter in the east.
The sun was rising with those very stars
That shone with God's great Love when Time began.
And so, despite the gay-skinned beast, I dared
To hope because it was an April dawn.   40
But oh, I hoped in vain, for now I paled
To see a lion planted in the path.
Enraged by hunger, with his head held high,
He moved against me, roaring as he came,
And seemed to terrify the air itself.   45
Then suddenly a she-wolf showed herself,
Bedeviled in her craving, rabid, gaunt,
The source of misery to many souls.
The sight of her so paralyzed my will,
I lost all hope of making the ascent.   50
Like one who greedily amasses gold,
Then, losing it, weeps inconsolably,
So was I rendered by this restless beast,
For on she came at me, relentlessly,

And down she drove me, down into the dark,   55
And down I fled to where the sun is silent.

As I was wandering in that vale of death
My eyes were startled by the sight of one
Whose voice, I thought, was weak from long disuse.
I watched him gliding dimly through the wasteland   60
And then in darkness I cried out to him:
"Take pity, you, whoever you may be,
A man perhaps, or shadow of a man!"

"No, I am not a man, though once I was.
I stem from Lombard stock: my parents both   65
Were born in Mantua. I saw the light
Of day in Julius Caesar's reign and lived
In Rome when great Augustus ruled the world
And men bowed down to base divinities.
I sang the exploits of Anchises' son,   70
Aeneas, fugitive from prideful Troy
Consumed in conflagration by the Greeks.
But you, returning to this evil wood,
Why not ascend the mountain of delight,
The origin of every human joy?"   75

I answered him: "Can you be Virgil, then,
That source of eloquence and silver speech?
Oh, glorious light of authors everywhere!
May all my studies and my love for you
Be useful now! Great prince of poetry,   80
From whom I gleaned the purity of style
That brings me fame, look at that animal!
I beg you, save me, wise and famous soul,
For fear and trembling bring me near to death!"

_____

Seeing my eyes well up with tears, he said: 85
"To flee the desolation of this wood,
You would do best to take another road.
This vicious beast who brings you so much grief
Lets no men pass this way, but slays them all.
Her nature is malevolent and vile.   90
Her appetite increases as she feeds,
And after she has fed, her hunger gnaws
At her more keenly than it did before.
This beast has mated many other beasts;
She'll mate with more, until the Greyhound comes   95
To punish her with pain and painful death.
He will not feed on nations or on wealth,
But be sustained by wisdom, virtue, love.
Between the Feltros is his native land,
And he will save that humble Italy   100
For whom so many perished: Turnus, Nisus,
The young Camilla, and Euryalus.
Through every city he will chase the wolf,
Until she falls into the flames of Hell
Whence Primal Envy loosed her on the world.   105

"Now let me tell you what I think is best:
I'll be your guide, and you will follow me,
And I will lead you through a world of pain
Where dead souls writhe in endless agony
And clamor, as they cry, to die again.   110
Then spirits of another sort you'll see,
Who find contentment in the fire and hope
One day to take their place among the blessed.
But I am not allowed through Heaven's gate
To see the city of Almighty God: 115
When I depart from you, one worthier
Than I must shepherd you through Paradise,

Because I was a rebel to God's law.
His throne is there; His realm is everywhere;
His reign is infinite in space and time;   120
Who dwells with Him dwells in beatitude!"

I said: "Escort me, Poet, through those worlds
Your words describe. I beg you, by that God
You never knew, to save me from this wood
And other evils that may lie in wait,   125
That I may see Saint Peter's gate and all
Those souls whose sadness you describe to me."

He moved on, and I followed close behind.

NOTES TO CANTO I

[SUMMARY OF THE CANTO: *It is just before dawn of Good Friday in the year 1300 A.D. Dante, who is the protagonist of his own poem, finds himself in a dark forest. Unable to comprehend how he got there, he is desperately seeking a way out. Seeing the rays of the rising sun shining on a nearby hill, he walks in that direction, but as he is about to climb it, he encounters three beasts in succession: a leopard, a lion, and a wolf; they block his path and force him back into the forest. At this point he meets the shade of Virgil, the great poet of ancient Rome, who tells Dante that he has come to guide him through the underworld and through Purgatory and that another soul will lead him through Heaven. Thoroughly bewildered, still frightened, but temporarily relieved because he has been saved from the threatening beasts, Dante follows Virgil out of the dreaded wood.*]

1 HALFWAY ALONG THIS JOURNEY OF OUR LIFE: See *Psalms*, 90:10: "The days of our years are threescore years and ten. . . ." (All Biblical quotations in the

notes are from the King James Version.) Since he was born in 1265, Dante is thirty-five years old at the beginning of the *cantica* (or "canticle", *i.e., Inferno,* the first of the three divisions of the *Commedia;* the other two are *Purgatorio* and *Paradiso*); this journey is thus taking place in the year 1300. The time is just before dawn of Good Friday (*i.e.,* the Friday before Easter Sunday).

2–3   I WOKE IN WONDER . . . FROM THE NARROW WAY: The sunless wood and narrow way echo Biblical thunderings against sin and exhortations to virtuous behavior: see *Proverbs* 2:13: "Who leave the paths of uprightness, to walk in the ways of darkness." Dante says he had "wandered" from the path of virtue; thus, he hopes to find his way back to it. The dark wood may also represent what Dante viewed as the tragic political condition of Florence.

6   THE VERY THOUGHT OF IT RENEWS MY FEARS: The word "fear" is a leitmotif that permeates the canto and, indeed, all of the *Inferno.*

13   . . . MY MIND WAS DRUNK WITH SLEEP: See *Ephesians* 5:14: "Awake thou that sleepest, and arise from the dead, and Christ shall give thee light." Sleep symbolizes the sinful state of the soul.

14   BUT, STUMBLING TOWARDS THE BOTTOM OF A HILL: The hill represents the virtuous life; and here it stands in opposition to the dark wood and the valley that have so frightened Dante.

16–18   . . . I LOOKED UP . . . ON EVERY ROAD: *Psalms* 121:1: "I will lift up mine eyes unto the hills, from whence cometh my help." The sun, called a planet (which means "wanderer") by medieval astronomers, symbolizes God, hope, etc.; it contrasts vividly here with the sunless wood of sin from which Dante is trying desperately to escape.

22   LIKE ONE WHO'S RESCUED FROM THE ANGRY WAVES: The *Commedia* is notable for the many hundreds of similes it contains. They are remarkable for their appropriateness and their beautiful simplicity.

29   MY RIGHT FOOT ALWAYS LOWER AS I CLIMBED: This odd image has been variously interpreted. It may be expressing the idea that Dante is climbing the hill in a counter-clockwise direction, or perhaps that he is climbing slowly, dragging one leg. One scholar, John Freccero, suggests that this image is a theological and philosophical reference to the operation of the fallen human will on human consciousness. On a more general symbolic plane, Dante's halting step suggests his, and humanity's, condition of sinfulness.

32   A LITHE, SWIFT LEOPARD WITH A DAPPLED HIDE: The leopard is the first of three beasts Dante encounters in this canto; the other two are a lion and a she-wolf. These may be viewed, respectively, as symbolizing incontinence, violence, and fraud; lust, pride, and avarice; or variations on these sins. They may

stand for Florence, the rulers of France, and Rome. The reader will discover still other meanings for the beasts. See *Jeremiah* 5:6: "Wherefore a lion out of the forest shall slay them, a wolf of the evenings shall spoil them, a leopard shall watch over their cities. . . ."

37–38   THE SUN WAS RISING . . . WHEN TIME BEGAN: That is to say, the sun is in the same zodiacal sign (Aries) as it was believed to have been at the Creation.

40   . . . BECAUSE IT WAS AN APRIL DAWN: Spring (and Easter) brings renewal of life and, with it, hope.

49   THE SIGHT OF HER SO PARALYZED MY WILL: Dante is still so steeped in sin that he cannot escape from it easily.

56   AND DOWN I FLED TO WHERE THE SUN IS SILENT: The words *the sun is silent* are an example of "synesthesia," a poetic technique characterized by the description of one sense impression in terms of another.

58   MY EYES WERE STARTLED BY THE SIGHT OF ONE: Dante now encounters Virgil, the great epic poet of ancient Rome. Though a pagan, Virgil was much respected by Christians who believed he had prophesied, in his fourth Eclogue, the coming of Christ. Virgil will be Dante's guide through *Inferno* and most of *Purgatorio;* to him Dante will turn continually for guidance and information, as a pupil turns to his teacher. In Canto II, Virgil will explain why he has come to rescue Dante.

59   WHOSE VOICE, I THOUGHT, WAS WEAK FROM LONG DISUSE: This may be a reference to the general neglect of classical studies in the medieval period, or it may suggest that Dante the sinner does not hear the voice of reason that Virgil symbolizes.

64   NO, I AM NOT A MAN, THOUGH ONCE I WAS. In 90 B.C., when Julius Caesar was alive, but before he actually ruled Rome, Virgil was born in the city of Mantua, located in the region of Lombardy in northern Italy. The emperor Caesar Augustus (Octavian), encouraged Virgil to write the *Aeneid.*

70–72   I SANG THE EXPLOITS OF ANCHISES' SON . . . PRIDEFUL TROY: Anchises' son is Aeneas, the hero of Virgil's epic. Having escaped from Troy at the end of the Trojan War (the setting for Homer's *Iliad*) while the Greeks were sacking the city, Aeneas arrives in Italy. En route, he has experienced many adventures, including a stopover in Carthage, where he has had a tragic love affair with Queen Dido. According to Virgil, Aeneas was the founder of Rome.

74   WHY NOT ASCEND THE MOUNTAIN OF DELIGHT: This mountain represents virtue (or perhaps philosophy) and stands opposed to the dark wood and the dark forest.

78   MAY ALL MY STUDIES AND MY LOVE FOR YOU: Dante had studied Virgil extensively. Virgil's *Aeneid*, Book VI, contains a description of the underworld from which Dante borrows many details visible throughout the *Inferno*.

95   SHE'LL MATE WITH MORE, UNTIL THE GREYHOUND COMES: Who is this greyhound? Many believe him to be Can Grande della Scala, a Veronese leader who was Dante's host for a time during the latter's exile, and who Dante hoped would bring order to chaotic Italy. The fact that "Can Grande" means "large dog" lends credence to the belief that he is the greyhound. Others believe the greyhound is Henry VII of Luxembourg, who became Holy Roman Emperor in Dante's time. Still others have thought that the animal refers to the Second Coming of Jesus Christ. Clearly, the question of the greyhound's identity has not been solved to everyone's satisfaction.

99   BETWEEN THE FELTROS IS HIS NATIVE LAND: By "the Feltros" Dante probably means the cities of Feltre and Montefeltro in northern Italy.

101–102   . . . TURNUS, NISUS, / THE YOUNG CAMILLA, AND EURYALUS: Turnus was King of the Rutulians in Italy when Aeneas arrived there; Aeneas later slew him. Nisus and Euryalus were good friends who left Troy with Aeneas and were killed during an attack on the Rutulians. Camilla was the daughter of an Italian king; she died helping Turnus fight the Trojans. All these characters are in the *Aeneid*.

105   WHENCE PRIMAL ENVY LOOSED HER ON THE WORLD: In the book of *Genesis*, envious Satan tries to destroy God's new creature, Man, by tempting Eve in the Garden of Eden. He succeeds, of course, in seducing her as well as Adam (the event is known as the Fall of Man). God then condemns the first couple (and all subsequent humanity) to suffer pain and know death. In Christian theology, Christ died in order to save humanity from the sin of Adam and Eve ("original," or "first," sin). Christ is thus often spoken of as the "Second Adam."

106–115   NOW LET ME TELL YOU WHAT I THINK . . . THE CITY OF ALMIGHTY GOD: Virgil tells Dante he will lead him below the earth through Inferno and then through Purgatorio. The latter is a place where, according to Catholic belief, the souls of those who have died penitent must undergo a period of purification (or "purgation," hence the place is called Purgatorio, Purgatory) before they can enter Paradiso (Heaven). The souls in Purgatorio suffer less than those in Inferno, not only because the punishments themselves are less severe, but also because their mental state is far healthier, since they know that, despite the torments they must endure, entrance into Purgatorio means automatic, if delayed, admission into Paradiso. Having been born before Christ's arrival on Earth, Virgil cannot enter Heaven; nor can any of the "virtuous pagans" (see Canto IV).

116–117 . . . ONE WORTHIER / THAN I MUST SHEPHERD YOU THROUGH PARADISE: The person who will conduct Dante through Heaven is Beatrice, the great love of Dante's life. She had died at the age of 24 in 1290, ten years before the action of the poem, and Dante has placed her, of course, in Heaven. Virgil will speak of her, though not by name, in the next canto, but she does not make her appearance in the *Commedia* until the late cantos of *Purgatorio*. In *La Vita Nuova,* a brief, lyrical, and crucial book of prose and poetry, composed long before the *Commedia,* Dante describes his love for her. The figure of Beatrice is central to the concept of the entire poem.

126 THAT I MAY SEE SAINT PETER'S GATE . . . : The gate of Purgatory or perhaps the gate of Heaven. It is conceivable that both are meant.

CANTO II

Daylight was fading, and the darkening air
Released Earth's creatures from their daily toil,
While I, removed from them, began to sense
How hard a journey was in store, how much
I would be moved by pity for the dead.   5
And memory shall tell the truth of this.

Oh Muses, lofty Genius, who inscribed
The things I saw, assist me now, I pray!
Here will be seen your true nobility!

I spoke: "My guide and master, hear me out: 10
Before you lead me on this arduous trip,
Consider: am I equal to the task?
The father of Sylvius, while his flesh
Was still corruptible, went down to see
The dead in the immortal underworld.   15
A reasonable man might understand
Why God, who hates all evil, chose Aeneas,
Considering what he was and what he wrought.
From him came Rome, from him the empire came.
So God Himself, from the Empyrean, picked   20
Him as father of Imperial Rome,
Established as the sacred site where sits
The latest occupant of Peter's throne.

Your art immortalized his trip to Hell
That brought him victory and brought to Rome   25
The mantle of the popes. From that domain
Of death the Chosen Vessel, Paul, came back
To bring us confirmation of the Faith
That points the way to every soul's salvation.
But who am I that I should make this trip?   30
Who gives *me* leave to go? Am I St. Paul?
Am I Aeneas? No. I am unworthy.
I yield to folly if I yield and go!
I've tried to speak my thoughts. My words are poor,
But you will understand because you're wise."   35

Like one whose will is weakened by new fears
And now no longer wills what once he willed,
So I, who quickly had agreed to go,
Was quick to let my resolution fade.
We paused on that bleak hill. My master spoke: 40
"If I have grasped the motive for your speech,
I'd say your soul is steeped in cowardice,
Which often holds men back from worthy deeds,
As horses shy at some imagined fear.
Well, let me free you from this dread of yours: 45
I'll tell you why I came to you and what
I heard when pity moved me to your side.

"While I was with the other souls in Limbo,
A lady came to me. She was so sweet,
So fair, I asked her to command my will.   50
With voice angelic she began to speak.
How gentle were her words and tone of voice!
How bright her eyes—more bright than Heaven's stars!
'Oh Virgil, noble soul of Mantua,
Whose fame endures and ever will endure   55

Through Time's unending stream, know that my friend,
Ill-used by Fortune and a prey to fear,
Is thwarted as he tries to climb the hill.
To judge from what was said of him above,
He is so lost, my help may be too late.   60
Go quickly to his side, help him escape,
And soothe him with your silver speech, I pray,
So that my own distress may be relieved.
For Love has moved me and has loosed my tongue.
Know that I who ask your help am Beatrice.   65
I long now to return to Paradise.
When next I stand before Almighty God,
I will commend your noble name to Him.'

"When she was silent, I began to speak:
'Virtuous soul, through whom mankind excels   70
All things within the smallest-circled Heaven,
So much has your request delighted me
That though I had already carried out
Your will, fulfilling it would seem too slow.
You need no further speak of what you wish.   75
But clarify one point: do you not fear
To come to this domain of pain and death
From Heaven, where you hunger to return?'

" 'Because you wish to learn these secret things
I'll tell you briefly why I have no fear   80
Of coming to this mournful place,' she said.
'Those things alone are to be feared
That have the power to harm, and nothing else.
God in His grace and wisdom made me such
That I am unaffected by the pain   85
Of Limbo or by Hell's eternal flames.
In Paradise a noble lady lives

Who felt so much compassion for that soul
Whose way is blocked upon the mountainside
That she transgressed the stern celestial law.   90
She called Lucia to her side and said:
"Your faithful friend is now in need of you.
To you I now commend him."

                                 " 'Lucia,
The enemy of cruelty, sought me
Where I sat with Rachel of antiquity.   95
"Beatrice," she said to me, "true praise of God,
Won't you assist the man who loved you so
That for you he shunned the vulgar multitude?
You surely hear his pitiful lament!
With death itself he struggles near the flood   100
Whose storms exceed the raging of the sea."

" 'Not ever in the world was anyone
So quick to follow good or flee from pain
As I when I had heard those pleading words.
I left my blessed seat and came to you,   105
Trusting the noble power of your speech
That honors you and all your listeners.'

"These were the words she spoke to me, and then
She turned aside her eyes, now bright with tears.
So I was moved to hasten to your side.   110
It is in answer to her will that I
Have saved you from the beast that turned you back
And would not let you find the shorter way
That would have led you to the mountaintop.
And so I ask: why do you hesitate?   115
Why harbor cowardice within your heart?
Why can't you be more bold, more free, when three

Celestial souls have shown their love and when
My words give promise of a world of good?"

And just as little flowers close and droop   120
In night's congealing air but then rise up
And stiffen on their stems and open wide
To greet the white rays of the morning sun,
So I, though drained of strength, found new resolve.

"Now I see the depth of her compassion,   125
And you yourself, most noble soul, have shown
Such courtesy and with such speed obeyed
My lady's will, that now my heart is filled
With new desire to follow where you lead.
Our wills are one, my master, guide and lord!"   130

Such were the words I spoke, and when he moved,
I followed on the wild and savage way.

NOTES TO CANTO II

[SUMMARY OF THE CANTO: *As Dante follows Virgil out of the forest, he is sud-
denly overwhelmed by fear of what may lie ahead for him. He expresses his feelings to
Virgil, who, upbraiding him for his cowardice, explains that it was Beatrice who asked
his help in saving Dante. Beatrice has learned of Dante's predicament from Saint Lucia,
who had in turn been asked by none other than Mary, the Mother of God, to take some
action to save his soul. Touched and encouraged by Virgil's narration, Dante resolves to
follow him wherever he may lead.*]

1   DAYLIGHT WAS FADING, AND THE DARKENING AIR: It is the evening of Good Friday. It is poetically fitting that Dante and Virgil should pass through the grim portals of Hell in the evening; it is symbolically fitting because it is the anniversary of Christ's crucifixion.

5   I WOULD BE MOVED BY PITY FOR THE DEAD: His pity will be for the souls of the dead whom he will see suffering in Hell.

7–8   OH MUSES . . . ASSIST ME NOW, I PRAY!: This invocation to the Muses is a standard feature of the epic poem (see the openings of Homer's and Virgil's epics), and Dante follows the tradition, despite the obvious pagan nature of these demi-deities.

10   . . . MY GUIDE AND MASTER, HEAR ME OUT: Dante will address, or refer to, Virgil with a variety of titles: "signore" ("lord"), "duca" ("leader"), "maestro" ("master"), "guida" ("guide"), etc. See line 130, where Dante employs three such appellations.

13   THE FATHER OF SYLVIUS . . . : Dante follows Virgil in calling Aeneas "the father of Sylvius." It was the legendary Aeneas who escaped from Troy at the end of the Trojan War and whose destiny it was to found the Roman Empire. In Book VI of the *Aeneid*, Virgil describes Aeneas' descent into the underworld; it is this journey to which Dante is referring. Dante mentions Aeneas' and St. Paul's visits to the other world, but not those of Hercules, Ulysses, Theseus, or St. Patrick. Clearly, Dante's interest lies primarily in ancient Christian and Trojan (*i.e.,* Roman) figures.

20   SO GOD HIMSELF, FROM THE EMPYREAN . . . : In the Ptolemaic model of the universe, which Dante and his contemporaries believed to be accurate, the Empyrean was the tenth and final sphere; God was thought to dwell there.

23   THE LATEST OCCUPANT OF PETER'S THRONE: Rome became the seat of the papacy after the Roman Empire converted from paganism to Christianity. Peter, one of the twelve apostles, and the one chosen by Christ (in the New Testament) to found the Church, was considered the first pope.

25–26   . . . AND BROUGHT TO ROME / THE MANTLE OF THE POPES . . . : Aeneas' founding of Rome eventually led to the establishment of the papacy in that city, which remains its home.

27   . . . THE CHOSEN VESSEL, PAUL . . . : At first, Paul persecuted the Christians, but later he became the most important spokesman of the early Church. See *Acts* 9:15: "He is a chosen vessel unto me."

48   "WHILE I WAS WITH THE OTHER SOULS IN LIMBO": Limbo (meaning "border") is a place in Dante's underworld reserved for the souls of the virtuous who were born before Christ. Also found there are those who were born in the

Christian era but were unbaptized. Dante and Virgil's journey will shortly take them into Limbo.

49–50   A LADY CAME TO ME . . . TO COMMAND MY WILL: This lady is Beatrice. (See Canto I, 116, and the note to I: 106–115.)

59   TO JUDGE FROM WHAT WAS SAID OF HIM ABOVE: "Above" refers to Heaven.

70–71   VIRTUOUS SOUL . . . THE SMALLEST-CIRCLED HEAVEN: Beatrice's surpassing purity and virtue are proof that human beings are superior to all other earthly creatures. The "smallest-circled Heaven," in the Ptolemaic system, is that of the moon and contains the Earth as well.

87   IN PARADISE A NOBLE LADY LIVES: This "noble lady" is the Virgin Mary. Neither her name, nor that of Christ, is uttered in the *Inferno*. It is through the direct intercession of the Virgin that Dante is being allowed to make his journey (and therefore to seek his salvation).

91   SHE CALLED LUCIA TO HER SIDE . . . : Saint Lucia (Lucy in English), of the city of Siracusa in Sicily, lived in the 3rd century A.D. during the reign of the emperor Diocletian and was martyred for her faith. She is the patron saint of those who suffer from eye troubles (as Dante did). Early Dante commentators thought she stood for "illuminating grace." One critic (Valli) believes Lucia to be an anagram of *acuila*, "eagle" (although the word is spelled *aquila* in both Italian and Latin) and that she thus symbolizes certain virtues of the Roman Empire, or perhaps the empire itself, for which the eagle was the traditional symbol. (See also *Purgatorio*, Canto IX.)

95   WHERE I SAT WITH RACHEL OF ANTIQUITY: The Biblical Rachel was the wife of Jacob; some see her as a symbol of the contemplative life.

100   WITH DEATH ITSELF HE STRUGGLES NEAR THE FLOOD: "Death" probably means damnation, or the death of the soul. The line may mean that his struggles are like those of a sailor caught in a terrible storm at sea, or it may refer to the fact that Dante is now close to the river Acheron in Hell.

125   NOW I SEE THE DEPTH OF HER COMPASSION: "She" is Beatrice.

"And who can these tormented people be?"

(30)

CANTO III

THROUGH ME THE WAY TO THE DOLOROUS CITY.
THROUGH ME THE WAY TO PAIN EVERLASTING.
THROUGH ME THE WAY TO THE SOULS OF THE DAMNED.
BY JUSTICE WAS MY HIGH CREATOR MOVED.
DIVINE OMNIPOTENCE CREATED ME,   5
AND THE HIGHEST WISDOM, AND PRIMAL LOVE.
BEFORE ME WERE CREATED ONLY THINGS
ETERNAL, AND ETERNAL I ENDURE.
ABANDON ALL HOPE, YOU WHO ENTER HERE.

These darkly colored words above a gate   10
Moved me to say to Virgil: "I'm afraid . . .
Those words . . . My lord, what do they signify?"

My master answered me, as one who knew:
"Now you must shed this cowardice of yours,
For we have reached the realm I told you of,   15
Where you will see the guilty souls of those
Who have lost the good of the intellect."

Then with a cheerful look he placed his hand
On mine to soothe my soul and mind—and then
He led me in among the secret things.   20

Loud lamentations, sighs, and cries I heard
Resounding harshly through the starless air:
I was unable to hold back my tears.
A babel of tongues, great shrieks of horror,
A pauseless, pitiless beating of breasts   25
Whirled about in the dark and timeless air,
Like sand that's swirling in a twisting wind.
My head was centered in a sea of pain.
I asked my lord: "What do these noises mean?
And who can these tormented people be?"   30

And he: "The miserable souls of those
Who lived on Earth neither in infamy
Nor praise are doomed forever to this place,
And mixed with them is that malefic choir
Of angels who, though faithless to their God,   35
Did not rebel but merely stood aside.
From Heaven banned, whose beauty they would mar,
They were not hurled into the pit of Hell,
For it was feared the wicked might exult."

"Why do they wail so loudly?" I inquired.   40

And he: "I will be brief: they have no hope
Of death. Their blind existence is so base,
They're envious of every other fate.
No mention of their name can be allowed;
By Mercy and by Justice they are scorned.   45
Let's speak of them no more but simply glance
And go our way."

                        A banner fluttered by,
Without a purpose and without a pause.
Such multitudes of dead were in its train,

I never would have thought Death had undone   50
So many. When I'd recognized a few,
I saw the craven soul of him who made
The great refusal. So I knew at once
This worthless band was made up of those souls
Abhorred by God and by God's enemies.   55
These wretches, who had never really lived,
Stood naked now. Their faces, pocked with stings,
Were bleeding so from wasp and hornet barbs
That, mixing with their tears, the blood streamed down
Their trunks and legs and, pooling at their feet,   60
Made food for loathsome worms. I saw some souls
Who neared a river, wide and dark as death.
I asked my guide, "Who can these people be?
Although the light is weak, it's clear to me
They want to cross. What law is driving them?"   65

"These things will be revealed when we have reached
The dismal shore of Acheron," he said.

Ashamed, my eyes downcast, I said no more
Until we reached the river, for I feared
More speech would give offense. And suddenly   70
A boat was coming at us. In the bow
A man with ancient hair stood grim and screamed:
"You misbegotten, God-forsaken souls,
Forever doomed! Heaven's beyond your hope!
I come to bring you to the other shore,   75
To fire and ice and everlasting night!
But wait—is that a living soul? Get out!
This is the kingdom of the dead and damned!"

I did not budge, and so he screamed again:
"You cannot cross the stream from here! Go find   80

Another way, another port, you hear?
A lighter boat will ferry you, not mine!"

My master chastened him: "Charon, be still,
For this is willed where what is willed must be.
Don't interfere, and seek to learn no more!"   85

These words of Virgil stilled the shaggy cheeks
Of Charon of the livid fen, whose eyes
Were wheels of flame, whose words, so hard and harsh,
Made all the sinners in this naked herd
Change color, gnash their teeth, begin to curse   90
The God who made them, curse their parents
And the human race, curse the place and time
And seed of their begetting and their birth.
Loud was their weeping as they came to crowd
The evil shore of Acheron, dead stream   95
Awaiting those who have no fear of God.

The boatman's demon eyes were burning coals
As, beckoning and herding all the damned,
He swung his oar and beat those slow to move.
As one by one the leaves in autumn drop   100
Until the branch has seen them on the ground,
All dead, so from the shore, on signal, one
By one the evil seed of Adam fling
Themselves: falcons summoned by a falconer.
Across black Acheron the shades are shipped,   105
Yet, long before they reach the farther shore,
Another swarm of sinners gathers here.

"My son," began my master courteously,
"The souls who perish in the wrath of God
Must all assemble here from every land,   110

All hurrying to cross this filthy stream,
For God's great justice spurs the spirits on,
Transmuting all their dread into desire.
No souls save evil ones may pass this way,
And so you understand what Charon meant."   115

When he had finished speaking, suddenly
The ground beneath us shook with violence.
(I sweat in terror at the memory!)
A blast of wind burst from the tear-soaked ground,
The air was rent by a vermilion flash,   120
And, all my senses failing me, I fell,
Oblivious, to the dark, dead floor of Hell.

NOTES TO CANTO III

[SUMMARY OF THE CANTO: *Dante and Virgil come to the gate of Hell, whose inscription terrifies the pilgrim. Once inside the gate, they hear the terrifying lamentations of the dead, which, together with the darkness and the whirling wind, overwhelm Dante. The first souls they see, Virgil explains, are those who, when alive, never took sides in important events or on questions of moral import. After spotting the soul of Pope Celestine V, they arrive at the river Acheron and see a group of souls waiting to be ferried across by Charon, the boatman. Because Dante is a living man, Charon loudly objects to transporting him, but Virgil silences him. The ground shakes violently, and Dante faints.*]

1–9   THROUGH ME THE WAY . . . YOU WHO ENTER HERE: These words are inscribed over the entrance to Hell. We are not yet in Hell itself but in ante-Hell or, as some call it, the Vestibule of Hell. The sinners whom Dante will see here are not worthy of being in Hell proper because they did not choose to do evil but to remain neutral on moral issues, or because they failed to take sides when doing so would have made a moral difference. Hell is designated as a city, called Dis, which is also another name for Satan, or Lucifer, or Beelzebub. All are used by Dante to refer to the arch-enemy of God and man and the chief occupant of the city of Hell. God's dwelling-place is also called a city (Canto I: 114).

4 BY JUSTICE WAS MY HIGH CREATOR MOVED: God made Hell because His justice demanded it; that is, as it was just to create Heaven for the angels, so it was equally just to create Hell for the fallen angels, including Satan.

5–6 DIVINE OMNIPOTENCE . . . PRIMAL LOVE: Omnipotence (God the Father), Wisdom (God the Son), and Love (God the Holy Spirit) are the Trinity. The figure of Satan, whom we shall meet in the last canto of Inferno (XXXIV), is the obscene obverse of this triune image.

8 . . . AND ETERNAL I ENDURE: The eternal things created before Hell (but not by much) are the elements, the angels, and the Heavens.

17 WHO HAVE LOST THE GOOD OF THE INTELLECT: To have lost "the good of the intellect" means to have lost the knowledge of God. The concept of this good is derived from the philosophy of Aristotle.

31–33 . . . "THE MISERABLE SOULS . . . TO THIS PLACE": These souls never took sides in momentous events in which their participation might have affected the outcome, for good or for ill.

34–36 AND MIXED WITH THEM . . . BUT MERELY STOOD ASIDE: This refers to those angels who neither supported God nor assisted Satan in his rebellion but stood by and did nothing.

39 FOR IT WAS FEARED THE WICKED MIGHT EXULT: Sinners in Hell are to be given no cause for gloating.

48 . . . A BANNER FLUTTERED BY: These souls, who would not commit themselves to any side, are now made to follow a banner that leads them nowhere. This is a good example of the idea of the *contrappasso*, or retaliation, according to which each soul in Hell is punished in accordance with the nature of the sin committed. This idea is traceable to certain Old Testament passages, *e.g., Exodus* 21:24, *Leviticus* 24:20, etc.

50–51 I NEVER WOULD HAVE THOUGHT DEATH HAD UNDONE / SO MANY: T. S. Eliot uses these words in his poem *The Waste Land*. He has thus made Dante's line into a familiar English phrase.

52–53 I SAW THE CRAVEN SOUL OF HIM WHO MADE / THE GREAT REFUSAL: This is probably Pope Celestine V, who resigned from the papacy in 1294 at the age of eighty. This act led to the ascension of Boniface VIII, whom Dante detested and often speaks of scathingly in *Inferno*. Although Celestine had the reputation of being a decent man (he was, in fact, canonized a couple of decades after his death), Dante viewed him as a coward, whose failure to live up to his pontifical responsibilities paved the way for what Dante viewed as the evil reign of Boniface. Some critics have suggested that this "craven soul" may be Pontius Pilate, or some other person, but Celestine seems the logical choice.

62   WHO NEARED A RIVER, WIDE AND DARK AS DEATH: The river is Acheron (Greek for "joyless"), the first of Hell's four rivers. See also Homer's *Odyssey*, Book XI; and Virgil's *Aeneid*, Book VI. In writing the *Inferno*, Dante borrowed many details from Virgil, though he transformed them to conform to his own vision and poetics.

72   A MAN WITH ANCIENT HAIR STOOD GRIM AND SCREAMED: This is the figure of Charon, the boatman of Acheron, from Greek mythology.

113   TRANSMUTING ALL THEIR DREAD INTO DESIRE: By sinning and dying unrepentant, the souls have *chosen* Hell; hence, they *desire* to cross over to it.

121–122   . . . I FELL, / OBLIVIOUS, TO THE DARK, DEAD FLOOR OF HELL: Dante faints and will awaken on the other side of the Acheron. We do not learn just how he gets across.

No sound of lamentation did I hear,
Only the sighs of women, children, men . . .
    (21–22)

CANTO IV

My sleep was shattered by a thunderclap.
I started, rose, and turned my rested eyes
Around me, wondering where I was. In truth,
I stood upon the brink of Hell's abyss,
The valley of despair, and from its throat   5
A thundering sound, the aggregate of all
The misery below, assailed my ears.
I stared into the pit but could not see:
It was too deep, the smoke and dark too thick.
"Down we go into a world of blindness,"   10
My master said, and he grew pale as death.
"I'll lead the way. Just follow me."

                                    When I
Observed the color drain from him, I said:
"How can I find the courage to descend
When you, my only comfort, are afraid?"   15

"You don't read fear upon my face, but pity
For many souls below. Our journey's long:
Let us begin."

                    Down he plunged, I followed,
And soon we stood inside the very first
Of all the circles girding Hell's abyss.   20

No sound of lamentation did I hear,
Only the sighs of women, children, men
That set the dark air trembling everywhere.
These souls are never punished physically
But sigh to be with God and sigh in vain.   25
My master said to me: "You haven't asked
Me who these people are. Before we move
Ahead, know that their lives were free of sin,
And yet, despite their virtues, it is willed
That they must suffer here, for back on Earth   30
Baptismal water of your faith did not
Cleanse them. They lived before Christianity
And so they did not rightly worship God.
This is the group to which I too belong.
For these defects and for no other wrongs   35
We dwell here in desire devoid of hope."

My heart was filled with sadness at his speech,
For many were the worthy souls I knew
To be in Limbo, neither saved nor damned.
"My lord, instruct me," I began, for I   40
Desire more understanding of the Faith
That triumphs over sin. "Did any soul
Depart from here through merit of its own
Or else because some power intervened?
Did any leave to live among the blessed?"   45

He, knowing what I really meant, replied:
"I had but newly come into this realm
When One descended, crowned in victory,
To take away the souls of Adam, Abel,
Noah, and Moses, giver of the Law,   50
Who served the Lord with such obedience;
Abraham the patriarch, King David;

Israel, together with his father,
His children, and Rachel, whom he would wed
Despite great obstacles; and many more,   55
And brought them all to Heaven, blessing them.
Before that time no soul was saved from Hell."

We kept on walking as he spoke and passed
A forest, so it seemed, of crowded souls.
When we had moved not far from where I'd slept,   60
The hemisphere of black was pierced by light.
Though still a little distant from the spot,
We could perceive it was inhabited
By honorable people, and I asked:
"My lord, who honor science and the arts,   65
Who are those noble figures set apart,
Apparently with honor, from the rest?"

"Their honorable fame," he said to me,
"Still echoes in your world, where it has earned
For them much favor in the eyes of God."   70

A voice, meanwhile, was heard to say: "The Prince
Of poets has returned. Let's honor him!"

The voice was still. The souls of four great men
Advanced toward us to greet my guide and me.
Their faces showed no sadness, showed no joy.   75
My good guide said: "Can you make out the one
With sword in hand who walks before the rest
As if he were their lord? His is the shade
Of Homer, poet without peer. That one
Is Horace, famous satirist. The third   80
Is Ovid. Lucan is the last of them.
One spirit called me poet: it is so.

All five of us are poets. They do well
To welcome me with honor in this way."

So here I saw convened the noble school   85
Of Homer, master of the epic form,
Who soars with eagle's wings above the rest.
They spoke awhile, and then they turned to me
And made a sign of greeting. Virgil smiled.
But in a greater way they honored me,   90
For I was welcomed to their group, and so
I made a sixth among such intellects.

We walked together onward toward the light
And spoke of things I will not speak of now,
Though they were fitting to that time and place.   95

A noble castle, ringed with seven walls,
Loomed up ahead of us. Around it flowed
A pretty rivulet, which we traversed
As if the ground were dry. With those wise men
I passed through seven gates until we came   100
To where a fresh and verdant meadow bloomed.
I saw a group of tranquil, solemn souls
Graced with an air of great authority,
Who seldom spoke and did so only gently.

We walked together to much higher ground,   105
An open place suffused with radiance,
Where we could view them all more easily.
Ahead on the enameled green I saw
Another group, of everlasting fame,
And I exulted at the sight of them.   110
I saw Electra: in her coterie
Were Hector, Aeneas, Julius Caesar

Of the hawklike eyes. I saw Camilla,
Penthesilea, on the other side;
And King Latinus, with Lavinia,   115
His daughter, sitting near. And I took note
Of Brutus (he who threw proud Tarquin out),
Lucretia, Julia, Marcia, Cornelia,
And, sitting by himself, the Saladin.
Looking up, I saw great Aristotle,   120
Acknowledged master of the wise, who sat
Among a philosophic family.
With honor and respect all gazed on him,
As Socrates and Plato stood nearby,
The worthiest of such proximity.   125
I saw Democritus, who claims the world's
All run by chance; Thales, Diogenes,
Anaxagoras and Empedocles,
Heraclitus and Zeno, and also
Dioscorides, he who gathered lore   130
Of medicine; and Linus, Orpheus,
Cicero, Seneca the moralist,
Euclid the geometer, Ptolemy,
Hippocrates, Avicenna, Galen,
Averroës, the famous commentator.   135
Of all those souls how can I fully speak?
My lengthy theme impels me to move on:
I must omit so many things I learned.

The company of six decreased to two;
My wise lord led me by another way   140
Remote from peaceful Limbo to a zone
Where dark and trembling air drowns every light.

NOTES TO CANTO IV

[SUMMARY OF THE CANTO: *Dante is awakened by a loud thunderclap. From the pit of Inferno, terrible wailing and lamentation rises up to assail his ears. Even Virgil grows pale at the thought of all the suffering that Hell contains. They descend into the First Circle, or Limbo, where dwell the sinless souls of those who were born without baptism and without Christianity. These people are never physically punished but suffer only from the realization that they will never be saved. Virgil and Dante converse with the souls of four virtuous pagan poets and walk and talk with them awhile in a pleasant meadow. Dante sees, but does not speak with, the souls of many other noble people from the ancient world. All too soon, Virgil leads Dante away so that the two may continue their descent.*]

1–3 MY SLEEP WAS SHATTERED . . . WONDERING WHERE I WAS . . . : How Dante gets across the Acheron is not explained. The thunderclap is the aggregate of all the lamentations and screams of the sinners in Hell. On the other hand, in Limbo (a place described not in the Bible but in the apocryphal *Gospel of Nicodemus*), where the poets will shortly arrive, there is no such wailing. That is because the souls in Limbo are not physically punished like the other occupants of Inferno.

16 "YOU DON'T READ FEAR UPON MY FACE, BUT PITY": Virgil's pity is no doubt reserved for the souls in Limbo, not for the sinners lower down. So often in the course of the journey Virgil upbraids Dante for showing pity for the sinners in Hell proper.

26–36 MY MASTER SAID TO ME . . . IN DESIRE DEVOID OF HOPE: We are in Limbo, the First Circle of Hell. The souls here are those of the virtuous pagans (the unvirtuous are punished farther down) who lived before the coming of Christ. Thus, they could not have been baptized into the Christian faith, which did not yet exist. Also found here are the souls of unbaptized infants and of those otherwise virtuous people born in the Christian era but not baptized into the faith. No matter how virtuous all these people in Limbo were, they cannot be saved, not having had the possibility of being redeemed by a knowledge of Christ.

48 WHEN ONE DESCENDED, CROWNED IN VICTORY: A reference to

Jesus Christ. (See *Peter* I 3:19). Christ's descent into the underworld was called the Harrowing of Hell, a story accepted as true by the Church.

49–54   TO TAKE AWAY THE SOULS . . . RACHEL, WHOM HE WOULD WED: All these are figures from the Hebrew Bible.

76–78   . . . "CAN YOU MAKE OUT . . . THEIR LORD?" . . . : Homer is shown holding a sword because he wrote about the Trojan War.

79–81   OF HOMER, POET WITHOUT PEER . . . LUCAN IS THE LAST OF THEM: Homer, the greatest of the Greek poets, wrote the *Iliad*, which takes place during the Greek war against Troy, and the *Odyssey*, which tells of the adventures of Odysseus ("Ulysses" to Dante—see Canto XXVI) during his long return home from the Trojan War. Horace was a Roman satirical poet. Ovid and Lucan were also Roman poets (the former's *Metamorphoses* was Dante's primary source for many of the mythological details in the *Divine Comedy*); Lucan's *Civil War* (often erroneously called the *Pharsalia*), an unfinished history of the conflict between Caesar and Pompey, was much admired by Dante.

96–101   A NOBLE CASTLE . . . A FRESH AND VERDANT MEADOW BLOOMED: The symbolism of the castle is vague. Since a favorite medieval symbolic number, seven, is mentioned here, we might be inclined to think of the seven cardinal virtues, the seven liberal arts, seven subdivisions of philosophy (ethics, metaphysics, etc.), and so on. The castle itself might stand for human reason. Why would such positive notions be associated with Hell? Perhaps Dante is trying to show his respect for the great figures of antiquity. In any case, no completely satisfactory explanation of the castle and its walls has yet been offered. The description of the setting is reminiscent of the Elysian Fields of classical myth.

111   I SAW ELECTRA . . . : This is not the famous Electra of the Greek tragedies, but the mother of Dardanus, founder of Troy.

112   . . . HECTOR, AENEAS, JULIUS CAESAR: Hector was the greatest of the heroes of Troy in the Trojan War. For Aeneas, see note to *Inferno* I:70–72. Julius Caesar was viewed, in the Middle Ages, as the founder of the Roman Empire.

113–114   . . . I SAW CAMILLA, / PENTHESILEA, ON THE OTHER SIDE: For Camilla, see note to *Inferno* I:101–102. Penthesilea was queen of the Amazons; she fought on the side of Troy in the Trojan War and was slain by Achilles.

115   AND KING LATINUS, WITH LAVINIA: Latinus was King of Latium (in Italy); his daughter Lavinia became the wife of Aeneas.

117   . . . BRUTUS (HE WHO THREW PROUD TARQUIN OUT): In the early

history of Rome, Lucius Junius Brutus (not the Brutus who assassinated Caesar—see Canto XXXIV) led a Roman revolt against Tarquin the Proud (last of the kings of Rome), founded the Roman Republic, and became First Consul.

118 LUCRETIA, JULIA, MARCIA, CORNELIA: These are the names of noted Roman women, models of the Roman concept of feminine virtue.

119 AND, SITTING BY HIMSELF, THE SALADIN: The Saladin was much admired in medieval Europe for his chivalrous ways (for instance, he often spared the lives of Christian soldiers captured in the Crusade), his wealth, and his skill as a leader.

120–124 . . . I SAW GREAT ARISTOTLE . . . AS SOCRATES AND PLATO STOOD NEARBY: Aristotle was one of the chief philosophers of ancient Greece. He had an enormous influence on medieval thought and on Dante. Socrates, an equally famous Greek philosopher, was immortalized by his pupil, Plato, in the latter's *Dialogues*. Dante had no direct knowledge of Plato's writings.

126–129 I SAW DEMOCRITUS . . . ZENO . . . : All of these men were ancient philosophers, mainly Greek.

130–131 DIOSCORIDES . . . OF MEDICINE . . . : Dioscorides was a Greek physician.

131 . . . AND LINUS, ORPHEUS: Linus was a mythical poet; Orpheus was a figure from Greek mythology whose skill with the lyre, a gift from Apollo, delighted all creatures. He descended into Hades and almost succeeded in bringing back his dead wife, Eurydice, but lost her at the last moment by looking back at her.

132 CICERO, SENECA THE MORALIST: Cicero was a Roman philosopher and orator whose works Dante studied closely. Seneca was a Roman playwright and philosopher.

133 EUCLID THE GEOMETER, PTOLEMY: Euclid was a Greek mathematician whose *Elements* is the classic work on geometry. Ptolemy was an Egyptian mathematician, cosmographer, and geographer. His concept of the structure of the universe was accepted in Europe for a thousand years and more, until it was exploded by the Copernican revolution in astronomy in the sixteenth century. Dante's idea of the universe is that of Ptolemy.

134 HIPPOCRATES, AVICENNA, GALEN: Hippocrates was a Greek physician, "the father of medicine." (Physicians in our time still take the Hippocratic Oath before they begin to practice.) Avicenna was an Arab physician and author of a text on medicine used in Europe until the Renaissance. Galen was a Greek physician and anatomical theorist whose frequently incorrect concepts of

anatomy (both of humans and of other animals) dominated European medicine for centuries.

135   AVERROËS, THE FAMOUS COMMENTATOR: Averroes was a Spanish/North African Arab philosopher, author of a commentary on Aristotle that Dante held in high regard.

"What tender dreams of Love, what desperate
Desire could bring these souls to such an end?"

(100–101)

CANTO V

Downward we journeyed to the second ring
That circumscribes less space but greater pain.
Here, spirits wail in anguish without end.
Here Minos stands, with minatory snarl,
Sin-seeker, judge, dispatcher of the dead.   5
Here, hapless spirits blanch before the beast,
Confessing all, while that inquisitor
Assigns each waiting shade its circled doom.
Around himself he wraps his restless tail,
The number of whose coils reveals the ring   10
Each soul is destined for. How anxiously
Around great Minos swarms the multitude,
To mark the judgment of the monster's tail!
They speak, they hear, and then are hurled below.

When Minos saw my form, he stopped his work.   15
"You living soul who dare to trespass here,
Beware of entering this realm of pain!
Beware of those in whom you place your trust!
Wide and deceitful is the entryway!"

My guide stood firm: "Why must you shout? Don't try   20
To stop the destined journey of this man,
For it is willed where what is willed must be.
Keep silent, then, and seek to learn no more!"

I now began to hear despairing cries.
My ears were pierced by lamentations, sounds   25
Unbearable, and every light was mute.
I heard a bellowing as when the sea
Is roiled by warring winds. In agony
The souls are driven, whirled, and buffeted
By storms that know no pity and no rest.   30
Wind-blown to where the edge of Hell's great sink
Begins, they shriek, they moan, they curse God's power.
How willingly these sinners of the flesh
Permitted reason to be passion's slave!
And just as flocks of starlings wing their way   35
Across the winter sky, so hosts of dead
And evil spirits hurtle in despair:
Here, there, above, below, bestormed they swirl,
Unsoothed by slightest hope of lesser pain.
Like cranes who chant their cries across the sky   40
In never-ending lines, so did they seem
Who wailed in winds that bore them darkly on.
I turned to Virgil: "Who are these, my lord,
Whom the dark fury of the tempest drives?"

"The first is Queen Semiramis, who ruled   45
Much land but who was slave to lechery
And who made licit the libidinous,
In her attempt to palliate her guilt.
As Ninus' widow, she succeeded him
And held the land where now the Sultan reigns.   50
That soul is Dido, suicide for love,
Unfaithful to the ashes of her spouse.
There's Cleopatra, the lascivious.
There's Helen, for whose sake much blood was shed
And for so long, and see Achilles there,   55

Whom love and treachery brought down to death.
Paris, Tristan. . . ."

       I saw a thousand shades
Whose lives had by the force of love been shattered,
And when my master had identified
Many a lord and lady of the past,   60
My heart felt pity, and my senses reeled.
I said: "If possible, I'd gladly speak
With those two spirits drifting in the wind
Who seem to float so lightly as they pass."

And he: "When they approach, ask them to pause   65
For love's sweet sake, whose law still leads them on,
And they will come."

       So when the wind had borne
Them close enough, I called: "Oh wearied souls,
If none forbid it, come and speak with us!"

My plea cut through the dark, malignant air   70
And they, like doves with steady wings outstretched,
Drawn sweetly to their nest by love's desire,
Borne swiftly by the will to love, broke off
From Dido's band and came to us. One spoke:

"Oh gracious living creature who have come   75
To witness this eternal night and wind
And visit us who stained the world with blood,
Were He who rules the universe our friend,
We'd pray that He might bring you peace of soul
Because of your compassion for our fate.   80
Of what you wish to hear we'll speak to you,

And we will hear whatever you would speak,
Now while the wind that punishes is hushed.

"The town where I was born sits by the sea.
Nearby the river Po descends to seek   85
Repose with all its tributary streams.
Love, the swift conqueror of gentle hearts,
Inflamed my lover with a carnal lust
For my fair form, of which I was deprived
In such a way as to offend me still.   90
Love, who makes the beloved love in turn,
Enchanted me and sealed our common doom.
In Hell we are as one, as once on Earth.
Love led us to one death: far, far below,
Caïna waits for him who spilled our blood."   95

Dark was the wind that carried these dark words,
And when I'd listened to that wounded soul,
I bowed my head, until the Poet asked:
"What are you thinking now?"

                       I answered him:
"What tender dreams of Love, what desperate   100
Desire could bring these souls to such an end?"
Again I turned to them and spoke: "Francesca,
Your story makes me sorrow, both for you
And for the one you love. But I must know:
When you and he had breathed those first sweet sighs   105
Of love, say how and when Love led you both
To taste his dubious desires."

                       And she:
"There is no greater pain than to recall
The happy past in times of misery.

Too well your teacher knows the truth of this!   110
But let me tell, though I must speak through tears,
The way Love came to nestle in our hearts.

"One day we sat and read for pleasure's sake
Of noble Lancelot, by Love possessed.
We were alone and mindless of the risk.   115
Some passage in the book would often cause
Our eyes to meet and from our faces drain
The blood. How quickly we were overwhelmed!
For when we read that Lancelot embraced
His Guinevere, his queen, his love, and kissed   120
Those long-desired, smiling lips, then he,
Who never shall be severed from my side,
All trembling, turned and kissed me on the mouth.
That writer and his book—what panderers
They were! . . . That day we read from it no more."   125

And while she spoke, the other spirit wept
And wept so pitifully that I felt
My senses failing me, like one near death,
And, like one dead, fell fainting to the ground.

NOTES TO CANTO V

[SUMMARY OF THE CANTO: *Descending to the Second Circle, the poets come upon Minos, judge of the damned, who tries unsuccessfully to prevent the living Dante from proceeding further. Dante and Virgil see swarms of spirits buffeted in the dark air by a never-ending storm. Virgil points out the shades of many famous people, here punished for the carnal sins they committed during their earthly existence. Among these are Cleopatra, Tristan, Helen, and Achilles. Dante then speaks with the soul of Francesca da Rimini, who tells him her tragic story while her lover, Paolo, looks on in silence. Overwhelmed by her tale, Dante falls fainting to the ground.*]

1   DOWNWARD WE JOURNEYED TO THE SECOND RING: Dante and Virgil are now in Circle Two of Hell, where the souls of those who committed sins of the flesh (*e.g.*, lust, adultery) are punished. It must be understood that Circles Two through Nine (the last) are divided into two parts: Circles Two through Five are reserved for the sins of incontinence, while Six through Nine are intended for those of malice (though some would argue that Circle Six, for the heretics, is *sui generis*). Sins of incontinence involve the lack of self-control, "sins of the individual man against the various parts of his own life and nature, by excess or defect," as John S. Carroll summarizes it. (See Select Bibliography.) Lack of control over one's appetites and passions are sins of sensuality and gluttony and are punished in Circles Two and Three, respectively; the sins of avarice and prodigality, or failure to control one's material possessions, are punished in Circle Four; anger and sullenness are reserved for Circle Five. In Circle Six are found the heretics, those who propagate and practice false belief. In the last three circles of Hell, Seven through Nine, are found those who sinned through malice, which is subdivided into violence, fraud, and treachery.

4   HERE MINOS STANDS, WITH MINATORY SNARL: Minos was a mythical king of Crete who was rewarded by Zeus for the justice of his earthly reign by being appointed the chief judge of Hades. He is found both in Homer's and Virgil's accounts of the underworld. However, Dante converts Minos into a demonic figure in keeping with the violence and malice of Hell as the poet conceives it.

16   "YOU LIVING SOUL WHO DARE TO TRESPASS HERE": This is the sec-

ond time some creature has tried to prevent Dante from passing through Hell (see Canto I).

19   "WIDE AND DECEITFUL IS THE ENTRYWAY!": *Matthew* 7:19: "Enter in at the strait gate: for wide is the gate, and broad is the way that leadeth to destruction, and many there be which go in thereat."

26   . . . AND EVERY LIGHT WAS MUTE: Another example of synesthesia (see Canto I: 56).

45   "THE FIRST IS QUEEN SEMIRAMIS . . .": Semiramis, the wife of Ninus, was queen of Assyria. She is alleged to have had an incestuous relationship with her son and to have tried to legitimize that ugly fact by making it a law in her realm that one could have sex with anyone at all.

51   THAT SOUL IS DIDO, SUICIDE FOR LOVE: In the *Aeneid*, Dido, queen of Carthage, has pledged to remain faithful to the memory of her husband, Sychacus. However, she falls in love with Aeneas when he arrives in Carthage with his men after their escape from Troy, and when he abandons her, she kills herself.

53   THERE'S CLEOPATRA, THE LASCIVIOUS: She was the lover of Julius Caesar (by whom she had a son) and then of Mark Antony. Egypt was an enemy of Rome, and Dante's stance is unshakably pro-Roman.

54   THERE'S HELEN, FOR WHOSE SAKE MUCH BLOOD WAS SHED: According to legend, beautiful Helen, a Greek married to the Greek Menelaus, was kidnapped by, or willingly ran off with, young Paris of Troy. The Greeks raised an army and sailed across the Aegean to Troy to get her back. The resulting ten-year war between Greeks and Trojans (won by the Greeks) is called the Trojan War, the subject of Homer's *Iliad*.

55   . . . AND SEE ACHILLES THERE: Chief of the Greek warriors during the Trojan War, Achilles was in love with Polyxena, a daughter of King Priam of Troy. Some versions of the story say that Achilles was slain by Paris in a temple to which the latter lured him with the promise of seeing Polyxena. Paris wounded Achilles in the heel, his only vulnerable spot.

57   PARIS, TRISTAN . . . : Concerning Paris, see the note to line 54, above. One of the most tragic and moving of medieval tales is that of the adulterous affair between Tristan, nephew of King Mark of Cornwall, and the latter's wife, Isolde, a story that had been told by many authors in several European languages before Dante's time.

63   . . . THOSE TWO SPIRITS DRIFTING IN THE WIND: These are the souls of Francesca da Rimini and her lover, Paolo Malatesta. The scandalous, somewhat sordid, story of their tragic love and death appears to be a true one, though

its details may have been exaggerated. Francesca's father, Guido Vecchio da Polenta, lord of Ravenna, promised her in marriage to Gianciotto, son of Giovanni Malatesta, lord of Rimini. Gianciotto's physical deformity, coupled with the fact that the marriage was not a love-match but was arranged, may explain why Francesca had an affair with Gianciotto's brother, Paolo, some years later. One day, probably sometime during the year 1285, Gianciotto discovered his wife and brother *in flagrante delicto* and slew them both. Dante probably heard of the tragedy soon after it occurred (he was a young man of twenty at the time). In any event, he would surely have heard about it toward the end of his life when he was a guest in Ravenna at the court of Guido, nephew of the late Francesca. It was there that Dante died and is buried. (Florence has never succeeded in getting back his remains.) Speculation has it that Dante included this story in *Inferno* to honor his hosts at Ravenna.

84 "THE TOWN WHERE I WAS BORN SITS BY THE SEA": The town is Ravenna, on the east coast of Italy.

95 CAÏNA WAITS FOR HIM WHO SPILLED OUR BLOOD: Caïna is one of the regions of the Ninth Circle, Cocytus. Francesca hopes (or simply states) that the soul of her husband, Gianciotto, both a uxoricide and a fratricide, will be hurled there after his death. In the year 1300, when Dante's voyage through Hell is supposed to be taking place, Gianciotto was still alive.

119–120 FOR WHEN WE READ THAT LANCELOT EMBRACED / HIS GUINEVERE . . . : These two are among the principal characters in the numerous versions of the popular King Arthur legends. Dante undoubtedly knew these quite well. He does not need to go into the details of the adulterous affair between Lancelot and Guinevere because his readers would have been quite familiar with the story.

CANTO VI

The lovers' melancholy fate had made
Me grieve and made my mind go dark. When I
Awoke, I was in Circle Three. No matter
Where I looked or walked or stared, I saw
New bands of sufferers and new suffering.   5

A steady deluge falls here, heavy, cold.
Its quality and rhythm never change.
Heavy the sleet and snow that mix with it,
A filthy rain that mercilessly drops
Through stinking darkness to the stinking ground.   10
Strange Cerberus, a beast with triple throat,
Barks doglike at the souls stuck in the mud.
The red-eyed brute, with black and greasy beard,
With swollen paunch and taloned hands, flays, claws
The spirits, rends them limb from limb, while all   15
Are howling in the rain like dogs gone mad.
Round and round spin the miserable damned
And try with half their bodies to protect
The other pelted half, but all in vain.
On spotting us, this great worm Cerberus,   20
Enraged and quivering, bared vicious fangs.
My master stretched his hands out to the ground
And grabbing fistfuls of the loathsome mud

Flung it at the monster's ravenous maws.
As dogs that bark for food are quieted   25
When meat's thrown to them and they start to chew
And focus only on devouring it,
So the snouts of the three-faced beast snapped shut
Whose thundering bark makes all the spirits wish
That they were deaf.

              We walked near rain-soaked shades,   30
Stepping upon their insubstantial forms
That sprawled before us in the filthy muck.
But one, on seeing us, sat up and said:
"You living creature being led through Hell,
I wonder if you know me? Maybe not,   35
For you were made before I was unmade."

I said to him: "Your anguish is a bar
To recognizing you. Your face to me
Is unfamiliar. Tell me who you are,
Confined to such a stinking place, condemned   40
To undergo disgusting punishment,
Though other kinds might cause you greater pain."

"Florence, the city of your birth," he said,
A city filled with envy, like a sack
That's overflowing, was a home to me,   45
And there I lived in sweet serenity.
Ciacco was the name all Florence called me.
Now for the piglike sin of gluttony
I lie stretched out in mud and whipped by rain.
Still, I'm not the only one tormented   50
In this way. All these souls surrounding me
Are punished for the same iniquity."

As he was silent for a while, I said:
"Your miserable state moves me to tears.
But tell me, Ciacco, if it's possible,   55
What fate awaits the anguished citizens
Of our divided city. Can one find
A single honest man within its gates?
What is the reason for such long discord?"

And he to me: "There will be violence;   60
Much blood will flow. Finally the rustic
Faction will force their city rivals out
Amid much havoc, but within three years
This party will in turn collapse and let
The other occupy the seat of power   65
Because of one who tacks between the two.
The prideful Blacks will hold their heads up high
And keep the Whites oppressed. What tears the Whites
Will shed, what anger they will show, what shame
They will experience! All this will not   70
Affect the Blacks at all. In Florence now
Live two who long for justice but are spurned
Because the Florentines, it seems, are moved
By envy, pride, and avarice alone."

His tearful speech concluded with these words.   75
And I: "There's more I'd like to learn about.
Please favor me by giving me more facts.
Say where great Farinata may be found,
Tegghiaio, too (both worthy men), and where
Jacopo Rusticucci, Arrigo,   80
Mosca, and others set on doing good
Are to be seen, for I would have you tell
If Heaven soothes or Hell unhinges them."

He said: "They dwell among the blackest souls
In Hell, for different crimes have dragged them down   85
Below. If you descend, you'll see them all.
But promise to remember me to men
And memory when you go back to all
The sweetness of the sunlit world. And now
I will not say another word to you."   90

He had been gazing fixedly at me,
But now he looked askance, then, dropping chin
To chest, he slipped into the stinking muck
Where other souls lay blindly on their face.

My guide spoke up: "He will not wake again   95
Until the day the Angel's trumpet sounds
And One inimical to these shall come.
Each to his dismal tomb will then return,
Put on his earthly flesh and form, and hear
The judgment sound through all eternity."   100

So through the filthy mix of shades and sleet
We made our way, discoursing for a time
About the life to come.

                    I spoke: "My lord,
On Judgment Day, will all these fiery pains
Grow more, grow less, or be the same as now?"   105

"Remember the science you have studied:
The closer something comes to being perfect,
The more its sense of pain and pleasure sharpens.
The damned cannot achieve that state but hope
They will come closer to it than they are."   110

CANTO VI

We went around the circle as we walked,
And spoke of many things I won't reveal.

At last we came to where the path led down,
There to find Plutus, the great enemy.

NOTES TO CANTO VI

[SUMMARY OF THE CANTO: *Dante awakens to find himself inexplicably in Circle Three. Rain, sleet, and snow are falling through the dark, foul-smelling air upon the sufferers whom Dante sees all around him. A bizarre doglike monster, Cerberus, is viciously attacking the souls; then, interrupting his deviltry, he snarls menacingly at Dante and Virgil. The latter silences him by flinging dirt at his triple gullet. One soul rises from the filthy mud to speak to the poets: it is Ciacco of Florence, who explains that he is in Hell because of his gluttony. Before sinking back into the muck once more, he foretells the fate of Whites and Blacks in the city of his birth. The poets move on and encounter the figure of Plutus as the canto ends.*]

2–3 ... WHEN I / AWOKE, I WAS IN CIRCLE THREE: Once again, Dante finds himself in a lower level of Hell without knowing how he got there (see the opening lines of Canto IV). Circle Three is reserved for gluttony, another sin of incontinence. For an interesting description of this sin, see Geoffrey Chaucer's "Parson's Tale," from the *Canterbury Tales*. See also *Philippians*, 3:18–19: "For many walk, of whom I have told you often, and now tell you even weeping, that they are the enemies of the cross of Christ: whose end is destruction, whose God is their belly, and whose glory is in their shame, who mind earthly things."

11 STRANGE CERBERUS, A BEAST WITH TRIPLE THROAT: Cerberus is yet another creature that Dante borrowed (and slightly altered) from the classic myths (see the *Aeneid*, Book VI).

20 ON SPOTTING US, THIS GREAT WORM CERBERUS: Dante also calls Satan a worm (see Canto XXXIV, in which Satan makes his appearance).

33   BUT ONE, ON SEEING US, SAT UP AND SAID: This is the shade of Ciacco, a Florentine of some distinction whose gluttony was well known (as was his wit). However, we know little else of him; we don't even know his full name (Ciacco, meaning "pig," is doubtless a nickname). Giovanni Boccaccio writes about the same character in the *Decameron*, IX:8.

36   FOR YOU WERE MADE BEFORE I WAS UNMADE: Ciacco means to say: "You were born before I died." Dante puns on the Italian words *fatto* ("made") and *disfatto* ("unmade").

43   "FLORENCE, THE CITY OF YOUR BIRTH . . .": Dante introduces the leitmotif of Florence for the first time in the poem; the city's name will sound and resound many times throughout the *Inferno*.

60 *et seq.* . . . "THERE WILL BE VIOLENCE": The souls in Hell, for some unexplained reason, have the power to see into the future. Ciacco tells Dante about events soon to transpire (but which had already transpired when Dante was writing the *Inferno*).

61–62   . . . FINALLY THE RUSTIC / FACTION WILL FORCE THEIR CITY RIVALS OUT: The "rustic faction" is that of the Whites (Bianchi in Italian), which was Dante's party, led by the Cerchi family. They are called "rustic" because they came originally from a rural area. The "rivals" are the Blacks (Neri in Italian), led by Corso Donati. (Dante's wife, Gemma, was a Donati.) These two divisions of the Guelf party were at each other's throats around the year 1300.

66   BECAUSE OF ONE WHO TACKS BETWEEN THE TWO: A reference to Pope Boniface VIII, whom Dante hated. Pretending that he merely wanted to restore peace to Florence, which was being wracked by clashes between the Blacks and Whites, Boniface sent Charles of Valois, brother of the king of France, to the city in 1301 to maintain order. However, no sooner had Charles arrived than he supported the Blacks, whose leaders had been exiled from Florence in 1300, during Dante's priorate. In 1302, more than five hundred Whites, Dante among them, were exiled in turn, and the exiled Blacks were readmitted into the city. Dante never returned to Florence. (See the *Cronica* of Giovanni Villani, who lived in Florence at the time of these events. Villani's account squares with Ciacco's.)

72   LIVE TWO WHO LONG FOR JUSTICE BUT ARE SPURNED: It cannot be said with certainty who these two just men are; however, some believe that Dante and his close friend, Guido Cavalcanti, are meant.

78   SAY WHERE GREAT FARINATA MAY BE FOUND: We shall meet the towering figure of Farinata degli Uberti in Canto X among the heretics. Though a Ghibelline, he saved Florence from destruction in 1260.

79–81   TEGGHIAIO . . . JACOPO RUSTICUCCI, ARRIGO, MOSCA: These men were all Florentines. Tegghiaio Aldobrandi tried, but failed, to dissuade the Florentines from attacking Siena in 1260; the attack resulted in the disastrous (for Florence) battle of Montaperti. Jacopo Rusticucci and another Florentine represented Florence in negotiations with other Tuscan towns. Arrigo has not been satisfactorily identified. Mosca dei Lamberti urged the murder of Buondelmonte de' Buondelmonti, who had dishonored a woman of the Amidei family. Tegghiaio and Rusticucci are found in Canto XVI amid the sodomites; Mosca dei Lamberti, in Canto XXVIII, among the sowers of discord. Dante does not speak of Arrigo again in *Inferno*, but some believe he is to be found in Mosca's circle.

87–88   BUT PROMISE TO REMEMBER ME TO MEN / AND MEMORY . . . : Similar requests to be remembered among the living will be made by other sinners as Dante proceeds through Hell. As he nears the bottom of the pit, however, Dante will meet sinners who hope he will say nothing at all about them to anyone, perhaps because their sin, and hence their shame, is greater.

97   AND ONE INIMICAL TO THESE SHALL COME: The "One" is Jesus, who will come to judge the living and the dead at the Resurrection. (Again, Jesus' name is not uttered anywhere in *Inferno*.)

106   "REMEMBER THE SCIENCE YOU HAVE STUDIED": By "science," Virgil means the ideas of Aristotle as they were filtered through to Dante and the medieval world by Thomas Aquinas.

107–110   THE CLOSER SOMETHING COMES . . . CLOSER TO IT THAN THEY ARE: An elaboration of an idea derived from Aristotle. Since, at the Last Judgment, the souls and their dead bodies will be reunited, it is assumed that the reassembling of the two parts will result in the sinners' suffering more acutely than they do now in Hell. Similarly, the blessed may experience even greater bliss.

114   THERE TO FIND PLUTUS, THE GREAT ENEMY: Some commentators believe that Dante confused the mythological figure of Pluto, god of the underworld, with that of Plutus, god of wealth. But Pluto would, for Dante, be associated with Satan, who is to be found at the bottom-center of Hell (Canto XXXIV). Plutus is, quite properly, found blocking access to the avaricious and the prodigals of Circle Four (Canto VII).

CANTO VII

"Pape Satàn, Pape Satàn, aleppe!"
Plutus the vigilant began to cluck.
My gentle guide, who knew all things, made haste
To comfort me: "Don't be afraid. His power,
Whatever it may be, cannot prevent   5
Our going down the cliff."

                              To Plutus then,
Whose face was puffed with rage, my guide cried out:
"You vicious wolf of Hell, choke on your words!
And may your wrath consume you from within!
There is a reason why he's come to see   10
This pit. For it is willed in that far realm
Where Michael executed God's command
Against the unfaithful host of angels!"

As sails inflated by the wind collapse
To the deck when the masthead snaps, so fell   15
Cruel Plutus to the ground, and we went on
To Circle Four, whose margins mournfully
Encase the malice of the universe.

Ah, Justice of great God, who is it crowds
Together all the punishments I saw?   20
And why do our transgressions break us all?

As when the waves above Charybdis meet
And shatter as they crash, so here the souls
Go round and round in never-ending dance.
On either side I saw more people here,   25
It seemed to me, than I had seen elsewhere.
Shouts filled the air, as, shoving with their chests,
They rolled great rocks and clashed with other souls,
Then, wheeling on the spot, turned back to scream:
"Why do you squander?" or "Why do you hoard?"   30

So back they went along the dismal ring
On either side to the opposing point,
Continuing to shriek the same refrains.
When through the semicircle they had come
To joust once more, they went right back again.   35
My heart was stricken by this sight. I spoke:
"Please tell me, master, who these sinners are,
And if the tonsured people on the left
Were priests."

         And he: "The minds of all of these
Were so distorted in their earthly lives   40
They could be nothing but extravagant.
Quite clearly do their voices bark this out.
When they have reached the circle's halfway point,
They are divided by the counter sin.
The ones with bald spots on their heads are priests   45
And popes and cardinals, whom avarice
Has mastered utterly."

         And I replied:
"Among this crowd I ought to recognize
A few who were corrupted by these sins."

And he: "A useless thought, for what they did   50
In life they did quite blindly, and so now
They can't be seen. Halfway around this ring
They will collide, through all eternity.
One group shall from the tomb arise with fists
Clenched tight; the other, with their hair all shorn.   55
These reprobates are barred from Paradise
By avarice and prodigality,
The forces that foment this endless strife,
Which I won't glorify with any words.
My son, you see how disillusioning   60
It is to have possessions, Fortune's toys,
For which the race of men forever vies.
Not all the gold that is, or ever was,
Beneath the moon could bring them any rest."

"This Fortune whom you speak of—can you tell   65
Me more of her? It seems the goods of all
The world are in her grip," was my reply.

And he to me: "Oh foolish creatures! See
How ignorance engulfs you! Mark these words:
Great God, whose knowledge transcends everything,   70
Created all the Heavens, and as guides
He made the angels, such that every part
Shines to every other part, with equal
Scattering of light. Correspondingly,
A guide and minister for worldly goods   75
He made, so that, from time to time, she might
Shift ownership of vain and worldly things
From race to race, from blood to blood, and far
Beyond the meddling of all human wit.
One people therefore rules, another's ruled,   80

And Fortune's choice, to us invisible
As serpents in the grass, can make it so.
Against her, knowledge is quite impotent.
Foreseeing, judging, she administers
Her reign just as the angels do their own.   85
Her permutations know no pause and so
Are implemented by Necessity
With speed. Thus change comes swiftly to mankind.
She is the one so frequently maligned
By those who ought to praise her but instead   90
Defame her. Blessed, she is oblivious
To them, and with the angels happily
She rolls her sphere, rejoicing in her bliss.

"And now we will descend to greater pain.
The stars that were ascending when I left   95
Are sinking, and we can't prolong our stay."

We crossed the circle to the other side
And found ourselves above a bubbling spring
Whose water flows into a ditch that leads
From it. That water was a darker hue   100
Than deepest purple. We were following
Its blackness and the going down was rough.
The murky stream, when it has reached the edge
Of dark and evil shores, melds with a marsh
That bears the name of Styx. Standing, staring   105
Fixedly, I could distinguish many
Spirits mired in the muddy swamp. Naked,
Their faces bestialized by twists of rage,
They beat like brutes at one another's forms,
Not only with their hands, but with their heads   110
And feet and chests, and furiously ripped
At one another with their feral teeth.

My master turned to me: "See there, my son,
Those souls whom wrath consumed, and understand
That deep beneath this water people sigh   115
Making the surface bubble with their breath.
This you may see no matter where you look.
These, stuck in slime, say: 'Sullen when on Earth,
Though every breath of air was honey-sweet,
Made happy by the sun, filling our hearts.   120
With sluggish fumes, here sullenly we lie
In mud.' This hymn comes gurgling from their throats:
No clearly spoken word can leave their mouths."

Between the dry bank and the pool we walked,
Along a lengthy portion of the ring,   125
And, watching those who feasted in the filth,
We came at last to where a tower rose.

NOTES TO CANTO VII

[SUMMARY OF THE CANTO: *The monstrous and frightening Plutus cackles
incomprehensibly at Dante and Virgil but is silenced by the latter's powerful words. They
move down to Circle Four, where they observe the strife between the avaricious and the
prodigal, who roll great weights toward one another around a circle, hurling insults, only
to go back the other way and repeat the performance in an endless dance. Virgil dis-
courses on the role of Fortune in human life. Continuing their walk, the poets come to
Circle Five, where they see the souls of the angry and the sullen submerged in the swamp
called the Styx. They then arrive at a tower.*]

1 PAPE SATÀN, PAPE SATÀN, ALEPPE: These words of Plutus, from no
known language, are unintelligible, although the meaning of word "Satàn"

seems obvious. Possibly, the first phrase is to be taken as the Italian words *Pap'è Satan,* short for *Il Papa è Satana* ("The Pope is Satan"). This is pretty strong stuff, but we know how Dante felt about many of the popes, especially Boniface VIII. Popes are found among the sinners in this canto, and the soul of Celestine V is probably dwelling in Canto III.

2   PLUTUS THE VIGILANT BEGAN TO CLUCK: As indicated in the note to line 115 of Canto VI, Dante, like many others (including some early commentators on the *Commedia*), may have confused Plutus, god of wealth, with Pluto, a name for the classical god of the underworld, Hades. Clearly, either would be a proper figure for this canto. In the last line of Canto VI, Dante calls him "the great enemy" (of mankind).

12–13   WHERE MICHAEL . . . HOST OF ANGELS: *Revelation* 12:7: "And there was war in Heaven; Michael and his angels fought against the dragon; and the dragon fought and his angels. . . ."

22   AS WHEN THE WAVES ABOVE CHARYBDIS MEET: Charybdis was the legendary name of a whirlpool (and simultaneously a monster) in the Strait of Messina between Sicily and the Italian mainland. The waters of that region are turbulent, for it is there that waters flowing from the Ionian and Tyrrhenian Seas meet. Attempting to avoid Charybdis, ships are said to have crashed on the rock (Scylla) on the opposite coast.

30   "WHY DO YOU SQUANDER?" OR "WHY DO YOU HOARD?": Each group of sinners berates the other for its sin: avarice or prodigality. No sinners are identified by name in this canto.

45–47   THE ONES WITH BALD SPOTS . . . HAS MASTERED UTTERLY: Dante was particularly outraged by what he viewed as the avarice of the clergy.

65   THIS FORTUNE WHOM YOU SPEAK OF . . . : Fortune was believed to be the handmaiden of God and had the status of an angel. She carried out God's will among humans on Earth; Dante's view of her is a far cry from the popular conception of Lady Luck. (In fact, luck is not involved.) There is a relevant poem on Fortune by Guido Cavalcanti, a friend of Dante's; Dante Gabriel Rossetti translated it into English as "Song of Fortune."

95–96   THE STARS . . . WE CAN'T PROLONG OUR STAY: It is now midnight. Dante and Virgil entered Hell early in the evening.

98   AND FOUND OURSELVES ABOVE A BUBBLING SPRING: The river Acheron circles Hell, then runs below ground and re-emerges to form the Styx.

104–105   . . . A MARSH / THAT BEARS THE NAME OF STYX . . . : Styx (meaning "hateful") is the river found in the underworld in the *Aeneid.* In the *Inferno,* it is a marsh encircling the city of Dis.

106–107   . . . I COULD DISTINGUISH MANY / SPIRITS . . . : These two new groups of souls, who bring us to Circle Five, are the angry and the sullen (or resentful). These represent the last of the sins of incontinence that we have been seeing since Limbo. The next group will be composed of violent sinners.

CANTO VIII

Continuing my story, I relate
That long before we reached the tower's base,
A pair of lights atop it drew our gaze,
While in the distant darkness dimly shone
Another light as if it answered these.   5
Of Virgil, sea of wisdom, I inquired:
"What is the message that these lights appear
To be exchanging, and who's sending them?"

                              He said:
"Above the filthy water you can see
What we are waiting for, unless the mist   10
That hangs above the marsh hides it from view."

No arrow ever shot from bow traversed
The air more quickly than the boat that rushed
At us across the river. In it stood
A single ferryman, who cried: "You have   15
Arrived, you wretched soul!"

                        And Virgil said:
"Phlegyas, Phlegyas, this shouting is in vain!
You'll have us only for the time it takes
To furrow through this filth!"

Discovering
He's been deceived, a man will often seethe   20
Resentfully. So with this ferryman,
Whose pent-up rage exasperated him.
My leader stepped into the skiff. I saw
That only after I had followed him
Did Phlegyas' boat show signs of bearing weight.   25
As soon as we had settled in the boat,
The ancient bark sped off, more deeply set
Into the fen than when it ferried souls.
While we were speeding through the stagnant marsh,
A mud-encrusted shade rose up and said: 30
"Who can you be that come before your hour?"

I answered him: "I'm here, but not for long.
But who are you, so ugly to behold?"

"You see before you one who weeps," he said.

"Then stay here weeping and in pain," said I.   35
"Detested soul! I know just who you are
In spite of all your filth!"

                              With both his hands
He grabbed the gunwale. Vigilant, my guide
Then shoved him back.

                              "Down with the other dogs!"
He said, then threw his arms around my neck   40
And kissed me.

                    "What worthy indignation!"
Virgil said. "Blessed is the womb that bore you!
On Earth he was a man of arrogance,

Who never did a kind or worthy deed,
And so his soul is wallowing in rage.   45
So many men on Earth now view themselves
As princes. Here they'll just be pigs in muck.
On Earth the only name they've left is mud."

I said: "My lord, before we leave this place,
I'd gladly see him choking in that soup."   50

And he: "Before we reach the other side you'll have
Your wish, the kind that ought to be fulfilled!"

The sinner's fellow-dwellers in the muck
Then set upon him so ferociously,
That to this day I thank and praise the Lord.   55
While they cried, "Get Filippo Argenti!"
The frenzied spirit of the Florentine,
In anguish and in anger, gnawed his flesh.
We journeyed on. I'll say no more of him.

New lamentations now assailed my ears.   60
I strained to see their source. My master said:
"We're coming quickly to the place called Dis.
Grave are its citizens, and powerful
Its demon garrison."

                "I can make out,"
Said I, "inside the valley many mosques,   65
Vermilion-hued as if they'd just emerged
From all the raging flames of Hell."

                     And he:
"The fire that burns so fiercely in their core
Lends them the crimson tint of Lower Hell."

We journeyed without pause until we stood   70
Amid the moats, so deeply dug, that ran
Around the gray and iron walls of Dis,
The city of despair, to which we gave
The widest berth before we came to shore.
Then Phlegyas thundered in a grating voice: 75
"Get out, get out! you're at the entrance now!"

More than a thousand angels could be seen,
The rebel crew expelled from Heaven's court.
They stood above the gates and screamed at us:
"And who is this that passes through the realm   80
Where dead men dwell, yet is not dead himself?"

My knowing guide advised the rebel band
That he would parley with them privately.
Their anger dimming, they replied: "We'll meet
With you, but as for your companion there,   85
Who boldly entered the forbidden realm,
He must retrace his steps along the path
That you and folly made him tread. You stay,
But through the darkness let him grope his way!"

Imagine, Reader, how these chilling words   90
Affected me: I thought I'd never see
The sunlit surface of the Earth again.
I quickly said: "My master and my lord,
Who more than seven times have rescued me,
Do not abandon me! If we cannot   95
Go on, then let's go back without delay!"

And he who'd led me all this distance said:
"Don't be afraid. No one can block our path,

For it is willed by One above. Wait here.
Let hope suffuse your mind and soothe your soul.   100
I shall not leave you in the jaws of Hell."

And so this gentle father went away
And left me in a state of agony.
I could not hear the words he spoke to them,
But soon the horde of ghouls was hurtling back   105
Helter-skelter through the hideous gates,
And in my master's face they shut them fast.
His eyes downcast, his face no longer bright
With customary boldness, he returned
With sad, slow steps: "See who blocks my entrance   110
To the house of pain!"

                    Then to me: "Don't fear
My growing wrath. I'll win no matter who
It is that bars my way. Their insolence
Is nothing new; at Hell's dark mouth they tried
This scheme before, but it is still unblocked.   115
Recall the marks of death above the gate.
Know, too, that while we wait, a figure now
Is dropping through the rings of Hell, and he
Will bring the power that will let us pass."

NOTES TO CANTO VIII

[SUMMARY OF THE CANTO: *Arriving at the edge of a marsh, Dante and Virgil find themselves at the base of a tower. As they observe what appear to be signal lights in the distance, a boat skims quickly over the water toward them. It is ferried by Phlegyas, guardian of Circle Five; he begins shouting, but Virgil silences him, and the poets enter the boat. As they cross the marsh, the soul of Filippo Argenti rises from the water and starts to speak with Dante, who reacts angrily. Virgil pushes Argenti back into the water, praising Dante for having spoken sharply. The sinner, meanwhile, is attacked by other souls from the marsh. Phlegyas deposits the poets near the entrance to the city where a host of devils say they will not allow them to enter Dis. Virgil tells Dante not to be concerned, for at that very moment help is on the way.*]

1   CONTINUING MY STORY, I RELATE: The three opening words seem to imply that some time elapsed between the writing of Cantos VII and VIII, although there is no hard evidence that there was such an interval; thus, the meaning of the words remains somewhat puzzling.

11   THAT HANGS ABOVE THE MARSH . . . : The marsh, again, is Styx (see note to line 104, Canto VII), representing Circle Five, reserved for those whose sin was either anger or sullenness.

16   . . . YOU WRETCHED SOUL!: Phlegyas here is speaking only to one figure, either Dante or Virgil (we cannot be sure which). Perhaps he recognizes that Dante is a living man and so ignores him.

17   "PHLEGYAS, PHLEGYAS, THIS SHOUTING IS IN VAIN!": Phlegyas is another figure from classical mythology. Angry because Apollo had violated his daughter, Phlegyas torched the god's temple at Delphi; for this, he was punished with death, and his soul was sent to Hades. In Dante's scheme, he represents immoderate wrath. The name Phlegyas comes from a Greek word meaning "I burn." It is instructive to compare the figure of Phlegyas to that of Charon, Plutus, and similar infernal monsters.

25   DID PHLEGYAS' BOAT SHOW SIGNS OF BEARING WEIGHT: A realistic touch designed to make the poem convincing in its immediacy.

30   A MUD-ENCRUSTED SHADE ROSE UP AND SAID: This is the soul of Filippo degli Adimari Cavicciuli—whose nickname, Argenti, appears to have been given to him by the Florentines because he used to shoe his horses with silver

(*argento* is Italian for "silver"). A nobleman of fiery temper, he was perhaps not untypical of the arrogant aristocrats of his day. There is a vivid contrast in this scene between Dante's ire, highly praised by Virgil, and Filippo's pathetic "You see before you one who weeps" (line 34). Dante demonstrates none of the pity that we saw in earlier cantos. Doubtless his heart becomes more hardened as he learns of increasingly graver sins in his descent through Hell. Another explanation for his hatred of Argenti may be the story that Argenti's brother, Boccaccio (not to be confused with the author of the *Decameron*), may have taken possession of Dante's goods when the latter was exiled from Florence. Another story has it that Argenti once slapped Dante in public. See Boccaccio's *Decameron*, IX, 8.

38   HE GRABBED THE GUNWALE . . . : It is when Argenti grabs the gunwale of the boat that we sense his anger. He has been provoked, it would seem, because Dante has recognized him and because Dante has spoken sharply to him: rage responds to rage. Contrast this encounter with Dante's conversation with Brunetto Latini in Canto XV.

42   . . . "BLESSED IS THE WOMB THAT BORE YOU!": See *Luke* 11:27: . . . "Blessed is the womb that bore thee, and the paps which thou hast sucked."

62   "WE'RE COMING QUICKLY TO THE PLACE CALLED DIS": Dis was the Roman name for Pluto, the ruler of the underworld. Dante also refers to him by the names Satan, Lucifer, and Beelzebub. (See Canto XXXIV for the figure of Satan.)

64–65   . . . "I CAN MAKE OUT / . . . INSIDE THE VALLEY MANY MOSQUES": The towers are probably called mosques because, as a result of the Christian crusades in the Near East, where European soldiers saw so many mosques, these came to symbolize the essence of things un-Christian, heretical. (See the figure of Muhammad in Canto XXVIII.)

113–115   . . . THEIR INSOLENCE . . . BUT IT IS STILL UNBLOCKED: A reference to the Harrowing of Hell by Christ (see Canto IV, note to line 48). Satan and other devils tried unsuccessfully to prevent Him from entering Hell.

117–118   . . . A FIGURE NOW / IS DROPPING THROUGH THE RINGS OF HELL . . . : This figure is an angel who will appear in Canto IX to force open the gates of Satan's city.

CANTO IX

The ghastly pallor of my face, brought on
By Virgil's turning back, now made my guide's
Seem much more normal in its hue than mine.
He stood attentive, listening. The dark,
The mist blocked everything from sight. He said: 5
"This battle must be won, or else . . . ! Just think
Of who it was that offered help! But why
This long delay in coming to our aid?"

I felt the shuffling in his words and so
I was afraid that what he'd left unsaid   10
Perhaps implied more than he really meant.
"Can any soul from Limbo come to this
Foul hollow? There, at least, the punishment
For sin is only loss of hope," I said.

And he: "The souls in Limbo rarely make   15
This journey to the city of despair,
As I do now, although I came here once
Before, conjured by the dread Erichtho,
Who reunites the spirit with its corpse.
My soul and body had not long been split   20
When she dispatched me into Dis to fetch
A soul from deep Judecca, lowest place,

And darkest, and most distant possible
From highest Heaven that encircles all.
I know the way; you may be sure of that.   25
This marsh, exhaling such a mighty stench,
Encoils this savage sink. On entering,
We'll stir up lots of wrath."

                              I don't recall
What else he said, for something caught my eye
Upon the looming tower red with flames.   30
Three hellish Furies, smeared with blood, appeared
And startled me. They had the shape of women.
Great green-skinned hydras slithered round their forms,
And on their heads, instead of hair, horned snakes
And tiny serpents grew. And then my guide,   35
Who knew so well these ghastly serving maids
Of Proserpine, the queen of endless grief,
Told me: "Those hags are the Erinyes:
Megaera on the left, and on the right,
Alecto weeping; and the center one's   40
Tisiphone."

                    He suddenly grew still.
They tore their breasts with savage fingernails
And beat themselves and screamed so stridently
I cringed and pressed much closer to my guide.
"Where's Medusa?" shrieked the Furies. "Let's turn   45
This wretch to stone! We should have sought
Revenge on Theseus and his bold assault!"

And Virgil: "Turn around and close your eyes,
For if the Gorgon comes and you but glance,
You'll be forever frozen on this spot."   50

He quickly spun me round, and then, because
He did not trust my hands alone, he cupped
Both of his tightly on my eyes. (All those
Whose intellects are sound will understand
The meaning that my cryptic verses veil.)   55
And now across the troubled waters came
A terrifying sound that shook each shore.
The blast was like a wind, made violent
When warm with warmer air conflicts, that whips
Across a wood, flings branches to the ground   60
And proudly sweeps them all away, swirling
In dusty clouds to scatter beasts and men.
My guide removed his hands and said: "Look now,
There where the mist is thick, across the scum
Of the primeval marsh."

                    Just as the frogs   65
Dive into water at a snake's approach
And squat in fear upon the bottom, so
I saw more than a thousand souls rush off
While from afar a figure came, who crossed
The Styx on feet the water could not wet.   70
The only sign of weariness he showed
Was when he waved away, with his left hand,
The wilted and miasmal air of Styx.
My guide instructed me to say no word
And made me bow. I sensed the messenger   75
Was Heaven-sent. About him was an air
Disdainful. Lightly with his wand he touched
The gate, and instantly it opened wide.
His will was law that no one could transgress.
He shouted at the rebel band: "Hear me,   80
You miserable dregs of Paradise!

How dare you demonstrate such insolence,
Dare kick against the unalterable will
Of Him whose purpose is immutable?
You've tried before; your punishment: more pain.   85
You'll get no benefit from fighting Fate.
Your pet fiend Cerberus still bears the scars
On neck and chin for trying to resist!"

Without a word, he made his way across
The fecal ooze of Styx, like one concerned   90
With weightier affairs. His holy words
Gave us the confidence to enter Dis.
No one prevented us from going in,
And I, who wanted to observe the state
Of sinners sealed inside these ugly walls,   95
Surveyed the scene. Around me stretched a plain
Of endless pain and cruel punishment.
As at Arles, where the water of the Rhone
Lies stagnant, or at Pola, on the gulf
Of Quarnero that shuts in Italy   100
And laves its boundaries, so here the ground
Lay pockmarked with innumerable graves.
But here they were more horrible, for flames
Were licking in between and made them glow
Like iron heated fiercely in a forge.   105
The lids of every tomb were opened wide
And pitiful the sounds that came from them,
The lamentations of the souls within.
"Who are the people buried in these tombs?"
I asked. "Who sighs in so much agony?"   110

He answered: "Herein lie great heretics
And with them their adherents. Like with like
Are buried in these crowded tombs, packed tight

With burning souls. How hot they are depends
Upon how heinously the sinner sinned."   115

Then when my leader circled to the right,
We passed between great walls and ghastly graves.

NOTES TO CANTO IX

[SUMMARY OF THE CANTO: *Virgil, who seems concerned as he and Dante await the arrival of the messenger, tells Dante that he has been in Hell once before, having left Limbo in order to bring back a spirit at the behest of Erichtho. When they catch sight of the horrible Furies on the tower of Dis, Virgil explains who they are. When these hags threaten to call in Medusa to turn Dante into stone, Virgil protects him by placing his hands over the pilgrim's eyes. Now, in a rush of wind, the angelic messenger appears. Scolding the rebel angels in Dis, he opens the gates with a touch of his wand. As the poets enter the city, they come upon a huge open area dotted with the fiery graves of the heretics.*]

7   OF WHO IT WAS THAT OFFERED HELP! . . . : The person who offered help is Beatrice (see Canto II).

17–18   . . . ALTHOUGH I CAME HERE ONCE / BEFORE, CONJURED BY THE DREAD ERICHTHO: There is no mention elsewhere of such a trip by Virgil. Erichtho was a legendary sorceress of Thessaly of whom the Roman writer Lucan speaks in his *Civil War.* The story of her alleged power to raise the dead derives from an incident recounted in Lucan: she is said to have revived a dead spirit in order to have it foretell, for Pompey, the outcome of the battle of Pharsalia.

22   A SOUL FROM DEEP JUDECCA . . . : The last division of the Ninth Circle of Hell (see Canto XXXIV) is called Judecca (Giudecca in Italian) after Judas Iscariot.

24   FROM HIGHEST HEAVEN THAT ENCIRCLES ALL: Heaven is the high-

est (outermost) sphere in the Ptolemaic concept, accepted in the Middle Ages as the model of the universe.

31   THREE HELLISH FURIES, SMEARED WITH BLOOD . . . : The Furies (or Erinyes—see line 38) are figures from classical mythology whose function is to hound sinners. (See, for example, the *Oresteia* of Aeschylus, in which Orestes is pursued by the Furies for his crime of matricide.) Dante probably derived his notion of these creatures from Virgil, Ovid, and Statius (all Roman authors).

37   OF PROSERPINE, THE QUEEN OF ENDLESS GRIEF: Proserpine (or Hecate) was the wife of Pluto and thus *ipso facto* Queen of Hades.

45   "WHERE'S MEDUSA?" SHRIEKED THE FURIES . . . : Medusa was one of the three Gorgons. Her head was horrible to look at (snakes, not hair, grew from her head); anyone who gazed upon her was turned to stone immediately.

46–47   ". . . WE SHOULD HAVE SOUGHT / REVENGE ON THESEUS AND HIS BOLD ASSAULT!": Theseus had tried to kidnap Proserpine and was punished by being kept in Hades. Hercules went to the underworld and managed to free him. Clearly, the Furies are still furious because Theseus escaped.

49   FOR IF THE GORGON COMES AND YOU BUT GLANCE: The Gorgon is Medusa.

53–55   . . . (ALL THOSE / WHOSE INTELLECTS . . . MY CRYPTIC VERSES' VEIL.): It is difficult to understand Dante's meaning here. One interpretation is that the Gorgon's ability to turn people into stone is symbolic of the power of sin to harden the heart against God.

58   THE BLAST WAS LIKE A WIND . . . : The blast of wind heralds the arrival of the angel who will open the gates of the city for the poets (see line 69).

65–66   . . . JUST AS THE FROGS / DIVE INTO WATER . . . : A passage in Ovid's *Metamorphoses* furnished Dante with several details about frogs that have their echo in a few cantos of *Inferno*, such as this one.

69   WHILE FROM AFAR A FIGURE CAME . . . : This figure is most likely an angel, although some have identified him with Mercury or Aeneas. Others have claimed he is Christ, perhaps because he seems to walk on water, but surely Dante would not have Jesus descend into Hell merely to open a gate! Furthermore, since Dante never mentions the name of Christ in the *Inferno*, it would be inconsistent to have him appear there.

87   YOUR PET FIEND CERBERUS STILL BEARS THE SCARS: Cerberus, whom we met in Canto VI, was wounded by Hercules when the canine monster tried to block him from entering Hades. Hercules wrapped a chain around the neck of Cerberus and pulled him outside Hades (this is the origin of Cerberus' "scars").

96 ... AROUND ME STRETCHED A PLAIN: The poets are now in Circle Six, where the heresiarchs (major heretics) are punished, together with all those the latter influenced. The circle is a huge cemetery, whose heated iron tombs enclose the sinners. Dante compares this infernal cemetery to those of Arles, in Provence (France), and Pola (in Istria, a region of northeastern Italy).

111–112 ... "HEREIN LIE GREAT HERETICS / AND WITH THEM THEIR ADHERENTS ...": "Great heretics" refers to famed members of the faith whose religious ideas ran counter to church teachings.

116 THEN WHEN MY LEADER CIRCLED TO THE RIGHT: Dante and Virgil have been consistently moving to the left as they walk along the circles of Hell. They walk one-ninth of the way around each circle before descending to the next one, and so when they arrive at the end of Circle IX, they have completed a full circle. Here, however, as in Canto XVII, the poets move to the right. The perhaps far-fetched explanation for these two exceptions is that they may signify the poets' honesty and sincerity.

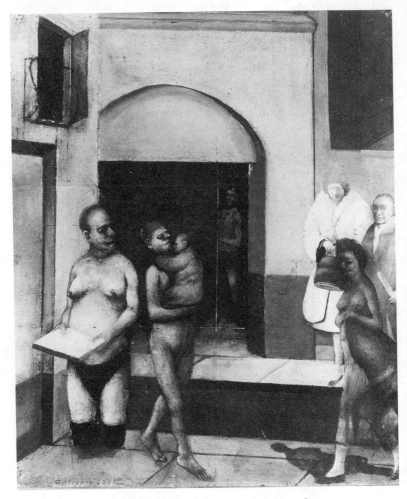

"The lids of those unguarded tombs are raised:
Am I allowed to see the souls inside?"

(8–9)

CANTO X

Between the sepulchers and city walls
We made our way, he first, I close behind,
Along a secret path my master knew.
I said: "My lord, in virtue unexcelled,
There are so many things I wish to learn,   5
So as you lead me through these evil rings,
Please satisfy my wish to understand.
The lids of those unguarded tombs are raised:
Am I allowed to see the souls inside?"

"They will be sealed when to Jehoshaphat   10
The ones who live in them return, bringing
Their bodies with them. Epicurus, he
Who spread the doctrine that the soul can die,
Here writhes in flame with all his followers.
Your question will be answered soon, and soon   15
Your secret wish will be fulfilled as well."

"I do not wish to hide my heart from you,"
I said, "but you've disposed me to be brief."

Suddenly I heard a voice: "Tuscan soul,
Who speak with reticence and trudge alive   20
Through Dis, the realm of fire, stay here awhile.

Your speech is manifestly Florentine.
Perhaps my treatment of that noble town
Was far too harsh."

        As from a tomb this voice
Eerily came forth, fearfully I moved   25
Much closer to my guide, whose words were sharp:
"What are you doing? Turn around! That soul,
The upper half of whom you soon will see,
Is Farinata, standing in his tomb."

I turned to stare at him, who raised his breast   30
And brow as if he held the universe
Of Hell in great disdain. The lively hands
Of Virgil thrust me boldly forth just then
Between the tombs. "Speak fittingly to him."

I reached the foot of Farinata's tomb.   35
In tone contemptuous, he spoke: "Tell me,
What's your lineage?"

        Anxious to obey,
I spoke to him quite openly. He said:
"They showed so much hostility to me,
My party and my ancestors, that twice   40
I sent your people into banishment."

"That may be so," I said, "but they came back
Both times, in any case. Apparently
Your people haven't yet picked up that art."

Then from the tomb another figure rose   45
Chin-high, for he was on his knees, I think.

He strained to see if someone else was there,
Someone he knew and loved. Not finding him,
He wept hot tears and said: "To this blind jail
Your brilliant mind has brought you. But if so,   50
Then where's my son?"

           And I replied: "It's not
Through any power of mine that I am here,
But someone's leading me. You see him there
Awaiting me. He's guiding me toward her,
Perhaps, for whom your Guido felt disdain."   55

His words and form of punishment revealed
His name to me. That's why my speech was frank.
In a moment he was on his feet. " 'Felt'?
Isn't he alive? Does the world's sweet light
No longer shine into his eyes?" he asked.   60

Because I paused before I answered him,
Back he fell into the flames and was seen
No more. The other soul, magnificent,
Impassive, neither bent nor turned his head,
But simply went on talking as before: 65
"To think that they have badly learned that art
Brings greater pain to me than does this bed.
The lunar face of her that reigns down here
Shall not reach fullness more than fifty times
Before you, too, shall learn how arduous   70
An art it is. And as you would return
To Earth, so sweet, so fair, I'd have you tell
Me why the Florentines use every law
To work against my family."

I said:
"The rout and carnage at the Arbia   75
   That dyed it red with so much blood gave rise
   To bloody prayers at temple."

                    Then he sighed
And said: "In that affair I did not act
   Alone, nor would I have allied myself
   With them in such a deed without great cause,   80
   But when they plotted Florence's destruction,
   I stood, one man alone, in her defense."

"May your descendants find repose," I said.
"And now, perhaps you can unloose a knot
   That binds my brain: from what I understand,   85
   You can foresee the future, yet it seems
   The present is inscrutable to you."

"Like some with faulty sight," he said, "we see
   What's far (God grants us this ability),
   But what's approaching us we cannot see: 90
   Our intellect is powerless, and so,
   For knowledge of the present world of men
   We must rely on those who relay news.
   So, when the door of future time is shut,
   We shall be blind, we shall know nothing more." 95

My conscience suddenly was pricked: "Please tell
   That other soul who fell into the tomb
   His son is still alive. I didn't tell
   Him so before because I was absorbed
   By all those doubts you've now cleared up for me." 100

Already Virgil was recalling me,
And so I begged the spirit tell in haste
Who lay with him. "More than a thousand souls
Here lie entombed with me. Among them are
The second Frederick and the Cardinal.   105
But of the rest I'll say no word."

                          Then down
Into the tomb he sank. I thought about
His hostile words while walking toward my guide,
Who started to move on, and as we went
Along he said to me: "You seem to be   110
Distracted. Why?"

                So I disclosed my thoughts.
"Remember well the words you've heard," he urged.
"And now attend to what I say." He raised
A finger. "When you stand before the soul
Of her whose spirit is so radiant,   115
Whose fair and brilliant eyes behold all things,
The journey of your life will be revealed."

He turned and started walking to the left.
We made our way along a lane that leads
To Dis and plunges headlong into Hell.   120

From where we stood we smelled its awful stink.

NOTES TO CANTO X

[SUMMARY OF THE CANTO: *As the poets make their way between the walls of Dis and the tombs, Virgil explains that the open tombs of this Sixth Circle of Hell will be closed forever on Judgment Day. Suddenly, one of the sinners, standing majestically in his tomb, calls to Dante. He is Farinata degli Uberti, a great leader of the Ghibellines and hence an enemy of Dante's. As Dante and Farinata converse, another soul, Cavalcante Cavalcanti, the father of Dante's good friend Guido, arises partially from the same tomb and asks Dante about Guido. Misconstruing Dante's hesitation in replying, he falls back into the tomb. Farinata, having utterly ignored Cavalcante, resumes his dialogue with the poet; he prophesies about Florence, explains the ability of a dead soul to see into the future, and tells who is in the tomb with him. Virgil calls out to Dante, who leaves Farinata, and the poets continue their journey.*]

10   "THEY WILL BE SEALED WHEN TO JEHOSHAPHAT": To the valley of Jehoshaphat all souls will be brought at the Last Judgment after they have been reunited with their bodies. *Joel* 3:2, 12: "I will also gather all nations and will bring them down into the valley of Jehoshaphat. . . . Let the heathen be wakened, and come up to the valley of Jehoshaphat: for there will I sit to judge all the Heathen round about." The appropriateness of the tradition, for Christians, is the fact that the Mount of Olives, from which Christ rose into Heaven, stands near the valley. It is also believed that the Mount of Olives is where Christ will descend to Earth at the Last Judgment.

12–13   . . . EPICURUS, HE / WHO SPREAD THE DOCTRINE THAT THE SOUL CAN DIE: Epicurus was a Greek philosopher (342–270 B.C.) who believed, in part, that happiness consists in the pursuit of pleasure (conversely, in the avoidance of pain). His followers added the idea that there is no afterlife. Dante classifies him as a heretic, but the label is inappropriate since he lived centuries before the birth of Christianity. The two characters with whom Dante converses in this canto were Epicureans. In his work, the *Convivio*, Dante says: "Of all possible stupid utterances, the most stupid, the basest, the vilest is that there is no life after this one, for when we read the writings of philosophers and other wise men, we find all of them agreeing that inside each person dwells something that will survive the death of the body."

16   YOUR SECRET WISH WILL BE FULFILLED AS WELL: Virgil frequently

seems to know what Dante is thinking. This serves to reinforce the medieval view of Virgil as a magician or sorcerer. And just what is Dante thinking of at this moment? Perhaps of Farinata, about whom he is curious (see Canto VI: 78) and whom he will, in fact, momentarily encounter.

22   YOUR SPEECH IS MANIFESTLY FLORENTINE: Dante is recognized as a Florentine because of his accent. Tuscan is the language of north central Italy, including Florence, but the Florentine accent is distinctive. Tuscan is synonymous with the language we now refer to as Italian, i.e., the official language of Italy. (Compare *Matthew* 26:73: "And after a while came unto him they that stood by, and said to Peter, Surely thou also art one of them, for the speech bewrayeth thee.") When he addresses Dante, Farinata uses the familiar form of the word for "you" in Italian (*tu*), but in responding to him Dante will use the then formal and more respectful word for "you" (*voi*).

29   . . . FARINATA, STANDING IN HIS TOMB: Farinata degli Uberti was a great leader of the party of the Ghibellines in Florence; thus, he and Dante were political enemies, since Dante was a Guelf. In the course of their dialogue, Farinata reminds Dante of the double expulsion of the Guelfs by the Ghibellines: once in 1248 and again, overwhelmingly, in 1260, after the battle of Montaperti. After that later Guelf defeat, many Ghibellines and their allies seriously contemplated the complete destruction of the city of Florence, but Farinata thundered against the idea and the city was saved. The Guelfs returned in 1266, after the defeat at Benevento of Manfred, son of the dead emperor, Frederick II. So strongly did many Florentines feel about Farinata that, almost twenty years after his death, he and his wife were condemned as heretics, and the inheritance of the surviving heirs was taken away from them. Despite the fact that Dante and Farinata are political enemies, it is clear that Dante has considerable respect for this distinguished leader of the opposing party and indeed feels a measure of awe in his presence. It is also true that Dante, in exile when he wrote the *Commedia*, had become significantly pro-Ghibelline in his sentiments. It was his own Guelf party, after all, that had exiled him from his native city.

42–44   "THAT MAY BE SO. . . . YOUR PEOPLE HAVEN'T YET PICKED UP THAT ART: The Guelfs returned in 1258, when the Ghibellines were expelled, and again in 1266 after the Ghibelline defeat at Benevento. The meaning behind the sarcasm of line 44 is that the Ghibellines never returned to Florence.

45   THEN FROM THE TOMB ANOTHER FIGURE ROSE: This is Cavalcante Cavalcanti, the father of the poet Guido, Dante's closest friend. The father was a Guelf whose homes were destroyed by the Ghibellines in 1267. Later, in an attempt at peacemaking, Cavalcante allowed his son to wed Farinata's daughter. Thus, Guido was the son-in-law of Farinata and the son of Cavalcante.

50–51 . . . BUT IF SO, / THEN WHERE'S MY SON? . . . : Not unreasonably, given the fact that Dante and Guido were such good friends, Cavalcante hopes that Guido has accompanied the poet in his journey to Inferno. Dante dedicated his book *La Vita Nuova* to Guido, who was also a poet of note. In that book, Guido is referred to several times as Dante's closest friend. As a Guelf and a member of a group called the Bianchi ("Whites"), Guido was involved in many political scrapes. See note to line 61.

54–55 . . . HE'S GUIDING ME TOWARD HER, / PERHAPS, FOR WHOM YOUR GUIDO FELT DISDAIN: "Her" refers to Beatrice. Guido's disdain is probably for theology, for Guido was an atheist, and theology is what Beatrice, in part, represents.

61 BECAUSE I PAUSED BEFORE I ANSWERED HIM: Dante hesitates to answer, probably because he is surprised that Cavalcante does not know if Guido is alive. Cavalcante interprets the hesitation as meaning that Guido is dead; agonized, Cavalcante falls back into the flames. Dante's hesitation may also be explained by the fact that Guido, in fact, had died just a few months after the supposed Dantean visit to the other world, and that Dante was himself partially responsible, as one of the political leaders of Florence at that time, for Guido's exile. Because Guido died of a malarial fever while in exile, Dante must have felt pangs of guilt.

63–65 . . . THE OTHER SOUL . . . WENT ON TALKING AS BEFORE: A demonstration of the haughty, self-centered character of Farinata, who gives no hint of having paid the slightest attention to Cavalcante during the preceding scene, for he now casually resumes his former conversation with Dante as if the soul of Cavalcante did not even exist. Cavalcante's son was Farinata's son-in-law.

68 THE LUNAR FACE OF HER THAT REIGNS DOWN HERE: The goddess Diana was believed to have three forms: that of Proserpine (or Hecate) in Hades, that of Luna in Heaven, and that of Artemis on Earth. These predictions of Farinata came true in reality, of course, for Dante is writing years after the occurrence of the events to which Farinata alludes. Compare his prognostications with those of Ciacco in Canto VI.

75 "THE ROUT AND CARNAGE AT THE ARBIA": The Arbia is the river near Montaperti where a great battle took place. (See note to line 29 above.)

105 THE SECOND FREDERICK AND THE CARDINAL: Frederick II was a towering figure in Italian politics in the thirteenth century. In fact, some called him Stupor Mundi ("wonder of the world") because of his accomplishments and the diversity of his talents; others believed him to be the Antichrist because of his constant struggles with the Church. His anti-Church stance may have strengthened the image of him as an unbeliever and a follower of Epicurus.

Emperor of Germany, King of Sicily, Frederick was the archenemy of the papacy and was excommunicated by the pope. He led one of the Crusades, encouraged the writing of poetry at his court in Sicily (thus affecting the course that Italian literature was to take), founded the University of Naples, was passionately interested in art, science, philosophy, non-Christian religions, literature, and the art of warfare, had a harem, etc. His policies, wars, political struggles, and stratagems affected all of Italy. Dante must have had mixed feelings about Frederick. In any case, the rigorous logic of Dante's system of punishments forces him to place Frederick in Circle Six. The cardinal referred to is Ottaviano degli Ubaldini, who died in 1273. He was a Ghibelline sympathizer and had the reputation of being an unbeliever.

115–117   OF HER WHOSE SPIRIT . . . WILL BE REVEALED: "Her" refers to Beatrice; the course of Dante's life will be "revealed" to him in Heaven, not directly by Beatrice, but by his ancestor, Cacciaguida, in *Paradiso*, Canto XVII.

121   The drama of the closing line of the canto is typically Dantean.

"Why is it that your thoughts have wandered far?
Why is your mind not focused properly?"

(80–81)

CANTO XI

High on the very edge of broken rocks
Set in a ring we stood and from that height
Looked down upon a herd who suffered
Greater pain in crueler pens. Oh, the stench
That wafted from the hole of Hell! It drove   5
Us both to hide behind a monument
Whose lid was blazoned thus: *"I contain Pope*
Anastasius, whom Photinus misled."

"We can't go down too fast," he said,
"Let's get accustomed to the fetor first,   10
And then we may proceed less cautiously."

"Some compensation should be found," I said,
"So that no time is lost."

         And he to me:
"That very thought is going through my mind.
My son, within these rocks three circles lie   15
One below the other, just like the ones
You've left. The souls contained in them are damned.
I'd have you understand the how and why
Of their confinement here. Thus, when you see
These souls you'll recognize them right away.   20
The aim of every sin that Heaven hates

Is injury, by fraud or violence,
To someone else. But, in the eyes of God,
A deed involving fraud is worse because
It stems from man alone. The fraudulent   25
Are therefore to a deeper circle sent
And plagued by God with harsher punishment.
The Seventh Circle holds the violent.
Since violence may be done against three
Persons, that ring contains three inner rounds.   30
Violence is done against the Deity,
Against one's self, against one's fellow man.
Even property itself is targeted.
(I'll shortly clarify all this for you.)
Men wound and kill their fellows and destroy   35
Their substance; they ravage and they burn it.
They resort to ravenous extortion.
And so, in varied groups, the first round wreaks
Its havoc on the murderer and all
Who harm maliciously, all plunderers   40
And pillagers. Against himself, against
His property a man may do great harm.
So in the second round are those who kill
Themselves and those who gamble, running through
The things they own. Such sinners shed hot tears   45
When, as we know, they should be filled with joy.
Those men who in their hearts deny their God
And utter blasphemies do violence
To Him, and so do those who demonstrate
Disdain for Nature and the good she brings.   50
Thus the smallest round sets its seal upon
The usurers of Cahors, and Sodomites,
And those whose hearts are set against their God.
Some practice fraud (grave sin that ought to prick
Our consciences) on those who trust them, some   55

On those who don't. This latter fraud would seem
To snap the loving link that's forged by Nature
And that binds all men. So in Circle Eight
Is where the hypocrites abide. Oh, what
A nest of flatterers, a den of thieves,   60
A place for sorcerers, simoniacs,
Pimps, barrators, and those who falsify,
And other filthy vermin of that sort!
The other kind destroys not only love
That's natural, but love that friendship adds   65
To form a special trust. So in the seat
Of Dis, the center of the universe,
Deep down, the ninth and smallest circle coils
Where traitors are eternally consumed."

I said: "Your discourse, Master, well explains   70
The various degrees of this abyss
And all the differences among its souls.
But tell me why the creatures in the marsh—
The ones the wind propels, the ones the rain
Bombards, the ones who fling such bitter words   75
At one another—tell me why they are
Not punished in the blood-red walls of Dis,
If God looks down on them with wrath? If not,
Then why must they sustain God's scourge at all?"

"Why is it that your thoughts have wandered far?   80
Why is your mind not focused properly?
Have you forgotten Aristotle's *Ethics*?
Remember that he notes those dispositions
Of the human mind (three of them there are)
That Heaven will not brook: incontinence,   85
Mad bestiality, and vice. God is least
Offended by incontinence, which brings

Less blame upon itself. If you consider
All those souls above, outside of Dis,
Who suffer for their sins, and if you give   90
The doctrine deeper thought, it will be clear
To you why those are set apart from these,
And why God hammers them less heavily."

"Oh Sun, who make all clouded vision clear,
Your clarity has pierced through all my doubts   95
And made me so content," I said, "that now
To doubt is not less pleasing than to know.
But please go back to what you said before
Of usury, offensive to our God.
Untie that knot for me," I said.

               And he: 100
"Philosophy, to those who understand
It well, explains, not solely in one place,
That Nature takes its course from God's own mind
And from His art. And if you will peruse
The *Physics* of the master, you will see,   105
Not many pages into it, that art
Is nature's faithful follower, just like
A pupil to his master. Art, therefore,
Is but the grandchild of Divinity.
If you remember *Genesis*, it is   110
From nature and from art that men must seek
To earn their bread and to advance themselves.
But usurers, proceeding otherwise,
Despising nature and her followers,
Rely on gullibility for gain.   115

"But now we must move on: the Fish begin
To quiver on the rim of the horizon.

The Great Bear now is lying over Caurus.
So follow where I lead. There, farther on,
We must climb down a steep and rocky path."   120

NOTES TO CANTO XI

[SUMMARY OF THE CANTO: *Dante and Virgil are standing on a cliff in Circle Six looking down into Circle Seven. Behind a tomb, they find temporary refuge from the stench that rises from below. While they are waiting to grow accustomed to the smell, Virgil explains the structure of the last three circles of Hell, describing Circle Seven, with its sins of violence; Circle Eight, with its sins of fraud; and Circle Nine, with its sins of treachery. He also discourses on the evils of usury.*]

1-4   HIGH ON THE VERY EDGE . . . IN CRUELER PENS . . . : Dante and Virgil are looking into Circle Seven, which represents the beginning of the lower division of Inferno. In this canto, Virgil's long disquisition on the structure of Hell is based largely on ideas Dante gleaned from Aristotle (via Thomas Aquinas), Cicero, and other sources. Whereas sins of incontinence are punished in earlier circles (Two through Five) and those of heresy in Circle Six, the sins of violence, fraud, and treachery are punished in Circles Seven, Eight, and Nine, respectively. To these we must add the souls of Limbo in Circle One and the neutrals of the so-called "vestibule" of Inferno (see Canto III). The sins of the last three circles are of a graver nature than those of incontinence; besides being more severely punished, those souls guilty of such sins are found in the deepest portion of Inferno. The sins of incontinence are represented by the leopard, the first beast Dante encountered in Canto I. The lion of Canto I stands for the sins of violence, and the she-wolf for those of fraud (see note to Canto I, line 32). Virgil does not here discourse upon the causes of sin; that discussion is left for *Purgatorio*. (One cannot hope to grasp the whole of Dante's thought without reading the entire *Commedia*.)

7–8 ". . . I CONTAIN POPE / ANASTASIUS, WHOM PHOTINUS MISLED":
By administering communion to a certain Photinus, who was a deacon from
Thessalonica in Greece, Pope Anastasius (*ca.* 497 A.D.) was said to have given tacit
approval to Photinus' heretical belief that Jesus was not the son of God.

22 . . . BY FRAUD OR VIOLENCE: Cicero, one of Dante's sources about the
nature of sin, divides it into two general categories: sins of violence and sins of
fraud.

31–32 VIOLENCE . . . AGAINST ONE'S FELLOW MAN: This tripartite dis-
tinction is made by Thomas Aquinas.

33 EVEN PROPERTY ITSELF IS TARGETED: Violence against persons and
against property amounts pretty much to the same sort of sin, according to
Dante. This idea may be, in part, a reflection of the fact that, since trade and
commerce were expanding rather rapidly in the late medieval period, the value
of property was increasingly impressing itself on the medieval mind.

52 THE USURERS OF CAHORS AND SODOMITES: The French city of
Cahors was infamous for its rapacious usurers. God destroyed the city of Sodom
because its inhabitants "sinned against nature," *i.e.*, practiced homosexuality,
which the Bible looks upon as a sin (see *Genesis*, chapter 19).

54–58 SOME PRACTICE FRAUD . . . THAT BINDS ALL MEN . . . : Dante dis-
tinguishes between those who defraud people they do not know and those who
defraud people they do know (friends, relatives, etc.). The latter kind of fraud is
punished further down, in Circle Nine, because it is more heinous in God's eyes.
The first kind of fraud, as Virgil says, breaks only the natural link between men
and not the stronger ties of family, friendship, etc.; the second involves the addi-
tional sin of betrayal or treachery.

61 A PLACE FOR SORCERERS, SIMONIACS: Simoniacs practice the sin of
simony, or the buying or selling of church offices, pardons, and indulgences. See
Canto XIX.

62 PIMPS, BARRATORS, AND THOSE WHO FALSIFY: Barrators made
money from the sale of public offices. In our time, the sin of barratry would be
called "graft."

67 OF DIS, THE CENTER OF THE UNIVERSE: The center of the universe is
the Earth; the bottom of Circle Nine, where Dis (Satan) is found, is the center of
the Earth. See Canto XXXIV.

73–76 . . . THE CREATURES IN THE MARSH . . . FLING SUCH BITTER
WORDS / AT ONE ANOTHER: The reason why the incontinent are not punished
as severely as other sinners is because incontinence is not a sin of malice and
therefore offends God less. This idea is an echo of Aristotle's *Ethics*, which Virgil
cites in line 84. "The creatures in the marsh" are those who sinned through anger

(Cantos VII and VIII); "the ones the wind propels" are the lustful (Canto V); "the ones the rain / Bombards" are the gluttons (Canto VI); "the ones who fling such bitter words / At one another" are the prodigal and the avaricious (Canto VII).

105   THE *PHYSICS* OF THE MASTER: The *Physics* is another work by Aristotle.

108–115   . . . ART, THEREFORE . . . ON GULLIBILITY FOR GAIN: God wants man to live his life according to nature and art (by "art" Dante here means applied craft and honorable work). Those who attempt to earn their living otherwise are contravening God's clearly stated command (*Genesis* 1:28, 2:15). Therefore, usury, which is unnatural and does not involve the kind of work of which God approves, offends God. It must be understood that by *usury* Dante means charging *any* interest at all on money that is loaned, not just excessive interest; he believed that earning money in such a way was immoral; it was a sinful practice because it was unnatural. No doubt he was influenced by Aquinas and Aristotle, who expressed similarly negative views about the practice. (See *Leviticus* 25:36–37: "Take thou no usury of him, or increase: but fear thy God; that thy brother may live with thee. Thou shalt not give him thy money upon usury. . . .")

116–118   . . . THE FISH . . . LYING OVER CAURUS: These references to the constellation (the Fish) and the wind (Caurus) tell us that it is now early Saturday morning, two hours before sunrise. Although the stars can't be seen from Inferno, Virgil does have the power to see them and repeatedly makes use of that power.

"Their deeds were merciless. Down here they moan."

(95)

CANTO XII

The rugged nature of the place that marked
The start of our descent offended sight,
As did the beast, its dread inhabitant.
Just like the landslide on this side of Trent
That struck the Adige, caused by a quake   5
Or water that erodes, a shattered cliff
Here stretches to the plain to form a path
One can descend. So down we climbed and saw
Along the fractured ground the beast of Crete,
Who was conceived inside a wooden cow.   10
He seethed on seeing us and sank his fangs
Into his flesh. My master spoke to him:
"You think the Duke of Athens, he who brought
You death on Earth, has now arrived? Not so.
Leave us, monstrosity! This man has not   15
Been tutored by your sister but has come
To see your punishments."

               Just like a bull
Whose head is hammered by a mortal blow,
The Minotaur broke loose and reeled, and then
My lord cried suddenly: "Be quick and run   20
That way while he's distracted by his rage!"

And so we made our way across loose rocks
That often slipped beneath my body's weight.
My master, seeing I was deep in thought,
Remarked: "This ruin, on which your mind no doubt   25
Is focusing, is guarded by the beast
Whose rage I quelled just now. Before, when I
Was here in lower Hell, this cliff still stood.
I think I know what happened here: not long
Before He came to take from Circle One   30
Of Dis the magnificent souls, the whole
Of this vile valley shook with violence,
As if the universe had felt God's love.
And so some think the world has often turned
To chaos. Here and elsewhere, at that time,   35
This primal rock rolled down; that's clear to me.
But look below you now: a stream of blood
Flows by, in whose red depths are drenched those souls
Who harmed their fellow men through violence."

Oh evil, blind, and mad cupidity   40
That drives us ever in our mortal life
To drown our souls with bitterness in Dis!
I saw, as Virgil said I would, a moat
Before me like a bow encircling all
The plain. Between the moat and cliff was seen   45
A file of centaurs racing on the plain,
With bows and arrows ready for the hunt.
While watching us come down they stood quite still.
Three centaurs from the group detached themselves,
With bows and arrows ready. Shouted one: 50
"What torments are you here to undergo?
Unless you speak from where you stand, I'll shoot!"

My guide to him: "I'll answer you when we
Are near, but it's to Chiron that I'll speak,
Not you, for you are ruled by recklessness."   55

My leader touched me: "That is Nessus,
He who died for lovely Deïaneira,
Yet who found revenge. The middle centaur,
Who looks as if he's studying his chest,
Is Chiron, shaper of Achilles' mind.   60
The other creature's Pholus, the enraged.
They turn in thousands round and round the moat
And shoot at any soul who dares to rise
Above the blood more than his crime allows."
When we were closer to the nimble beasts,   65
Chiron chose a shaft and with its notch he brushed
His beard back, and we saw his mouth. He said
To his companions: "Look at him! You see?
It's obvious that anything he treads
On moves. I mean that one standing behind   70
His guide. The feet of dead men can't do that."

To this, my guide, now near the centaur's chest
Just where the beast and man parts join, replied:
"He is indeed alive, and since he is
Alone, it's fitting that I be his guide   75
The length of all the valley of black Hell.
Necessity compels him, not delight.
A lady left off singing hymns of praise
And begged me to perform this novel task.
He's no villain; I'm no thieving shade.   80
Now by that Power impelling us through Hell's
Wild road, I ask you to select one beast
To bring us to a ford, and let him bear

This man upon his back, for he cannot,
Like spirits, glide through air."

                   So Chiron wheeled   85
And said to Nessus on his right: "Go back
With them and take them where they wish to go,
And keep all other groups away from them."

The centaur guiding us, we made our way
Along the margin of the roiling red   90
Whose boiling victims scarred the air with screams:
A number were submerged up to the brow.
The monstrous centaur spoke: "Those tyrants dipped
Their hands in blood and plundered what they could.
Their deeds were merciless. Down here they moan.   95
Great Alexander's swimming in that flood
And cruel Dionysius, who brought
Long years of suffering to Sicily.
See the black-haired shade? That's Azzolino.
And the blond one is Opizzo of Este,   100
Whose stepson slew him."

                 I said to Virgil:
"Please let the centaur guide you first, then me."

A little farther on the creature stopped
Above a crowd immersed up to their necks
Inside the boiling pool. Now pointing to   105
A shade who stood alone, the centaur said:
"In God's own house, this sinner stabbed the heart
That still is dripping blood upon the Thames."

I saw some spirits, some of whom I knew,
Holding head and chest above the water.   110

Then bit by bit the stream grew shallow till
The feet alone of the tormented boiled
In blood, and it was here that we could cross.
Once on the other side, the centaur said:
"The bubbling water on this side is not   115
As deep as on the other where its bed
Grows deeper by degrees and comes once more
To join the spot where tyranny must groan.
Attila, earthly scourge, is scourged in turn
By God's just wrath. Also scourged are Sextus   120
And Pyrrhus: fast flow the tears and endlessly
(The boiling flood's the cause) from two who made
The roads run red with blood: Rinier Pazzo
And, boiling with him, Rinier da Corneto."

Then Nessus left us and recrossed the ford.   125

NOTES TO CANTO XII

[SUMMARY OF THE CANTO: *As the poets begin to climb down the fallen rocks,
they encounter the Minotaur, who threatens them. But no harm comes to them, for Virgil
speaks sharply to the creature. They arrive at the first round of Circle Seven. Here, sin-
ners who committed deeds of violence against their fellow man are sunk eternally in a
river of boiling blood. Bands of centaurs rove about, shooting arrows at any soul who
tries to remain surfaced for too long. Virgil asks Chiron, the leader of the centaurs, to
choose one of these creatures to convey the poets across the river. Nessus is chosen, and as
he transports Dante and Virgil, he comments on some of the souls in the river. Among
these are Alexander the Great, Attila the Hun, and a number of Florentines. The poets
are deposited on the other side, and Nessus crosses back.*]

4–5 JUST LIKE THE LANDSLIDE ON THIS SIDE OF TRENT / THAT STRUCK THE ADIGE . . . : Trent (Trento in Italian) is a city; the Adige, a river. Both are in northern Italy.

9 . . . THE BEAST OF CRETE / WHO WAS CONCEIVED INSIDE A WOODEN COW: This beast is the Minotaur of classical mythology, a creature half-man and half-bull. Sometimes he is described as having a bull's head and a man's body, but Dante's creature is just the reverse. He was the product of the union between Pasiphaë, the wife of King Minos of Crete, and a white bull, for which she had developed an unnatural passion. Daedalus, the famed artificer, contrived to make a wooden cow into which Pasiphaë was inserted so that she could be conveyed to the bull and receive his ardor. Dante makes the Minotaur the guardian of this circle, the prison of the violent.

13–14 "YOU THINK THE DUKE OF ATHENS . . . HAS NOW ARRIVED?" . . . : After Pasiphaë gave birth to the Minotaur, Minos had Daedalus construct a labyrinth where the beast was placed. Minos then required the city of Athens, which he had defeated, to send him an annual tribute of seven young men and seven young women. Placed in the labyrinth, from which escape was virtually impossible, they were eaten by the Minotaur. This horrible practice was terminated by Theseus, the legendary hero and "Duke of Athens," who killed the Minotaur. With the help of the famous thread of Ariadne, the daughter of Pasiphaë and King Minos (and thus half-sister of the Minotaur), Theseus found his way out of the intricate labyrinth.

25–26 THIS RUIN, ON WHICH YOUR MIND NO DOUBT / IS FOCUSING . . . : For an observation on Virgil's ability to read Dante's mind, see note to Canto X, line 16.

27–28 . . . BEFORE, WHEN I / WAS HERE IN LOWER HELL . . . : Concerning this earlier trip of Virgil's, see Canto IX, line 17 *et seq.*

30 BEFORE HE CAME TO TAKE FROM CIRCLE ONE / OF DIS THE MAGNIFICENT SOULS: Another reference to the Harrowing of Hell by Christ (see Canto IV; line 47 *et seq.*).

31–32 . . . THE WHOLE / OF THIS VILE VALLEY SHOOK WITH VIOLENCE: The implication is that the earthquake that shattered the cliff and caused the landslide is the same one that occurred when Christ was crucified; it is reported in the New Testament (see *Matthew* 27:50–51).

33–35 AS IF THE UNIVERSE . . . TO CHAOS . . . : This is an allusion to an idea of Empedocles' that when the world is made harmonious through love, the elements become as one, *i.e.,* they lose their individual nature that makes our world what it is, and so the world returns to a state of primordial chaos.

37 BUT LOOK BELOW YOU NOW: A STREAM OF BLOOD / FLOWS BY ... : This stream is identified in a later canto as the river Phlegethon (Greek for "burning" or "boiling"). In the *Aeneid,* the river is on fire; here it is a river of blood.

46 A FILE OF CENTAURS RACING ON THE PLAIN: These creatures were half-man, half-horse. See Canto XXV for a further reference to them.

51 "WHAT TORMENTS ARE YOU HERE TO UNDERGO?": The centaurs believe Dante and Virgil are newly arrived sinners, ready for punishment.

56–58 ... "THAT IS NESSUS ... YET WHO FOUND REVENGE": Nessus, a centaur, tried to violate Deïaneira, the wife of Hercules, but the latter slew him with a poisoned arrow. Before expiring, Nessus gave Deïaneira his bloody shirt and told her that if Hercules were to wear it his love for her would not diminish. When Hercules put it on, however, he went mad and immolated himself; Deïaneira consequently committed suicide.

60 ... CHIRON, SHAPER OF ACHILLES' MIND: Chiron, portrayed in myth as a learned centaur, was supposedly a musician, an astronomer, and a physician, and was the tutor of Achilles, the Greek hero.

61 THE OTHER CREATURE'S PHOLUS, THE ENRAGED: Pholus was present at the wedding of Pirithous and Hippodamia; he attempted to rape the bride and other women present.

78 A LADY LEFT OFF SINGING HYMNS OF PRAISE: The lady is Beatrice, who temporarily stopped the singing of hallelujahs to God to come to Dante's aid.

96 GREAT ALEXANDER'S SWIMMING IN THAT FLOOD: This is Alexander the Great of Macedon, who in his short life conquered much of the Eastern Mediterranean world and beyond. According to Seneca, Orosius, and other ancient writers, Alexander's rule, romanticized by posterity, was characterized by frequent acts of cruelty and violence.

97 AND CRUEL DIONYSIUS ... : This may be a reference either to Dionysius I or his son, both Sicilian tyrants in the fourth century before the Christian era.

99 SEE THE BLACK-HAIRED SHADE? THAT'S AZZOLINO: Ezzelino da Romano (1194–1259), considered by contemporary chroniclers to be the cruelest prince of the Italian peninsula, was known as the "child of the Devil" and was responsible for the deaths of thousands of people. The son-in-law of Emperor Frederick II, he ruled portions of northern Italy.

100 AND THE BLOND ONE IS OPIZZO OF ESTE: This is Obizzo d'Este of Ferrara, a thirteenth-century tyrant. He is said to have been killed by his own son.

106–108   A SHADE WHO STOOD ALONE . . . DRIPPING BLOOD UPON THE
THAMES: The shade is Guy de Montfort, who avenged the death of Simon de
Montfort, his father, by killing King Henry III's cousin during a church cere-
mony at Viterbo in 1272. Allegedly, the heart of Guy's victim was sealed in a
golden cup and set atop a column along the Thames, where it dripped blood—
that is, cried out for vengeance.

119   ATTILA, EARTHLY SCOURGE, IS SCOURGED IN TURN: The famed
Attila the Hun, who ravaged much of eastern Europe and even invaded Italy in
452 A.D.

120–121   . . . ALSO SCOURGED ARE SEXTUS / AND PYRRHUS . . . : Sextus
Pompeius, after his father's death, continued the fight against Julius Caesar.
(Some believe this soul is Sextus Tarquinius, son of the last of the early Roman
kings.) Pyrrhus was king of Epirus around the end of the fourth century B.C. He
fought against Rome and Greece and was responsible for devastating Italy and
Sicily. He, too, had a reputation for extreme cruelty. (Some believe this shade to
be that of an earlier Pyrrhus, the son of Achilles.)

123–124   RINIER PAZZO / AND, BOILING WITH HIM, RINIER DA COR-
NETO: Rinier Pazzo was a notorious thief. In 1268, he attacked and robbed a
bishop and his entourage, killing some of them; for this he was excommunicated
by the pope and banned from the city of Florence. Of Rinier da Corneto very lit-
tle is known, other than that he was also a famous robber of Dante's time.

CANTO XIII

Not yet had Nessus reached the other side
When we set foot inside a pathless wood.
Not green, but darkly tinted was each leaf.
Not smooth, but gnarled and rough each branch, bearing,
Instead of fruits, thorns poisonous to touch.   5
Wild beasts avoiding cultivated land
That lies between Cecina and Corneto
Don't rove through growth so thorny or so thick.

Here the hideous Harpies nest who drove
The Trojans from the Strophades and told   10
Them of impending doom. Their wings are broad,
Their faces and their necks are human, feet
Sprout talons, feathers grow from swollen guts,
And from the twisted trees in which they perch,
What sorrow-burdened shrieks now pierce our ears!   15

"Before you go much further," Virgil said,
"I'd have you know this is the second round,
Where you'll remain until you see the sand
That looks disgusting. Be observant now
And watch for things that might belie my words."   20

Around me I could hear laments, but those
Who made them were not visible, and so

"And can

A soul break free from such captivity?"

(86–87)

I paused, confused by what was happening.
I am convinced he thought that I believed
The groans I heard were issuing from shades   25
Who hid from us behind the trees.

                                        "If you
Should break a twig from any tree, you'd see
That what you're thinking now is false," he said.

I stretched my hand out to a thorny tree
And plucked a twig. Promptly I heard a voice: 30
"Why break my branch?"

                            It was the trunk that spoke,
And when its blood had turned a darker hue,
It spoke again: "How can you be so cruel?
So pitiless? Once all of us were men,
But now we've been transformed into these trees   35
You see surrounding you. You would have been
More merciful had we been souls of snakes!"

A twig of greenish wood, one end on fire,
Will bubble at the other end and hiss
As steam bursts out; just so this broken twig   40
Spewed forth both blood and words, and when it did,
I dropped it quick and stood there stupefied.
My master spoke to it: "Oh wounded soul!
If this man had been able to believe
What he'd not seen save in my poetry,   45
His hand would not have harmed you in this way.
To him, the notion was far-fetched and so
He acted, but I prompted him to do
The deed, and this has grieved me very much.
But tell him who you were so that, to make   50

———

Amends, he may restore your name above
Where Heaven wills him to return."

                                    The tree
Replied: "Your gentle words appeal to me.
And so I won't be silent. I will hope
It won't displease you if I speak at length.   55
Both keys to Frederick's heart were in my hands.
Softly I turned them in the wards: I locked
And I unlocked. I kept so many people
From his person! With what fidelity
I always did my duty to my prince!   60
But what a price I paid! I was deprived
Of sleep and sapped of all my energies.
The harlot, Envy, who with vice and death
Poisons every court, cast her meretricious
Eyes on Caesar's courtiers, kindled minds   65
Against me. So enkindled, these in turn
Now kindled great Augustus, turning joy
And honor tart. Indignation mastered me,
And hoping to escape the world's disdain,
I was impelled, though once by justice ruled,   70
To do an unjust deed. I swear to you
By this tree's roots: I never did betray
My master, whom I honored and revered.
And now I ask but this: if one or both
Of you return to Earth, restore my name   75
That Envy sullied with a vicious swipe."

He broke off. Virgil said: "He's quiet now.
Because your purpose is to learn, you must
Converse with him, so seize the chance."

And I:
"I pity him; I cannot speak a word.   80
  Please ask him about anything you think
  Would satisfy my wish to know."

At that
My master turned to him: "This man will do
Quite freely what you ask of him. So now,
Bound spirit, tell us, if you will, just how   85
The souls are trapped within these trunks. And can
A soul break free from such captivity?"

The trunk blew hard, the wind became a voice:
"I'll answer briefly. When the savage souls
Have from their earthly body torn away,   90
Minos remands them to the seventh ring.
They fall quite randomly into this wood,
And sometime later they begin to sprout
Like grains of spelt, swell to sapling size,
Then swell to trees. Feeding on their foliage,   95
The Harpies harrow them with pain. In us
They make these cracks for painful cries. Like souls
Elsewhere, we'll come back to the world to seek
Our bodies once again, but all in vain.
We can't put on our flesh, for Justice won't   100
Permit the repossession of the forms
We willfully abandoned. So we'll drag
Them to this wood to hang in timbered gloom,
Each on the tree of its antagonist."

We waited by the trunk, expecting it   105
To tell us more, when suddenly a noise
Surprised us both, like hunters in a wood

Who hear the tumult of a wild-boar chase
When beasts come crashing through the underbrush.
Two spirits on our left came running past 110
Whose naked flesh was bleeding as they rushed
Headlong and broke through bramble and through branch.

"Come quickly, quickly, Death!" the first one cried.

The other, trailing, said: "Lano, your legs
At the Toppo couldn't carry you this fast!" 115

And seeming to be out of breath, he rolled
Into a bush. Black bitches followed fast,
Like unleashed greyhounds, ravenous and swift,
And, dismembering the imprisoned soul,
They dragged its bleeding limbs away.

                                  My guide 120
Now took my hand and led me to the bush
To hear it wailing through its bleeding wounds.
"Jacomo da Sant'Andrea, tell me:
Why use me to protect you thus? Your life
Was filled with guilt. I played no role in it." 125

Above the bush my master stood and said:
"You there, breathing blood and speech profusely
Through your cracks, tell us who you were."

                                And he:
"Oh spirits who have come to contemplate
The stark atrocity that stripped away 130
My leaves, please heap them at this bush's base
In which my soul lies ever prisoner.
My native town first chose, as patron, Mars,

But, later, John the Baptist took his place.
Enraged, the god swore Florence would be marked   135
To live in misery forevermore,
And were it not that some small part of Mars
May still be seen by Arno's banks, the men
Who in Attila's wake rebuilt the town
Would all have worked in vain. And what of me?   140
There, in the very house in which I lived,
I looped a deadly noose around my neck."

NOTES TO CANTO XIII

[SUMMARY OF THE CANTO: *The poets are now in the second round of Circle Seven in the Wood of the Suicides and the Violent against Property. They see Harpies eating the leaves of trees in which the souls of the suicides are imprisoned. Dante speaks with one of the latter, Pier delle Vigne. The poets also come upon the shades of Jacopo da Sant'Andrea and Lano da Siena, who are being chased through the woods by greyhounds. Lano's body is torn to pieces by the dogs, who carry his limbs away. The poets then hear from the spirit of an anonymous Florentine.*]

6–8   WILD BEASTS AVOIDING . . . SO THORNY OR SO THICK: The sense of the passage is that this wild region is more thickly overgrown and more savage than the area known as the Maremma, near Livorno in northern Italy.

9–15   HERE THE HIDEOUS HARPIES . . . THE STROPHADES . . . NOW PIERCE OUR EARS: The Harpies, who appear in Book III of the *Aeneid*, are mythological creatures with the bodies of birds and the faces of women. Like so many such creatures in *Inferno*, these cannot, or will not, express themselves in intelligible speech. In Virgil's poem, the bird-women foul the food of the Trojans, who then attack them. The Strophades are the two islands in the Ionian Sea where this event occurs. Dante makes the Harpies guardians of the suicides.

24　I AM CONVINCED HE THOUGHT THAT I BELIEVED: This odd line is, in the original Italian, *"Cred'io ch'ei credette ch'io credesse,"* literally, "I believe that he believed that I believed." Such word play was not uncommon in medieval writing and was, indeed, much admired. Some propose that this line and one or two other similarly artificial ones in the canto are Dante's imitations of Pier delle Vigne's poetic style.

52–53　. . . THE TREE / REPLIED . . . : The soul imprisoned in the tree is that of Pier Delle Vigne, one of Emperor Frederick II's most trusted counselors. For unknown reasons, he was accused of treason and was also the target of slander in Frederick's court. Pier tells us that this slander was the fruit of envy. Imprisoned and blinded at Frederick's order, he committed suicide in 1248 by dashing his head against a prison wall. He is also remembered for his Italian poems and Latin letters. Because Dante places Pier in this circle, it may mean that he did not believe Pier betrayed Frederick, for if he did, he would have put Pier in the last circle along with the traitors: in the Dantean hierarchy of sins, treachery is a graver sin than suicide.

63　THE HARLOT, ENVY, WHO WITH VICE AND DEATH: Virgil mentions envy as early as Canto I.

65–67　. . . CAESAR'S COURTIERS . . . GREAT AUGUSTUS . . . : The use of the names of Caesar and Augustus is appropriate: the Holy Roman Emperors, including Frederick II (it is he, of course, who is meant here) were often addressed by these titles, which came to signify great leaders.

110　TWO SPIRITS ON OUR LEFT CAME RUNNING PAST: These two figures running through the wood are Lano da Siena and Jacopo da Sant'Andrea. The former (from Siena, as his name implies) was a notorious spendthrift. He lost all his money through his own folly. Convinced that death was the only way out of his misery, he decided he would try to die in battle. Therefore, in 1288, he fought as a soldier in the Sienese expedition against Arezzo and was granted his suicidal wish. Jacopo da Sant'Andrea, from Padua, wasted and destroyed both his own and others' property, even resorting to arson, for motives that border on the irrational. There is a story that, while visiting Venice, he one day threw many gold coins into the water just to see them dance on the waves. The tyrant Ezzelino da Romano, whose soul is also in Hell (see Canto XII), had Jacopo killed. These men acted violently: against themselves, against their property (or the property of others—it was viewed as an extension of the self), or against both; hence their relegation to this circle. They resemble the prodigal sinners of Circle Four (Canto VII) but differ from them by virtue of the violence of their deeds.

122　TO HEAR IT WAILING THROUGH ITS BLEEDING WOUNDS: This is the soul of an unknown Florentine.

133 MY NATIVE TOWN FIRST CHOSE, AS PATRON, MARS: In ancient times, Mars was indeed the patron god of the city of Florence. Later, in Christian times, a church was constructed over the former temple that had been dedicated to the god. According to Dante and others, when the city was invaded by Attila and his hordes, the statue of Mars that is referred to here fell into the Arno River. (In fact, Attila never attacked Florence, though Dante and his contemporaries believed he had.) Later, the remains of the statue were set up in Florence's Ponte Vecchio. It was widely believed that if the Florentines had not done so, they would have been unable to reconstruct their damaged city. Because Mars had been deeply offended, they believed, the city continued to suffer from civil disruptions.

142 I LOOPED A DEADLY NOOSE AROUND MY NECK: This Florentine who committed suicide has not been identified.

CANTO XIV

Moved by love of the city of my birth,
I gathered all the leaves, and to the soul
Whose voice was growing fainter I restored them.
We left him. The third round lay ahead: there
A dread device of justice was revealed.   5
I shall relate the strange new things I saw.

We reached a plain whose soil rejects all plants.
The wood of misery loops round it like
A garland. By the mournful ditch the wood
In turn is fringed. At the perimeter   10
We paused. The deep, dry sand was not unlike
The sand that Cato trod. (Vengeance of God!
How much you must be feared by all who read
Of everything that was revealed to me!)
I saw great herds of naked souls who wept   15
In wretchedness and who by different laws
Were mastered: some lay supine, others ran;
Still others crouched; most numerous were those
Who ran in circles; fewest, those who lay
In torment, but how loud their shrieks of pain!   20

Slow, slow, like Alpine snow in windless air,
Broad flakes of fire were falling. It is said
That in the hotter zones of India,

Great Alexander saw unbroken flames
Fall groundward. So his troops were quickly told   25
To trample on the flames before these merged
Into a single sheet. And here, the heat,
Relentless and eternal, fell and fell,
Redoubling every torment, firing sand
As flint fires wood. The spirits' dancing hands   30
Perpetually, pitifully strove
To quench the deadly flames without success.

Then I began: "My lord, who have the power
To vanquish everything, except the fiends
Who moved against us at the gate of Dis,   35
Who is that figure lying there? He seems
Indifferent to all this falling fire.
His glowering, disdainful look is proof
The burning flakes can't soften him."

                                    The shade,
Who understood it was of him I spoke,   40
Cried out: "I was in life what now I am
In death. Let Jove fatigue his armorer,
Whose thunderbolt he seized to cut me down
On my last day. And let him, if he will,
Exhaust the laborers who work by turns   45
At Mongibello's murky forge. And as
At Phlegra, where he called to Vulcan, 'Help,
Good Vulcan, help!' so let him cry and hurl
His mighty bolts. No sweet revenge for him!"

My master then, with most surprising force,   50
Addressed the spirit thus: "Capaneus,
This inextinguishable arrogance
Intensifies your punishment. You rave

And rage; such fury is the only pain
Sufficient for your guilt."

            My lord then turned   55
To me, with gentler look, and said: "He was
Among the ancient group of Seven Kings
Who levied war on Thebes. He held and holds
God in disdain, shows Him no reverence.
His spite's the best adornment for his breast.   60
Now follow me. Avoid the burning sand
And edge the wood."

          We walked without a word
And came upon a rivulet that ran
Across the sand. Its redness haunts me still.
It called to mind the little streams that flow   65
From the Bulicame, shared by prostitutes.
Because its sides and bed were petrified,
I saw that both my guide and I might walk
Along the river's stonied edge. He spoke:
"Among the many things I have disclosed   70
To you since first we came inside the gate
Through which all men are free to pass, not one
Is worthier of note than this red stream
That snuffs out every flame above its flow."

My appetite was whetted by these words,   75
And so I asked my leader for the food.
He gave it: "In the middle of the sea
Lies Crete, now desolate. In ancient times,
Beneath its king's dominion, all the world
Was pure. The mountain there, named Ida, once   80
Glowed joyfully with field and stream but lies
Deserted now. The goddess Rhea chose

This island as a cradle for her son.
To make the hiding-place more safe, she had
Bacchantes drown his cries by clamoring.   85
Inside the mountain stands a grand old man
Who toward Damietta keeps his shoulders turned
And looks at Rome as if into a glass.
Of finest gold his head is formed; his arms
And chest are silver and his trunk is bronze.   90
Of iron are his legs and his left foot;
His right foot is, however, made of clay,
And that's the one on which he leans his weight.
In every part, except the gold, is found
A fissure dropping tears. Collecting, these   95
Cut through the cavern floor and drop down here.
As streams descend from rock to rock, they form
The rivers Styx, Acheron, and Phlegethon
And then continue down this narrow way
That leads to Hell's deep heart, the frozen lake   100
Of Cocytus. Soon you will understand
What sort of lake it is, but not just yet."

"Why is this stream seen only here between
  Two circles if it has its origin
  On Earth above?" I asked.

                          And he replied: 105
"You know the shape of Hell is circular,
  But even though we've journeyed very far
  (And leftward made our way in the descent),
  We've never made the circuit of one ring.
  Why, then, does novelty surprise you so?"   110

And I, persisting: "Where are Phlegethon
  And Lethe to be found? You haven't said

A word about the latter. And you say
That Phlegethon is made from fiery rain?"

"I find your questions pleasing, but the first   115
Might have been answered by the boiling stream
Of red. You won't see Lethe's waters here,
Not in this hellish pit, but there where souls
Can cleanse themselves when all their guilt's removed
And they've been purified by penitence.   120

But now's the time for us to leave this wood.
Be sure to stay behind me as we walk
Along the unburned path that skirts the bank.
Each flake of flame above us will be quenched."

NOTES TO CANTO XIV

[SUMMARY OF THE CANTO: *Having gathered up the leaves of the anonymous Florentine, Dante goes with Virgil to the third round of Circle Seven. They cross a desert plain surrounded by the Wood of the Suicides, which is in turn encircled by the river Phlegethon. The poets see a number of sinners arranged in various positions. On these souls flakes of fire fall continuously. The travelers meet the shade of Capaneus, who sinned against divinity. When they come upon a streamlet whose bed and banks are stony, Virgil tells of the Old Man of Crete, who is the origin of the waters of the rivers of Hell.*]

7   WE REACHED A PLAIN WHOSE SOIL REJECTS ALL PLANTS: The poets are now in the third round of Circle Seven.

12   THE SAND THAT CATO TROD . . . : In his *Civil War*, the Roman historian Lucan tells how Cato, a noble Roman renowned for his stern moral princi-

ples, marched across the desert of Libya in 47 B.C. Dante and Virgil will meet Cato in *Purgatorio.*

15   I SAW GREAT HERDS OF NAKED SOULS WHO WEPT: Three classes of sinners are described: blasphemers, usurers, and sodomites. The first group, on their backs, suffer the most, for their sin against God is the most heinous of the three.

24   GREAT ALEXANDER SAW UNBROKEN FLAMES: The story was a popular one in the Middle Ages. It derives from a spurious letter of Alexander's addressed to his tutor, the great Aristotle. In it, the Macedonian conqueror describes this phenomenon.

36   WHO IS THAT FIGURE LYING THERE? . . . : This shade is Capaneus, one of the kings who besieged Thebes, the famed city of ancient Greece. He had the reputation of being a blasphemer of the ancient gods, even of Zeus himself. According to the legend, which Dante read in the *Thebaid* of the Latin poet Statius (an important figure in *Purgatorio*), Capaneus jeered at the gods as he scaled the walls of Thebes and was immediately struck dead by a thunderbolt from Zeus. Dante tends to use the Latin forms of the names of the ancient gods, because he knew that language and because he would only rarely come across the original Greek names. The influence of Latin in every field of human thought was all-pervasive in Dante's time. Even in English the Latin forms of the names of the Greek gods prevail: Neptune for Poseidon, Bacchus for Dionysus, and so on.

42   . . . LET JOVE FATIGUE HIS ARMORER: This armorer of Jove's is Vulcan, who made thunderbolts for him in his forge at Mount Etna.

46–47   AT MONGIBELLO'S MURKY FORGE. AND AS / AT PHLEGRA, WHERE HE CALLED TO VULCAN . . . : Mongibello is a Sicilian name for Mount Etna, located near the city of Catania in the northeast corner of Sicily. Phlegra (a Greek word) means "place of burning" and is related to the name of one of the infernal rivers, Phlegethon, as well as to the name of Phlegyas, the ferryman of Styx. It was at Phlegra that Zeus was attacked by the Cyclopes whom he fought with and killed.

66   FROM THE BULICAME, SHARED BY PROSTITUTES: The Bulicame is a hot spring of sulphurous water near the city of Viterbo.

74   THAT SNUFFS OUT EVERY FLAME ABOVE ITS FLOW: The hot water of the river turns to steam, which extinguishes the falling flames.

79–80   BENEATH ITS KING'S DOMINION, ALL THE WORLD / WAS PURE . . . : Saturn, king of Crete, lived in the legendary golden age when ". . . all the world / Was pure. . . ."

82–83   THE GODDESS RHEA . . . A CRADLE FOR HER SON: Rhea was the wife of Saturn. Having learned that one of his sons would destroy him, Saturn gobbled up his children as they were born. To save their son Jupiter (Jove), Rhea fooled her husband by wrapping a stone in child's clothing and giving it to the god. Believing it to be a baby, Saturn gulped it down. Rhea then fled with the real child to Mount Ida in Crete.

84–85   . . . SHE HAD / BACCHANTES DROWN HIS CRIES BY CLAMORING: The Bacchantes, or Corybantes, as they are often called, were devotees of the goddess Rhea. Whirling in wild dances to the tune of frenzied music, they would follow her as she walked at night over the wooded hills.

86   INSIDE THE MOUNTAIN STANDS A GRAND OLD MAN: The Grand Old Man of Crete, described here, represents various stages in human history. He is an echo of the passage in the *Book of Daniel* (2:32 *et seq.*) in which Daniel interprets a dream of Nebuchadnezzar's. The Old Man is looking toward Rome, which symbolizes the future of civilization and the Church. "Damietta" stands for the older civilizations of the East. The metals and the clay that make up different parts of his body are a reference to the ancient idea of the various ages of man, mentioned by such writers as Ovid (*Metamorphoses*, Book I). The tears of the old man, Dante tells us in his creative way, eventually form the rivers of Hell. Their source, then, is human sin and suffering.

98–101   THE RIVERS STYX, ACHERON, AND PHLEGETHON . . . COCYTUS . . . : Virgil names the four "rivers" of Hell, which are really more like moats. Dante and Virgil have now seen the first three of them. In the very bottom of Hell, Dante will find Cocytus, a frozen lake in which Satan is embedded.

III–II2   . . . WHERE ARE PHLEGETHON / AND LETHE TO BE FOUND? . . . : Dante has already seen Phlegethon; it is the river of blood in the first round of Circle Seven. As for Lethe (meaning "forgetfulness"), it will be found in the Terrestrial Paradise (in *Purgatorio*), and Dante will see it when he arrives there. In a fine Dantean touch, the river, bringing with it the sins washed out of the sinners, is made to flow down to Hell, where the sins are forever frozen into the ice of Circle Nine that surrounds the massive figure of Satan (see Canto XXXIV). In classical mythology, the dead souls who arrived in Hades drank from Lethe's waters, thereby forgetting their earthly existence.

CANTO XV

Now while we're borne along the stony bank,
The mist above creates so thick a shade
That stream and banks from falling flames are screened.
As Flemings, up between Wissant and Bruges,
Fearing the flooding tide that rushes in,   5
Build bulwarks that will keep the sea away,
As Paduans along the Brenta build
Their high embankments to contain the floods
That come when snows of Chiarentana melt
In spring and swell the stream, so here the banks   10
Were by some unknown architect designed,
Though made less massive and less high.

                                 We'd come
Some distance from the wood. It was too far
Behind us to be seen. We saw some souls
Who walked along the bank and stared at us,   15
Just as, at evening, when the moon is new, men
Will stare at one another and will squint,
Like aging tailors threading needles' eyes.
And while they peered at us, one recognized
My face, and suddenly he grabbed my hem.   20
"What miracle is this?" he said and stretched
His hand toward me. When I had scanned the scorched
Flesh of his countenance, I realized who

He was, despite his burns, and lowering
My hand to that familiar face, I said,   25
"Are *you* here, Ser Brunetto?"

He replied:
"My son, I hope you will not be displeased
If Brunetto Latini lingers here
With you and lets the group move on."

And I:
"I hope and pray you can, and if you wish,   30
I'll gladly sit here with you for a while,
If he with whom I travel doesn't mind."

And he: "If any spirit dared to pause,
He would be forced to lie upon the ground
A hundred years, unable to protect   35
Himself from tongues of flame. Keep moving on
While I stay at the level of your hem,
And then I will rejoin that walking band
Who weep and wail their everlasting doom."

I did not dare descend to walk with him   40
But kept my head bowed reverentially.
He spoke: "What fate or fortune can have brought
You here before you're dead? And who's your guide?"

I answered him: "Back in the tranquil life
On Earth, before my age was at the full,   45
I strayed into a valley. Yesterday
At dawn I turned my back on it. And he,
My guide, appeared when I was drifting back.
Along this path he's leading me back home."

"Keep following your star," he said to me.   50
"If I foresaw correctly back on Earth,
    The port of glory will be yours one day.
    Had I been granted longer life, I would
    Have given you encouragement in all
    Your work, since Heaven chose to smile on you.   55
    But those ungrateful and malicious folk
    Of Florence, who came from Fiesole
    Of old and still retain the qualities
    Of mount and rock, will be your enemies
    Because of your good deeds. For fig trees can't   60
    Bear fruit where sour-apple trees abound,
    As all men know. Proverbially blind,
    The Florentines are greedy, envious,
    And arrogant. See to it that you cleanse
    Yourself of all their ways. Your fortune shows   65
    That honor is your destiny. Both sides
    Will hunger after you, and yet, how far
    The goat will graze from where the grass sprouts up!
    Let the Fiesolan beasts make fodder
    Of themselves and not desecrate the plant   70
    (If any on their dungheap put forth leaves)
    That still contains the noble Roman seed
    Of those who stayed in Florence when that town
    Became a nest of such iniquity."

"If all my wishes were fulfilled," I said,   75
"You would not yet be banished from the Earth,
    For in my memory, your countenance—
    So dear, so good, so fatherly—is fixed,
    And fills my heart with sadness. Back on Earth,
    You spent so many hours teaching me   80
    How man creates his immortality.
    As long as I have life, the words I write

———

Will show how much I value what you taught.
The things you say about me I shall set
In memory together with a text   85
That will be glossed by one who'll know their sense,
If ever I succeed in reaching her.
There's one thing you must know, and I must hope
My conscience will not trouble me for this:
Whatever fate great Fortune has in store   90
I'm ready to receive it. Let it come:
I've heard such prophecies so many times.
So, as she wills, let Fortune turn her wheel.
Let peasant with his mattock turn the soil."

Then, turning to his right, my master said: 95
"Good listeners remember what they hear."

Despite this I continued on my walk
With Ser Brunetto, asking him to say
Which of his companions were illustrious.
And he: "It would be right to speak of some   100
Of them, but not of all. The time is short,
Too short for so much talk. In brief, all these
Were churchmen and great scholars of much fame,
And all have been corrupted by one sin.
Priscian is found in that polluted crowd   105
And Francesco d'Accorso. Farther on,
If interested in such filth, you'd see
A bishop, who from the river Arno
To the Bacchiglione was forced to shift
His see by the servant of all servants,   110
And there he left behind, perversely stretched,
The vitiated muscles of his rump.
I'd tell you more but can no longer talk
Or walk with you. Ahead I see the dust

Arising from the sand. I'm not allowed 115
To mingle with the souls who've just arrived.
My life and fame endure in my *Tesoro*,
And I commend it to you now; of you
I ask no more than this."

              He turned away,
And sped off like a runner at Verona 120
Competing at the Palio. And I thought
He looked like one who'd win, not lose, the race.

NOTES TO CANTO XV

[SUMMARY OF THE CANTO: *The poets follow the banks of the little river and are protected from the falling flakes of fire by the steam rising from the boiling water. They meet a group of souls who are walking. Among them is Brunetto Latini, a beloved teacher of Dante. Brunetto speaks to him for a while about the past, about Dante's talents and future, and discusses some of the other sinners in Brunetto's group.*]

1   NOW WHILE WE'RE BORNE ALONG THE STONY BANK: The poets are still walking along the stream as they were at the end of the previous canto; its steaminess protects them from the falling fire.

4–9   WISSANT AND BRUGES . . . BRENTA . . . CHIARENTANA . . . : Dante compares the banks along this stream to similar constructions near the city of Bruges, in Belgium; and near the city of Padua, along the Brenta, in Italy. Chiarentana (Carinthia) is the upland region that is the source of the Brenta.

12–14   WE'D COME . . . TO BE SEEN . . . : This is a good example of Dantean style, which incorporates dense and complex layers of theological and psychological meaning within a direct, transparently effortless statement whose simple, literal meaning remains undisturbed and miraculously self-sufficient.

20 . . . AND SUDDENLY HE GRABBED MY HEM: Dante, of course, is wearing a gown, normally worn by scholars and certain other men of the time.

26 ARE *YOU* HERE, SER BRUNETTO? . . . : This figure, who dominates the canto, is that of Brunetto Latini (1220–1294), one of the truly memorable characters of the *Commedia*. He is found here among those who did violence to nature. The sketch of Brunetto is a poignant one, and it is clear that Dante has immense respect for the man who taught him so much through his writings and his character (he was not Dante's teacher in the traditional sense of the word). He was a notary in Florence and, as a Guelf, was politically active. In 1260, he was sent to the court of Alfonso X of Castile as ambassador but did not immediately return to Florence after his mission, for in that year the Guelfs were defeated at the battle of Montaperti. Instead he went to Paris, where he remained until 1266, when the Ghibellines were defeated at Benevento. (See Notes to Canto X for details about some of these events.) He continued to hold important posts in the Florentine government. In his writings, Brunetto strove to impart knowledge to the people; he regarded his writings as practical and didactic. His most famous book is *Li Livres dou Tresor*, a kind of encyclopedia, which he wrote (in French) while he was in France. From it he later made a shorter Italian version, *Il Tesoretto*. In politics, he was obviously one who revered his city and who worked for peace and harmony among the warring factions. Thus, Dante could and did admire Brunetto greatly for his artistic and civic ideals. The question arises: Why does Dante place such a decent man in Hell? Apparently, Dante knew of Brunetto's homosexuality; since that practice is, in Dante's system, a terrible sin, the rigidity of his system cannot permit Dante to place him anywhere else except in Inferno. Clearly, however, his portrait of Brunetto is reverential (*But [I] kept my head bowed reverentially*). He even addresses Brunetto with the polite form *voi*, just as he addressed Farinata (but no one else in *Inferno;* see Canto X, note to line 22). The word *ser* is short for *messere*—often shortened to *messer*. It was an honorific title that probably derives from *mio signore*, meaning "my lord." The word is used in modern Italian only humorously or ironically.

56–57 BUT THOSE UNGRATEFUL AND MALICIOUS FOLK / OF FLORENCE . . . : Tradition has it that Florence was originally an amalgam of Romans and people from the nearby hill town of Fiesole. Dante seems to think that the endless civil strife in Florence is traceable to this dual strain in the population. Dante himself traced his roots to Roman, not Fiesolan, stock.

61 . . . WHERE SOUR-APPLE TREES ABOUND: In the Italian, the reference is to "sorbs," a kind of sour apple.

62 PROVERBIALLY BLIND, / THE FLORENTINES . . . : A number of stories are told as to why the Florentines are dubbed with the epithet "blind." One such

story involves their being hoodwinked by the Paduans. The reference to Florentines as "ungrateful and malicious" reflects the bitterness of Dante's years of exile.

66–67 ... BOTH SIDES / WILL HUNGER AFTER YOU ... : It is unclear how these lines are to be taken: will both sides hunger after Dante because they will want to bask in his future fame, or will they simply hunger to annihilate him? The two parties are the Whites and the Blacks.

86 THAT WILL BE GLOSSED BY ONE WHO'LL KNOW THEIR SENSE: A reference to Beatrice who, according to Virgil (Canto X: 114–116), will tell Dante about his future life.

90–91 WHATEVER FATE ... I'M READY TO RECEIVE IT ... : Dante seems to adopt a show of bravado.

92 I'VE HEARD SUCH PROPHECIES SO MANY TIMES: This probably refers to the prophecies made to Dante by Ciacco (Canto VI) and Farinata (Canto X).

105 PRISCIAN IS FOUND IN THAT POLLUTED CROWD: Priscian was a well-known grammarian who lived many centuries before Dante and who taught at Constantinople. Why Dante chooses to place him here is not known; no historical records show Priscian to have been a homosexual.

106 ... AND FRANCESCO D'ACCORSO: He was a famed professor of law at the University of Bologna and later at Oxford.

108–110 A BISHOP ... BY THE SERVANT OF ALL SERVANTS: The use of the names Arno and Bacchiglione, instead of the cities they flow through, is a case of metonymy—the use of the name of one object or concept for that of another to which it is related. The Arno flows through Florence; the Bacchiglione, through Vicenza. The "bishop" was Andrea de' Mozzi, transferred by Pope Boniface VIII at the request of the former's brother who, reportedly because of Andrea's brainlessness and homosexuality, could not tolerate him. By "the servant of all servants" Dante means Boniface. The epithet is one of the papal titles, but Dante's sarcasm is palpable.

111–112 AND THERE HE LEFT BEHIND ... OF HIS RUMP: Dante employs a roundabout way of referring to the bishop's homosexuality.

120 AND SPED OFF LIKE A RUNNER AT VERONA: In Verona, on the first Sunday in Lent, it was traditional to hold a foot-race. The winner received a piece of green cloth; the runner who came in last got a rooster.

"I guessed that people such as you would come,
Whose sad condition made me sorrowful
And not contemptuous . . ."

(48–50)

CANTO XVI

I'd come upon a spot where water rushed
And rumbled down, cascading to the ring
Below and humming like a swarm of bees,
When toward us ran three souls who'd left a band
Of spirits passing us in fiery rain.   5
They called to me to stop: "Your way of dress
Is proof you come from our corrupted town!"

It wounds me to remember how their limbs
Were seared and scorched by fire, with scars both old
And new! When he had heard their cries, my master   10
Turned to me and spoke: "Courtesy demands
We pause to speak with them. And were it not
For all those flames that seem so natural,
I'd say that haste to show some reverence
Would become you more than them."

                                                    When we paused,   15
The three began lamenting as before.
They came to where we stood, and holding hands,
They formed a wheel, like champion wrestlers stripped
And oiled who seek advantage for a grip
Before the interchange of thrust and blow.   20
As these three spun, each showed his face to me,
Their necks turned one way and their feet another.

"If the misery of this sandy spot,"
One said, "and these our baked and hairless forms
Cause us and what we ask for to be scorned,   25
May you, whose living feet are leading you
Through Hell with such security, be so
Disposed as to disclose your name to us.
This one, whose footprints I am trampling on,
Was of a higher rank than you might think,   30
Though he is naked and his skin is peeled.
Guido Guerra is his name, a grandson
Of good Gualdrada; he accomplished much
In life through wisdom—yes, and with the sword.
The other, treading on the sand behind me,   35
Is Tegghiaio Aldobrandi, whose voice
Should have been valued in the world above.
Jacopo Rusticucci is my name,
Thrust in this place of torment with the rest.
Still, my ferocious wife did me more harm   40
Than all of these."

                If from the fire I'd been
Protected, I'd have leaped into their midst
(I think my teacher would have let me jump),
But since this would have cooked and burned my skin,
My feelings of goodwill that made me yearn   45
To be affectionate were overcome
By fear. I said: "When Virgil spoke to me,
I guessed that people such as you would come,
Whose sad condition made me sorrowful
And not contemptuous, and I am sure   50
It will be long before my pity fades.
I, too, am Florentine, and I have heard
Your honorable names and told your deeds
To men. I hope to leave the bitter gall

Behind to seek the sweet fruit that my guide   55
Has promised me, but first I must climb down
To reach the very center of the Earth."

And he: "Long may your body house your soul!
Long may your fame shine after you! But now,
I want to know if still within the heart   60
Of Florence courtesy and virtue dwell
As once they did, or are those qualities
Extinct? For Guglielmo Borsiere, he
Who recently arrived to share our pain
(The one you see back there among our friends),   65
Has grieved us with reports of her sad state."

"Oh, Florence! New citizens and new wealth
Are what have made you newly arrogant,
Immoderate, and this has made you weep!"

I spoke those words, my head held high, while they,   70
Who understood my speech as a response,
Now stared at one another, having guessed
The truth, and said: "If you, at other times,
Have satisfied, at no real cost to you,
Men's wish to know, then you are fortunate   75
Indeed to speak as freely as you do.
And so, if you escape from this dark hole
To see the beauty of the stars once more,
And you are moved to tell the world that you
Were here, I beg you—speak of us."

                              They broke   80
Their wheel and fled; their nimble legs seemed wings;
They disappeared as fast as one might say
"Amen."

Now Virgil thought it best to leave.
I followed him, and soon we came upon
A waterfall whose thunder was so loud   85
It would have drowned out any spoken words.
Just like the stream that flows from Monte Viso
In the east, left of the Apennines, but
Higher up is called the Acquacheta
(The first to form a single stream before   90
It rushes headlong to its bed below),
And after Forlì takes another name,
And leaps in thunder from the Alpine heights
At San Benedetto, then drops alone
(Though for a thousand such there's space enough),   95
So from a high, steep cliff that cataract
Rushed down to meet the valley floor. In awe
We watched it fall whose roar could make one deaf.

Now round my waist a cord was hanging; once
I'd hoped to snare the dappled beast with it.   100
My guide demanded that I take it off, and so
I looped the knotted cord into a coil
And handed it to him; then, turning right,
He hurled the cord some distance from the edge
Far down into the darkness of the pit.   105
"No doubt," I told myself, "this falling cord
My master keenly follows with his eye
Will have some consequence I can't foresee."

We must be careful in the company
Of those who watch the things we do and have   110
The intellect to read our thoughts to boot!
"The thing you dream of and that I await,"
He said, "will be revealed to you quite soon."

Always a man should close his lips to truths
That sound like lies, though he be innocent,   115
For shame will overwhelm him in the end.

But I cannot be still: Reader, I swear
By all the verses of my *Comedy*
(May they enjoy long favor in the world),

A form that would appall the strong of heart   120
Swam upward through the murky air like one
Who, having dived into the waves to free

An anchor snagged beneath a rock or stuck
Some other way, begins resurfacing
And lifts his arms while drawing up his feet.   125

NOTES TO CANTO XVI

[SUMMARY OF THE CANTO: *The poets walk along the same river bank as in Canto XV and are able to hear the sound of the stream falling into the next circle. A group of three souls approaches them: Guido Guerra, Tegghiaio Aldobrandi, and Jacopo Rusticucci. The last of these speaks to Dante and reveals the identity of all three. Virgil urges Dante to treat these men with courtesy, despite their sins, for they were respected figures in Florence. Dante is moved to tell them, in fiery words, of the degraded moral condition of contemporary Florence. The souls then leave the poets, who, continuing on their way, arrive at the point where the Phlegethon drops with a roar into Circle Eight. Virgil instructs Dante to remove from his waist the cord with which Dante had apparently tried to snare the leopard in Canto I. To Dante's astonishment, Virgil drops the cord into the abyss. As if on signal, the monster Geryon rises from the deep.*]

4   WHEN TOWARD US RAN THREE SOULS . . . : The sinners run toward Dante, whom they recognize as a living soul, so as to catch him before he leaves

the area. They recognize Dante's manner of dress as that of a typical Florentine ("our corrupted town," line 7). Nearly all the souls in Hell are naked, so someone wearing clothes makes a startling impression.

8   IT WOUNDS ME TO REMEMBER . . . : Once again we are witness to Dante's compassion, in this case for three noted Florentines. See also lines 42–47.

11–12   COURTESY DEMANDS / WE PAUSE TO SPEAK WITH THEM . . . : Virgil is aware that these three souls merit a certain deference, and he therefore urges Dante to meet with them.

18   THEY FORMED A WHEEL, LIKE CHAMPION WRESTLERS STRIPPED: The sinners keep moving in a circle. As we learned in the last canto from Brunetto, the sinners in this round are forbidden to stop moving.

23   IF THE MISERY OF THIS SANDY SPOT: The sinner who addresses Dante and speaks for all three is Jacopo Rusticucci (see note to line 38).

26–27   MAY YOU, WHOSE LIVING FEET ARE LEADING YOU / THROUGH HELL . . . : There is pathos in this and the ensuing lines. Jacopo is all too conscious of the fact that, unlike himself, Dante is alive, is not being punished, and will soon leave Inferno.

29   THIS ONE, WHOSE FOOTPRINTS I AM TRAMPLING ON: Jacopo is stepping on the footsteps of the soul in front of him (Guido Guerra) in an apparent effort to place his feet on sand that he thinks may be less scorching.

32–33   GUIDO GUERRA IS HIS NAME . . . : Guido Guerra was a wise counselor. In 1260, along with others, he urged the Florentines not to fight the Sienese. They did not take his advice, however, and the result was the disaster of Montaperti, after which the Guelfs were exiled from Florence. He participated heroically in the battle against the Ghibellines at Benevento in 1266 and helped defeat Manfred. The good Gualdrada was his grandmother, noted for her exceptional virtue.

36–37   . . . TEGGHIAIO ALDOBRANDI, WHOSE VOICE / SHOULD HAVE BEEN VALUED: Tegghiaio Aldobrandi was another Guelf leader. He, too, tried unsuccessfully to dissuade the Florentines from invading Siena in 1260 (see note to Canto VI, lines 79–81).

38   JACOPO RUSTICUCCI IS MY NAME . . . : Jacopo Rusticucci was appointed by the Florentines to represent the city in negotiations with other Tuscan towns. Some time after the Ghibellines had won the battle of Montaperti, his house was destroyed, as were those of Tegghiaio Aldobrandi and other Guelfs (see Canto VI, note to lines 79–81). The allusion to his wife is not entirely clear, but he appears to be blaming her for causing him to hate women and (rather implausibly, it would seem) to turn to homosexuality.

42   . . . I'D HAVE LEAPED INTO THEIR MIDST: Once more, Dante's pity

for some sinners, mingled with his respect and admiration for them, despite their sins, is made evident. As noted earlier, Virgil himself is sympathetic to these three men (lines 11–12).

58–59 . . . LONG MAY YOUR BODY HOUSE YOUR SOUL: Jacopo's response to Dante's little speech (lines 47–57) is gracious. Since Dante's words have been courteous and kind, even sensitive to the sinner's feelings, Jacopo answers in a similar tone. Good responds to good.

63–64 . . . GUGLIELMO BORSIERE, HE / WHO RECENTLY ARRIVED: was reputed to be a pursemaker (*borsiere* in Italian) of Florence. He was viewed as a man of peace, was of some influence in the Florentine government, and is mentioned with esteem in Boccaccio's *Decameron.*

67 OH, FLORENCE! NEW CITIZENS AND NEW WEALTH: These new citizens are people from the surrounding countryside, who had come to live in Florence. The new wealth is considered to be of a sordid kind. (Dante speaks of these new Florentines in *Paradiso,* Cantos XV and XVI.)

77–80 . . . IF YOU ESCAPE FROM THIS DARK HOLE . . . SPEAK OF US: The effect of these lines is, once again, to arouse pity, which is increased by the fact that they are spoken by a sinner rather than by either of the poets. On the other hand, as we have already seen (and as we shall see in later cantos), Dante is sometimes unsympathetic, or at least indifferent, to the sufferings of the damned. As for the allusion to the stars, see the last line of the *Inferno.*

87–98 JUST LIKE THE STREAM . . . COULD MAKE ONE DEAF: This is an image of Homeric dimensions. Dante frequently refers to the geography of Italy, especially the northern part of the peninsula. This is not only an indication of his encyclopedic knowledge but also a reminder of how much he had traveled in that region during the twenty years of his exile.

99 NOW ROUND MY WAIST A CORD WAS HANGING . . . : The image of this cord has been the subject of endless critical commentary. Some view it as an allusion to the possibility that Dante was at one time a Franciscan monk (Franciscans wore such cords). In any case, it seems to be associated with sexual chastity; as such it would be appropriate to link it, as Dante does, with the leopard ("the dappled beast") of the first canto, who represents the sins of lust. (Dante says nothing in Canto I about trying to snare the leopard.)

125 Dante leaves us dangling at the end of the canto. When the story resumes, we learn that the creature who is rising to meet the poets is Geryon.

CANTO XVII

"Behold the beast with pointed tail, the one
Who passes mountains, pierces walls and weapons,
And leaves a stain upon the world!"

                              My guide
Began to speak to me this way and then
He beckoned to the beast, bade him approach   5
The bank, right at the rocky pathway's end.
So fraud's repellent image came to us,
Who laid his head and trunk upon the bank,
But not his tail. Honest seemed his face, mild
Its expression, but all the rest of him   10
Was serpent-like, while his paws were hirsute
To the armpits, and painted knots and rings
Bedizened breast and sides and back. No Turk
Or Tartar ever made a cloth so rich
In color or design, and on her loom   15
Arachne never wove a web like this.

In Germany, where people drink a lot,
Boats at times lie half ashore, half in water,
And beavers do the same to snatch their prey;
So on the rocky sand-retaining edge   20
The loathsome beast now lay, as in the void.

The sharp point of his twisting tail whirled high,
A fork envenomed like a scorpion's.

"We've got to alter course," my master said,
"To reach the vicious beast who's lying there."   25

Turning to the right, we walked ten paces
On the edge, thus avoiding sand and flames.
When we had reached the beast, I saw, not far
Away, some people sitting on the sand
Near the abyss. My leader said to me: 30
"It's good to learn from what you see and hear
Within this circle's compass. Go and see
What state they're in, but don't converse too much.
Meanwhile, I'll urge the beast to let us use
His broad back's strength."

          So then, without my guide,   35
I made my way along the boundary
Of Circle Seven, where I came across
Some souls who sat in abject misery.
Their eyes gushed grief as frantically they tried
To fend off flames or shield themselves against   40
The burning soil. They acted just like dogs
In summertime who chew and scratch at bite
Of fly or flea.

          I searched each face to see
If any were familiar, but not one
Of these on whom the fatal fires descend   45
Was known to me. Around each neck there hung
A pouch with special hues and special marks.
On this their gaze was fixed, it seemed. As I
Approached I saw upon a yellow pouch

An azure shape with lion's face and form.   50
On one, as red as blood, was drawn a goose
Of whiter hue than any butter known.
One pouch displayed a pregnant azure sow.
The soul who wore it said: "Why are you here?
Get out! You have no business in this pit!   55
And since you are alive, I'll let you know
That Vitaliano, who's my countryman,
Will sit here on my left. I'm Paduan
And sit with Florentines who often shout
Into my ears and almost deafen me: 60
'Let the sovereign cavalier come and bring
His three-goat pouch!' "

                Twisting his mouth, he stuck
His tongue out like an ox that licks its nose.
I was afraid to stay lest I displease
My lord, who'd told me not to linger long.   65
From these unhappy souls I turned away
To find my master, who already sat
Upon the monster's back.

               "Be brave and bold,"
He said. "From now on this is what we'll use
For stairs. Climb up and sit in front of me;   70
I'll perch here in the middle to protect
You from the tail."

             I started trembling then,
Like someone shaking with malaria
Who shivers uncontrollably, whose nails
Turn livid, and who, strangely, fears the shade.   75
When Virgil scolded me, I felt the sort
Of shame that often makes a servant bold

Before his lord, and so I forced myself
To mount the back of the repugnant beast.
I would have asked my lord (but couldn't get   80
My voice to work) to clasp me in his arms
And shield me, yet I knew he'd helped before
When danger threatened me. As I sat down,
In fact, he held me tightly in his arms.
"Geryon," Virgil said, "fly up, but make   85
Wide turns and slow descents, for on your back
There sit extraordinary passengers."

The beast moved slowly off, just like a boat
That backs out slowly, slowly, from its berth,
And when Geryon felt that he was free   90
To fly, he curled his tail up to his chest
And stretched it like an eel's to all its length
While paddling with his paws through Hell's black air.

When Phaeton loosed the sun-car's reins and set
The sky afire (the Milky Way is proof)   95
His fear was less than mine; and Icarus,
Unlucky man, whose waxy wings unglued
While Daedalus cried out, "Destruction lies
That way, my son!" could not have taken fright
As much as I, suspended in mid-air,   100
All things invisible to me, save him,
Slow swimmer in the dark, who turned and turned
And dropped through space. Yet little did I feel,
Except to sense the wind upon my face
Or underneath, while far below me, far,   105
I heard a whirlpool's terrifying roar,
And, stretching out my head and looking down,
I trembled as I held on tight, for I
Could see the flames of endless fires and hear

The ceaseless lamentations of the lost.   110
I knew that we were dropping down and down,
For nearer, ever nearer to me drew
Hell's inconceivable malignity.
Just as a falcon, long aloft, who's spied
No bird or lure, impels the falconer   115
To cry, "Bad luck! You're falling!" and descends
Exhausted, spiraling, then to alight
Upon the lift-off spot it left so quick,
And, sullen, scornful, shuns its master's call,
So at the bottom of the rocky cliff   120
Geryon set us down, and, rid of us,
Rushed off, like an arrow shot from a bow.

NOTES TO CANTO XVII

[SUMMARY OF THE CANTO: *Geryon rises from the depths. While Virgil negotiates with him to transport the poets to the next circle, Dante is instructed by his guide to go off by himself to see some of the sinners in the third and last round of Circle Seven. Dante comes across a group of usurers, and although he cannot recognize who they are, he describes the heraldic devices visible on the pouches hanging from their necks. Thus the reader can identify the families of these usurers. One of the sinners speaks curtly to Dante and tells of two souls who will soon arrive to join this band of usurers. Dante leaves this unpleasant group to find Virgil again, who is now astride Geryon, ready to be brought down to Circle Eight. Dante mounts the back of the beast, and Geryon wheels downward into the next circle.]*

1   BEHOLD THE BEAST WITH POINTED TAIL . . . : This is Geryon, who will fly down to Circle Eight carrying the poets on his back. He was, in classical mythology, a king of Spain. Dante describes Geryon's body (which was actually three bodies, each with its own head, all somehow knit together) as being part

reptile, part scorpion (the tail), part lion (the paws), and part human (the face). Geryon is said to represent fraud—the sin and its many variations that will be punished in the ten ditches (*malebolge*) of Circle Eight. The deceptively honest face of the beast reinforces the idea of fraud, for those who practice fraud aim to deceive—just as Geryon, in one of the stories told about him, used to rob those he enticed into his territory. Dante's concept of Geryon is largely of his own invention but is reminiscent of the ninth chapter of *Revelation*. (See also *Genesis* 3:1: "Now the serpent was more subtil than any beast of the field which the Lord God had made. . . .")

13–14 . . . NO TURK / OR TARTAR EVER MADE A CLOTH SO RICH: Turks and Tartars were reputed to be excellent weavers.

16 ARACHNE NEVER WOVE A WEB LIKE THIS: Arachne, in Greek mythology, knew how to weave beautifully. Excessively proud of her skills, she challenged the goddess Athene to a weaving competition. The goddess saw that Arachne's work, into which she wove pictures of the gods' love-lives, was wonderfully done; in a jealous rage, however, Athene destroyed it. Arachne subsequently hanged herself, though Athene saved her at the last minute by changing the rope into a cobweb and metamorphosing Arachne into a spider. There is a similarity between the intricacy of weaving and the intrigue associated with fraud. "Oh, what a tangled web we weave / When first we practice to deceive," says Sir Walter Scott.

17 IN GERMANY, WHERE PEOPLE DRINK A LOT: The Germans had the reputation of being heavy drinkers, but the inclusion of this characteristic seems somewhat gratuitous.

19 AND BEAVERS DO THE SAME TO SNATCH THEIR PREY: It was believed in Dante's time that beavers could fish by dipping their tails into the water, using them to hurl fish out of it, as bears do with their paws.

29 . . . SOME PEOPLE SITTING ON THE SAND: In this third round are the usurers, the final group whom we encounter among the violent of Circle Seven. Dante will recognize no one here.

49–50 . . . I SAW UPON A YELLOW POUCH / AN AZURE SHAPE . . . : The heraldic device on the pouch shows this sinner to be a representative of the Gianfigliazzi family of Florentine Guelfs, probably Catello di Rosso Gianfigliazzi, who practiced usury in France.

51–52 ON ONE, AS RED AS BLOOD, WAS DRAWN A GOOSE: The device identifies the sinner as being, most likely, Ciappo Obriachi, also a well-known usurer. The Obriachi family was Ghibelline. (Dante is impartial in his condemnation of usury.)

53–58 ONE POUCH DISPLAYED . . . WILL SIT HERE ON MY LEFT . . . : The device on the pouch reveals that this sinner is probably Reginaldo dei Scrovegni, whose family was from Padua. He speaks to Dante quite rudely, as we see. He suddenly predicts that one of his fellow townsmen, Vitaliano del Dente, or possibly Vitaliano di Jacopo Vitaliani (about whom almost nothing is known, except that he appears to have been a usurer), will one day be seated beside him. The Florentines around Scrovegni are shouting for the arrival of the still living Giovanni Buiamonti, a Ghibelline leader whose family arms were three goats. Buiamonti was also a usurer, of course, and also gambled, losing heavily. Buiamonti died in misery in 1310, two years after being charged with various financial irregularities and ten years after the supposed events of the *Commedia*. The irony of a man of such character having been knighted by Florence as a "cavaliere" is not lost on Dante. The only usurers Dante mentions are Italians of the nobility: by their practices they tainted their good name and social rank. For Dante, nobility of blood should be matched by nobility of deed. Those who occupy privileged positions in society, whether they be noblemen or priests (especially priests), had a special obligation to act morally and be above reproach. Sinners from those two groups, therefore, always receive greater Dantean scorn and contempt.

62–63 . . . TWISTING HIS MOUTH / HE STUCK HIS TONGUE OUT LIKE AN OX . . . : This action is Scrovegni's attempt to taunt Dante about the fact that so many Florentine usurers are in this round.

67–68 . . . WHO ALREADY SAT / UPON THE MONSTER'S BACK . . . : While Dante has been speaking with Scrovegni, Virgil has been making arrangements with Geryon to transport the poets to Circle Eight. He is now astride Geryon as Dante approaches.

73 LIKE SOMEONE SHAKING WITH MALARIA: Dante's Italian refers to "quartan" fever, whose symptoms are like those of malaria.

94–95 WHEN PHAETON LOOSED THE SUN-CAR'S REINS . . . THE MILKY WAY . . . : Phaeton was the son of Apollo. He was granted permission to take the reins of the chariot from his father and drive the sun across the sky but was unable to control the horses. Rather than risk having the Earth destroyed by conflagration, Zeus killed the boy with a thunderbolt. The Pythagoreans used to say that the Milky Way was that part of the sky that was burned when Phaeton's chariot went careening off course.

96–97 . . . AND ICARUS, / UNLUCKY MAN . . . : Icarus was the son of Daedalus, the great artificer of classical mythology. Trapped in the labyrinth at Crete, Daedalus made wings for himself and his son so that they might escape. He attached the wings to their bodies with wax. Unfortunately, Icarus flew too close to the sun, and so the wax melted; the young man was cast into the sea and met a watery death.

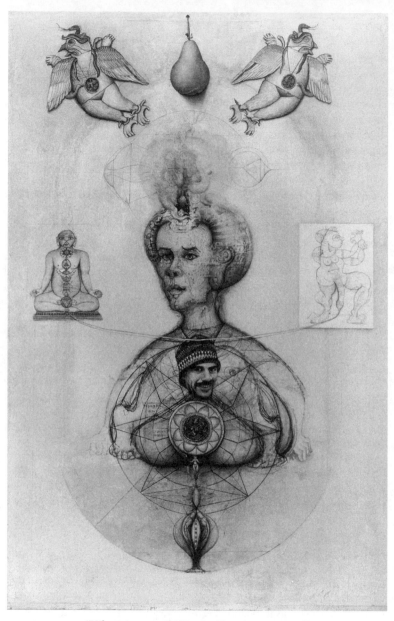

"Why stare, you ask? Because I knew you once . . ."

(110)

CANTO XVIII

There is a place of iron-colored stone
In Hell called Malebolge. With this tint
The cliffs enwalling it are tinged. A pit
Yawns wide and deep in this malevolence
To form its center. Later on, when it's   5
Appropriate, I'll speak of its design.

Round is the zone between the rocky cliff
And pit. Ten ditches can be counted there,
Like moats successively encircling walls
Of castles as protection. A fortress   10
Has a drawbridge that when down can link it
With the distant bank; here it was the same,
For bridgelike crags extended from the cliff
Across each bank and ditch to reach the pit,
The hub of all the spokes of one great wheel.   15

When from his back Geryon shook us off,
We stood and stared in awe. Leftward my guide
Began to walk; I followed in his wake.
Fresh misery assailed me on the right,
Fresh torments, fresh tormentors I perceived,   20
As we stared down into the first dark ditch.
Naked malefactors prowled the bottom:
Half the sinners faced us as they walked, while half

Were walking with us, taking longer strides.
So the Romans do in time of Jubilee   25
To deal with crowds who press across the bridge;
One group walks toward Castel Sant'Angelo
And St. Peter's, while on the other side
The pilgrims amble toward the Capitol.
On both sides of the blackened rock, I saw   30
Horned demons scourging sinners from behind;
The devils beat their backs so forcefully
That every shade was lifted off his heels,
And no one stayed to take a second stroke.

I struggled on and suddenly began   35
To stare at someone who returned my look;
I quickly said, "I've seen this man before,"
And stopped to scrutinize the sinner's face.
Virgil paused, letting me retrace my steps.
The soul in torment tried to hide his face,   40
To no avail, and I called out: "You there,
You staring at the ground! You're Venedico
Caccianemico, or your features lie!
What put you in such piquant sauce?"

                                        And he:
"You've spoken bluntly, forcing me to speak   45
And to remember what a world I left.
My answer will be given grudgingly:
No matter how the story has been told,
I made my sister, Ghisolabella,
Give in to the Marchese's will. But look,   50
These other Bolognesi weep as well;
This place is crawling with them, so much so
That between Savena's stream and Reno's
You couldn't find so many tongues who've learned

To say the word for 'yes' in Bolognese.   55
Do you need proof of this? Just call to mind
Their avaricious nature, if you will."

Just then a demon lashed his back and yelled:
"Move on, you miserable pimp! You'll find
No ladies here to prostitute for cash!"   60

I then rejoined my guide; we walked a bit
And found a reef that jutted from the bank.
We climbed it easily, and to the right
We crossed the toothy ridge, leaving the damned
To trudge the deep trench of their destiny.   65
Beneath us at one point a passage yawned
Through which the scourged could come and go at will.
My master said: "Stop here and look upon
The faces of those souls you couldn't see
Because their movement was away from us."   70

From where we stood we saw the sinners tread
In our direction, driven by the lash.
Before I'd said a word, my master spoke:
"Observe that mighty figure. Not a tear
Rolls down his cheeks despite his suffering.   75
See what a regal look he still retains!
He is the soul of Jason who by force
And cunning took the Golden Fleece from Colchis.
He it was who passed the isle of Lemnos
Where men were put to death by women's hands.   80
Though other women were deceived by young
Hypsipyle, she was seduced by Jason
Who made her big with child and desperate.
For such deception, and deceitful deeds
Against the proud Medea, he must pay   85

The penalty of everlasting pain.
And there dwell those who dealt in similar
Deceit. It will suffice for now for you
To know of this first ditch and all the shades
Of evil men its famished jaws hold fast." 90

When we had come to where the narrow path
Intersects the second crag to make it
The abutment of an arch, we could hear
The groans of people in the second ditch.
They snorted through their snouts, and with their palms 95
They smacked their trunks and limbs. A mold, produced
By exhalations from below, beslimed
The ditch's banks. It stank and burned our eyes.
How deep and dark a ditch! The only way
To peer into its bottom was to mount 100
The apex of the overhanging arch
And have a look from there. That's what we did
And from that vantage-point saw people steeped
In human excrement. I scanned the ditch
And saw a soul whose head was smeared with shit. 105
Impossible to tell if he were priest
Or layman. Seeing me, he shouted up:
"Why look at me? Why don't you save your stares
For all the culprits flopping in this filth?"

"Why stare, you ask? Because I knew you once 110
In Lucca; you're Alessio Interminei.
But won't you please refresh my memory?
I don't remember that your hair was *quite*
So greasy in those days, don't you agree?
Well, now you know the reason why I stare!" 115

He started battering his head and moaned:
"My tongue spewed flattery in floods. That's why
I'm here; that was the sin I wallowed in."

My master spoke to me: "Look over there
And cast your eyes upon the filthy face   120
Of that disheveled bitch. She either squats
Or stands and, with her shit-clogged nails, this whore
Scratches her dirty body. She's Thaïs.
One day her lover sent to her, as gift,
A slave, and when he asked her if her thanks   125
Were deep, she said: 'My thanks are bottomless.'
Now let our sight be satisfied with this."

NOTES TO CANTO XVIII

[SUMMARY OF THE CANTO: *Geryon deposits Dante and Virgil at the edge of Malebolge, Circle Eight, which is composed of ten concentric rings. Each of these is like a deep ditch and contains souls who are being punished for various kinds of fraud. In the first ditch, the poets see pimps and seducers who walk in two lines while they are lashed by devils. Dante recognizes Venedico Caccianemico and taunts him. The sinner points out other Bolognesi who are in the ditch along with him. The poets proceed across a bridge that joins the first and second ditches. In the second, containing flatterers, they see the legendary Jason, Alessio Interminei, and Thaïs.*]

1–2   THERE IS A PLACE . . . CALLED MALEBOLGE: This is Dante's name for Circle Eight, which is composed of ten concentric *bolge,* or ditches. (*Male* is Italian for "evil," and *bolge* is the plural form of the word *bolgia,* meaning "bag" and also "ditch"; no one word in English is a precise equivalent of *bolgia; ditch* seems to be an acceptable English equivalent.) As Dante points out, the last ditch surrounds a pit that constitutes Circle Nine, containing the treacherous. In Malebolge, those who practiced fraud of one kind or another are punished. The various subcategories of this sin will be catalogued for us as we descend from ditch to ditch with the poets. The first ditch is made up of two groups: pimps and procurers; and seducers. The poets also see, from the bridge above it, the second ditch, where flatterers are punished.

21   AS WE STARED DOWN INTO THE FIRST DARK DITCH: Dante and Virgil peer into the first ditch of Malebolge and see, walking in contrary directions, two lines of sinners, whom devils are lashing. Dante compares the two lines to the crowds crossing the bridge in Rome over the Tiber River during the Jubilee Year of 1300 (proclaimed such by Boniface VIII, probably to attract more pilgrims, and their money, to Rome), the very year in which Dante is making his fantastic journey. Thus, we can visualize real people walking in Rome on their holy pilgrimage while these souls in Malebolge are walking in a kind of diabolical parody of their living counterparts.

31   HORNED DEMONS SCOURGING SINNERS . . . : This is the first time we have encountered the devils of Hell. They are seen here doing their job: ascertaining that no soul in Inferno has even momentary reprieve from his or her (note how rarely women sinners are mentioned) punishment, whatever it is. We will see other devils further down.

42–43   . . . YOU'RE VENEDICO / CACCIANEMICO, OR YOUR FEATURES LIE!: Venedico Caccianemico was a Guelf nobleman of Bologna who held a number of important positions in various Italian cities during his lifetime. He persuaded his sister, Ghisolabella, to sleep with Obizzo II, a nobleman of Ferrara, and he accepted money for having done so. It is possible that Dante met Venedico at Bologna or Pistoia. In any case, since there is no source for this story other than the *Commedia*, Dante may have known of it firsthand. Dante speaks in a contemptuous way to Venedico, whose manner is abject and shamefaced. Whereas in previous cantos sinners seemed eager to speak with Dante, sinners in the lower parts of Hell are more reluctant to do so and appear to be more aware of the magnitude of their crimes. Whereas sinners in the upper circles ask to be remembered, sinners in lower Hell are anxious for their names and deeds to be erased from human memory.

51–57   THESE OTHER BOLOGNESI . . . THEIR AVARICIOUS NATURE . . . : The sense of these lines, which Dante intends as an insult to the Bolognesi (that is, people from Bologna, which lies between the Savena and the Reno rivers), is this: the city is so corrupt that here in Malebolge there are more souls from Bologna than there are people living in the city at this time. The Bolognesi were notorious in the Middle Ages for their alleged cupidity. The comment about the word "yes" in Bolognese is a reference to the fact that Italy had (and has) many languages (some prefer to call them "dialects"). While a Bolognese and a Florentine could certainly understand each other's "dialect," there were, and are, differences in pronunciation and vocabulary between them (and among all the other languages of Italy). Probably a parallel for an English-speaking person would be, say, the difference between the way English is spoken by people in Dallas, Edinburgh, Canberra, Liverpool, and New York. Many Italian languages are, however, much more divergent: for instance, the difference between Venetian and Sicilian is quite striking. In our times, these linguistic differences are fading in Italy, because of improved communication, universal education, and, above all, television. The official, and dominant, language of Italy is Tuscan (a word that, linguistically speaking, means "Italian"), whose roots are in the region called Tuscany, of which Florence is the main city. Like all the Italian languages, Tuscan (Italian) derives from Latin, as do French, Spanish, Portuguese, Rumanian, etc. Those languages also have variations: Provençal or Catalan, for instance.

77–85   HE IS THE SOUL OF JASON . . . AGAINST THE PROUD MEDEA . . . : Jason is another figure from classical mythology. He is punished in Inferno because he was a seducer of women: first, Hypsipyle, of the isle of Lemnos; then Medea, daughter of the king of Colchis. Medea helped Jason obtain the Golden Fleece and bore children by him. However, he abandoned her in order to marry Creusa, daughter of another king. Virgil admires Jason (lines 74–76) despite the latter's sins.

91   WHEN WE HAD COME TO WHERE THE NARROW PATH: The poets are now on the bridge overlooking the second ditch, where flatterers are punished. The description here is particularly repellent. I have used the precise English equivalent, in lines 105 and 122, of Dante's words, still used today in Italy: *merda* and *merdose*.

111–112   . . . YOU'RE ALESSIO INTERMINEI: Of Alessio Interminei of Lucca not much is known, except that he seems to have had a reputation for outrageous flattery, as he confesses in lines 117–118.

120–121   . . . THE FILTHY FACE / OF THAT DISHEVELED BITCH . . . : Thaïs, so graphically described, is a prostitute in a play of Terence's, *Eunuchus*, which contains the little scene incorrectly reported in lines 119–126. Dante learned about her from a work of Cicero's, but he erred in thinking that it was she who says the words he attributes to her. Even though she was a courtesan, Thaïs is not in Hell for that reason, for Dante would then have placed her in Circle Two. Instead, Dante focuses on her sin of flattery.

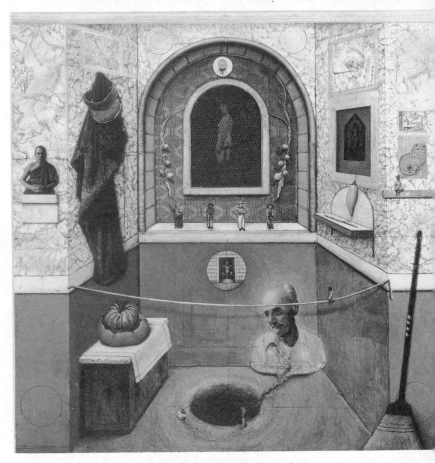

"If you prefer, I'll take you down
That steep decline so you may ask that soul
About his life on Earth and earthly crimes."

(31–33)

CANTO XIX

Simon Magus, and you his followers,
Who should be wed to goodness but instead
Adulterate the things of God through greed
For gold or silver, now in this third ditch
The trumpet shall be sounded for you all!   5

At the next tomb we now arrived; we'd climbed
The crag to where it hangs above the mid-
Point of the ditch.

              Supreme Wisdom of God!
The greatness of your art is shown on Earth,
In Paradise, and in this realm of sin!   10
How just the acts of your omnipotence!

Round holes, all of the same circumference,
Punctured the livid rock on every side
And on the ground. At San Giovanni's church,
So beautiful to me, the holes where priests   15
Who baptize stand are also of this size.
Not many years ago, I broke through one
Of these to save a drowning child. (And let
My declaration undeceive all men!)

From every hole a sinner's legs stuck out 20
Up to the calf. Their feet were all aflame.
In futile efforts to relieve the pain,
The sinners' legs were jerking back and forth
With force enough to break a binding rope.
When oily things are burning, all the flames 25
Are seen to flicker superficially,
And this was how the feet burned, heel to toe.
"My lord," I said, "who is that writhing soul
Who seems to struggle more than all the rest
And who is licked by far more vivid flames?" 30

And he: "If you prefer, I'll take you down
That steep decline so you may ask that soul
About his life on Earth and earthly crimes."

And I: "Whatever you decide is fine.
You are my lord; your will is mine; you know 35
The thoughts and wishes that I don't express."

At the fourth bridge we turned and started down
And leftward made our way among the holes
Along the narrow bottom of the ditch.

My master didn't set me down until 40
We neared the hole of him who twitched in pain.
"You miserable soul," I said to him,
"Whose body's planted upside down, just like
A fencepost in an ugly hole, speak up,
If possible, and tell me who you are!" 45

I felt just like a monk who hears the last
Confession of a killer; suddenly,
The doomed one, ready to be thrust alive

Into a hole, calls back the shriving friar
To delay his death.

               The soul cried: "Boniface,   50
Can it be you? Are you already here
In Hell? Has Fate deceived me by some years?
Have you been glutted then with all the wealth
You took so fearlessly from Mother Church,
The lady whom you treated like a whore?"   55

I stood there in bewilderment. His words,
So mocking, made no sense. What could I say?
My master spoke: "Reply at once and say,
'I'm not the person who you think I am.' "

I did as I was told, and as I spoke,   60
The spirit moved his feet convulsively
And sighed, and then in a lamenting tone
Replied: "What do you want from me? You want
To find out my identity? Is that
Why you came down the bank? I'll tell you then: 65
I wore the sacred mantle of the popes
And as a son of the Orsini clan
Schemed to better all the bear cubs' lot.
I stuffed my money pouch with so much coin
That now in Hell they've stuffed *me* in a pouch!   70
Simoniacs who predeceased me lie
Below my head, pressed down through cracks in rocks.
Someday I, too, will be mashed down, when *he*
Shows up, the one I took you for when I
Abruptly asked if you were Boniface.   75
But I've already been here upside down,
My feet on fire, a longer stretch of time
Than *he'll* be planted here with burning feet,

For from the West will come a pastor steeped
In lawlessness, who's done some ugly deeds   80
And who will cover Boniface and me.
He'll be another Jason, whom we read
About in *Maccabees*. His king, we know,
Was pliant, just as this one's king will be,
The King of France, I mean."

                       I was too bold,   85
Perhaps, but boldly answered him: "When God's
Great son made Peter keeper of the keys,
Did He demand a payment? Not at all!
He simply said to Peter: 'Follow me.'
And Peter and the others took no gold   90
Or silver from Matthias, who was picked
To take the place of vile Iscariot.
So roast forever in your hole! How just
A punishment! And please do guard with care
The filthy coin that made you bold with Charles!   95
Know one more thing: that if the reverence
For God's great keys, which you had sworn to keep,
Did not prevent my saying so, I'd speak
Severer words. The vicious avarice
Of tainted priests exalts iniquity   100
And tramples every good into the ground.
It was precisely pastors of your kind
Whom the Evangelist was thinking of
When he observed the lady (she who sits
Upon the waters) fornicate with kings,   105
That woman who was born with seven heads,
Whose strength derived from ten great horns, so long
As virtue was her spouse's impetus.
The god you've made is made of gold and silver.
If so, is there some difference between   110

Idolaters and you? Not much. Just this:
You worship one, and they a hundred things.
Oh, Constantine! What evils have been sired—
No, not by your conversion to the Faith
But by the dowry Mother Church's first   115
Rich father took from you who offered it!"

And while I sang out all these words to him,
Pope Nicholas kicked viciously, bestirred
By rage or pangs of conscience to react.
My master, I believe, was pleased with me,   120
For as he listened to my speech he wore
A look of satisfaction on his face
Nor interrupted all the truths I spoke.
He grasped me with both arms and lifting me
Climbed up the bank and went the very way   125
He'd come when climbing down. He did not tire
But brought me to the summit of the arch
That to the fifth bridge leads and gently set
Me down, for here the cliff is high and steep
And rugged: goats would find the climbing hard.   130

I dared looked down, and deep below me yawned
The monstrous maw of yet another ditch.

NOTES TO CANTO XIX

[SUMMARY OF THE CANTO: *Dante and Virgil arrive at the third bolgia, or ditch, where simoniacs are punished. The sinners are stuck upside down in holes, their burning feet (more precisely, just the soles) protruding. One shade in particular catches Dante's attention because he is kicking more violently than the others. The poets descend to speak with this soul, who turns out to be Pope Nicholas III. The pope at first thinks Dante is Pope Boniface VIII, who has at last come to replace him as the topmost person in the hole. Realizing his error, he tells Dante about his sinful deeds when he was pontiff and also takes swipes at Boniface and at still another pope, Clement V. Dante replies with a tirade against the corruption of the papacy. Virgil then carries Dante back up to the bridge and Dante gazes into the next ditch*].

1   SIMON MAGUS, AND YOU HIS FOLLOWERS: Simon Magus, whose name gives us the word *simony*, is a New Testament figure who tried, without success, to buy certain spiritual powers from the apostles Peter and John; for this, Peter roundly criticized Simon (see *Acts* 8). Simony is the sin of profiting by the sale—for money or favors—of church preferments, benefices, etc.

8–11   SUPREME WISDOM OF GOD! . . . YOUR OMNIPOTENCE: Once again Dante expresses the idea that God's punishments are always just.

14–19   . . . AT SAN GIOVANNI'S CHURCH . . . UNDECEIVE ALL MEN!: The church of San Giovanni (Italian for Saint John) in Florence, is where Dante was baptized. He mentions the church nostalgically several times in the *Commedia*. Priests stood in holes at the baptismal font (destroyed in 1576) so as to be protected from the crowds, for on the two days each year when baptisms were performed, many babies and their families were present. Dante reports that he saved a boy from drowning in one of these holes by breaking the surrounding marble and freeing him. Dante seems to be somewhat defensive about this action; apparently, a false report of what really happened had been in circulation: he may have been accused of having committed some irreverent act or other. Lines 18–19 seem to reinforce the idea that Dante is taking this opportunity to lay out the truth of the event.

28–30   . . . THAT WRITHING SOUL . . . LICKED BY FAR MORE VIVID FLAMES?: This is Pope Nicholas III, who occupied the throne from 1277 to 1280.

41   WE NEARED THE HOLE OF HIM WHO TWITCHED IN PAIN: This is Pope Nicholas again, with whom Dante will shortly speak.

46–50   I FELT JUST LIKE A MONK . . . TO DELAY HIS DEATH . . . : It was precisely in this grotesque manner that assassins were punished in Florence: placed head first in a hole, they suffocated to death. Often, such criminals would seek to delay their death by calling for a confessor. They were then removed from the hole and allowed to speak with the priest for a time before being put back in.

50–51   . . . THE SOUL CRIED: "BONIFACE, / CAN IT BE YOU? . . . : Pope Nicholas III now speaks. Having spotted him from above, Dante and Virgil have climbed down the side of the ditch and are standing next to the soul "who seems to struggle more than all the rest" (line 29) of the sinners around him. He is, in fact, punished more severely because his sins were greater; we will also learn that his feet are burning more fiercely than those of the other sinners. A member of the powerful Orsini family of Rome, he had the reputation for doing whatever he could (legally and otherwise) for his family; specifically, he was accused of simony. His hatred for Boniface VIII is palpable in the scene. (See the notes to Canto III, lines 52–53; Canto VI, line 66; Canto VII, line 1; and Canto XV, lines 108–110.) Mistaking Dante for Boniface, Nicholas is surprised that the pope is already in Hell, for he had not expected him to die until sometime later. (Remember that the souls are able to see into the future.) Dante uses strong language to address the figure whom he thinks is Boniface. The language expresses Dante's own sentiments.

68   SCHEMED TO BETTER ALL THE BEAR CUBS' LOT: The reference to bear cubs alludes to the family name of Nicholas, Orsini, which means "little bears" or "bear cubs."

79–80   . . . A PASTOR STEEPED / IN LAWLESSNESS . . . : The pastor is Pope Clement V, a Frenchman, who sat on the papal throne from 1305 to 1314. He was the first pope to reign in Avignon, in France, rather than in Rome, and thus his reign initiated the period known as the "Babylonian Captivity" (1309–1378), when the papal see was located in the French city. Clement, it seems, was the puppet of the French king. At the time of Dante's visit, Nicholas is occupying the top spot in his hole. When Boniface dies (that event would occur in 1303), he will replace Nicholas in the top position and push his predecessor further down into the hole, where there are already many other souls. The soul of Clement will then replace Boniface's in the uppermost spot in the hole, pushing Boniface further down. Between Boniface and Clement another pope, Benedict XI, reigned for a period of nine months. Dante does not place every dead pope in

Hell, but there is a vivid contrast between Dante's manner of addressing some clerics and his deferential attitude toward nonclerical figures like Francesca da Rimini (Canto V) or Brunetto Latini (Canto XV).

82   HE'LL BE ANOTHER JASON . . . : Nicholas is speaking of Clement V, whom he compares not to the Jason of the Medea story but the Jason of the Biblical *Book of Maccabees,* who became high priest by offering a bribe of 360 talents.

83–84   . . . HIS KING . . . WAS PLIANT: This king was Antiochus Epiphanes. Nicholas says that Clement, in like fashion, will become pope through unfair and immoral means—that is, through the machinations of King Philip the Fair of France.

86–89   . . . WHEN GOD'S / GREAT SON MADE PETER KEEPER OF THE KEYS . . . "FOLLOW ME": For the Biblical sources of these allusions, see *Matthew* 4:19 and *John* 21:19.

91–92   OR SILVER FROM MATTHIAS . . . VILE ISCARIOT: Matthias was chosen to replace Judas Iscariot, who had hanged himself after betraying Jesus. (See Canto XXXIV for the figure of Judas, who is punished more horribly perhaps than any other soul in Inferno.)

95   THE FILTHY COIN THAT MADE YOU BOLD WITH CHARLES!: Nicholas attempted to arrange a marriage between his niece and Charles of Anjou. When the plan fell through, Nicholas gave secret support (in exchange for money) to the Sicilian revolt against Charles. The uprising is known as the Sicilian Vespers.

103   WHOM THE EVANGELIST WAS THINKING OF: This is based on *Revelation,* Chapter 17. Dante is accusing the Church of avarice.

113–116   OH, CONSTANTINE, WHAT EVILS . . . YOU WHO OFFERED IT!: This is a reference to the famous document called the "Donation of Constantine." Undoubtedly a forgery, it nevertheless had profound consequences. By the terms of the document, Constantine supposedly gave to Pope Sylvester I all temporal authority over the Western Empire. The Church's principal excuse for claiming such authority, however, was Constantine's conversion to Christianity. Dante is saying that, over the centuries, the Church's meddling in temporal matters has resulted in its corruption, thus deflecting it from its primary mission.

132   THE MONSTROUS MAW OF YET ANOTHER DITCH: This will be the fourth *bolgia.*

CANTO XX

To furnish matter for the twentieth
Canto of this first canticle of mine,
I'll versify about new punishments
I saw among the spirits who are damned.

I placed myself in such a way that I   5
Could peer into the ditch below that seemed
Suffused with tears of anguish from the doomed.
Along the valley vast and circular,
The spirits walked in silence and in tears,
Slow-paced, as people in processions do.   10
Observing them more closely, I could see
Bizarre distortions in their forms between
The chin and chest: their heads were twisted round
So that their faces were above their backs,
And backwards they were forced to walk, for they   15
Were not allowed to look ahead of them.
A paralytic might be twisted so,
In time, but I have never seen a case
To rival these and doubt I ever will.

If God allows it, Reader, garner fruit   20
From what you read: how could I help but weep
When I had seen their forms perverted so?
The tears of all these sinners down their backs

Were flowing, trickling through their buttocks' crack.
I leaned against the rocky bridge and wept.   25

And Virgil said: "Are you some sort of fool?
Pity must die that piety may live!
To be compassionate toward those whom God
Has doomed! Why, there's no greater sin than that!
Lift up your head! Lift it and look at him!   30
Earth opened wide its jaws for him at Thebes;
Townsmen taunted: 'Amphiaraus, where
Are you falling to? Giving up the war?'
He fell far down to where great Minos stands
Who catches everybody in his grip.   35
You see? He's made a chest out of his back.
Because he sought to see too far ahead,
He looks behind and walks a backward path.
See blind Tiresias? He changed his sex
(Strange transformation of his body's parts!).   40
Later, before he could become a man
Again, he had to use his wand to smite
Two serpents' bodies that were intertwined.
Aruns there, whose back is near the belly
Of Tiresias, dwelled in Luni's hills   45
At whose feet Carraresi work the soil.
Amid white marble in a cave he lived;
From there he saw, quite clearly, sea and stars.

"That woman there, whose long hair covers up
Her breasts, which you can't see, is hirsute   50
On her other side. She is Manto, who
Through many lands progressed and settled down
In Mantua where I was born: let me
Say something of her now. Her father dead,
And Bacchus' city, Thebes, enslaved, she took   55

To wandering a while about the world.
In northern Italy, so beautiful,
There lies a lake named Benaco above
The Tyrol, set below the Alpine Chain
That shuts in Germany. A thousand springs   60
Or more, whose waters mingle in this lake,
Wash Apennino, spur of Rhoctian Alps,
Between Val Canonica and Garda.
Now in that lake an island lies, and here
The bishops of Verona, Brescia, Trent   65
Give blessings if they pass that way. A fine,
Strong fortress called Peschiera rises up
Where the shore is low. It faces Brescians
And the Bergamesi. Precisely here
The water that Benaco can't contain   70
Flows out to form a stream whose winding course
Traverses verdant fields, and where the stream
Begins its flow it's called the Mincio, not
The Benaco. It goes to join the Po
At Governo, and after it has flowed   75
A little way, it finds a lowland spot
Where, spreading out, it turns into a swamp,
A place unhealthy in the summertime.

"A cruel virgin, as she passed this way,
Chanced upon a strip of land unpeopled   80
And untilled. Here, to shun humanity,
She lived with many slaves and worked her arts.
She left her soulless body in that place.
Then, people living in that region came
Together at that spot, protected well   85
By virtue of the bog surrounding it.
There Mantua was built above the bones
Of Manto, with no further augury.

Its population was much greater once,
Before stupidity on Casalodi's   90
Part assisted Pinamonte's treachery.
I warn you if you hear another tale
About my native city's origin,
Do not let falsehood undermine the truth."

And I: "For me, my lord, your story rings   95
With truth. So much am I convinced, that tales
That contradict it would be burnt-out coals.
But tell me of these people walking past,
For now my mind is focusing on them."

And he: "That one, whose beard is covering   100
The dark skin of his back, was augur once,
When Greece was drained of almost all its men;
In cradles, even, few males could be found.
When first the cables of the ships were cut
At Aulis, he and Calchas gave the sign.   105
I know you've read my epic carefully
And so remember well the passage where
One Eurypylus, as he's called, appears.
That other soul, so lean about the loins,
Was Michael Scott, who mastered every fraud   110
The art of magic brews. Guido Bonatti
Is in that crowd; Asdente, too, a soul
Who wishes now he'd stuck to all his thread
And leather, for repentance comes too late.
See women who abandoned needle, loom,   115
And shuttle, all to truck in prophecies
And cast vile spells with images and herbs.

"But now we must move on, for I see Cain
And all his thorns up in the moon that sits

Between the hemispheres, silvering waves   120
Below the Pillars of great Hercules.
Last night the moon was full, and you'll recall,
When you were in the sunless wood, its light
Helped guide you through the dark."

                                While Virgil spoke,
We moved our feet along the floor of Hell.   125

NOTES TO CANTO XX

[SUMMARY OF THE CANTO: *Dante and Virgil are on the arched bridge above the fourth ditch. Below them the souls of sorcerers, diviners, and soothsayers are walking in a slow procession, weeping as they go. Their heads are twisted around so that their faces are above their backs instead of their chests. Thus, they appear to be walking backwards and cannot see ahead of them. Virgil rebukes Dante for feeling pity for these souls and then names many of them: Amphiaraus, Tiresias, Aruns, Eurypylus, Michael Scott, Guido Bonatti, Asdente. Virgil tells the story of Manto, the Theban prophetess. Aware, as always, of the passing of time, he urges Dante to hurry on with him.]*

2   . . . THIS FIRST CANTICLE OF MINE: The first canticle is *Inferno;* the second, *Purgatorio;* the third, *Paradiso.*

6   COULD PEER INTO THE DITCH BELOW: Dante is on the bridge above the fifth *bolgia.*

10   . . . AS PEOPLE IN PROCESSIONS DO: Dante is referring to religious processions that wind their way slowly through the streets of a town or village.

12   BIZARRE DISTORTIONS IN THEIR FORMS . . . : The strange condition of these sinners is another example of the *contrappasso,* or retaliation: these false prophets, who pretended to see into the future, are now punished by having their heads turned around so that they can only see behind them as they walk.

Just as they were never able to see ahead of them in time, so they are now unable to see ahead of them in space as well. (See lines 37–38.)

24   . . . TRICKLING THROUGH THEIR BUTTOCKS' CRACK: The grotesque punishment is made vivid for us by this unforgettable image.

26   . . . ARE YOU SOME SORT OF FOOL?: Virgil scolds Dante, whose tears of pity (line 25) are a form of disobedience to God's system of justice.

32   . . . AMPHIARAUS, WHERE / ARE YOU FALLING TO? . . . : Amphiaraus, with Capaneus (Canto XIV), was one of the seven kings of Thebes. Having had a foreboding of his death during this struggle, he attempted to flee the war and his destiny. But his wife betrayed him. As Amphiaraus fled in his chariot, Zeus cast a thunderbolt that opened up a crack in the earth into which Amphiaraus fell to his death. Dante's version of the story is rather different, as we see here.

39   SEE BLIND TIRESIAS? . . . Tiresias, of ancient Thebes, is one of the most famous figures in Greek myth. In the tale reported here, he found two serpents intertwined. Separating them, he was metamorphosed into a woman. Seven years after this event, he found the same serpents, again intertwined. When he once more separated them, he became a man again. Tiresias appears as a character in several Greek plays, including *Oedipus the King* and *Antigone.*

44   ARUNS THERE, WHOSE BACK IS NEAR THE BELLY / OF TIRESIAS . . . : Aruns was an Etruscan who predicted the battle between Caesar and Pompey and said it would lead to Caesar's victory and Pompey's death. Lucan tells the story in his *Civil War.* Dante says that, near his cave, Aruns could see the stars clearly, enabling him to make his astrological predictions.

45   . . . DWELLED IN LUNI'S HILLS: Luni was an ancient and powerful city of the Etruscans.

46   AT WHOSE FEET CARRARESI WORK THE SOIL: The Carraresi are the people of Carrara, a city still noted for its marble.

49 *et seq.* THAT WOMAN THERE . . . : The long recital about Manto that begins here is based on a passage in Book X of Virgil's *Aeneid,* although what Virgil says here contradicts what he says in his own poem. Manto was a prophetess of Thebes and was the daughter of Tiresias; her name is the origin of the name of the city of Mantua (Mantova in Italian). Virgil seems to go out of his way to show that the city was only named after Manto, not really founded by her. Nor, curiously, does Virgil mention his earlier account in the *Aeneid,* where the city is said to have been founded by one Ocnus, the son of another Manto, also a prophetess (but not the one Dante portrays). It is as if Dante wishes to avoid the association of Virgil's city with sorcery and divination, which are sins in the eyes of the Christian God; he may be attempting to clean up the reputation of Virgil who for centuries had been regarded as a magician and a sorcerer. This would

help to explain Virgil's stern rebuke of Dante's misplaced pity (line 24 *et seq.*). Divination, sorcery, etc., may be viewed, after all, as attempts to assume God's power. What such sins really involve is the larger sin of pride.

55   AND BACCHUS' CITY, THEBES, ENSLAVED . . . : Thebes had become enslaved because of the tyranny of its king, Creon.

58   THERE LIES A LAKE NAMED BENACO . . . : Benaco was the old name of the lake now called Lago di Garda in northern Italy, near Mantua. Various places associated with that lake are mentioned in these lines.

64   NOW IN THAT LAKE AN ISLAND LIES . . . : This island was the junction of three overlapping bishoprics. Thus, all three bishops mentioned here had ecclesiastical authority over the church on the island.

68–69   IT FACES BRESCIANS / AND THE BERGAMESI . . . : Brescians are people from the city of Brescia; Bergamesi are those from Bergamo.

79   A CRUEL VIRGIN, AS SHE PASSED THIS WAY: The "cruel virgin" is, again, Manto, who is the subject of the entire lengthy passage that follows.

87   THERE MANTUA WAS BUILT . . . : See the note to lines 49 *et seq.* Virgil stresses the fact that witchcraft and sorcery had nothing to do with the founding of his native city.

90–91   BEFORE STUPIDITY ON CASALODI'S / PART . . . : Albert, Count Casalodi, Guelf leader of Mantua, was influenced by Pinamonte dei Buonaccorsi, a Ghibelline, to exile all the nobles of Mantua. As soon as Casalodi had done so, Pinamonte led a revolt against the count and won control of the city for himself.

100–101   . . . THAT ONE, WHOSE BEARD IS COVERING / THE DARK SKIN OF HIS BACK . . . : This is Eurypylus, who was an augur in ancient Greek myth. An augur's job was to decide when a ship could set out on its voyage. Dante says, through Virgil, that Eurypylus, together with Calchas the priest (famous for his role in the *Iliad*), decided when Agamemnon should leave the port of Aulis en route to Troy. It was at Aulis, of course, that Agamemnon was persuaded to sacrifice his daughter, Iphigenia, in order that the Greek fleet might continue to sail toward Troy. This sacrifice was one reason why Agamemnon's wife, Clytemnestra, murdered him upon his return home after the Trojan War had ended. Dante's version of the story is somewhat inaccurate, but we must remember that his direct access to the literature of Greece was limited.

102   WHEN GREECE WAS DRAINED OF ALMOST ALL ITS MEN: Many Greek men had gone off to Troy to fight.

110   . . . MICHAEL SCOTT, WHO MASTERED EVERY FRAUD: Michael Scott was a noted Irish scholar who, in addition to his conventionally acceptable work (such as his translations of Aristotle), also studied forbidden things, *i.e.,* the

occult. He spent some time in Sicily at the court of the Emperor Frederick II. To delve into occult matters was a sin in the eyes of the medieval Church. Compare the story of Faust, so dear to the hearts of the Romantic Era.

III–II2   . . . GUIDO BONATTI / IS IN THAT CROWD . . . : Guido Bonatti was an astrologer at the court of Guido da Montefeltro (see Canto XXVII).

II2–II7   . . . ASDENTE . . . CAST VILE SPELLS WITH IMAGES AND HERBS: Asdente (meaning "toothless") was a popular prognosticator of late-thirteenth-century Parma. Originally a humble maker of shoes (hence the reference to "thread and leather"), he rose to fame by virtue of his alleged powers as a soothsayer. The herbs are probably magic love-philtres (compare the story of Tristan and Isolde: their illicit love begins when they drink such a philtre). "Images" refer to figures made of wax or silver, which, when burned, are supposed to destroy the life of the person in whose image they are made. These are some of the black arts that Dante and the Church condemned.

II8–II9   . . . I SEE CAIN / AND ALL HIS THORNS . . . : Cain with his bush of thorns was like our modern "Man in the Moon." (See Shakespeare's *A Midsummer Night's Dream*, Act III, Scene i.) The time is now early Saturday morning.

I2I   BELOW THE PILLARS OF GREAT HERCULES: For Europeans, the Pillars of Hercules (at Gibraltar) represented, until the fifteenth century, the western limits of the known world. (See the story of Ulysses, Canto XXVI.) Dante actually says "Seville," not "Pillars of Hercules." Seville is inland and somewhat north of Gibraltar, but "Seville" then referred to a whole region of Spain.

I23   WHEN YOU WERE IN THE SUNLESS WOOD: A reference to Dante's struggle in the dark wood of Canto I.

CANTO XXI

So on we walked, my guide and I, and talked
Of things this *Comedy* of mine is not
Concerned to sing about.

                 To the fifth bridge
We came. We halted, and we stared in awe
Into another ditch of Malebolge,   5
Our ears assailed by futile lamentations
Of the dead, all drowned in darkness palpable.

In winter, at the Arsenal in Venice,
They boil a sticky pitch to caulk the ships
That cannot sail the seas when it is cold.   10
So some construct new ships, while other men
Repair those vessels that have traveled far.
Some men swing heavy hammers at the prow;
Some, at the stern. One fellow fashions oars,
Another twists new rope, some work to mend   15
The tattered jib or mainsail of a ship.
So in the ditch, far down below the arch
On which we stood, there bubbled viscous pitch,
Not heated by men's fire but by God's craft.
But when I tried to see what lay within   20
The sludge that slimed both banks, I only saw
The bubbles rise and burst, the huge mass heave,

Contract, heave, and contract repeatedly.
While I was staring at this ooze, my guide
Burst out: "Watch out! watch out!" and pulled me close   25
To where he stood.

              Like one who's curious
To see the thing he's forced to flee, and thus
Unmanned by fear, runs off but looks behind,
I ran, and looking to the rear made out
A monstrous devil racing on the bridge.   30
How fierce the black beast seemed to me, how cruel,
Who ran so trippingly with wings outspread!
Across his shoulders, which were square and sharp,
He'd slung the haunches of a luckless soul
And by the tendons firmly clutched his feet.   35
He cried to other devils from the bridge:
"Malebranche! A senator is here
From Santa Zita! Stick him in while I
Go back for more to Lucca, which I've stocked
With barrators like him, a bunch of crooks,   40
Except Bonturo. Everybody knows
In Lucca 'no' can turn to 'yes'—for gold!"

Flinging down the soul, he turned back upon
The bridge. No unleashed mastiff ever raced
So fast to catch a thief as did this beast.   45
The sinner plunged into the pitch and then
Rump first, resurfaced. High up on the bridge,
Where devils hid, they screamed: "Think you can pray
To Lucca's Holy Face down here or swim
In Serchio's stream? And would you like to feel   50
Our hooks? Just stick your head above the muck!"

They pricked the sinner with a hundred prongs
And said: "Below the surface you can dance
And do your dirty business secretly!"

They were like cooks who tell their kitchen help   55
To keep the meat deep down inside the pot
And not to let it float up to the top.
My caring master spoke to me: "Go hide
Yourself behind that rock so that these beasts
Don't know you're here. Whatever they may do   60
To me, don't be afraid. Once I was here
In circumstances similar to these."
He crossed the bridge and on the sixth bank stepped,
Where he'd need every strength of mind and soul.
Just as, when beggars come, the dogs rush out   65
In rage and make them beg from where they've stopped,
So devils from beneath the bridge charged forth
At him and brandished ugly hooks.

                    And he:
"Don't try to do me harm; before you touch
Me with your hooks, let one of you step forth   70
To hear me out. Then see if you're inclined
To tear my flesh."

                    A shout came from the fiends:
"Let Malacoda go!" and one came forth;
  The others didn't budge. The devil said:
"This won't do any good!"

                    My master said: 75
"So, Malacoda, do you think I've come

This far, quite safe till now from all your tricks,
Without the potent help of Heaven's will
And favorable Fate? We can't be stopped,
So let us pass! It has been willed on high   80
That I conduct this man along the way
Of horror and despair."

                          The devil's pride
Was pricked. He dropped his hook and said to all
The other beasts: "Leave him alone for now!"

Then turning up to me, my leader called: 85
"Come down, you, flattened out among the rocks!
It's safe!"

                    I rose and quickly went to him,
But now the devils threatened, rushing forth,
And I was sure they'd break their word. I once
Saw soldiers at Caprona on the march   90
Blanch fearfully when greeted by the sight
Of such a number of the enemy.
I moved as close to Virgil as I could
And kept my eyes glued on that grisly crew.
Leveling their prongs, they kept repeating: 95
"Say, shall I prick him in the rear?" Their mates
Replied: "Yes, stick him hard!"

                              The devil now
Conversing with my leader spun around
And shouted: "Scarmiglione! Calm yourself!"
Then turned to us: "You can't move forward here.   100
The sixth bridge at the bottom of the ditch
Now lies in ruins. If you want to forge
Ahead, then walk along this cliff. You'll find

A bridge that's passable, for yesterday,
Five hours later than the present one,   105
One thousand two hundred and sixty-six
Years were completed since the bridge collapsed.
I'm sending out a bunch of devil scouts
To see if any soul inside the pitch
Is seeking respite from his misery   110
By surfacing down there. So go with them.
No harm will come to you. Alichino!
Calcabrina! and you, too, Cagnazzo!
Step forward and let Barbariccia lead
Ten of you; take Libicocco with you,   115
And Draghignazzo, and Ciriatto
(With his tusks), Graffiacane, Farfarello,
And mad Rubicante. Search carefully
Around the bubbling pitch, and leave these two
Alone. Let them attain the other bridge   120
Whose span above the ditches is intact."

And I: "But master, what is this I see?
Let's find our way without these fiends as guides!
If you're as keen as ever, can't you see
Those gnashing teeth, those brows that menace us   125
With evil?"

              "Let the demons gnash their teeth!
Their threats are for the spirits in the pitch!"

The beasts turned left upon the ridge, but first
Each squeezed his tongue in signal to the chief.
His answer was to trumpet through his ass.   130

NOTES TO CANTO XXI

[SUMMARY OF THE CANTO: *From the bridge above the fifth ditch, Dante glances down and sees that the ditch is filled with boiling pitch. He watches as a devil, carrying a newly arrived soul, flings him into the pitch. Other devils torment the sinner physically and verbally when he bobs to the surface. Virgil descends to speak to the devils, who rush to attack him but are stopped short by his words and demeanor. Having made the way safe for Dante, Virgil beckons him to descend from the bridge, where he has been cowering in fear. Malacoda, spokesman for the other devils, tells Dante and Virgil that the bridge to the sixth ditch is in ruins; he will, however, allow a group of devils to escort the poets to the next ditch.*]

8　IN WINTER, AT THE ARSENAL IN VENICE: Venice was one of the leading maritime powers of the Mediterranean. Its noted shipyard, where weapons were also manufactured, was called the Arsenal.

37　MALEBRANCHE! A SENATOR IS HERE: Malebranche, a plural word addressed to more than one devil, means "evil claws"; it is a generic term that includes all devils. The devils in this and the next canto have quaint names of this kind, though not all the names have clearly discernible meanings.

37–38　... A SENATOR IS HERE / FROM SANTA ZITA ... : Santa Zita was the patron saint of Lucca; hence, her name is used to stand for that city. The senator's crime is barratry (the sin of this *bolgia*)—what we would call graft.

40–41　... A BUNCH OF CROOKS, / EXCEPT BONTURO ... : This is meant sarcastically, for Bonturo Dati was an outrageously corrupt Luccan politico.

48　... THINK YOU CAN PRAY / TO LUCCA'S HOLY FACE DOWN HERE ... : The sinner is bent over and looks like he's praying; hence the devil's taunts. The Holy Face ("Santo Volto") was an old Byzantine wooden image of Christ to which the Luccans prayed. This irreverent comment by the devils is what one would expect from them.

49–50　... OR SWIM / IN SERCHIO'S STREAM ... : The Serchio is a river north of Lucca.

63　HE CROSSED THE BRIDGE AND ON THE SIXTH BANK STEPPED: The sixth bank also forms the lower bank of the fifth ditch, where Virgil is now.

73　LET MALACODA GO! ... : Malacoda means "evil tail" (see note to line 37).

85–87 . . . MY LEADER CALLED. . . . IT'S SAFE!: There is a complex mix of comedy and grimness in these lines. Dante was exiled from Florence on a trumped-up charge of barratry. Thus, despite the farcical element ("flattened out among the rocks"), the fear he demonstrates has its origin in the events of his real life. There is an air of mock trepidation about the scene, as if Dante were pointing up the absurdity of the charge leveled against him.

89–92 . . . I ONCE . . . SAW SOLDIERS . . . OF THE ENEMY: Dante was apparently a soldier for Florence when the city successfully helped the Guelf Luccanesi (people of Lucca) and other Tuscan Guelfs in 1289, in their battle to take the fortress of Caprona on the Arno river in Pisan territory.

101–107 THE SIXTH BRIDGE . . . COLLAPSED: The bridge, this devil says, was destroyed by a quake, the same one that occurred at the Crucifixion and preceded the entrance of Christ into Hell (the Harrowing of Hell). He also says it was the cause of the rockfall that occurred between circles Six and Seven (see Canto XII, note to lines 31–32). Since Dante accepts the year 34 A.D. as the year of the Crucifixion, then 1,266 years later brings us to the year 1300, the year of Dante's journey.

130 HIS ANSWER WAS TO TRUMPET THROUGH HIS ASS: Dante uses the word *cul* (the shortened form of *culo*), which is equivalent to *ass* (British "arse") in the vulgar sense.

CANTO XXII

I've seen the infantry break camp, engage
The enemy, hold muster, or retreat
To save themselves, and I've seen cavalry,
Oh people of Arezzo, overrun
Your land. I've witnessed soldiers pillaging,   5
Seen tournaments and jousts where trumpet sounds
Or bells were heard or sounds of banging drums
And starting signals from the castle walls,
And other methods, common or bizarre,
But never heard of horsemen who set out   10
Or infantry who marched at such a call,
Or heard of ship that sailed by any sign
From star or shore that rivals Malacoda's
Braying rump!

      With the devils we set out.
A beastly crew! But, "In the church with saints,   15
In taverns with the gluttons," as they say.
Now on the burning sand and on the pitch
I focused, and on all the burning souls.
As dolphins sign to sailors with their backs
By arching them, preparing mariners   20
For being saved, so every now and then,
To ease his pain, a sinner floated up
And showed his back, then dove again, as fast

As lightning strikes. And just as frogs in moats
Lie at the water's edge with only snouts   25
Exposed, hiding their legs and all the rest,
So was it with the spirits on all sides.
But when with cohorts Barbariccia came,
They quickly hid their heads within the pitch.
Some frogs stay surfaced for an instant more,   30
One soul was seen to hesitate that way
And in a flash (I shudder as I think
Of it), the devil Graffiacane hooked
The soul and dragged him from the sludge: the wretch
Looked like an otter with his gluey hair.   35

By now I knew the names of all the beasts
(When Malacoda called them each by name
I listened carefully, as well as when
They spoke to one another). Suddenly
The fiends in chorus yelled: "Rubicante! Stick   40
Your talons in his back and tear his flesh!"

And I: "My lord, can you learn anything
About that miserable soul attacked
By such a band of enemies?"

                    And so
My guide approached and asked where he was from.   45
He answered: "In the Kingdom of Navarre
I saw the light of day. My mother gave
Me over to a lord to serve, for she'd
Conceived me to a wretched man who ruined
Himself and all he owned. In later years   50
I served the good King Thibault; it was then
I practiced barratry: I pay the price
By being boiled forever in this pitch."

Ciriatto, from whose ugly snout stuck out
Two boar-like tusks, tore into him (so mouse   55
Was caught by evil cat). Barbariccia
Locked him in his arms and said: "Get back there
While I hold him!" And turning to my guide:
"Quick! if you want to learn some more from him,
Ask now, before the others rip him up!"   60

My master asked: "Among the guilty souls
Down there with you, who is from Italy?"

"A short while back I was with a Sardinian.
If only I could be with him right now
Than have to face these hellish hooks and claws!"   65

Libicocco spoke: "Let's get on with it!"
He hooked the sinner by the arm and tore
Away a piece of muscle. Draghignazzo,
I believe, would have torn into his leg,
But suddenly their leader turned and glared.   70
When he had calmed them down, my master spoke
To him who gaped in horror at his wound:
"Who was the spirit whom you left to come
Ashore unluckily?"

                    And he replied:
"His name was Fra Gomita of Gallura,   75
Who had his hand in every fraud and had
His master's every enemy in hand.
He dealt with them in such a way that all
Were full of praise for him. How happily
He took their cash, how smoothly let them off,   80
As he himself has said! This friar was
No petty crook but King of Barrators!

———————

Don Michel Zanche of Logodoro
Is down there with him. Endlessly they talk
Of their Sardinia. Oh, misery!   85
Look at that devil grind his teeth! I'd tell
You many things, but I believe he plans
To scratch my itchy skin!"

Barbariccia,
Leader of the beasts, turned to Farfarello,
Whose demon's eyes were gleaming, for he wished   90
To strike, and shouted at him: "Stand aside,
You evil hawk!"

The terror-stricken soul
Spoke up again: "If you desire to speak
With Tuscans or with Lombards, I will have
Some come to us, but make these Malebranche   95
Stand aside; their vengefulness is threatening.
From where I sit, I'll whistle for my friends,
And seven will appear. We all do that
Whenever any of us surfaces."

Cagnazzo raised his snout and shook his head: 100
"Just listen to his cunning plan to plunge
Headlong into the muck!"

The soul replied:
"Yes, I'm really evil, for my plan will cause
My friends more misery!"

Alichino
Could not keep still: he had to speak his mind: 105
"If you jump down, I promise to pursue
You fast, not with my feet, but double-quick

With wings. We'll leave this height, and place ourselves
Behind the bank, and then we'll see if you
Can match us."

              Reader, here's a sport that's new!   110
The beasts looked at the other side, and he
Who'd shown reluctance most was first to go.
His feet now firmly set, the Navarrese,
Biding his time, leaped in a flash and freed
Himself at once from Barbariccia's grasp.   115
The fiends felt shame and anger, it was clear,
And Alichino more than all the rest.
He'd bungled badly; therefore now he leaped
Ahead to chase the soul and cried: "You're caught!"
But he was wrong: the soul was spurred by fear   120
And fast outran the devil's beating wings.
The soul dived headlong, sinking in the pitch,
And made the demon check his downward plunge
And sweep back up. Just so do wild ducks dive
When falcons swoop, and so the birds of prey   125
Must soar away in anger and defeat.
Calcabrina, whom the sinner's craftiness
Enraged, flew after him, but he escaped,
And yet the beast was pleased, for he could pick
A fight with Alichino now. So when   130
The sinner dropped into the pitch, the beast
Dug talons in his equal and they clawed
Each other as they fiercely fought aloft.
But strong and hawklike Alichino hooked
His razor talons in his comrade's flank   135
Till both beasts lost control and plummeted
Into the pitchy pond below. The muck's
Great heat soon loosened both the demons' grasp,
Yet each of them, unable to unstick

His gluey wings, was powerless to rise.   140
Lamenting wildly with his team, the chief
Dispatched four devils to the other shore
So that, in haste, from either side, with hooks,
The beasts poked in the pitch at the belimed,
Who now were baked inside their crusts.

                                        We left   145
To let them stew in their predicament.

NOTES TO CANTO XXII

[SUMMARY OF THE CANTO: *Still astonished by Malacoda's bizarre and vulgar signal at the end of the last canto, Dante watches the devils hook a sinner in the pitch who had tried to stay surfaced too long. At Dante's request, Virgil approaches the sinner, who tells his story. Meanwhile the devils begin tormenting the soul. Virgil, however, manages to get him to talk more about himself and other nearby sinners while a devil holds another shade captive. After telling about two other souls in the pitch, Fra Gomita and Michele Zanche, the sinner plays a trick on the devils by escaping from them and diving into the pitch, leaving them frustrated and angry. They fight among themselves as Dante and Virgil move on.*]

1   I'VE SEEN THE INFANTRY BREAK CAMP . . . : The reference is to the battle of Campaldino in 1289, in which Dante may have fought. The Florentine Guelfs fought with the Aretine Ghibellines—those from Arezzo. The Guelfs eventually won the fight.

8   AND STARTING SIGNALS FROM THE CASTLE WALLS: These signals were made by smoke in the daytime and by fire at night.

15–16   . . . "IN THE CHURCH WITH SAINTS / IN TAVERNS WITH THE GLUTTONS . . .": This proverb is more or less equivalent to: "When in Rome, do as the Romans do."

19 AS DOLPHINS SIGN TO SAILORS WITH THEIR BACKS: It was commonly believed that dolphins behaved this way. In fact, Brunetto Latini, whom we met in Canto XV, mentions this bit of dolphin lore in his *Li Livres dou Tresor.*

42–43 . . . CAN YOU LEARN ANYTHING / ABOUT THAT MISERABLE SOUL . . . : This soul has not been positively identified, though he may be a certain Ciampolo of the Kingdom of Navarre in Spain. Despite the fact that almost the entire canto is devoted to him and his shenanigans, nothing is known of him. Wishing to escape from the devils, who caught him when he stayed out of the pitch too long, the spirit makes a pact with them: if they will let him go, he will call some fellow sinners out of the pitch, and the devils will then be able to attack them at will. However, as soon as the devils agree and hide themselves to await the appearance of the other sinners, Ciampolo (if that is who he is) dives into the pitch. A devil pursues him in vain. This escape causes a fight between two of the devils, who then become stuck in the pitch and must be rescued by their fellows.

51 I SERVED THE GOOD KING THIBAULT . . . : Thibault was king of Navarre from 1253 to 1270. He was the son-in-law of Louis IX of France (Saint Louis) and was also a well-known poet.

75 HIS NAME WAS FRA GOMITO OF GALLURA: Fra Gomita served under Nino Visconti of Pisa, who governed Gallura, a province of Sardinia, a Pisan possession. Although Visconti knew that Gomita had been guilty of barratry for some time, he did nothing about it. But when he learned that Gomita had accepted a bribe to allow prisoners to escape, he had the friar hanged.

83 DON MICHEL ZANCHE OF LOGODORO: Michel is a form of Zanche's first name, Michele: in Italian, final vowels or syllables are sometimes omitted to satisfy the demands of euphony (or, in poetry, the needs of meter); *e.g.,* the title *dottore* changes to *dottor* in front of the person's family name. Michel Zanche was seneschal of Enzio, the king of Sardinia, and an illegitimate son of the emperor, Frederick II. When Enzio went to war, he appointed Zanche vicar. After the king was captured in Bologna, Zanche arranged for Queen Adelasia to divorce the king; he then married her himself. Enzio died soon afterwards in prison. In 1290, Zanche was murdered by his son-in-law, Branca d'Oria, whom we learn about in Canto XXXIII. (Some recent commentators discount this entire story of Zanche's intrigues.)

CANTO XXIII

Silently, alone, and unescorted,
We journeyed on, he first and I behind,
As friars of a minor order walk
Along a road.

      The fight we'd seen now made
Me think about a fable Aesop told   5
About a frog and mouse; not more alike
Are "at this time" and "at this hour" than are
That fable and the episode, if one
Compares the start and end of both, and just
As from one thought another soon erupts,   10
So from my first a second flared, and all
My fears intensified. I thought: "No doubt
We've made the demons look and feel like fools,
For they've been mocked and wounded quite a bit,
And they are much provoked; if to the mix   15
We add their wrath, how pitiless they'll be
If they begin to chase us both! They'll be
Like dogs in hot pursuit of hares, I'd say!"

By now, my skin was goose-flesh as I looked
Behind me anxiously. To Virgil then: 20
"My lord, we've got to hide; I'll have no peace
Just thinking of the devils in our rear:
I seem to see and hear them even now!"

"If I were like a mirror," said my lord,
"Your outward form would not reflect itself 25
  More quickly than your thoughts; just now our minds,
  In kind and in intensity, were one,
  And both have merged to form one resolution:
  If that cliff's slope upon the right is not
  Too steep, we can descend and flee the beasts." 30

He'd hardly finished speaking, when I saw
Not far away, the devils in pursuit,
Their wings outstretched, their only thought to pounce
And snap us up. My guide took hold of me.
Just as a mother, stirred from sleep by roar 35
Of flames, scoops up her son and flees the house,
Without a stitch of clothing on, for his
Security is all that's on her mind,
My master grabbed me on the rocky ridge
And slid upon his back right down the cliff 40
That forms the wall of the ensuing ditch.
No water ever rushed so fast through sluices
To turn the wheel of water-mill as did
My guide when sliding down the wall, who held
Me close to him as if I were his son. 45
His feet hit bottom as the demons reached
The spot we'd fled, but here we felt no fear,
For Providence, which made them guardians
Of the preceding ditch, gave them no power
To leave its boundaries.

                In this sixth ditch 50
We came upon a crowd of painted souls
Who crept ahead with pitiful slow steps,
They wept, they were exhausted and undone.

Great mantles draped their forms and hoods concealed
Their eyes; the monks from Cluny look like this.   55
Each mantle glittered with its painted gold,
But each was lined with lead and weighed so much
That Frederick's, to these, would be like straw.
How heavy are these robes they'll never doff!
The souls turned to the left, and so did we   60
And listened to their chorus of lamenting.
The weighty mantles slowed their pace so much
We met new groups of souls at every step.
Then to my guide I said: "Please scrutinize
These people as we walk and try to find   65
A soul whose name or deeds we've heard about."

A soul who overheard our Tuscan speech
Called out: "You spirits racing through the dark,
If you'll slow down, I may just tell you both
Some things you'll want to know!"

                                        At this, my guide   70
Said: "Wait until that spirit catches up.
Walk with him at whatever pace he sets."

Now two of them seemed eager to approach,
I thought, but oh, how ponderous their pace,
Slowed by their weight and by the crush of souls!   75
At last they joined us, but they looked at me
Askance and uttered not a syllable.
I heard them speaking to each other then:
"That one's alive; the way he moves his throat
Is proof. Still, if the two of them are dead,   80
They should be wearing heavy robes like ours.
Whence this dispensation?"

                They turned to me:
"Oh Tuscan, visiting this crawling swarm
  Of hypocrites of mournful countenance,
  Do not refuse to tell us who you are."   85

"I saw the light of day in that great town,"
  I said, "that graceful Arno's stream flows through.
  This body is the body of my birth.
  But who are you whose cheeks are wet with tears
  Of pain that flow in floods? And please explain   90
  The glitter of the robes that punish you."

One soul replied: "These orange-colored cloaks
  Are made of lead; they are so thick, our limbs
  Creak with the weight, like overloaded scales.
  We're from Bologna. We were Jovial Friars.   95
  I'm Catalano; he's Loderingo.
  One man alone is usually picked
  To keep the peace in Florence, but instead
  The two of us were chosen for that task.
  The fruit of all our deeds is visible   100
  Around Gardingo."

               I began to say:
"You Friars whose evil deeds . . ."

                   My words now froze,
  For suddenly I saw upon the ground
  A soul who was by three stakes crucified.
  He glanced at me. His body writhed in pain,   105
  And long and deep he sighed into his beard.
  Observing me, Friar Catalano said:
"You're gaping at the soul of Caiaphas
  Who's nailed in agony. This wretch advised

The Pharisees to sacrifice one man   110
For the sake of the people and the state.
Behold him now! All naked in the road,
And on him all the sinners step who pass
This way and press him down with all their weight.
The father of his wife, and those who formed   115
The Council (what an evil seed they were
For all the Jews!) are also punished here."

In wonder Virgil stared at him who formed
A despicable cross upon the ground,
Eternal exile in the house of Hell.   120
He then addressed the friar: "Are you allowed
To tell if over to the right there is
Some aperture by which we may escape
This ditch so that the fallen angels don't
Come down to get us out?"

                                  "There is a bridge   125
Nearby," the friar said, "that branches from
The huge encircling cliff and stretches out
Across those ditches dense with misery.
Though here the bridge is down, you still can climb
The mass of rocks that formed the bridge and now   130
Lies in a pile against the ditch's slope."

My leader stood awhile, head bowed, then said:
"That devil over there, the one who hooked
The souls, withheld the truth about all this."

"When I was in Bologna," said the friar,   135
"I heard the Devil called by many names:
The Great Deceiver, Father of all lies."

My guide strode off, with anger in his face.
Then I, too, left these burdened souls behind
And walked in my beloved Virgil's steps.   140

NOTES TO CANTO XXIII

[SUMMARY OF THE CANTO: *As the poets journey away from the devils toward the next ditch, they suddenly see the devils pursuing them. To escape them, Virgil takes hold of Dante and slides down the sloping wall of the ditch; they come to a stop at the bottom of the sixth ditch. Here they come upon the hypocrites, dressed in hoods and capes of lead. One of them, Friar Catalano, tells Dante about himself and his companion, Friar Loderingo. Before leaving, the poets see the soul of Caiaphas crucified upon the ground.*]

1   SILENTLY, ALONE, AND UNESCORTED: Dante and Virgil are no longer being escorted by the band of ten devils.

3   ... FRIARS OF A MINOR ORDER ... : The reference to friars foreshadows the meeting, in this canto, with the Jovial Friars: Catalano and Loderingo.

5   ... THINK ABOUT A FABLE AESOP TOLD: This fable does not appear to be one of Aesop's, although it is found in collections of Aesop from the medieval period. In this fable, a mouse, trying to cross a river, encounters a frog, who offers to transport him to the other side and persuades him to tie his foot to the frog's; the mouse consents. They start out, but the frog soon dives into the water to try to drown the mouse. Observing the struggle in the water, a passing bird of prey snatches the mouse and, of course, the frog to which the mouse was tied. The fable was later masterfully retold by Jean de la Fontaine, whose refashionings of Aesop's originals are miniature masterpieces.

6–9   ... NOT MORE ALIKE ... THE START AND END OF BOTH ... : In other words, Dante sees a parallel between the fable and the episode concerning the Navarrese and the devils in the previous canto.

37   WITHOUT A STITCH OF CLOTHING ON ... : Sleeping in the nude may have been a fairly common practice at this time, as it had been in antiquity.

39   MY MASTER GRABBED ME ON THE ROCKY RIDGE: An element of grim farce is once more injected into the proceedings. The picture of Virgil sliding down on his back is a tad Chaplinesque!

46   HIS FEET HIT BOTTOM . . . : The poets land at the bottom of the sixth ditch, where the mood is much more somber. Here the hypocrites are punished.

55   . . . THE MONKS FROM CLUNY LOOK LIKE THIS: They look like monks because of their mantles and hoods. Monks from Cluny, in France, were notable for their somewhat luxurious robes.

58   . . . FREDERICK'S, TO THESE, WOULD BE LIKE STRAW: Legend (and that is all it is) has it that Frederick II punished those guilty of treason by encasing them in lead. The traitors were then placed in a cauldron, which was heated until the lead (and the victim's flesh) melted.

67   A SOUL, WHO OVERHEARD OUR TUSCAN SPEECH: On several occasions we have met souls who recognize Dante by his Tuscan speech.

68   . . . YOU SPIRITS RACING THROUGH THE DARK: The pace of the hypocrites is so slow that, to them, Dante and Virgil appear to be running.

86   I SAW THE LIGHT OF DAY IN THAT GREAT TOWN: Florence is the town referred to.

95   WE'RE FROM BOLOGNA. WE WERE JOVIAL FRIARS: The Jovial Friars (a nickname) were a military-religious order (Ordo Militiae Beatae Mariae), founded in 1261 in Bologna. Its purpose was to protect the weak and to help settle disputes between parties. Although the order became famous, it also became corrupt, so that its members soon began to be called Jovial Friars (Frati Godenti in Italian) because of the easy lives that the monks of the order led and also because of the spirit of joy that seemed to characterize the monks (they were also dubbed Capons of Christ!). Catalano dei Malavolti came from a Guelf family in Bologna, while Loderingo degli Andalò was from a Ghibelline family there. They were appointed jointly as *podestà* of Florence in 1266; that is, they were asked by Pope Clement IV to rule the city after the battle of Benevento. Though they were from Bologna, these friars were chosen to govern Florence because it was thought they might rule more objectively than Florentines. In reality, the pope favored the Guelfs and persuaded the friars to favor them, too, though they feigned neutrality (more hypocrisy!). Both friars were soon accepting bribes. Dante places them here, rather than among the barrators, because of their religious affiliation.

100–101   THE FRUIT OF ALL OUR DEEDS IS VISIBLE / AROUND GARDINGO . . . : Gardingo was a section of Florence where the houses of Farinata degli Uberti and his clan had stood before being torn down by the Florentine Guelfs during the anti-Ghibelline rule of the two friars.

103–104   . . . I SAW UPON THE GROUND / A SOUL WHO WAS BY THREE STAKES CRUCIFIED: This soul is Caiaphas, chief priest of the Jews, who urged that Christ be killed.

109–110   . . . THIS WRETCH ADVISED / THE PHARISEES . . . : See *Matthew* 23:27: "Woe unto you, scribes and Pharisees, hypocrites! for ye are like unto whited sepulchres, which indeed appear beautiful outward, but are within full of dead men's bones, and of all uncleanness."

111   FOR THE SAKE OF THE PEOPLE AND THE STATE: Caiaphas had said, ". . . Ye know nothing at all, nor consider that it is expedient for us, that one man should die for the people, and that the whole nation perish not." (*John* 11:49–50)

115   THE FATHER OF HIS WIFE . . . : His father-in-law was Annas, the judge who pronounced the death sentence against Jesus.

115–116   . . . AND THOSE WHO FORMED / THE COUNCIL . . . : This Council was the Sanhedrin.

118   IN WONDER VIRGIL STARED AT HIM . . . : Virgil stares in wonder because, during his first trip to Inferno, Caiaphas, of course, had not yet arrived.

133   THAT DEVIL OVER THERE . . . : This is Malacoda.

137   THE GREAT DECEIVER, FATHER OF ALL LIES: See *John* 8:44: "Ye are of your father the devil, and the lusts of your father ye will do. He was a murderer from the beginning, and abode not in the truth, because there is no truth in him. When he speaketh a lie, he speaketh of his own; for he is a liar, and the father of it."

CANTO XXIV

When, in the still-young year, the frigid sun
Beneath Aquarius begins to warm
His locks, and when the long dark nights begin
Their movement to the south, and when the frost
Designs the image of the snow (her sister)   5
On frozen ground (though soon her point grows blunt),
The peasant then, provisions low, looks out
Upon the whitened fields, then smacks his thigh
And turns into the hut to pace and fret,
Desperate, uncertain what to do. Then   10
He gives another glance and gathers hope,
For now the face of Earth is changed, and so
He takes his staff and leads his sheep to graze.

Just so, on seeing Virgil's face, I trembled
Apprehensively. But how quick the wound   15
Was soothed because the bandage was applied!
For when we reached the broken bridge, he wore
A sweet look on his face, as at the hour
When first I felt its radiance near the hill.
He paused in thought, surveyed the ruined bridge,   20
Then opened wide his arms and held me tight,
And like a man who has a job to do
And plans against catastrophe with care,

My guide observed a nearby crag as toward
The summit of a peak he carried me.   25
He said: "Climb over to that rock, but first
Be sure it's strong enough to bear your weight."

Those souls with hoods of lead could never tread
This bridge, for even we—my guide (a shade)
And I, pushed up by him from rock to rock—   30
Had trouble climbing to the top, and if
The cliff had not been relatively low,
The climb would have defeated me, but since
The ditches of this ring do clearly lean
In the direction of the furthest pit,   35
The outer cliffs are high; the inner, low.

At last we reached the summit of the heap.
By now my lungs were screaming for more air
So, out of breath, I sat upon the ground.
"Do not succumb to sloth; the road to fame   40
Lies not in downy bed or quilt; what trace
Is left by lives unmarked by fame? The same
As smoke on wind or foam upon the wave.
Stand on your feet, therefore," my leader said,
"And strive to overcome this lethargy   45
By strength of soul that flesh cannot drag down.
There is a longer ladder to be climbed;
For merely to have left these hypocrites
Is not enough. Well, if you understand,
Then take some action that will profit you."   50

So spurred, I rose and, steadying myself,
Pretended to be breathing easier.
I said: "Let's move ahead; I'm feeling strong
And now I have no fear of anything."

We made our way across the bridge. It was   55
More steep than the preceding one and far
More rugged, narrow, arduous. I spoke
While walking so as not to seem too weak.
Suddenly, from the seventh ditch, we heard
A voice that issued inarticulate.   60
Already on the summit of the bridge
I stood, yet could not understand the words,
But he who spoke them snarled in angry tones.
Over the ditch I bent and stared but could
Not see the ditch's bed; it was too dark.   65
I said to Virgil: "Master, please move on
And let's go down the next cliff's wall; I hear
A voice but cannot understand the words;
I try to see but only see the dark."

"My answer," Virgil said, "will be to do   70
The thing you ask, since what you ask is fit.
In silence, then, the deed should be performed."

We went into the ditch just where the bridge
Links up with the ensuing cliff. And then
The ditch's horrors were revealed to me: 75
Within, a slimy swarm of serpents writhed.
(Just thinking of them makes my blood run cold!)
Let sandy Libya cease her boastful ways,
For though she brought forth chelydri, jaculi,
Phareae, cenchri, and amphisbaena,   80
She never showed (nor Ethiopia,
Nor all the lands that by the Red Sea lie)
So many plagues of such malignant kind.

Among this loathsome, savage swarm of snakes
Ran naked people, frightened to the core,   85

Who had no place to hide and had no help
From magic heliotrope. Their hands were bound
Behind their backs with snakes whose heads were pushed
Between the sinners' loins and in the front
Were twisted into knots. A darting snake,   90
As quick as lightning, pierced a sinner's flesh
Where neck and shoulders join. No quill could write
An *o* or *i* more quickly than the time
It took for all his body to ignite
And burn and turn to ash. Yet almost instantly   95
The ashes reunited and reformed
Themselves into the same tormented shape.

The phoenix, sages tell us, in the same
Way dies, to be reborn when she is near
Five hundred years of age. This bird feeds not   100
On grass or grain but only on the tears
Of frankincense or amomum, and when
She dies her shroud is precious wood and myrrh.

When he arose, the soul resembled one
Whom spasms overwhelm, who's pulled perhaps   105
By demon power to the ground or bound
By some obstruction of his vital force,
Who, rising, stares around with vacant look,
Stunned by the suffering he's undergone.

How stern the power of Almighty God   110
Who crushes sinners with such righteous blows!

My guide asked who he was. The soul replied:
"I washed into this gorge of cruelty
From Tuscany, not long ago. I found
Great pleasure in the bestial life I led,   115

Bastard that I was. I'm Vanni Fucci,
A beast. Pistoia was a fitting den
For me!"

      I turned to Virgil: "Tell that shade
He must not slip away from us, and ask
What sin it was that doomed him to this ditch.   120
I used to know him as a man of blood
Consumed with rage."

          The soul was listening.
His look did not belie my words, and while
He stared at me his face turned red with shame.
"For you to catch me in my misery   125
Torments me more than my disgraceful death.
I can't, however, turn you down. I'm thrust
This deep in Hell's great hole because I stole
Some jewelry and silver from the church,
A theft for which another man was hanged.   130
But maybe if you leave black Hell you'll feel
A sense of triumph that I'm buried here?
I won't let that take place! You will not gloat
When I have shown you what the future holds!
Pistoia first will thin herself of Blacks.   135
Your native town will change its governors
And ways of governing. From Val di Magra,
Mars will launch a thunderbolt of war wrapped
In clouds of turbulence, and in a storm
Of savagery a fight will pierce the mist   140
On a field at Piceno. Oh, how red
With wounds the bodies of your Whites will run!
I hope this statement stings you to the quick!"

NOTES TO CANTO XXIV

[SUMMARY OF THE CANTO: *Having climbed with difficulty to the seventh bridge, the poets hear a voice from the ditch below. Descending, they see a swarm of serpents amid whom a host of sinners are running, their hands bound by twisted snakes. One soul, who continuously burns to ash and is then resurrected before their eyes, is that of Vanni Fucci of Pistoia. He tells the story of his sinful deed and then cruelly torments Dante by prophesying the doom of the White party.*]

1–13   WHEN, IN THE STILL-YOUNG YEAR. . . . HIS SHEEP TO GRAZE: This is another extended image of the kind often found in the epic poets of antiquity. In late January and most of February the sun is in the constellation of Aquarius. As the calendar in Dante's time was somewhat different from our own, the climate then was warmer in the February of the Italian calendar.

8–9   THE PEASANT . . . THEN SMACKS HIS THIGH: This action is a way of expressing one's grief in Italy.

19   WHEN FIRST I FELT ITS RADIANCE NEAR THE HILL: A reference to the hill of Canto I.

47   THERE IS A LONGER LADDER TO BE CLIMBED: This ladder may be an allusion to their upcoming voyage through Purgatory, the locale of the second canticle of the *Commedia*.

79–80   . . . CHELYDRI . . . AMPHISBAENA: Lucan mentions these monstrous creatures in his *Civil War*.

87   . . . MAGIC HELIOTROPE: Many believed this stone had the power to render invisible anyone who carried it on his person. It also was believed to cure snake bites. (In the Third Story of the Eighth Day of Boccaccio's *Decameron*, the alleged power of this stone is used to great comic effect.) In this passage, the meaning is clear: these miserable sinners cannot escape their fate in any way, and Dante has no pity for them.

98   THE PHOENIX, SAGES TELL US . . . : Dante once again employs a bird image. The Arabian phoenix, a mythical bird, is said to have burned itself to death once every half millennium. It then arose from its ashes and became whole once more. Dante's version of the phoenix myth is derived, no doubt, from Ovid's *Metamorphoses*. Wallace Fowlie (in *A Reading of Inferno*) points out

that the death and resurrection of the phoenix in this ditch are an infernal travesty of the Resurrection of Christ.

103   . . . HER SHROUD IS PRECIOUS WOOD AND MYRRH: The Italian says "nard and myrrh."

104–105   . . . THE SOUL RESEMBLED ONE / WHOM SPASMS OVERWHELM . . . : The spasms may be those experienced during an epileptic seizure. Demons were thought to cause these seizures.

116   BASTARD THAT I WAS. I'M VANNI FUCCI: He was one Fuccio de' Lazzeri, a nobleman of Pistoia. With others, Fucci robbed the treasures of the cathedral of San Zeno in Pistoia in 1293. Rampino di Ranuccio and other men were accused of the crime, for which one of these men is said to have been hanged. One of Fucci's colleagues in crime later confessed to the theft, but Fucci himself fled. He belonged to the Black party of Pistoia and so was *ipso facto* an enemy of Dante.

135–143   PISTOIA FIRST WILL THIN HERSELF OF BLACKS. . . . STINGS YOU TO THE QUICK!: The "prophecy," like nearly all those found in *Inferno*, has already been fulfilled, since Dante is writing from the vantage point of the future. Fucci seems to enjoy making this prophecy, knowing it will disturb Dante. In any case, the prophecy is not entirely clear; perhaps it is intentionally a bit obscure. In 1301, Florentine and Pistoian Whites threw out the Blacks from Pistoia; the exiles went to Florence and allied themselves with the Florentine Blacks. In 1301, Charles of Valois was permitted to enter the city with the avowed purpose of maintaining peace between the warring parties. Instead of acting impartially, however, he favored the Blacks. Their leader, Corso Donati, who had been exiled, now reentered Florence and liberated all the Blacks who were in prison. These men devastated many houses of the Whites over the next week, while Charles sat idly by and let the atrocities be committed. The Whites, including Dante, were exiled the next year. Piceno was the site of a battle between Whites and Blacks in 1302 (the Blacks won). The thunderbolt and clouds of turbulence stand for the Blacks; the mist, for the Whites. The final line of the canto reveals Vanni Fucci's malign nature. Since Dante was a member of the Whites, Fucci's prophecies are obviously unpleasant for Dante to hear. Furthermore, Dante hated the city of Pistoia, for it was there that the White and Black factions originated, a party division that was to bring great grief to Dante. (See Canto XXV.)

CANTO XXV

His speech had ended. Suddenly he raised
His hands and made the fig-sign with them both.
"Here, God, take these! They're both for you!" he cried.

From then on all the serpents were my friends,
For one coiled round his neck as if to say: 5
"Don't speak another word!"

               A second one
Now coiled around his arms and held them fast
By clinching near his paunch.

               Ah, Pistoia,
Pistoia, why not burn yourself to ash
And disappear, since you outdo your seed   10
In evil deeds? In all the rings of Hell
I saw no soul so arrogant toward God,
Not even he who fell from Theban walls.

He fled and said no more. A centaur then
Appeared who shouted angrily: "Direct   15
Me to the soul that dares such blasphemy!"

Maremma does not hide so many snakes
As crawled the beastly portion of his back.

And on his shoulders, just across the neck,
A dragon draped, its wings spread wide, who sets   20
Ablaze all creatures in its path. My guide
Explained: "That centaur's Cacus, he who caused
The pooling of so many lakes of blood
Below the rock where Aventino lies.
His brethren tread another road; he's here   25
Because he fraudulently stole a herd
Of cows, a deed that proved to be his last,
For he was clubbed to death by Hercules,
Who dealt a hundred blows, though ten sufficed."

As Virgil spoke, the centaur raced away.   30
Three spirits from below approached us now,
Though we were not aware of them until
They shouted: "Who are you?"

                       So Virgil ceased
His tale and to this trio we gave ear.
I knew not who they were, but then by chance   35
One spirit called another by his name
And said: "Where can Cianfa be?"

                        Then, to make
My leader listen to their words, across
My lips I stretched my finger nose to chin.   40
(My readers may be hard-pressed to believe
The tale I'll now relate; and, truth to tell,
I sometimes wonder if it did occur.)
As I looked on, a serpent with six feet
Began to coil itself around one soul.   45
Its midfeet clutched the sinner's abdomen;
Its forefeet held his arms as into both
His cheeks it bit. Across the sinner's thighs

Its hind feet stretched; between his thighs it shoved
Its tail. No ivy ever twined around   50
A tree as tightly as this serpent wrapped its form
Around the soul. Like heated wax, they seemed
To melt and merge as all their color mixed,
And each was altered from its former state.
Just so a paper's whiteness dies away   55
And dims to brown when held above a flame.
The other two looked on and cried to him:
"Agnello! Right before our eyes you change!
You're neither one nor two!"

                        By now their heads
Had joined as one, their faces mingling so   60
That neither one was recognizable.
The soul's arms and the forelegs of the beast
Had formed new limbs. Appendages that no
Man's eyes had ever seen before grew out
Of blended legs and thighs, of chest and paunch.   65
The features of each face had been erased.
The now perverted shape resembled both,
Yet also neither. Then, transmogrified,
The creature limped away. As in the heat
Of dog-days lizards leaping hedge to hedge   70
Resemble lightning flashes when they cross
The road, a fire-breathing snake appeared,
As black and livid as a peppercorn,
And darting toward the bellies of the two
It pierced, in one of them, the part we're fed   75
Through in the womb, then fell upon the ground.
The wounded soul said not a word, stood still,
And stared, then yawned, like someone overcome
By sleep or fever-fit. The snake and he
Now eyed each other, as, from spirit's wound   80

And serpent's mouth great clouds of smoke poured out
That blended as they billowed forth.

                              And you,
Oh Lucan, hold your tongue about Sabellus
And Nasidius, and listen to my words!
And Ovid, with your metamorphoses of Cadmus   85
And of Arethusa—one changed to snake,
The other changed to fountain—what of that?
I'll not be envious; *you* never showed
The transmutation of two natures such
That *both* their substances were interchanged!   90

Each closely to the other's ways adhered:
The serpent's tail divided into legs.
The wounded spirit's feet closed up to form
A tail. The limbs cohered so that no joint
Between the two was visible to me.   95
The tail, now forked, assumed the shape the soul
Was losing fast. The serpent's skin grew soft;
The spirit's hardened to a scaly coat.
The arms into the armpits shrunk, while both
The serpent's feet, quite short, began to stretch   100
To make up for the spirit's shortened arms.
And what a transformation now occurred
As, blending, both the hind feet of the snake
Became the organ Adam's seed conceals,
And in its place the miserable shade   105
Displayed two desiccated serpent's feet.
By smoke each one was veiled with colors new.
The man grew hirsute and the snake grew bald.
One fell upon the ground, the other rose,
Yet neither at his consort ceased to stare.   110

Behind their eyes that burned ferociously
The face of each had changed forevermore.

The snake, erect, now toward his temples pulled
His muzzle, from whose fleshiness there grew,
Upon the cheeks that had been featureless,   115
A pair of ears. The flesh in front now shaped
Into a nose; the lips now thickened out.
The soul upon the ground thrust forth his snout
And drew his ears into his head, as snails
Pull in their horns. His tongue, like tongues of men,   120
Had been a single piece of flesh and made
For speech, but now it split into a fork.
The serpent's meanwhile healed into a whole.
And then there came an end to all the smoke.

The shade that had become a beast now fled   125
Along the ditch and hissed, and as he ran
The other chased him, spitting as he spoke,
And turning on his new-formed neck he said:
"Along the road I'll make this Buoso run
On all four legs, as I have had to do!"   130

And so I witnessed many changes of all kinds
Among the cargo of the seventh ditch,
But if my pen seems far-removed from truth,
I plead the novelty of all I saw.
And though my sight and mind were both confused,   135
Both Buoso's flight and Guercio's could not mask
The view of Crippled Puccio: only he
Among the first three souls had undergone
No change of any sort. The other one
Was he who brought such mourning to Gaville.   140

NOTES TO CANTO XXV

[SUMMARY OF THE CANTO: *When Vanni Fucci makes an obscene gesture toward Heaven, snakes entwine his body and he runs off. Cacus the centaur appears and follows Fucci in order to punish him further for his blasphemous gesture. Dante and Virgil witness the fantastic transformations of the souls of several Florentine noblemen.*]

1   HIS SPEECH HAD ENDED. . . . HE . . . MADE THE FIG-SIGN . . . : This canto continues the action of the previous one. Committing incredible blasphemy, Vanni Fucci inserts his thumbs between the forefinger and middle finger of each hand and points both hands at God in the vulgar, sexually suggestive gesture still in use among Italians.

4   FROM THEN ON ALL THE SERPENTS WERE MY FRIENDS: The serpents are Dante's friends because they punish Fucci for his vile gesture.

10   . . . SINCE YOU OUTDO YOUR SEED / IN EVIL DEEDS? . . . : By "seed," Dante means the founders of the city, who were thought to have been soldiers from the army of the defeated Catiline, conspirator against the Roman state in the first century B.C. Dante deeply resented Pistoia because it was there that the parties of Whites and Blacks originated. (See Canto XXIV, note to lines 135–142.)

13   NOT EVEN HE WHO FELL FROM THEBAN WALLS: A reference to Capaneus, whom we encountered in Canto XIV.

17   MAREMMA DOES NOT HIDE SO MANY SNAKES: The Maremma is a swampy malarial region of Italy.

22   . . . THAT CENTAUR'S CACUS . . . : Dante errs in calling Cacus a centaur: he was a giant. The error seems to stem from Dante's misreading of a passage in the *Aeneid*. In Greek myth, Cacus appears in the stories of the Twelve Labors of Hercules. An inhabitant of a cave at Mount Aventino, Cacus stole some cattle that Hercules was transporting from Spain. Cacus brought them to his cave, but Hercules, hearing the cattle low, found the cave, dispatched Cacus, and took back his booty.

25   HIS BRETHREN TREAD ANOTHER ROAD . . . : Cacus' brethren are the other centaurs, found in the Seventh Circle.

29   . . . THOUGH TEN SUFFICED: Cacus died after the tenth blow from Hercules' club. Apparently, Hercules kept clubbing him long after Cacus was dead.

31 THREE SPIRITS FROM BELOW APPROACHED US NOW: These three souls are those of Agnello Brunelleschi, Buoso degli Abati, and Puccio Sciancato. Along with two other Florentine noblemen, Cianfa Donati and Francesco de' Cavalcanti, they are the group whose transformations we witness in this canto. Agnello is changed into a serpent, exchanging forms with Cianfa Donati. Buoso then becomes a serpent, exchanging forms with Francesco de' Cavalcanti. Puccio undergoes no transformation.

44 AS I LOOKED ON, A SERPENT WITH SIX FEET: This is Cianfa Donati, who changes from a serpent into a man. He was of the family of Gemma Donati, Dante's wife, and had the reputation of being a great thief.

58 AGNELLO! RIGHT BEFORE OUR EYES YOU CHANGE!: Agnello dei Brunelleschi came from a distinguished Florentine family. He was suspected of having stolen public monies.

72 . . . A FIRE-BREATHING SNAKE APPEARED: This snake is Francesco de' Cavalcanti.

75–76 IT PIERCED, IN ONE OF THEM, THE PART WE'RE FED / THROUGH IN THE WOMB . . . : The one who is pierced is Buoso degli Abati. The "part we're fed / through, in the womb" is the navel, to which the umbilical cord is attached.

83 OH LUCAN, HOLD YOUR TONGUE . . . : In his *Civil War*, a work mentioned several times already in these notes, Lucan tells of soldiers bitten by serpents in Africa. Sabellus melted into a pool of liquid flesh, while Nasidius' body swelled so grotesquely that it burst through his armor.

85–86 AND OVID, WITH YOUR METAMORPHOSES OF CADMUS / AND OF ARETHUSA . . . : In the *Metamorphoses* (Books IV and V), Ovid tells of Cadmus, metamorphosed into a serpent, and of Arethusa, changed into a fountain.

125 THE SHADE THAT HAD BECOME A BEAST NOW FLED: This is the spirit of Buoso degli Abati.

127 THE OTHER CHASED HIM, SPITTING AS HE SPOKE: The other shade is Francesco de' Cavalcanti. It was thought that snakes found human spit poisonous.

137 . . . THE VIEW OF CRIPPLED PUCCIO: This is the spirit of Puccio Sciancato, whom Dante did not recognize earlier.

140 . . . HE WHO BROUGHT SUCH MOURNING TO GAVILLE: The serpent who bit Buoso has now become Francesco de' Cavalcanti. The latter was killed by the inhabitants of Gaville, on the river Arno, because he had treated its inhabitants so harshly. His family took revenge on the townspeople by killing a number of them; hence the comment about the town's mourning.

CANTO XXVI

Great Florence! How you must exult, whose wings
Are beating over land and sea and whose
Renown has reached down to the depths of Hell!
Among Hell's thieves I found five Florentines—
Not commoners but men from noble stock.   5
What shame I feel! How low your honor aims!
But if near dawn one's dreams are true, quite soon
You'll feel what Prato and some other towns
Would like your destiny to be. And if
You'd met that fate already, rest assured: 10
Not soon enough could it have come for them.
I wish it had, since it must come to pass.
No doubt of that, for as this head grows gray
I find it harder to accept your grief.

We left that place and Virgil climbed the rocks   15
That we had used as stairs for our descent.
He drew me up. Our solitary way
We made among the bridge's jagged rocks,
Though foot could not proceed without the hand.
I felt much sorrow then and feel it now   20
When I remember all the things I saw,
And more than is my custom I must check
My genius: if it speeds too quickly on,
Sweet virtue may not be its guiding light.

So then, if some good star has graced my mind   25
I must not, through some act, disgrace that gift.

Just as the peasant—resting on the hill
That time of year when he that lights the world
Stays with us long each day, and flies give way
To gnats—sees myriads of fireflies   30
Along the valley where he tills the fields
And tends the vine, so here in this eighth ditch
I saw, when I was in a spot to see
Its depths, the glare of endless flames.

And just as old Elisha, he who used   35
The bears to take revenge, watched Elijah's
Chariot depart, his horses rearing up
To Heaven as he rode, but could not trace
Him far into the sky and noted but
A little fire that seemed a wispy cloud,   40
So all along the bottom of the ditch
I saw red flames. Yet none reveal what they
Entomb: the burning spirits of the damned.

Positioned on the bridge to see, I stood
So straight I would have dropped into the depths   45
Without a push had I not quickly clutched
A rock. My leader saw how much the scene
Below absorbed my mind and said: "The fires
Contain the spirits, each enveloped fast
In flames that scorch his form."

                    And I to him: 50
"Your words confirm my thoughts; I was in fact
About to ask who's trapped within that flame
Approaching us that's split on top as if

It had arisen from the famous fire
On which the bodies of Eteocles   55
And Polynices burned, the cursed sons
Of Oedipus the King."

                    And Virgil said:
"Within that fire writhe two tormented souls:
One Ulysses, the other Diomedes,
In God's just vengeance joined, as once in wrath.   60
Engulfed in flames, they mourn the Trojan horse
That served the great Aeneas as a gate
To slip through, seed of all the race of Rome.
There they weep for all Deidamia's wiles,
Who, though dead, laments her lost Achilles,   65
And there they also pay the penalty
For having stolen the Palladium."

"My lord, I pray, and hope each prayer may count
For yet a thousand more, that I may stay
Right here until that forked flame comes to us.   70
You see the strength of my desire."

                              And he
Replied: "Your prayers, in truth, deserve much praise,
And so I yield. I understand your wish,
But you must hold your tongue with them. I'll speak
Instead—they're Greeks, remember, and may scorn   75
Your speech."

                    So when the flame had reached the spot
My guide judged most appropriate, he spoke:
"Oh you who burn together in one flame,
If I deserve some merit in your eyes
For what I wrote of you on Earth in lines   80

_____

That live, pause here awhile. Ulysses, tell
Us of your final voyage and your death."

The higher horn of flame was flickering
And murmuring as if just then a wind
Had ruffled it quite suddenly, and now   85
The tip moved up and down just like a tongue,
As out of it a voice began to speak:

"When I had left enchanting Circe's isle
Beside Gaeta, which Aeneas was
To name, where she had kept me for a year,   90
Not fondness for my son Telemachus,
Nor reverence for him who fathered me,
Nor love for my Penelope, whose heart
I would have filled with joy, could overcome
The deep desire in me to know the world,   95
To visit all the haunts of men and see
Their vices and their virtues for myself.

"I put to sea in but one boat, on board
With me a faithful company of men.
I visited the lands on either coast: 100
Sardinia, Morocco, Spain we saw,
And many islands sparkling in the sea.
Old men we were, slow and deliberate,
But finally we came to that famed strait,
The outlet to the sea where Hercules   105
Has placed the Pillars, signs to every ship
That none shall pass those boundaries of stone.

"Off to the right I passed Seville and had
Already passed Ceuta when I said:
'Brothers, who have reached the West and escaped   110

A hundred thousand dangers—in the time
That yet remains to us, no longer young,
Let's not deny ourselves the matchless joy
Of following the setting sun to lands
Where no man lives, far out to sea beyond   115
The Pillars of the god that shut us in.
Think, my friends, of the seed from which you've sprung:
You were not made to live like beasts, but men—
To follow virtue and to strive to know.'

"These words had their effect; they'd sail with joy;   120
No force on Earth could hold my comrades back.
We turned our stern toward where the morning breaks
And veered to port as on and on we sailed:
In this mad flight, our oars seemed changed to wings!

"Night now revealed to us the southern stars,   125
While bright Polaris dropped beneath the waves.
It never rose again from ocean's floor.
Five times the moon's cold light shone down on us;
Five times its light was drowned since first we'd dared
To enter on that deep and deadly sea,   130
When, misty in the dark ahead of us,
A mountain loomed: no higher had I seen
In all my days. It filled our hearts with joy!

"But joy soon turned to grief, for from that strange
New land a great wind rushed upon our ship,   135
And struck our bow, and wheeled us thrice about,
And when again it whirled us down a wave,
Our stern was pointing to the sky, our prow
Toward death (that day Another sealed our doom),
And over us the seas forever closed."   140

NOTES TO CANTO XXVI

[SUMMARY OF THE CANTO: *Dante begins the canto with an outburst against his native Florence. Now in the eighth ditch, the poets are among the evil counselors. Dante sees a double flame containing the souls of Ulysses and Diomedes. Unwilling to allow Dante to speak with them, Virgil addresses the soul of Ulysses, urging him to tell of his final days. The famed Greek hero tells of his last voyage, in which he and his men, sailing beyond Gibraltar and into the Southern Hemisphere, drowned near the mountain of Purgatory.*]

7   BUT IF NEAR DAWN ONE'S DREAMS ARE TRUE . . . : It was an old belief that the dreams that came to one just before dawn had a prophetic quality.

8–9   . . . WHAT PRATO AND SOME OTHER TOWNS / WOULD LIKE YOUR DESTINY TO BE . . . : Prato and other towns hated Florentine dominion in Tuscany. Some commentators believe that the Prato referred to here is not the town, but a cardinal by that name whom Pope Benedict XI picked to help settle differences between warring parties. However, because the cardinal did not succeed in his mission, he cursed Florence, placing it under an interdict. A number of disasters that occurred in the city not long after were thought to be the direct result of the priest's interdict.

25–26   . . . IF SOME GOOD STAR . . . DISGRACE THAT GIFT: Dante is saying that he must not use his intellectual gifts for immoral or criminal ends.

28–29   . . . WHEN HE THAT LIGHTS THE WORLD / STAYS WITH US LONG . . . : A reference to the sun and to the longer days of summer.

35   . . . OLD ELISHA, HE WHO USED / THE BEARS TO TAKE REVENGE . . . : The book of *Kings* in the Hebrew Bible tells how Elisha watched as Elijah was taken up into Heaven in a chariot of fire. A group of children then jeered at Elisha, wishing aloud that he, too, had disappeared along with Elijah. When Elisha uttered some imprecations against them, two "she-bears" immediately appeared and ate up forty-two of the unfortunate children.

55–56   ON WHICH THE BODIES OF ETEOCLES / AND POLYNICES BURNED: Eteocles and Polynices were the sons of King Oedipus. They forced their father to give up the throne of Thebes and agreed to rule during alternate years. (After being forced from the throne, Oedipus prayed that his sons would always hate each other.) When Eteocles did not step down after his year was up,

Polynices led the so-called Seven against Thebes in a civil insurrection against his brother. Fighting hand-to-hand, the brothers killed each other. According to the Latin poet Statius, their bodies were placed on the same funeral pyre; however, their mutual hatred had been so great during their lives that the flames from the fire would not coalesce but remained as two separate "horns," not unlike the two horns of flame containing the souls of Ulysses and Diomedes in this canto.

59–67 WITHIN THAT FIRE . . . HAVING STOLEN THE PALLADIUM: Ulysses (the Latin form of the Greek name Odysseus) and Diomedes fought with the Greeks against Troy in the Trojan War. Together they devised a number of schemes (Ulysses the plotter, Diomedes the agent, in most cases), that Dante believed merited Hell's severe punishment. For instance, the two devised the idea for the Trojan Horse, by means of which the Greeks were able to enter the gates of Troy and sack the city, bringing the Trojan War to an end. Ulysses also stole the Palladium, or statue of Pallas Athene, which was thought to be protecting the Trojans from harm. Before the war, Achilles' mother, Thetis, in order to protect her son from battle, had hidden him at the court of King Lycomedes of Skyros, where Achilles dressed in woman's clothing to further conceal his identity. He seduced Deidamia, a daughter of the king, and had a son, Pyrrhus, by her. Ulysses and Diomedes found out where Achilles was hiding, however, and tricked him into revealing who he was, so that he had to accompany them to Troy and the war. When Achilles departed, the grief-stricken Deidamia died. Naturally, Dante would view the exploits of Ulysses as crimes, for the poet, as we have so often seen, favors the Trojans whenever possible. However, others see in the wiles of Ulysses the laudable efforts of a hero to win the war for his side, and this view of the Greek warrior has surely been the prevalent one since Dante's time. In Dante's view, Ulysses' sin, in the episode that the latter relates, seems to be that he counseled his men to embark on a foolish voyage that was doomed from the start. In broader terms, Ulysses represents the arrogance and pride of intellect that does not, or will not, realize or admit that God has set limits to the human capacity for thought, knowledge, and understanding.

75–76 . . . THEY'RE GREEKS, REMEMBER, AND MAY SCORN / YOUR SPEECH . . . : The Greeks would despise Dante because he was an Italian (i.e., his ancestors were Trojans, who had lost the Trojan War to the Greeks). Furthermore, Dante did not know the Greek language, ancient or contemporary. His rather sketchy knowledge of Greek literature was derived from Latin translations. Much ancient Greek literature, known to Roman civilization, had been lost or neglected during the Dark Ages. In Europe, it would be rediscovered during the Renaissance in the two centuries that followed Dante's death.

88 WHEN I HAD LEFT ENCHANTING CIRCE'S ISLE: The magnificent final

portion of the canto, which begins at this line, is a monologue by Ulysses, in which he tells of his final days. The account by Dante differs radically from Homer's tale of Ulysses' return from Troy to Ithaca, his homeland, for, in Dante's version, Ulysses and his men never return home, but go directly across the Mediterranean and out into the Atlantic to their doom. There is no authority for the story of this final voyage, which Dante has almost certainly invented. Circe kept Ulysses on her island in the Aegean and changed Ulysses' men into swine. She was finally persuaded by Zeus (through Hermes) to let him go.

89–90   BESIDE GAETA, WHICH AENEAS WAS / TO NAME . . . : Gaeta is a town in the southeast corner of Italy. In his *Aeneid*, Virgil tells us that Aeneas named the town after his nurse, Caieta.

92   NOR REVERENCE FOR HIM WHO FATHERED ME: Ulysses' father was Laertes.

93   NOR LOVE FOR MY PENELOPE . . . : Penelope was Ulysses' wife. In Homer's *Odyssey*, she is depicted as an extraordinarily patient and devoted wife, who, with their son, Telemachus, waits twenty years for her husband to return from Troy. Meanwhile, she ignores the insistent and insolent urgings of many suitors, who harass her and her family, trying to convince her that Odysseus must be dead and that she ought to marry one of them. Upon his return, Odysseus slays the suitors. This entire aspect of the Odysseus-Ulysses story is ignored by Dante, who did not know the *Odyssey* and based his own version of the hero's end on non-Homeric sources and his own imagination.

100   I VISITED THE LANDS ON EITHER COAST: The coasts, that is, of the Mediterranean.

105–106   . . . WHERE HERCULES / HAS PLACED THE PILLARS . . . : These pillars are now called the Strait of Gibraltar, the narrow arm of water between Spain and Africa. It was considered folly even to think of voyaging past them into the Atlantic, for surely one would not come back alive if one did so. (Incidentally, Dante and his contemporaries were not "flat-earthers." The idea that Columbus's fifteenth-century notion of a spherical earth was a radical belief is false.)

108   OFF TO THE RIGHT I PASSED SEVILLE . . . : That entire area of Spain was then called Seville.

108–109   . . . AND HAD / ALREADY PASSED CEUTA . . . : Ceuta is in Morocco on the Strait of Gibraltar.

125   NIGHT NOW REVEALED TO US THE SOUTHERN STARS: Polaris, the North Star, is no longer visible in the night sky because Ulysses and his men have sailed so far south.

128   FIVE TIMES THE MOON'S COLD LIGHT SHONE DOWN ON US: This signifies that five months have passed.

131–132 . . . MISTY IN THE DARK AHEAD OF US, / A MOUNTAIN LOOMED . . . : This is the mountain of Purgatory, which Dante believed to be the only piece of land to be found in the entire Southern Hemisphere.

139 . . . (THAT DAY ANOTHER SEALED OUR DOOM): By "Another" Ulysses means God.

CANTO XXVII

The flame, now silent, stood up straight and still
And, with my guide's approval, moved away.
But now another flame came close to us
Whose tip sent forth a sound so strange we stared
At it, surprised. Like that Sicilian bull   5
Whose bellowing came roaring from the throat
Of him who with his file had fashioned it
(How just this was!) that sounded and resounded
With piercing screams of those he'd shut inside
To roast (it seemed to suffer pain itself,   10
Though formed of brass), so here the cheerless words
That had at first no way of issuing
From that eternal flame changed into sounds
Of riffling fire. But when they'd made their way
Up through the fiery tip, the tongue that shook   15
With words from him within, we heard him say:
"Oh you to whom I speak and who just now
Were talking in the tongue of Lombardy
(You who said: 'Go, I will not urge you more'),
Though I perhaps have come a little late,   20
If it is not displeasing, stay and speak,
For I won't be displeased, although I burn.
To this blind world you have perhaps been dropped
From that sweet land of Italy, the land
Of all my sins. If so, then tell me now   25
If fair Romagna's fate is peace or war.

For I was born in hilly land between
Urbino and that mount where Tiber's stream
Begins to flow."

        As I was bending low
Upon the bridge to catch the sinner's words,   30
My master touched my side and said: "He is
Italian; speak to him."

         I had prepared
A speech and spoke to him without delay:
"Oh spirit hidden from the sight of all,
When has Romagna ever known a time   35
Untouched by war, for which its tyrants long?
Yet I was there not long ago and saw
No open war, at least. Ravenna is
Exactly as she's been for years. Above
Her broods the famous eagle of Polenta   40
Who over Cervia also spreads his wings.
And Forlì, former victim of the siege
That piled the bloody bodies of the French
Before her walls, is struggling yet again
In the clutch of the Ordelaffi clan.   45
At Verrucchio, the young and ancient dogs
Of the Malatestas (cruel maltreaters
Of their prisoner, Montagna) now rule
With canine teeth, as they have always done.
The cities on the banks of the Lamone   50
And the Santerno reel beneath the reign
Of Little Lion of the White Lair, he
Who changes sides with every season's change.
And just as Cesena, washed by the Savio,
Is set between the mountain and the plain,   55
So it lives in freedom tinged with tyranny.

"The time has come to tell us who you are.
Now speak up, for I've been frank with you,
So that on Earth your name may long endure!"

The flame then in its fashion roared awhile,   60
The sharp point licking back and forth, and then
It breathed these words:

                    "If I believed
That what I say were being said to one
Who might return one day to Earth, my flame
Would cease its flickering, but since I know,   65
If what I hear is true, that never once
Has anyone returned alive from Hell
To Earth, I'll speak and fear no infamy.

"I was at first a man of arms and then
A monk of the Franciscan order; thus,   70
I thought, I'd make amends. I would have, too,
But I was lured by Boniface the priest
(I hope he burns forevermore in Hell!),
For he enticed me back to sinful ways.
And I will tell you how it came about.   75

"When I still had the form of flesh and bone
My mother blessed me with, I did not act
As lions do but as a cunning fox.
I knew each ruse, each wile, each secret way
And used them all: my fame spread far and wide.   80
But when the years began to take their toll,
When it was time to lower sail, to take
In rope, those things I'd taken pleasure in
Now made me penitent. So I confessed,
Made peace with God, became a holy monk.   85
This would have saved my soul! (Oh, misery!)

"Pope Boniface, Prince of the Pharisees
Of modern times, fought the Colonna clan.
No, he did not combat Jew or Saracen,
For only Christians were his enemies,   90
None of whom had caused grand Acre's loss
Or carried on forbidden trade with Muslims.
With dirty hands he sullied Peter's chair.
He broke his sacred vows, had no respect
For that Franciscan cord I wore, a cord   95
That once could make its wearers look so lean
And zealous in their work. That priest, I say,
Like Constantine who went to see Sylvester
In Soracte to be cured of leprosy,
Called me (was I the pope's physician now?)   100
To cool the fever of his evil pride.
He asked me what to do in such-and-such
A case. I did not answer him, for all
His words were like the ravings of a sot.
And then he said: 'Just place your trust in me;   105
Tell me how Penestrino can be seized,
And all your sins, I swear, will be absolved
From this time forth! For in my hands I hold,
As you must know, two massive keys, the ones
My predecessor failed to use. I have   110
The power to open Heaven's gates with one,
And with the other I can lock them tight.'

"His arguments convinced me that to say
No word would be unwise, and so I spoke:
'Since, Father, you'll forgive the sins I will   115
Commit, I say then: promise what you must,
But plan to break your word. The papal seat
Will triumph in the end.'

"Then at my death,
Saint Francis came to take my soul, but oh,
A grinning night-black angel intervened: 120
'You will not cheat me of my prey; he'll join
Us down below where all my minions play,
For ever since he hissed his evil words
I haven't left his side, and now he's mine!
Without repentance, none can be absolved.   125
None can repent before a sin is done.
No reasoning could be more fraudulent!'

"Oh what a rude awakening I had
When, clutching me, he said: 'So then, perhaps
You didn't think I could chop logic, too?'   130

"Then down he bore me to where Minos waits,
Who wound his tail around his scaly back
Eight times for me, and bit his tail in rage,
And roared: 'He's destined for the thievish fire!'

"And so you see me here among the damned;   135
How bitter is my fate! I burn, I burn!"

When he had ceased to speak, the anguished flame
Sped off, its sharp horn twisting every way.
My guide and I then walked along the bridge
And reached an arch that spans another ditch.   140

Here writhe the shades who reaped a dreadful doom,
For in the world they sowed immense discord.

NOTES TO CANTO XXVII

[SUMMARY OF THE CANTO: *As the flame of Ulysses and Diomedes moves away, another enters the scene. Within it is the spirit of Guido da Montefeltro, a well-known leader of the Ghibelline faction in the province of Romagna. In reply to a request from Guido, Dante tells of the present condition of the people of that region. Guido, in turn, tells the reasons why he is being punished in Hell, blaming Pope Boniface VIII for his loss of salvation. The poets then journey on toward the next ditch.*]

3 ... ANOTHER FLAME CAME CLOSE TO US: This is the soul of Count Guido da Montefeltro, the leader of the Ghibelline party in Romagna during the last quarter of the thirteenth century.

5 ... LIKE THAT SICILIAN BULL: This gruesome brass bull, designed to torture people, was fashioned by a certain Perillus for a Sicilian tyrant named Phalaris in the sixth century B.C. The victim was placed inside the bull, which was then heated over a fire, roasting the occupant, whose cries allegedly resembled the bellowing of a bull. (Phalaris tested Perillus' creation on Perillus himself.)

18 WERE TALKING IN THE TONGUE OF LOMBARDY: Virgil, whose native town was located in what was later to be the province of Lombardy, is supposedly speaking in the Lombard language, a "dialect" of Italian.

26 IF FAIR ROMAGNA'S FATE IS PEACE OR WAR: Romagna is a province of Italy south of the Po River and lies to the east of the Apennine chain. Ravenna is its chief city.

38–39 ... RAVENNA IS / EXACTLY AS SHE'S BEEN FOR YEARS ... : Ravenna was ruled for the better part of two centuries (1270–1441) by the lords of Polenta, whose symbol was an eagle.

41 WHO OVER CERVIA ALSO SPREADS HIS WINGS: Cervia had recently come under the dominion of Ravenna, which lies south of it.

42 AND FORLÌ, FORMER VICTIM OF THE SIEGE: In 1282, Guido da Montefeltro protected the town of Forlì against an invasion by French troops, sent by Pope Martin IV. In a political turnabout typical of the time, Forlì leagued itself with the pope in 1285 and expelled Guido.

45 IN THE CLUTCH OF THE ORDELAFFI CLAN: The Ordelaffi ruled Forlì by the year 1300, the time of Dante's voyage.

46–49 AT VERRUCCHIO . . . AS THEY HAVE ALWAYS DONE: Malatesta
and his son, Malatestino, Black Guelfs of the city of Rimini, imprisoned Mon-
tagna de' Parcitati, leader of the Ghibelline party of the city. Montagna was mur-
dered by Malatesta's son. Verrucchio was the Malatesta castle.

52 OF LITTLE LION OF THE WHITE LAIR . . . : The Little Lion is
Mainardo Pagano, lord of Faenza and Imola (the former on the Lamone, the lat-
ter on the Santerno), who appears to have done a good deal of political shuffling
between Guelf and Ghibelline.

54 AND JUST AS CESENA . . . . The town of Cesena reputedly underwent
continual changes in its government.

62–68 . . . IF I BELIEVED . . . AND FEAR NO INFAMY: Guido does not
believe that Dante is a living man, but one of the infernal souls. Dante makes no
attempt to show him that he is mistaken—a just revenge on an evil counselor.
(These words are quoted in Dante's original Italian at the head of T. S. Eliot's
"The Love Song of J. Alfred Prufrock.")

70 A MONK OF THE FRANCISCAN ORDER . . . : Having made up his differ-
ences with the Church, which had twice excommunicated him, Guido became a
Franciscan in 1296, two years before his death.

72 BUT I WAS LURED BY BONIFACE THE PRIEST: Here again the name of
Boniface VIII is invoked; he hovers over Inferno like an evil spirit. The story told
here concerning Guido's advice to Boniface on how to capture Penestrino by
trickery appears to be a true one.

87 POPE BONIFACE, PRINCE OF THE PHARISEES: We can hear Dante's
own animus in Guido's diatribe against Boniface, which occupies nearly all the
remainder of this canto.

88 . . . FOUGHT THE COLONNA CLAN: The Colonna family and Boniface
had long hated and fought with each other. Guido da Montefeltro did in fact
counsel the pope on how to take the fortress of the Colonnas at Penestrino. The
Colonnas had their revenge years later in 1303, when one of the family impris-
oned the pope at the behest of King Philip of France.

89–92 . . . HE DID NOT COMBAT JEW OR SARACEN . . . TRADE WITH
MUSLIMS: This passage refers to the retaking of the city of Acre by the Saracens
in 1291. They were assisted both by some Jews and by Christians who supplied
the Saracens with war matériel.

98–99 LIKE CONSTANTINE . . . CURED OF LEPROSY: According to an
apocryphal story, the emperor Constantine, who had contracted leprosy
(allegedly because he had been persecuting Christians), had Pope Sylvester I
brought to his court from a cave at Mount Soracte near Rome, where the pope
had been in hiding. Sylvester converted the emperor to Christianity and cured

his disease. The grateful Constantine supposedly gave to the Church the so-called Donation of Constantine (discussed earlier—see Canto XIX, note to lines 113–116). In similar fashion, Boniface sent for Guido, who was then a Franciscan monk at Assisi.

110   MY PREDECESSOR FAILED TO USE . . . : Boniface's predecessor was Celestine V, whom we met in Canto III (note to lines 52–53).

119   SAINT FRANCIS CAME TO TAKE MY SOUL . . . : This is the same Francis who founded the Franciscan Order of monks, which Guido joined late in life.

120   A GRINNING NIGHT-BLACK ANGEL INTERVENED: The night-black angel is, of course, a devil.

CANTO XXVIII

No man could ever tell in full detail,
Not even using words that have been freed
From poetry's strict laws, the blood and wounds
I witnessed now. In that attempt all tongues
Would fail: our understanding is too weak,   5
Our speech inadequate for such a task.

Were all the people of Apulia,
(That fated land) assembled once again—
Those men who mourned the blood the Romans, sons
Of Troy, made flow, or blood they lost in that   10
Long war fought with the Carthaginians
(Unerring Livy tells us that great heaps
Of golden rings were gathered in that duel);
Those men who fought Guiscard and suffered wounds;
Those men whose bones at Ceperano lie,   15
Where all Apulians proved traitorous;
Those men who fell at Tagliacozzo's towers,
Where old Alard de Valéry was victor
By subterfuge but not by soldier's skill—
Were all those men, I say, brought to one place   20
To show their wounds and amputated limbs,
The sight would be as nothing when compared
To all the horrors of the great ninth ditch.

But I remained to stare at all the damned
And saw a thing I'd fear to tell about
Without more proof . . .

(113–115)

No cask with missing cover-board or stave
Could gape as wide as did a soul I saw   25
Whose frame was cleft from chin to where he farts.
His guts were hanging down between his legs
And I could see the body parts inside
The filthy paunch that churns all food to shit.
I gaped at him and he at me, and then,   30
With both his hands he opened wide his chest
And said these words: "See how I tear my flesh;
I have endured such mutilation here!
I, Muhammad, and he in front of me,
Alì, my son-in-law, whose face from scalp   35
To chin is sliced in half (just hear those screams!).
These others stirred up schism and discord
And so their fate is to be split and cracked.
Behind us lurks a devil with a sword
Who cuts us cruelly, swinging at our forms   40
As we complete each turn around this trench,
For all our wounds are healed before we're forced
To pass this grinning demon once again.
But you there, staring down at us, you think
Perhaps by staying on the bridge you'll stall   45
The punishment that Minos meted out
When you confessed your earthly sins to him?"

Said Virgil: "No, he hasn't yet been snared by death,
Nor have his crimes delivered him down here,
But I, a soul from Limbo, must escort   50
This man through all the rings of Hell so that
He learns from what he sees and what he hears.
Make no mistake: my words are full of truth."

When they had heard my guide, a hundred souls
Stood still in that black ditch, forgot their pain,   55

And stared wide-eyed at me. Muhammad spoke:
"You living soul, who may be privileged
To see the sun again, tell Fra Dolcino,
Who is now besieged, to store more food; or,
When snow is on the ground, Novara's men,   60
Who might have trouble otherwise, will take
The town and doom the heretic to Hell."

These words he'd uttered with one foot in air
As if to start to walk. When he was done,
He placed it on the ground and moved away.   65
Another soul, whose throat was cut, whose nose
Was missing from the eyebrows down, whose head
Had lost one ear, now stopped to stare in awe,
Then from his windpipe wiped away the blood
That smeared his neck and spoke before the crowd: 70
"Oh you, whom sin has not condemned to pain
And whom I've seen in Italy (unless
You look like someone else I know), if you
Return to see the smiling Lombard plain
That from Vercelli slopes to Marcabò,   75
Remember me: Pier da Medicina.
If prophecy be valid here in Hell,
Then let the two best men of Fano know,
Both Messer Guido and Angiolello,
That they'll be thrown into the sea and drown   80
Near La Cattolica, through treachery
Of vile, despotic Malatestino.
Between the isles of Cyprus and Majorca
Great Neptune never saw so vile a crime
Committed in his realm by Greek or pirate.   85
That tyrant, sightless in one eye, the lord
Of Rimini, a town that one down here
Now vainly wishes he had never seen,

Will send for them, pretending that he wants
To parley. Then he'll drown them both and they   90
Will never need to pray that they be saved
From Mount Focara's sharp, ferocious winds."

And I: "I'll bring back news of you to Earth,
But first reveal to me the name of him
Who looks on Rimini with bitterness."   95

He grasped a sinner's jaw and opening
The mouth, this Piero said: "This is the one;
But look inside his mouth; he cannot speak.
Chased out of Rome, he made great Caesar think
That he who hesitates is lost, and so   100
The mighty Julius crossed the Rubicon."

How horrible to look at Curio,
Once bold of tongue, whose tongue had been cut out!
I saw a shade with lopped-off hands who raised
His stumps high up into the darkened air,   105
So that his face was splattered with their blood.
"You will remember Mosca, he who said:
'A deed once done is done once and for all':
Dark seeds of evil for the Tuscan race."

"And death to all your family!" I said,   110
And he, who'd piled up misery on misery,
Now rushed away like one insane with grief.

But I remained to stare at all the damned
And saw a thing I'd fear to tell about
Without more proof, but I am reassured   115
By conscience, friend to men, who makes them bold
Beneath their breastplate of integrity.

I saw, in truth, and seem to see it still,
A headless trunk that with the tristful crowd
Kept pace, and he was holding, by its hair,   120
His severed head, as if it were a lamp.
It stared at us and said, "Oh misery!"
And so it made a lantern of itself
And they were two in one and one in two:
And only God can say how this could be.   125
So toward the bridge's base he walked and then
He raised the arm that grasped the head so we
Might hear his words more clearly, and he said:
"You living creature in the land of death,
Can you conceive of torture worse than mine?   130
I beg you: tell my story on the Earth.
Bertrand de Born am I, who planted thoughts
Of rank revolt in Henry's mind, the son
Of England's king, against his father's crown.
I made them enemies. Ahithophel,   135
With evil whisperings to Absalom,
Divided him from David just as I
Divided king from prince. And so it is
That I, who broke the bond between those two,
Must hold my brain dissevered from its root   140
In this dead trunk. In me is seen at work
God's just law of perfect punishment."

NOTES TO CANTO XXVIII

[SUMMARY OF THE CANTO: *Dante and Virgil are astounded by the large number of mutilated souls they now see in the ninth ditch. The poets encounter the spirit of Muhammad and that of the latter's son-in-law, Alì, both of whom are being punished as schismatics. They also come upon the souls of Pier da Medicina, Curio, Mosca de' Lamberti, and Bertrand de Born, each punished for having caused divisions of one sort or another: religious, political, or familial. Except for Alì, each soul makes some comment about his condition or his past, asks to be remembered, or gives advice to Dante to be transmitted to some living person.*]

7   WERE ALL THE PEOPLE OF APULIA: Apulia is the older name for the region now called La Puglia in southeast Italy. The events alluded to in this passage occurred there.

9–13   THOSE MEN WHO MOURNED . . . GATHERED IN THAT DUEL: The Romans were thought of as the descendants of the Trojans. The wars alluded to in these verses are the Roman wars against the Samites in the fourth century B.C. and against the Carthaginians in the third century B.C. (the Second Punic War). Livy, the ancient Roman historian, tells us that so many Romans were killed at the terrible battle of Cannae (216 B.C.) in that war that the fingers of the dead yielded several bushels of gold rings to Hannibal, leader of the Carthaginian invasion force. (We are uncomfortably reminded of the horrors of the Nazi concentration camps of World War II.) Tens of thousands of soldiers were reputed to have died in that battle. Hannibal's invasion of Italy remains one of the most astounding stories in military history.

14   THOSE MEN WHO FOUGHT GUISCARD AND SUFFERED WOUNDS: Robert Guiscard, famed Norman conqueror of southern Italy, fought against both Greeks and Saracens in the eleventh century A.D. His soul is found in *Paradiso*.

15–16   THOSE MEN . . . PROVED TRAITOROUS: Manfred was deserted by the barons of Apulia at the pass of Ceperano. The result was that Charles of Anjou was able to get through and then defeat Manfred at the battle of Benevento in 1266. (See the Introduction to the present volume.)

17–19   THOSE MEN WHO FELL . . . NOT BY SOLDIER'S SKILL: Conradin, nephew of Manfred, was defeated at Tagliacozzo by Charles of Anjou who, acting on the advice of Alard de Valéry, pretended to retreat, and, when the enemy broke formation and began to plunder, wiped them out.

25 . . . A SOUL I SAW: This is Muhammad, whom Dante views as a schismatic, *i.e.,* one who brought division to the Catholic Church by founding a new religion. It must be recalled that in Dante's time many believed Muhammad to have been a Christian—in fact, a cardinal of the Church with papal aspirations. This odd story has it that, thwarted in his ambition to sit upon the throne of Peter, he sought revenge by founding the new religion. In Dante's view, shared by nearly everyone else in Europe at the time, there could be only one religion: Catholicism.

35 ALÌ, MY SON-IN-LAW . . . : Alì Ibn-abi-Talib, husband of Fatima (Muhammad's daughter), was also a schismatic, for some thought he did not have the right to become caliph. As a result, Islam was divided into two principal sects: the Shiites and the Sunnites, and Alì's punishment derives from his having been seen as the cause of the schism.

58–59 . . . TELL FRA DOLCINO, / WHO IS NOW BESIEGED . . . : Fra Dolcino Tornielli, of the sect of Apostolic Brothers, was an early social and religious reformer. Excommunicated by Pope Clement V for alleged heresy (though it appears that the Brothers wished merely to purify the Church in various ways), Dolcino (together with Margaret of Trent, reportedly his mistress) held out for a year against troops sent to overthrow him and his followers in his stronghold near Novara. On June 1, 1307, the same year of his defeat and capture, Dolcino, Margaret, and some followers were burned at the stake for crimes against the Church. The question arises: why should Muhammad care about Fra Dolcino? The answer is that if we accept the logic of Dante's beliefs about Muhammad, the latter would have been motivated by a desire to see greater schism among the Christians. Dolcino's battle with the pope could only widen Christian division; thus, the longer the fight lasted, the better, as far as Muhammad was concerned.

66 ANOTHER SOUL, WHOSE THROAT WAS CUT . . . : This is the soul of Pier da Medicina of the Biancucci family of Medicina near Bologna. The emperor Frederick II took away his praetorship in 1287 and exiled his family from Romagna. Pier then sowed discord among different rulers of Romagna, turning the Polentas and Malatestas against each other.

79 BOTH MESSER GUIDO AND ANGIOLELLO: Malatestino Malatesta of Rimini invited Guido dal Cassero and Angiolello da Carignano, both leading men of the town of Fano, to attend a meeting at La Cattolica, located on the Adriatic Sea. Then, in a truly ignoble act, he had both men drowned.

86   THAT TYRANT, SIGHTLESS IN ONE EYE . . . : This tyrant is Malatestino (see note to line 79 above).

92   FROM MOUNT FOCARA'S SHARP, FEROCIOUS WINDS: It was near Mount Focara that Guido and Angiolello were drowned (see note to line 79 above).

96   HE GRASPED A SINNER'S JAW . . . : The sinner whose mouth is forced open is Curio, who counseled Julius Caesar to cross the Rubicon, an event fraught with fateful consequences for Rome and for Caesar himself. Caesar's crossing of the river, which is near Rimini, and was the northern boundary between Italy and so-called Cisalpine Gaul (*cisalpine* means "on this side of the Alps"), was considered an act of war against the Roman state. Curio seems to have believed he would profit personally from Caesar's action and so was greatly motivated by self-interest.

107   YOU WILL REMEMBER MOSCA . . . : Mosca dei Lamberti, mentioned in Canto VI, advised that Buondelmonte de' Buondelmonti be killed in retaliation for the latter's having jilted a woman of the Amidei family. Mosca's words, which were the Italian equivalent of "A thing once done is done once and for all," meant that the killing should be done and done quickly. The jilting and the slaying of the jilter gravely divided Florentines; the rift led to the establishment of two parties, the Guelfs and Ghibellines. Their mutual hatred was to intensify in the ensuing decades of the thirteenth century.

119–135   A HEADLESS TRUNK. . . . I MADE THEM ENEMIES . . . : This head and trunk belong to Bertrand de Born, a soldier and also a troubadour (*i.e.*, a poet who wrote songs and poems dealing largely with themes of courtly love) from the region of Périgord in France. The allusion to his having caused, when in England, a division between King Henry II and his son (also a Henry) appears to be true. Bertrand ended his days as a monk.

135–138   . . . AHITHOPHEL . . . DIVIDED KING FROM PRINCE: The story of Absalom and Ahithophel is told in the second book of *Samuel,* Chapters 15–17. One of King David's advisors, Ahithophel urged David's son Absalom to revolt against his father and, in fact, to try to kill him.

"Our fate is this disfigurement—just look!
But who are you that ask?"

(81–82)

CANTO XXIX

The hordes of people with their horrid wounds
Had filled my eyes with tears to overflowing.
I only wished to look at them and weep.
But Virgil asked: "Why stare down there so much?
Why gawk at these disfigured, groaning shades?   5
The other ditches didn't make you act
Like this! Is it your plan to count these souls?
Consider this: the circuit of the ditch
Is two and twenty miles. What's more, the moon
Is now beneath our feet; we're running out   10
Of time and still have many things to see."

And I: "If you had taken note of why
I stared, you might have pardoned my delay."

But he kept walking while I spoke, and as
I followed in his tracks, I said to him: 15
"Within that ditch down which I looked so long,
I think there prowls a relative who grieves
Because his sin produced such misery."
And he to me: "Don't be concerned with him;
Attend to other things: leave him to Hell.   20
He pointed at us from the bridge's base
And shook his fist to threaten us. His name
Is Geri del Bello; but you had fixed

Your eyes on him who holds his bloody head,
And when you looked where Geri was, he'd gone."   25

"My lord, his death, so violent, has not
Yet been avenged by those who share his shame
And so resentment clouds his face. That's why
He went away without addressing me.
All this has made me pity him the more."   30

We came, while we were speaking, to a ridge
Where we could see another ditch, and if
We'd had sufficient light we could have seen
Into its depths. So there we stood atop
The final round that, cloister-like, contained   35
The brothers whom we glimpsed from our high perch.
Their screams of pain like arrows pierced my soul
With pity; to my ears I pressed both hands.
It was as if the illness from the wards
In Valdichiana in the summertime   40
And all Maremma's maladies, as well
As all Sardinia's, were gathered here.
The stench was like the stink of gangrened limbs.

Then, keeping to the left, my guide and I
Plunged down into the final ditch, and as   45
We neared its floor, I saw with clarity
The counterfeiters, all of whom are tracked
By Justice, God's unerring aide, who deals
Out punishment appropriate to each.

The sight of all Aegina's sick, back when   50
The air malevolently struck with death
All life (from tiny worms to men who then
Were resurrected from the seed of ants,

As poets tell) could not, I think, compel
Compassion more than these bereft of God.   55
How much more pitiful were these, piled up
In heaps along the murky ditch, where some
Lay prone, some leaned against another's back,
Some slithered on the fetid floor of Hell!
As step by step we moved, without a word,   60
We marveled at the sick, who could not rise,
And listened to their moans.

                          I saw two shades
Who leaned against each other, like two pots
Propped close upon a grate to share their heat.
Their bodies were a mass of scabs, and I   65
Had never seen a stable-boy, afraid
To keep his master waiting, or a man
Who's kept awake against his will, apply
A currycomb so energetically
As they, who scratched their ulcered, bleeding skin   70
In frenzied efforts to obtain relief
From an eternal, agonizing itch
And ripped the scabs off with their nails,
As knives would scrape away a fish's scales.

"You there, whose pincer fingers tear the shirt   75
Of mail you wear, tell us if we can find
A spirit in this ditch who's an Italian—
And may your nails last to eternity!"
Said Virgil then to one of them.

                       That soul,
Who wept, replied: "We're both from Italy.   80
Our fate is this disfigurement—just look!
But who are you that ask?"

My leader said:
"I make the long descent from ring to ring
With him, this living soul, to show him Hell."

The two shades, all atremble, broke apart   85
And came toward me, as did some other souls
Who'd overheard my master's every word.
And then, approaching me, my leader said:
"Now speak to them as freely as you wish."

I took my cue from him and said these words: 90
"Long may the memory of you be fresh
In human minds and live for many suns!
Who are the two of you? What race is yours?
Don't let your loathsome punishment prevent
You both from baring all to me."

                              One spoke: 95
"Arezzo was my native town. It was
Through spite of Àlbero, a Sienese,
That I was put to death by being burned
Alive. And yet the crime for which my flesh
Was charred was not the one that brought me here;   100
The truth is I was telling him one day
(In jest, please understand) that I could rise
From Earth and fly into the air, and he,
A man of curiosity, I'll grant,
But dim of wit, asked me to teach him how   105
To fly. (Was I to make him Daedalus?)
He told his father, bishop of the town,
What I had said, and so the latter flung
My body to the flames. But Minos dumped
Me in this ditch, the last of ten, because   110
I practiced alchemy: he never errs."

I turned to Virgil: "Never have there been
A people vainer than the Sienese.
They're even vainer than the French, I'd say!"

At this, the other leprous soul spoke up: 115
"This condemnation of Siena's folk
Cannot include, of course, the Spendthrift Club:
Like Stricca, who so wisely spent his funds,
As everybody knows! Like Niccolò,
Who grew and used expensive spices, all   120
The rage among Siena's many fools;
Like Caccia, squanderer of woods and vines;
Like Brilliant Bartolomeo, what a
Blunderer that fellow was!

                "And now,
I'm sure you want to know just who it is   125
That shares your point of view about that town.
Look at me carefully so that you read
My face correctly: I'm called Capocchio,
Who made false metals, mainly gold, through skill
In alchemy. For this I, too, was burned.   130
But bear this fact in mind as you depart:
They called me 'Ape of Nature without Peer!' "

NOTES TO CANTO XXIX

[SUMMARY OF THE CANTO: *As Dante and Virgil leave the ninth ditch, Dante is filled with pity for the suffering souls. He is particularly touched by the sight of a relative of his, Geri del Bello, a sower of family discord, whose murder has not yet been avenged by Dante's family. From the bridge above the tenth ditch, which the poets are now approaching, they hear the agonized screams of the souls below. Once in the ditch, the poets come across a vast number of sinners, all of them falsifiers of one kind and another. Two of them, tormented by leprous sores, speak in turn: Griffolino d'Arezzo and Capocchio da Siena.*]

9 ... TWO AND TWENTY MILES ... : It has not been possible to make precise calculations about the size of Dante's Hell, though many have tried to do so, probably foolishly. That Hell in the poem often seems so measurable is a tribute to the power of Dante's art.

10–11 ... WE'RE RUNNING OUT / OF TIME ... : As he has done many times during the journey, Virgil reminds Dante of the passing of time and hastens him on. Obviously, the Mantuan has a timetable to which he must adhere, but whose details he does not reveal to Dante. His tone here seems particularly scolding. According to those scholars who have been able laboriously to determine what time it is at various stages in the poets' journey through Hell, it is now around one o'clock in the afternoon on Saturday, the day before Easter Sunday.

16 WITHIN THAT DITCH DOWN WHICH I LOOKED SO LONG: Dante is speaking of the ninth ditch; the poets have not yet come to the tenth.

17 I THINK THERE PROWLS A RELATIVE WHO GRIEVES: As we shall shortly learn, this relative turns out to be Geri del Bello, a cousin of Dante's father. Reputedly, he got into trouble all his life. At the time of Dante's journey, Geri's murder by a member of the Sacchetti family had not been avenged: thirty-five years were to pass from the time of his death to the avenging of the murder. Geri is in the ninth ditch for having sown discord within his family.

23–24 ... BUT YOU HAD FIXED / YOUR EYES ON HIM WHO HOLDS HIS BLOODY HEAD: Virgil means that Dante was preoccupied with Bertrand de Born at the moment when Geri del Bello was carrying on in the manner Virgil describes.

26–27 ... HIS DEATH ... HAS NOT / YET BEEN AVENGED ... : To seek vengeance on someone (or on some family or town) was viewed as perfectly legitimate; indeed, it was considered a sacred duty. Not to take revenge was shameful, unthinkable. As we see in the present case, however, vengeance was not always swift. Vengeance could be taken on a member of the family of the doer of the avengeable deed and not necessarily on the doer himself. Geri is angry with Dante because, as a member of the family, Dante ought to have already avenged his murder.

31   WE CAME . . . TO A RIDGE: It is at this point that the poets come to the tenth ditch, the last one of Circle Eight.

40–42   IN VALDICHIANA . . . AS WELL / AS ALL SARDINIA'S . . . : The places Dante mentions in these lines were notoriously unhealthy, particularly during the summer months. Both Valdichiana and Maremma had an abundance of marshy areas, breeding grounds for mosquitoes that carried malaria.

45   PLUNGED DOWN INTO THE FINAL DITCH . . . : The final ditch is, of course, the tenth. After this, there is one final circle in Hell.

50–53   THE SIGHT OF ALL AEGINA'S SICK . . . RESURRECTED FROM THE SEED OF ANTS: In the *Metamorphoses* of Ovid, the Latin author tells of a plague sent to the island of Aegina (named after a woman) by Juno, the wife of Jove (Jupiter, Zeus). Juno had been angered by the fact that the young woman had allowed Jove to make love to her. Jove transformed ants into humans (called Myrmidons, made famous in Homer's *Iliad* as the soldiers of Achilles) to repopulate the disease-ravaged island.

62   . . . I SAW TWO SHADES: These two, Griffolino d'Arezzo and Capocchio da Siena, are infected with a leprous condition, as the description of their bodies will bear out. Each speaks to the poets in turn, beginning with Griffolino.

96   AREZZO WAS MY NATIVE TOWN . . . : The soul who now speaks is Griffolino d'Arezzo. An alchemist, he slyly obtained large sums of money from a certain Àlbero (a young man said to be the son of the bishop of Siena) by pretending to be able to do all sorts of wonderful things, including teaching the young fellow how to fly. When it became clear to the fatuous Àlbero that Griffolino would be able to do no such thing, the lad complained to his father, who promptly had the unfortunate Griffolino burned at the stake as a sorcerer. It is because of his falsifications that Griffolino is in Hell, however, and not because of any sorcerous practices.

106   . . . WAS I TO MAKE HIM DAEDALUS?: Dante has mentioned Daedalus and his son earlier in *Inferno:* see Canto XVII, note to line 96.

109–111   . . . BUT MINOS . . . HE NEVER ERRS: Griffolino was burned by the bishop for sorcery or perhaps heresy, but Minos (Canto V), whose word is final, sent Griffolino's soul to this ditch for the sin of alchemy.

115   AT THIS, THE OTHER LEPROUS SOUL SPOKE UP: This is Capocchio da Siena, a Florentine, who now speaks. According to some, he was a friend and fellow student of Dante's.

117   . . . THE SPENDTHRIFT CLUB: This club ("La Brigata Spendereccia" in Italian) was a late-thirteenth-century organization made up of a dozen young Sienese who did precisely the kind of extravagant things that Capocchio speaks of here so ironically. They contributed large sums of money to the club and built a palace in which each of them had a resplendent bedchamber for himself. They also prepared extravagant meals; at the end of these they frequently flung the cutlery and glassware out the window—a wasteful defenestration indeed! Stricca was a lawyer; Niccolò dei Salimbeni is responsible for the custom of stuffing pheasants with costly spices. The club lasted for a little under a year, collapsing finally from ridicule and lack of funds. In Canto XIII, we heard of a certain Lano, who, it appears, also belonged to the club.

129–130   . . . THROUGH SKILL / IN ALCHEMY . . . : In Siena, in 1293, Capocchio was burned at the stake for alchemy, but in Hell he is being punished for falsifying.

131   . . . APE OF NATURE WITHOUT PEER: It seems that Capocchio was given this sobriquet either because he was an excellent mimic or because he drew so skillfully.

CANTO XXX

Against the Thebans, Juno often flashed
Her godly anger; once, she was enraged
With Athamas, who'd broken all the vows
He'd made to Semele, his wife, and so
She made the wretch go mad. His wife approached   5
One day with their two sons, whose hands she held.
"The time has come to spread the nets and catch
The lioness and cubs," he said. He seized
His little boy Learchus in his claws
And dashed his brains out on a rock. His wife   10
Then drowned her other son and drowned herself.

And when the bold and haughty Trojan race
By fate was humbled (Priam and his clan
Destroyed), the grieving Hecuba became
A captive of the Greeks. But when she saw   15
Her Polyxena dead and saw the corpse
Of Polydorus on the beach, her mind
Became disordered by her grief, and she
Began to bark as if she were a dog.

Still, no one ever saw in Troy or Thebes   20
A fury, whether shown toward beast or man,
To rival that displayed by two down here,
Both pale, both naked, running like two pigs

Unpenned that root and snap at everything.
One sank his fangs into Capocchio's neck   25
And dragged the wretch so that his belly scraped
Along the stony floor. The Aretine,
Meanwhile, whose every limb was trembling, turned
To me and said: "That beast is Gianni Schicchi,
Who butchers every soul in just that way."   30

And I: "Please tell me, if you will—who is
That other beast? (May you escape its clutches.)
Speak up, now, quick, before it goes away."

He said: "That soul is Myrrha, she of old
Who loved her father in forbidden ways;   35
To sleep with him, she falsely took the form
Of someone else. Old Gianni Schicchi there,
To steal the herd's best mare, disguised himself
As Buoso Donati, already dead,
And made a phony will in Buoso's name   40
In proper legal form."

                    When finally
The rabid souls, on whom I kept an eye,
Moved on, I fixed my gaze on other shades
Among this misbegotten horde. One soul
Was shaped just like a lute, from head to crotch   45
At least. His limbs from dropsy were misshaped
Because the humors act malignantly
Upon the human frame, and so his head
Was out of all proportion to his paunch.
The illness made his lips hang open wide   50
Like one who has the hectic fever's mark.
His form was shriveled up from thirst. He curled

One lip to chin, the other lip to nose and said:
"You there, who seem (I don't know why) to go
Unpunished in this place of pain called Hell,   55
Just take a look at me! I'm Master Adam.
I satisfied my every wish on Earth,
But here I suffer so! If only I
Could drink the smallest drop of water now!
I think of all those little streams that flow   60
From Casentino's green, luxuriant hills
And join the Arno to refresh both bed
And bank with liquid cool; such thoughts torment
Me without end. Their image seems to dry
My body even more than this disease   65
That ravages my face. Strict Justice thus
Employs the very region where I lived
My life of sin to make me long in vain.
There lies the Castle of Romena where
I counterfeited coins, the ones that show   70
The head of John the Baptist on one side.
That's why they burned my body in the world.
But if I were to see the soul of Guido
Here, or of his brother Alessandro,
Or the other, Aghinolfo, why then   75
I'd not give up that sight to quench my thirst
At Branda's fount! And one of them is here,
If I can credit what these raging souls
Have said—though what's the use of that to me,
Whose limbs hang useless from disease? If I   80
Could only weigh a little less! If I
Could even move an inch per century,
Why then, I'll have you know, I'd start upon
The path to seek him out amid this pack
Of twisted souls, though it's eleven miles   85

Around this ditch and half a mile across.
Those brothers made me forge the coins with base
Alloy; they brought me to the depths of Hell."

And I: "Who are those wretched souls who lie
So close together on your right, whose hands   90
Are smoking like wet hands in wintertime?"

"I found them in that spot when I arrived;
They haven't budged since then; I doubt they will
For all eternity," he said. "That one
Is she who falsely spoke of Joseph, son   95
Of Jacob. Sinon is the other shade,
Who fooled all Troy about the wooden horse.
A fever makes them stink like this, you know."

Then Sinon, who at Adam's words no doubt
Had taken umbrage, smacked him on the paunch.   100
The sound was like a drum's, but Adam's arm
Was harder than the other's fist; he aimed
A mighty blow and hit him in the face.
"Although these arms of lead are hard to lift,
I still can swing them at the likes of you!"   105

"Your arms were no protection from the stake
When they were tied behind your back! But, ah,
They were so useful when you made your coins,
I'll bet!"

            To which the dropsied one replied:
"You speak the truth for once, but back at Troy,   110
You showed how great a liar you could be!"

"What if I did? *You* counterfeited coins!
 I may be here for one offense, but *you*,
 My friend, are here for doing more than all
 The other demon denizens of Hell!"   115

The swollen-bellied soul shot back: "Recall
 The Trojan horse, you lying beast! Rot here
 Forever, knowing all the world's aware
 Of your unparalleled deceit!"

                    And Sinon:
"Oh bitter be the thirst that cracks your tongue,   120
 Bitter the liquid of your paunch, so huge
 It blocks your vision like a monstrous hedge!"

And Adam said: "As usual your mouth's
 A gaping hole that does you in; and, yes,
 It's true I thirst, and humors stuff my frame,   125
 But you're consumed with burning and your head's
 A vise of pain; no one need ask you twice
 To lick the limpid stream Narcissus kissed!"

I was intently listening to them
 When Virgil spoke: "Go on: provoke my wrath   130
 By staring at these miserable curs!"

When I had heard his angry words, I turned
 To him and felt such shame that even now
 The memory whirs through my mind; like one
 Who dreams an evil dream and, dreaming, hopes   135
 It is a dream, I wanted my good guide
 To pardon my offense. No words would flow,
 But he could read the shame upon my face.

My master said: "Less shame than this can wash   140
Away a far more grievous fault; therefore
Divest yourself of sorrow. Don't forget,
That if you come to where two souls contend,
I am with you: it is a base desire
To want to listen to them quarreling."   145

NOTES TO CANTO XXX

[SUMMARY OF THE CANTO: *Two rabid spirits rush in while Capocchio is ending his speech; one bites into his neck and drags him off. In response to a question from Dante, Griffolino explains that the two maddened spirits are those of Myrrha and of Gianni Schicchi, who spend their time racing around the ditch, grabbing at spirits and ripping at their flesh. Dante and Virgil now come upon the misshapen soul of Master Adam, a famed counterfeiter, who tells the poets about himself and points out two other souls: Potiphar's wife and Sinon. The latter and Master Adam exchange insults as Dante, transfixed, looks on. Virgil upbraids Dante for listening to their verbal duel, but forgives him when he shows remorse.*]

1–2   . . . JUNO OFTEN FLASHED / HER GODLY ANGER . . . : The wrath of the goddess Juno (Hera, to the Greeks) was often provoked by the infidelities of her husband (Jupiter, Jove, or Zeus), and many ancient myths tell of her acts of vengeance, mainly against women whom Jupiter had seduced. Jupiter had impregnated Semele of Thebes, who gave birth to the god Bacchus. Juno therefore avenged herself upon the house of Thebes in a variety of ways. In the tale as told by Dante, Juno caused Athamas to go quite mad, so that one day he did the insane deed recounted here. Athamas' wife was Ino, the sister of Semele. The other child of Ino and Athamas was named Melicertes.

14–19   . . . THE GRIEVING HECUBA . . . AS IF SHE WERE A DOG: At the end of the Trojan War, when Troy had been taken by the Greeks, Hecuba, the wife of Priam, king of Troy, was enslaved and brought to Greece together with her daughter, Polyxena. The latter was slain in a sacrificial ceremony. When the grief-stricken mother went to the seashore to wash away the blood of Polyxena from her hands, she saw the corpse of her son Polydorus, who had been murdered by the king of Thrace, the very man who was supposed to protect the youth. She subsequently went out of her mind from the double loss. (Hecuba's tragic fate at the end of the Trojan War is vividly told by perhaps the greatest antiwar play ever written: Eurpides' *The Women of Troy*.)

27–28 ... THE ARETINE, / ... WHOSE EVERY LIMB WAS TREMBLING .... This is Griffolino d'Arezzo, from Canto XXIX.

29 ... THAT BEAST IS GIANNI SCHICCHI: Upon the death of a certain Buoso Donati of Florence, his nephew Simone, afraid that his uncle, in his will, might have tried to return some of the goods the old man had illegally amassed, went to see Gianni Schicchi for counsel. Since only Simone and Schicchi knew that Buoso was dead, Schicchi impersonated Buoso and drew up a will that left almost everything to Simone—and something for himself (including the "best marc" among Buoso's horses). Some believe this Buoso to be the Buoso degli Abati of Canto XXV. Schicchi's tale is charmingly told in Giacomo Puccini's one-act opera, *Gianni Schicchi*.

34 ... THAT SOUL IS MYRRHA ... : Myrrha's story is found in Ovid. She committed incest with her father, king of Cyprus, by disguising herself and entering his bed. When her father realized whom he had made love to, he wanted to kill her. Escaping, she disguised herself as a stranger but was transformed into a myrtle bush. From her trunk was born Adonis. In one of his letters, Dante calls Florence an "accursed, impious Myrrha."

44–45 ... ONE SOUL / WAS SHAPED JUST LIKE A LUTE ... : The soul who now takes center stage is that of Master Adam, a notorious thirteenth-century counterfeiter whom the counts of Romena (family name, Guidi) induced to counterfeit gold florins (coins of Florence). So many false coins were made that severe financial turmoil ensued. Caught trying to pass the false coins, Adam was burned at the stake in 1281.

61 FROM CASENTINO'S GREEN, LUXURIANT HILLS: Casentino is a lush hilly area where the Guidi family's Castle of Romena (line 69) was located. Dante knew the region because he had traveled there at least twice.

70–71 ... THE ONES THAT SHOW / THE HEAD OF JOHN THE BAPTIST ... : The florin did indeed display the head of John the Baptist on one side; on the other was a lily, the emblem of Florence. The city's name derives from the Latin word for "flowering."

73–75 ... GUIDO ... ALESSANDRO ... AGHINOLFO ... : These are the Guidi brothers who pushed Adam to commit his sins (see lines 87–88).

76–77 . . . TO QUENCH MY THIRST / AT BRANDA'S FOUNT . . . : Either of two fountains with that name may be meant; one is at Siena, the other may have been near the Castle of Romena.

95 . . . SHE WHO FALSELY SPOKE OF JOSEPH . . . : Joseph was falsely accused by Potiphar's wife of sexual assault (see *Genesis* 39:7–23).

96–97 . . . SINON IS THE OTHER SHADE: When the Greeks pretended to sail away and quit the Trojan War, they left behind the famous wooden horse. Also purposely left behind was Sinon, who told the Trojans that he had deserted the Greek army and that the Greeks had gone for good; he persuaded the Trojans to drag the horse inside the city gates. Greek soldiers hiding in the belly of the horse issued from it in the middle of the night, opened the gates, and let in the rest of the Greek army, which had not really left the area. The result was the destruction of Troy and Greek victory in the war.

128 TO LICK THE LIMPID STREAM NARCISSUS KISSED: Narcissus became enamored of his own reflection in a pool of water. Consumed with a self-love that paralyzed his will and made him ignore the advances of poor Echo, he was metamorphosed into a flower.

130 . . . GO ON: PROVOKE MY WRATH: Virgil's wrath may be provoked by what he views as Dante's sympathy for the sinners. Virgil wants Dante's moral sense to be strict and severe.

144 I AM WITH YOU . . . : Virgil, as we have seen from Canto I, represents reason; therefore, these words of Virgil's mean that reason will always be available to Dante to guide him.

CANTO XXXI

I was wounded by my master's tongue;
It made me blush with shame, and yet it brought
Forgiveness for my sin, just as the lance
Of great Achilles and his sire could cause
Grave wounds but also heal them rapidly.   5

We turned our backs at last upon the tenth
And final ditch of misery, and crossed,
Without a word, the cliff that circles it.
Less dark than night it was, less light than day,
And so I could not see too far. But soon   10
I heard a blast as if from some great horn,
A sound much louder than a thunderclap
And with my eyes could trace it to its source.
Not even Roland's horn, when Charlemagne
Lost all the Paladins, blared out so loud.   15

I stared in that direction for a while
And seemed to see what looked like lofty towers.
I asked: "What is that city over there?"
"You strain to see too far into the dark,"
He said, "So distance plays a trick on you.   20
As you come closer, it will all be clear.
Walk on."

Then tenderly he took my hand:
"Before we move ahead, let me explain,
So that the sight will seem less strange to you,
That those are not high towers you see, but forms   25
Of awesome giants, standing in a pit,
Their navels level with the circling bank."

As when a fog is lifting and the eyes
Begin to give a shape to everything
The thickened air conceals, so as I moved   30
Through mist and darkness and approached the bank,
I saw more clearly, though my fear grew great.
As towers ring Montereggione's wall,
So here, high up above the bank that skirts
The pit, the giants loom with half their forms,   35
Whom Jove still threatens with his thunderclaps.

Now I was close enough to see the face,
The shoulders, paunch, as well as chest and arms
That hung along the sides of one of them.
How wise of Nature not to make more beasts   40
Like this who might have done whatever Mars
Desired. You thoughtful men will see that while
She harbors no regrets at having made
The whale and elephant, the deadly mix
Of malice, mind, and might the giants owned   45
Would have been more than men could have withstood.
Just like the pinecone cast in bronze that's found
In Rome before St. Peter's church, his face
Was long and wide. His frame was in proportion
To his face, and it bulked above the bank   50
(To him, an apron from his middle down).
So large a part of him we saw that if
Three men from Frisia stood on top of one

Another here, they would not reach his hair,
Boast as they might. And where I stood I saw   55
Full thirty spans of him from where a man
Would buckle up his cloak down to his feet.
His beastly mouth, where no sweet psalm would sound
Appropriate, now screamed out words of no
Known tongue: *"Rafèl maỳ amèch zabì almì."*   60

Then Virgil said to him: "You brainless soul!
Go blow your horn when you are full of rage
Or when some other fit of passion swells
Your being; vent your feelings in that way.
Just feel your neck, bewildered soul, and you   65
Will find the strap to which the horn is tied
That's draped around your massive chest."

                                    My guide
Then said to me: "His own strange words condemn
That bestial soul. He's Nimrod, who designed
The evil tower that brought a multitude   70
Of tongues to Earth. Let's leave him be and not
Waste words: they'd seem to him as his to us,
Mere gibberish."

                    So to the left we walked
About the distance of a crossbow shot,
And there a larger giant stood, by far   75
More savage than the first. Whose could have been
The master hand that bound this beast? Behind
His back his right arm was made fast. In front,
His left was shackled with a chain that stretched
From neck to trunk and wound around his chest   80
Five turns. My leader spoke: "This proud one, called
Ephialtes, tried testing all his strength

Against great Jove himself. See his reward!
With all the other giants of that time
He moved against the Gods who feared these beasts.   85
But never shall he move those arms again
That once were raised against divinity."

And I to him: "If possible, I'd like
To see the huge Briareus."

          He said:
"Not far from here we'll come upon Antaeus,   90
A beast unbound who speaks with clarity,
And he will set us down into the well
Where evil reigns supreme. Briareus
Is found much further on. However, he
Is bound. He looks like this one, but his face   95
Is surely most ferocious of the three."

Ephialtes now violently strained
To free himself: no earthquake ever shook
A castle tower so forcefully, and had
I not perceived the chains that held him down,   100
I would have thought my hour of death had come.
Ahead of us Antaeus loomed, who stood
Five ells above the rock (and that does not
Include the giant head.)

          "Antaeus, you
Who took a thousand lions as your spoil   105
Along that valley where great Scipio
Was glorified when Hannibal fell back
With all his host, and who, if you had joined
The battle of your brothers when they fought
Against great Jove, would easily have tipped   110

The fight to favor them, do not refuse
To place us two below where Cocytus
Is bound in ice. Don't make us go to Typhon
Or Tityus. This living soul can speak
Of you to men when he returns to Earth   115
(A thing you much desire). Don't sneer at us,
For he can yet restore your name to fame,
Since he's alive and will be so for years,
Unless he's called by Grace before his time."

Thus Virgil spoke to him, and as he did,   120
Antaeus, stretching forth those hands that once
Encircled mighty Hercules himself,
Now clutched my guide, who turned to me and said:
"Come here so that I may take you with me now."
My lord so managed it that he and I   125
Were like one bundle in the giant's grip.
And just as Carisenda's tower looks
When over it a cloud is seen to hang,
So seemed to me this strange gigantic beast
When he was bending forward (how I wished   130
I'd walked a different road!).

                      The creature placed
Us gently in the deepest pit of Hell
That swallowed Lucifer and Judas both.
Nor did Antaeus, thus bent over, stay,
But quickly raised his mighty form   135
As if he were the mainmast of a ship.

NOTES TO CANTO XXXI

[SUMMARY OF THE CANTO: *Dante and Virgil cross the embankment that separates Circles Eight and Nine. Hearing the sound of a horn in the dimly lit region, Dante tries to determine its source. He sees in the distance what appear to be lofty towers but are in reality giants buried in the ground up to their waist. The poets approach these creatures and are able to observe each one minutely. Virgil tells Dante about each of them: Nimrod, Ephialtes, and Antaeus. The giants do not speak to the poets, although Nimrod utters one unintelligible phrase. Virgil flatters Antaeus into lifting him and Dante into the air in order to deposit them in the pit of Cocytus.*]

3–4   . . . JUST AS THE LANCE / OF GREAT ACHILLES . . . : According to legend, Achilles, Greek warrior of the war against Troy, had received a magic lance from his father, Peleus; its power was such that, if it wounded anyone, it could heal that person if it touched him again. ("Whose smile and frown, like to Achilles' spear, / Is able with the change to kill and cure." Shakespeare, *Henry VI, Part II*, V, i.)

6–7   WE TURNED OUR BACKS AT LAST UPON THE TENTH / AND FINAL DITCH . . . : The poets have now passed out of Malebolge, or Circle Eight, with its ten *bolge* or ditches.

14–15   NOT EVEN ROLAND'S HORN . . . BLARED OUT SO LOUD: After Charlemagne had fought in Spain against the Saracens, he and his army began their long journey back to France. As they crossed over the Pyrenees, which divide the two countries, his nephew Roland, leading the rearguard of the army, was betrayed by Ganelon. As Roland lay dying, he blew upon his horn in an attempt to summon Charlemagne to the rear. (Roland was later to become the popular hero of Italian Renaissance epics.) The sound that Dante hears comes from the horn of Nimrod, whom the poets will shortly encounter.

33   AS TOWERS RING MONTEREGGIONE'S WALL: Montereggione is a multiturreted castle located not far from Siena. Most of its dozen or so towers are no longer standing.

47   JUST LIKE THE PINECONE CAST IN BRONZE . . . : Outside the old church of St. Peter's in Rome, in the time of Dante, an eight-foot image of a pinecone cast in bronze was to be found. It is now in the Vatican.

53   THREE MEN FROM FRISIA . . . : Frisian men were known for being exceptionally tall.

60   . . . RAFÈL MAÝ AMÈCH ZABÌ ALMÌ: No one has succeeded in deciphering these words. Probably, as Virgil says in line 73, they mean nothing at all.

69–70   . . . HE'S NIMROD, WHO DESIGNED / THE EVIL TOWER . . . : Nimrod (meaning "rebel") is the first of three giants whom the poets will encounter. These creatures are the custodians of the Ninth Circle. A king of Babylon, Nimrod is mentioned in *Genesis* in the story of the Tower of Babel, which some believe he was instrumental in building. There is no hint in the Biblical account that he may have been a giant, nor does it say that he built the tower. Patristic and medieval tradition, however, depict him as a giant who promoted its construction. Because Genesis says that Nimrod was a hunter, Dante depicts him with a horn.

81–82   THIS PROUD ONE, CALLED / EPHIALTES . . . : Ephialtes, the son of the sea-god Poseidon (Neptune in Latin), and his brother were giants who battled the Olympian gods, trying to pile mountains atop one another—Ossa on Olympus and Pelion on Ossa—in order to reach Heaven. They were killed by Apollo. See *Genesis* 6:4: "There were giants in the earth in those days. . . ."

88–89   . . . IF POSSIBLE, I'D LIKE / TO SEE THE HUGE BRIAREUS . . . : The son of Tellus (the Earth) and Uranus, Briareus also fought alongside Ephialtes against the gods. He is said to have had a hundred heads and a hundred hands, but Dante makes him less fantastic. Virgil dissuades Dante from seeing this creature (lines 93–96).

90   NOT FAR FROM HERE WE'LL COME UPON ANTAEUS: Antaeus, the son of Tellus and Poseidon, could not be defeated so long as his feet remained on the earth. Hercules vanquished him by lifting him off the ground and then crushing him to death in the air. Antaeus was not involved in the battle with the gods, which explains why he is not chained. The story of his slaying of a thousand lions is found in the *Civil War* of Lucan; the deed supposedly took place near the site of the later battle of Zama (see note to lines 106–107).

97–98   EPHIALTES NOW VIOLENTLY STRAINED / TO FREE HIMSELF: Ephialtes probably does this because his pride has been wounded, for he has heard Virgil say that Briareus is more ferocious than he.

106–107   . . . WHERE GREAT SCIPIO / WAS GLORIFIED . . . : Scipio was the savior of Rome by virtue of his having defeated Hannibal, the famed Carthaginian general, at the battle of Zama in Libya. The archenemy of Rome, Hannibal had earlier invaded Italy, causing tremendous destruction and loss of life.

112–113   . . . WHERE COCYTUS / IS BOUND IN ICE . . . : Cocytus is a frozen lake in the deepest region of Hell.

113–114   DON'T MAKE US GO TO TYPHON / OR TITYUS . . . : These were two other sons of Tellus. Having angered Jupiter, they were cast into Mount Etna, the volcano near Catania, Sicily.

134   THAT SWALLOWED LUCIFER AND JUDAS BOTH: Lucifer is, of course Satan (he has several names). Judas Iscariot was the betrayer of Christ. Both characters will make their appearance in Canto XXXIV.

136   . . . THE MAINMAST OF A SHIP: In Dante's time, masts were not permanently attached to ships but were raised at the beginning of a voyage and lowered at the end.

CANTO XXXII

Had I some harsh and disharmonious rhymes
To match that murky hole weighed down by all
The other rocks, I would extract the juice
Of all the creativity my mind
Contains, but since I do not own such rhymes,   5
I speak reluctantly of what I saw,
For light or childish speech cannot depict
This nadir of the Lord's creation. Still,
May all those Muses give my words new wings
Who helped Amphion build the walls of Thebes   10
With magic lyre, so that the tale I tell
Be told in words of truth.

                  Better for you
To have been born not men but goats or sheep,
You misbegotten souls who dwell down deep
In Hell's remotest reaches that defy   15
Description!

               Down below the giants' feet,
Far down inside the infernal sink I stood,
And as I wondered at the lofty wall
That stretches round the pit, I heard a voice
Cry out: "Watch where you walk, or you will tread   20
Upon the heads of miserable brothers!"

I turned and saw, before me and below,
A frozen lake whose surface seemed like glass.
In winter, never did so thick a sheet
Of ice as this, in Austria, seal up   25
The surface of the Danube or the Don
Far north beneath the frozen Russian sky.
A slide of rocks from Mount Tambernicchi
Or Mount Pietrapana would not have caused
The edges of this lake to creak or crack.   30

And as in summertime, when farmers' wives
Dream deeply of rich garnerings of grain,
The frogs are seen to squat, with muzzles out
Of water as they croak, so seemed the shades
Down here, who groaned, immersed up to the neck   35
In ice, their frozen bodies blue, though still
Their faces flushed with crimson out of shame.
Each head was bowed, and, storklike in the cold,
Their teeth were chattering, while in their eyes
Great tears bore silent witness to their grief.   40
Then looking down, I saw the forms of two
So closely pressed together that their hair
Was interwoven in one gelid mass.
"You souls whose bodies are compacted so,"
I said, "tell me who you are."

                              Bending back   45
Their necks, they looked at me, and now the tears
That filled their eyes gushed forth in streams to wet
Their cheeks and flow across their lips and freeze
And bind the duo like two wooden boards
Squeezed tightly in a vise. This roused their wrath   50
So that, like angry goats, they butted heads.
A nearby shade who'd lost both ears to frost

Addressed me with his head bowed down: "Why stare
At us that way? If you would like to know
Just who those spirits are, I'll tell you now: 55
Their father Albert and his wretched sons
Possessed the vale where the Bisenzio
Begins its journey toward the Arno's stream.
One woman bore them both, and though you search
Throughout Caïna's realm you'll find no souls   60
Who merits more this fix in solid ice
Than these, not even Mordred who was slain
By Arthur with a blow that split his chest
And let the sunlight through; not Focaccia;
Not this one here, a murderer of kin,   65
Who blocks my vision with his head; his name
(If you're a Tuscan, you will know it well)
Was Sassol Mascheroni. Now I'll tell
You who I am, so that you won't keep forcing
Me to speak: I'm Camicion dei Pazzi.   70
Carlino I await, whose crime, more vile
Than mine, will help exonerate my own."

I saw a thousand spirits purple-faced
From frost. I shiver at the memory
The sight of frozen fords brings back to me.   75
Now toward the center of the universe,
To which all weight is drawn, we made our way.
How chilled I was from that eternal cold!
And as we stepped among the heads locked fast
In ice, my foot (was it God's will, or chance,   80
Or destiny?) kicked hard against the face
Of one of them, who wept and screamed at me:
"Why are you kicking and molesting me?
Are you exacting even more revenge
For the victory at Montaperti?"   85

I said to Virgil: "Wait for me, my lord;
There's something I must clarify with him;
And then I'll move as quickly as you like."

He waited as I turned to see the shade,
Who still was cursing bitterly, and said: 90
"Why such reviling of the other souls?
Who can you be?"

             "And who are you?" he said,
"That move through Antenora striking cheeks
Much harder than a living man would do?"

"I am alive," I said, "and it may be   95
Of no small worth to you that I will add
Your name to others I will sing about,
That is, if fame is what you want."

                  And he:
"I want the opposite; get out of here!
Give me no further reason to complain!   100
You're not much good at flattery down here."

I grabbed him by the hair and said: "Tell me
Your name, before I pull out every hair!"

And he: "Do what you will, but I won't tell
You who I am or show my face, though you   105
Should pluck a thousand hairs from me!"

               By now
I had already torn from him at least
One tuft, while he, head bowed, howled like a dog.
The other soul cried out to him: "Hey, Bocca!

What's eating you? Isn't it enough for you   110
To make all kinds of music with your jaws?
Why must you yelp those doggy sounds as well?
What devil is attacking you?"

                    And I:
"You traitor! Not a word do I demand
From you, but I will tell the world the truth   115
Concerning you!"

                    "Just go away, and say
Whatever pleases you, but don't hold back
From telling everything about that one
(Provided you escape from here, of course)
Whose tongue was set to speak. He wails and wails   120
About the coins the Frenchman slipped to him,
And you can say: 'I saw Buoso da Duera
In Hell, where sinners shiver in the ice.'
And if you're asked who else you met, tell them
You came across the abbot Beccheria,   125
Whose head the Florentines lopped off. And here
You'll find Gianni de' Soldanieri, too,
And Charlemagne's betrayer, Ganelon.
Here's Tebaldello, traitor to his town,
Who opened up Faenza's gates to Guelfs   130
From Bologna while all his townsmen slept."

We had already left him when I saw,
Inside a hole, two frozen souls, so close
Together that the head of one was like
A hood that hung above the other head,   135
And, just like one who's famished and devours
A piece of bread, the upper spirit chewed
The head of him below, sinking his teeth

Into the very spot where brain meets nape,
In just the way the dying King Tydeus   140
Raging, gnawed the skull and chewed the brain
Of Theban Menalippus. Then I spoke:
"You there, who show such hatred for that soul
That you are eating him as if you were
Not human but a beast, explain this deed,   145
And understand that in the world I may
Repay you for it, knowing who you are
And what he did, if my poor tongue does not
Completely wither in this world of Hell."

NOTES TO CANTO XXXII

[SUMMARY OF THE CANTO: *Dante tells the reader that he fears he may not be able to express adequately what he saw in Circle Nine, the last circle of Hell, and therefore asks for help from the Muses. The two poets are now walking on a plain of ice in the region of Caïna, the first part of Cocytus, where sinners against kin are stuck fast in the icy bottom. Dante learns about several sinners from Camicione de' Pazzi who talks of the Alberti brothers, Mordred, Focaccia, Sassol Mascheroni, and Carlino de' Pazzi. Moving to the next region, Antenora, the poets meet sinners who betrayed their homeland. Dante abuses one of them both verbally and physically before learning from Buoso da Duera that Dante's victim is Bocca degli Abati, whose actions at Montaperti helped defeat the Guelfs. Bocca tells Dante of other sinners in the vicinity: Tesauro de' Beccaria, Gianni de' Soldaneri, Ganelon, and Tebaldello de' Zambrasi. Dante and Virgil then come upon two sinners, one of whom is gnawing at the other's head: in the next canto they will be identified as Count Ugolino and Archbishop Ruggieri.]*

2   TO MATCH THE MURKY HOLE . . . : The hole is Cocytus, the lowest point of Inferno. It is divided into four regions: Caïna, Antenora, Ptolomea, and

Judecca. At its very center is Lucifer. Cocytus is a lake into which the rivers of Hell empty their waters. The water here is frozen, however, because of the cold wind that blows through all the region. The wind comes from the incessant beating of Lucifer's wings (see Canto XXXIV.)

10–11 WHO HELPED AMPHION BUILD THE WALLS OF THEBES: Amphion, from Greek myth, was inspired by the Muses to play the lyre so enchantingly that blocks of stone were magically removed from Mount Cithaeron. The stones then arranged themselves so as to form the walls of the city of Thebes.

26 THE SURFACE OF THE DANUBE OR THE DON: The Danube runs through Austria and other countries of southeast Europe before emptying into the Black Sea; the Don, in Russia, empties into the Sea of Azov.

28 . . . MOUNT TAMBERNICCHI / OR MOUNT PIETRAPANA . . . : Tambernicchi may refer to a mountain in Slavonia or perhaps to one in the Alps. Pietrapana (today known today as Pania della Croce) is near the city of Lucca in Tuscany.

38–39 . . . STORKLIKE IN THE COLD, / THEIR TEETH WERE CHATTER-ING . . . : Storks make a clacking sound with their beaks. The verb *crepitate*, from the Latin, seems aptly to describe the noise, and in fact it is the word Ovid uses, in his *Metamorphoses*, to describe the sound: *crepitante* ("chattering"). Again, Dante resorts to animal imagery, a salient feature of his poem.

41 . . . I SAW THE FORMS OF TWO: The forms are those of Alessandro and Napoleone, the sons of Count Alberto degli Alberti; Alessandro was a Guelph; Napoleone, a Ghibelline. They fought with each other continually while alive and, after a fight about their inheritance and their political differences, managed to murder each other.

52 A NEARBY SHADE WHO'D LOST BOTH EARS TO FROST: This spirit is Camicione di Pazzi (see note to line 70).

57–58 . . . WHERE THE BISENZIO / BEGINS ITS JOURNEY . . . : The Bisenzio is a small river that empties into the Arno.

59–60 . . . THOUGH YOU SEARCH / THROUGHOUT CAÏNA'S REALM . . . : Another region of this Ninth Circle, Caïna is named after the Biblical Cain, slayer of his brother, Abel.

62–64 . . . NOT EVEN MORDRED . . . LET THE SUNLIGHT THROUGH . . . : Mordred was King Arthur's nephew who planned to kill the king. Arthur therefore attacked him, wounding him with his lance. Immediately, a shaft of light shone through Mordred's large wound. Before dying, however, he did kill Arthur. The story is from the medieval poem, *Lancelot du Lac*, which seems to have been the book that Francesca and Paolo were reading in Canto V. (There is another link between the cantos: Francesca tells Dante that the region of Caïna is awaiting the soul of her husband, Gianciotto, who murdered both her and her lover.)

64   . . . NOT FOCACCIA: In Pistoia, Vanni dei Cancellieri, called Focaccia, cut off his cousin's hand and murdered his uncle, exacerbating the tensions between the Whites and Blacks of that city. When the Florentines were called in to help settle the dispute, the White-Black friction spread to Florence and became a feature of that city's life for some time thereafter.

66–68   . . . HIS NAME . . . WAS SASSOL MASCHERONI . . . : Having been chosen as the guardian of his nephew, Mascheroni killed his ward so as to obtain the young man's inheritance. (Again, treachery against kin is the sin involved here.)

70   . . . I'M CAMICION DEI PAZZI: Alberto Camicione dei Pazzi of Valdarno murdered a member of his own family. (Here Dante spells Camicione without the final "e"; final vowels in Italian may be dropped under certain circumstances.)

71   CARLINO I AWAIT . . . : Carlino dei Pazzi, a relative of Camicione, was defending a castle in Valdarno for the White cause. However, after being bribed, he surrendered the castle to the Blacks of Valdarno. Since his crime is that of treachery to one's country, he properly belongs in Antenora, situated lower down in Hell. Thus, Camicione seems to take satisfaction in the knowledge that Carlino will be more severely punished than he himself.

76   . . . TOWARD THE CENTER OF THE UNIVERSE: In the medieval conception, the center of Hell is the center of Earth and the center of the universe. All gravity is therefore concentrated in that point, the center of all the guilt and sin of humanity. The central figure of Hell, quite literally, is Lucifer, emperor of the realm of pain and of the guilty dead.

79   AND AS WE STEPPED AMONG THE HEADS . . . : Dante and Virgil unceremoniously leave Caïna, the first region of Cocytus, and enter Antenora. There is no visible boundary between the two regions.

82   . . . ONE OF THEM, WHO WEPT AND SCREAMED AT ME: This is Bocca degli Abati, who, supposedly fighting for the Guelfs, betrayed them by cutting off the hand of the Florentine Guelf standard-bearer during the battle of Montaperti. This caused confusion among the horse soldiers, who no longer had a flag around which to rally; the Guelfs lost the battle.

93   THAT MOVE THROUGH ANTENORA . . . : This region is named after Antenor, who betrayed his city, Troy, to the Greeks in the Trojan War.

122   . . . I SAW BUOSO DA DUERA / IN HELL . . . : Buoso da Duera (or Dovera) was from the city of Cremona in northern Italy. At the time of the bat-

tle between Charles of Anjou and Manfred, Buoso was ordered to prevent Charles's army from entering Parma. Instead, Buoso accepted a bribe, and so the French entered.

125 YOU CAME ACROSS THE ABBOT BECCHERIA: Tesauro dei Beccheria of the city of Pavia was the papal legate of Pope Alexander IV to Florence. Having been found guilty of conspiring with the exiled Florentine Ghibellines against the Guelfs, he was summarily decapitated.

127 YOU'LL FIND GIANNI DE' SOLDANIERI, TOO: He was a well-known Florentine Ghibelline who deserted his party and, following the defeat of Manfred at Benevento in 1265, became a Guelf leader.

128 AND CHARLEMAGNE'S BETRAYER, GANELON: We have encountered the name of Ganelon before. See note to lines 14–15 in Canto XXXI.

129 HERE'S TEBALDELLO, TRAITOR TO HIS TOWN: Tebaldello de' Zambrasi of Faenza betrayed the city to the Guelfs of Bologna in order to avenge himself, it would appear, on the Lambertazzi family, who were Ghibellines.

140–142 ... THE DYING KING TYDEUS ... THEBAN MENALIPPUS ...: The king killed Menalippus during a battle. Though he had been wounded by Menalippus, Tydeus asked, as he himself lay dying, that Menalippus' head be brought to him. He then began to chew on it in blind fury, ripping the brains out of it (see Statius' *Thebaid,* Book Eight). The last lines of the canto (starting with line 132) lead into the story of Count Ugolino and Archbishop Ruggieri, which will be fully told in Canto XXXIII.

CANTO XXXIII

Up from that savage meal the sinner raised
His blood-stained mouth and wiped it on the hair
Of that same head whose nape he chewed upon.
He said to me: "You want to stir my mind
Once more with misery that knows no end!   5
The memories alone are merciless
And wring my heart before I even speak.
But if my words will be the seeds that bear
The fruit of infamy for him whose head
I gnaw, I'll speak and weep, if it must be.   10

"I don't know who you are, nor how you came
To be among the dead, but, by your speech,
Truly it seems to me you're Florentine.
Count Ugolino was my name, and he
Who lies in agony beneath me here,   15
Once archbishop, bears the name Ruggieri.
I'll tell you why the two of us are joined
Forever in this way. I need not speak
Of how I trusted him and how his deeds
Of evil led me to be seized and killed.   20
But what you do not know is that I died
A death of cruelty beyond belief.
I'll tell you how it was; you be the judge:

"I had observed, from where I lay inside
  The tower (now known as Hunger, all because   25
  Of me), through slits cut in those stony walls
  Which will entomb still other prisoners,
  That several moons had waxed and waned. One night
  There came to me an evil dream that rent
  The future's veil: this beast, Ruggieri, he   30
  Whose hateful head I gnaw, appeared to me
  As if he were a lord and led a hunt
  For wolf and whelps toward San Giuliano's height
  That hides the town of Lucca from the Pisans.
  Ruggieri loosed his swift, lean, well-trained hounds   35
  And sent Gualandi, Sismondi, Lanfranchi,
  To run before the dogs. It was not long
  Before the father and his sons were weak
  And near exhaustion. Then I seemed to see
  The sharp-toothed hounds rip deep into their flesh.   40

"When I awoke before the dawn I heard
  My sleeping boys, who'd been locked up with me,
  Cry out for bread. You must be cruel indeed
  If that same thought that overwhelmed my heart
  With dread does not move you to weep, and if   45
  You cannot weep at such a thought, then what,
  In all the world, can wet your eyes with tears?"

"The boys were now awake; the time for food
  Had come, though each of them was sick at heart
  Because of what they'd dreamed. Then came the sound   50
  Of hammering: the men were nailing shut
  The prison door.

                "Without a word I gazed
  Into the hungry faces of my boys.

I could not weep; I had become a stone.
The boys were crying; little Anselm said: 55
'My father, what is wrong? You look so ill.'

"No tears, not even one, flowed down my cheeks
And no word passed my lips that day
Nor all that night, until another sun
Had risen on the world. No sooner had   60
Its light pierced through our dismal prison-cell
Than I observed the faces of my sons,
The living mirrors of my misery.
I gnawed my hands in anguish and despair.
But they, perceiving this to mean that I   65
Was ravenous with hunger, said: 'It will,
Dear father, give us much less pain if you
Would eat our flesh; for it was you who gave
Our bodies life. So take and eat and do
As you judge best.'"

                    "I struggled hard to calm   70
Myself and not intensify their pain.
We spoke no word that day nor all the next.
(Cruel Earth! Why did your jaws not open wide
And swallow us at once!) The fourth day came:
My little Gaddo dropped down at my feet.   75
'Why don't you help me, Father?' were the words
He whispered as he died. Just as you see
Me here, I saw, with numbing clarity,
My three remaining sons collapse, between
The fifth day and the sixth. And then, made blind   80
By lack of food, I groped about the cell
To touch the bodies of my little boys.
I called them each by name, but each was dead.
And on the eighth day hunger conquered grief."

When he had said these things, his eyes askance,   85
He seized Ruggieri's skull and chewed on it
With teeth that tore more strongly than a dog's.

Ah Pisa! Nest of vipers in the land
Of Italy, your neighbors are too slow
To punish you! Oh, may Gorgona's isle,   90
Capraia's, too, dam up the Arno's mouth
To make it overflow and drown you all!
Though Ugolino had betrayed your town,
How vile it was to torture all his sons!
You modern Thebes! It's clear their tender age   95
Meant Uguccione and Brigata both
Were guiltless as their brothers, whom my song
Has named.

        My guide and I walked on and found
Souls fast in ice; their faces were upturned;
Their frozen tears dammed up the flow of others.   100
Their grief, blocked up, increased their pain. The tears
That first flowed down had formed a knot and, like
A crystal visor, filled the cup that formed
Beneath the eyebrows of these sufferers.
Although, as in a callus, now there was   105
No feeling in my face at all, because
It was so cold, I thought I felt a wind
And said: "My lord, there isn't any sun
To heat the air down here; whence comes this wind?"

And he: "You soon will come to where your eye   110
Will see the source of all the winds that chill
This realm of ice, and you will understand."

Then from the icy crust a soul was heard:
"You evil souls, whose home is now the deep
Of Hell, please break for me these frozen clumps   115
That block my tears, and let me weep to vent,
However briefly, all the agony
That weighs upon my heart until my tears
Congeal once more!"

         "If you would have my help,
Tell me your name; if then I do not loose   120
Your tears, may I be dragged into the depths."

He spoke: "I'm Brother Alberigo, he
Who's famous for the evil fruits. When I
Give figs, I get back dates.

         "You're dead? How can
This be?"

         "I do not know a single thing   125
About my body back on Earth. You see,
This region, Ptolomea, has such power
That often souls come here before they're sent
By Atropos. And let me add, so that
You will more willingly pluck off these tears   130
Of glass, that when a soul like mine has sinned
In treachery, a devil rules the body
And will not leave it till the body dies.
To this cold pit my soul has plummeted.
Perhaps the body of that nearby shade   135
That's wintering in Hell is still on Earth.
You must know who he is, if you've just come:

He's Branca d'Oria. So many years
Have passed since he was shut into the ice!"

"I think you are deceiving me," I said,   140
"For Branca d'Oria's not dead at all.
He eats and drinks, he sleeps and wears
His clothes just like a living man."

         And he:
"In Malebolge, in that ditch where pitch
Is bubbling, Michel Zanche had not yet   145
Arrived when this one left a fiend inside
His earthly form and also in the form
Of one, a relative, who helped commit
A parricide. And now stretch out your hand
And open up my eyes."

         I didn't, though,   150
And took much pleasure in my cruelty.

You men of Genoa, who do not know
What virtue means, who wallow in your vice,
If only God would sweep you from the world!
Down here, besides this guilty friar's soul,   155
I've come upon the shade of Branca d'Oria,
Your kin, a man so vile, his soul's consigned
To frozen Cocytus, while back on Earth
His soulless body breathes as if alive!

NOTES TO CANTO XXXIII

[SUMMARY OF THE CANTO: *The sinner whom Dante had seen gnawing on some-one's head in the last canto now begins to speak. He reveals himself to be Count Ugolino della Gherardesca, and the head he is chewing on is that of the Archbishop Ruggieri degli Ubaldini. Ugolino tells Dante how he and his sons and grandsons died of starvation at the hands of the archbishop. The count's story moves Dante to utter a violent invective against the city of Pisa. Now the poets arrive at the next region of Cocytus, Ptolomea, where they come upon Fra Alberigo, stuck fast in ice, and learn that while his soul is in Inferno, his body, taken over by a demon, is still alive on Earth. Marveling at this phe-nomenon, Dante is moved to lash out with another invective, this time directed at the Genoese.*]

1 UP FROM THAT SAVAGE MEAL THE SINNER RAISED / HIS BLOOD-STAINED MOUTH . . . : This canto is dominated by the figure of Count Ugolino della Gherardesca, whom we first saw at the end of the previous canto gnawing on the head of his enemy, Archbishop Ruggieri degli Ubaldini. A Guelf leader in Pisa, Ugolino conspired with the archbishop to eliminate his own grandson, Nino dei Visconti (see *Purgatorio,* Canto VIII), so as to become sole leader of the Guelf party. The conspiracy was successful; however, Ruggieri then turned on Ugolino and in this double cross threw him, his two sons, and two grandsons into prison. (Ugolino was accused of having given over some castles to Florence and Lucca— see note to line 93 below.) One day, many months later, the prison was nailed shut; eight days later it was opened and all those inside were found dead of starvation. (Ugolino and his kin were imprisoned in 1288 and died early the following year.)

25–27 THE TOWER . . . WILL ENTOMB STILL OTHER PRISONERS: The tower continued to be used as a prison only until 1318, three years before Dante died.

28 . . . SEVERAL MOONS HAD WAXED AND WANED . . . : That is, a few months had passed.

32–33 . . . AND LED A HUNT / FOR WOLF AND WHELPS . . . : The wolf and whelps of the dream are, of course, Ugolino and his children.

36 AND SENT GUALANDI, SISMONDI, LANFRANCHI: The three men were Ghibelline nobles of Pisa and allies of Ruggieri. They appear in the dream as hunters.

42 MY SLEEPING BOYS, WHO'D BEEN LOCKED UP WITH ME: The boys consisted of Ugolino's two younger sons and his two grandsons. None of them was as young as Dante's tale seems to suggest. The youngest, Anselm, was probably fifteen years old.

62 . . . I OBSERVED THE FACES OF MY SONS: As we have seen (note to line 42), two sons and two grandsons of Ugolino were with him in the tower.

84 AND ON THE EIGHTH DAY HUNGER CONQUERED GRIEF: This line has caused considerable comment among critics over the centuries. Does Dante wish to say that Ugolino resorted to cannibalism? If so, would not Ugolino be punished elsewhere, that is, in Circle Seven? Dante does not specifically mention the sin of cannibalism anywhere in the *Inferno*. Most interpreters take the line to mean that hunger, not grief, killed Ugolino.

88–95 AH PISA! . . . YOU MODERN THEBES! . . . : There is a Biblical quality to Dante's invective. Compare the quality of his imprecations with the tone of the prophetic thunderings in, for example, the Biblical books of *Isaiah* and *Jeremiah*. As for Thebes, the ancient Greek city was renowned for the terrible things that had happened there, beginning with the murder by Oedipus of King Laius (his father).

90–91 . . . OH, MAY GORGONA'S ISLE, / CAPRAIA'S, TOO, DAM UP THE ARNO'S MOUTH: At this time, Pisa owned these islands, which are situated at the mouth of the Arno River.

93 THOUGH UGOLINO HAD BETRAYED YOUR TOWN: Ugolino had in fact yielded several castles to the cities of Lucca and Florence, probably to ensure that they would remain neutral in Pisa's war against Genoa. Ugolino was thus guilty of treason to country, which explains his presence in Antenora.

96–97 . . . UGUCCIONE AND BRIGATA BOTH . . . / WERE GUILTLESS . . . : Uguccione was one of Ugolino's sons; Brigata, one of his grandsons (see note to line 62).

98 . . . MY GUIDE AND I WALKED ON . . . : The poets now leave Antenora and enter the region of Ptolomea, probably named after a certain captain named Ptolemy (1 *Maccabees* 16) who invited the high priest, Simon, to a dinner along with Simon's sons and murdered them. In Ptolomea those who sinned against guests are punished.

114–115 YOU EVIL SOULS, WHOSE HOME IS NOW THE DEEP / OF HELL . . . : The sinner believes that Dante and Virgil are also sinners and that they are headed for punishment in Judecca (Dante's spelling is actually "Giudecca"), the lowest spot in Hell.

120–121 . . . IF THEN I DO NOT LOOSE / YOUR TEARS, MAY I BE DRAGGED INTO THE DEPTHS: These lines show a clear intent to deceive on

Dante's part. He knows very well that, in order to escape from Hell, he must travel as far down into it as he can; furthermore, he must be aware that the sinner, believing Dante to be a soul like himself, will interpret Dante's words to mean: "May I be punished in an even deeper part of Hell if I am lying."

122–123   . . . I'M BROTHER ALBERIGO, HE / WHO'S FAMOUS FOR THE EVIL FRUITS . . . : Alberigo, of the city of Faenza, was a Jovial Friar, like Catalano and Loderingo of Canto XXIII. In 1284, during the course of a quarrel with his brother, Manfred, the latter hit him. A year later, Alberigo invited his brother and his brother's son to a dinner and had them killed. "Bring the fruit" was the signal for the killings. Thus, Alberigo's words in this line become clear. From this chilling incident, a proverbial saying arose in Italian: "The evil fruit of Friar Alberigo." There is, furthermore, another Italian saying, "To give back dates for figs," which means to be punished in like manner, and then some, for an evil deed (or to be paid back with interest). Dates, not grown in Italy, were more expensive than figs.

128–129   . . . BEFORE THEY'RE SENT / BY ATROPOS . . . : In Greek mythology, Atropos was one of the three Fates; her job was to sever the thread of life.

138   HE'S BRANCA D'ORIA . . . : He was a Ghibelline from Genoa. Not unlike the crime that Alberigo committed, his own consisted of inviting his father-in-law, Michel Zanche, to a dinner during which Zanche and his friends were killed (hence the allusion to *parricide* in line 148). See Canto XXII, note to line 83.

CANTO XXXIV

" 'The banners of the King of Hell' advance
   Against us; see if you can make him out,"
   My master said.

             It seemed to me I saw
A structure loom ahead that looked just like
A windmill dimly seen from far away,   5
Whose blades are churning in the misty air
Or in the dark when evening starts to shroud
The hemisphere, and since I could not hide
From that sharp wind, I crouched behind my guide.

I now had come (and with what fear I write!)   10
To where the souls are all immersed in ice,
Resembling straws in glass. Some seem to stand,
While some lie supine; some are upside down,
Some right side up; some are doubled over,
Their faces to their feet, like archers' bows.   15

When we had moved so far that Virgil felt
I should be shown the creature, once so fair,
He made me stop: "There's Satan, King of Hell.
And now is when you'll need great strength of soul."

I froze and weakened then, but do not ask   20
Concerning this, oh reader: hard it is
To write of it: all words would prove too poor.
I did not die nor was I quite alive;
Imagine if you can what I, at such
A time, became: unliving yet undead.   25
Stuck in ice to the middle of his chest
He stood, emperor of the world of pain,
And I am closer to a giant's size
Than giants to his arms. Just think how huge
His body is, to correspond to such   30
A part. If once he was as pure as now
He's hideous, and dared to take up arms
Against the Sovereign of the universe,
We well may understand that he's the source
Of every evil in the world.

                             He had   35
Three faces on his head, and much I marveled
At this sight; the face in front was red in hue;
The other two were centered over each
Of Satan's shoulders. All of them were joined
Atop his head. His right face was a shade   40
Of yellow-white; his left one had the tint
Of men who live where Egypt's Nile descends.
Two mighty wings grew out beneath each face,
The size of them befitting such a bird;
No larger sails I ever saw at sea.   45
His batlike wings were plumeless, leathery,
And as they beat, three fierce and icy winds
Blew out to freeze all Cocytus. His six
Eyes wept, besliming triple face and chin
With tears, with pus, with foam of brilliant red.   50
In each of his three mouths he crunched a soul

Between his teeth, like heckles combing flax;
And so he chewed, and still he chews, three souls
Who writhe in pain that cannot end. The soul
In front, I saw, was suffering much more,   55
For all the skin upon his back was clawed
And flayed by Dis.

           My master said to me:
"The soul you see up there who suffers most
Is that of Judas, who betrayed the Lord.
His head's inside the mouth of Lucifer;   60
His feet are dangling from the mouth. Of all
These three, his pain is most intense. The one
That's hanging from the darkest snout is Brutus,
Twisting in silent agony. The last
Of these is Cassius, he of sturdy limb.   65

"But now night's come again, and we must go;
We've seen all that we came to see in Hell."

He made me put my arms around his neck,
Then, waiting until Lucifer's great wings
Were open to their widest point, he grasped   70
The demon's shaggy sides, and, climbing down
From clump of hair to clump, he worked his way
Between the demon and the frozen crusts.
And where the thigh on haunch's thickness turns,
My guide, who panted hard, now bent his head   75
To where his legs had been and turned them up
And grabbed the hair of Lucifer, as if
To climb: was he returning into Hell?
"Hang on!" he cried, exhausted. "By these stairs
We'll free ourselves from Hell's malignity."   80

He crawled out from a fissure in a rock
And made me sit upon the edge of it.
Then he himself came out and walked toward me.
Expecting to see Lucifer as I
Had left him, I looked up, and, puzzled, saw   85
Instead his legs protruding from the ground.
(I'll let the dullards judge what point I'd passed.)
"Up on your feet," my master said. "It's time!
The way from here is long, the road is hard;
And we're already at midmorn."

                     We found   90
Ourselves not in a palace hall but in
A dungeon made by nature, roughly floored
And dimly lit. Then, standing up, I said:
"Before I tear myself from Hell, my lord,
Please speak to me and clarify some things.   95
What happened to the ice? And Lucifer—
How comes it that he's upside down? And tell
Me how the sun can possibly have gone
From night to day so soon?"

                  And he to me:
"You think you're on the center's other side,   100
Where I was clinging to the clumpy hair
Of that vile worm who penetrates the world.
You were indeed, but only to the point
Where I went down, and when I turned around,
You passed the center of all gravity.   105
So now you stand below the hemisphere
That's opposite the one that overspreads
The great dry land of Earth, and underneath
Whose zenith He, immaculately born,
And sinless in His death, was crucified.   110

You stand upon the little sphere that forms
Judecca's underside. Here it is dawn
When there it's night; the beast of Hell whose hair
We used like steps is stuck fast in the ice.
He fell from Heaven on this side. The Earth,   115
Till then protruding here, hid in the sea
And then heaved up to join your hemisphere.
Perhaps then, to escape from him, the land
On this side fled this monstrous hole and leaped
Up high to form the Mount of Purgatory."   120

As far from Beelzebub as his tomb
Extends, a place is found where darkness reigns.
Still, one can hear the stream that runs along
A hollowed rock that by the water's course
And slope has been eroded. Here, my guide   125
Ahead, we walked along a secret road
And thus could find our way back to the world
Illumined by the sun. We did not care
To rest, but climbed and climbed until we saw
An opening, and through it were laid bare   130
Eternal beauties that the Heavens hold.

And walking out, we saw once more the stars.

NOTES TO CANTO XXXIV

[SUMMARY OF THE CANTO: *Dante and Virgil see a huge structure in the distance, which Dante thinks is a windmill. Chilled by a cold blast of wind, he seeks protection behind Virgil. As they approach the large object, Dante realizes that what seemed to be a structure is the body of Satan himself, half-imbedded in the ice. Dante sees the souls of Judas, Brutus, and Cassius, each in one of the three mouths of the Devil. The poets climb on the body of Satan and escape from Hell through the narrow fissure between Satan's body and the ice in which he is stuck fast. Once on the other side, they see Satan's legs dangling upside down, for they are now at the center of Earth. They begin a long climb out of Hell and eventually arrive at the island on which the mountain of Purgatory is situated. With immense relief, they look up at the sky and see the stars of Heaven.*]

1   'THE BANNERS OF THE KING OF HELL' . . . : Virgil quotes the opening line of a noted medieval Latin hymn by one Fortunatus, *"Vexilla Regis prodeunt,"* which means "The banners of the king advance"; but to this first line Dante has Virgil add the Latin word *inferni* ("of Hell"). Virgil's words are therefore intended ironically. The "banners" would be the wings of Satan.

4   A STRUCTURE . . . THAT LOOKED JUST LIKE / A WINDMILL . . . : This structure is, of course, not a windmill, but the body of Satan (Lucifer), as Dante will shortly discover.

18   . . . THERE'S SATAN, KING OF HELL: Dante uses four names to refer to the Devil: Satan, Lucifer, Dis, and Beelzebub. (See Canto III, note to lines 1–9.) Some critics find the character of Satan curiously flat and not particularly exciting when compared to other characters we have encountered in Hell. Perhaps there is some merit to the notion that Satan has been defeated and is therefore shown as utterly bestial, mindless, trapped, prosaic—a creature of matter and not of spirit. An argument can also be made that the last canto of *Inferno* is, after all, not the last canto of the *Commedia,* and that it must be seen, in fact, as a prologue to the remaining two canticles.

31   . . . IF ONCE HE WAS AS PURE AS NOW / HE'S HIDEOUS . . . : Satan was once quite beautiful to look at; he was first among the angels. After his revolt against God, the ugliness of his spirit became manifest on his face and body.

35–36 . . . HE HAD / THREE FACES ON HIS HEAD . . . : Satan's three faces are a perverse and blasphemous parody of the heavenly Trinity composed of God the Father, God the Son, and God the Holy Spirit. The three colors of the faces may symbolize the races of humanity. The faces may also represent such qualities as Hatred, Ignorance, and Impotence, the opposites of the Divine attributes. They may also stand for the political powers that dominated northern Italian affairs in Dante's time: thus, the black face represents Florence; the yellow-white, France; the red, Rome.

43 TWO MIGHTY WINGS GREW OUT BENEATH EACH FACE: Satan has wings because he was once an angel. He has six wings altogether.

50 WITH TEARS, WITH PUS, WITH FOAM OF BRILLIANT RED: These unpleasant dribblings of pus and foam are no doubt coming from the bodies of the sinners whom Satan is chewing.

59 . . . JUDAS, WHO BETRAYED THE LORD: Judas Iscariot was the disciple who betrayed Christ.

63–65 . . . THE ONE . . . IS BRUTUS. . . . THE LAST . . . IS CASSIUS: Brutus, along with Cassius and others, assassinated Julius Caesar on the Ides of March, 44 B.C. Dante, who believed that the Roman Empire was ordained by God to be the universal government that would bring order and peace to the world, saw in the murder of Caesar (regarded as the founder of the empire) a crime whose depravity was rivaled only by Judas's betrayal of Jesus (see note to line 59). (Other than Brutus, Cassius, and Judas, Dante does not name any other sinners in Judecca.) Cassius is described as being of sturdy limb because his skin has been ripped off by Satan and his bare muscles make him look strong.

66 BUT NOW NIGHT'S COME AGAIN . . . : It is approximately six o'clock on Saturday evening.

89 AND WE'RE ALREADY AT MIDMORN . . . : Dante designates the time as "mid-tierce." In the system of counting the hours used by the Catholic Church, this would be about half past seven in the morning. The poets, in leaving Hell, have moved ahead by twelve hours, so that while it was Saturday evening when they left Satan, it is now Sunday morning; in fact, it is Easter Sunday.

106–120 SO NOW YOU STAND . . . TO FORM THE MOUNT OF PURGA- TORY: Virgil explains to Dante that when God expelled Satan from Heaven after the revolt of the rebel angels, the dry land of the Southern Hemisphere rushed away from this terrible fallen creature and went to the Northern Hemisphere. The ocean then poured into the hole left by the land that had fled. The interior of Earth, also wishing to avoid being anywhere near Satan, leaped upward toward the southern part of the globe, there to become an island mountain, on top of which the Earthly Paradise was situated. This mountain was to become the first home of humanity and, later, the Mountain of Purgatory. Dante believed that this was the only piece of land in the entire southern Hemisphere. The empty hole in the Earth became Inferno.

121–122   AS FAR FROM BEELZEBUB AS HIS TOMB / EXTENDS . . . : Beelzebub is one of the four names Dante uses for Satan.

123   . . . ONE CAN HEAR THE STREAM . . . : This is the river Lethe. In the mythology of Greece and Rome, a soul would drink of the water of this stream before entering a human form. In Dante's world, the water of Lethe flows downward from the mountain of Purgatory and washes out the memory of all sin from the souls who have been purged in the Purgatorial process. The memory of sin is then carried to Inferno, the center of all the sins of the world.

132   AND WALKING OUT, WE SAW ONCE MORE THE STARS: It is now, most fittingly, early in the morning of Easter Sunday. Because the poets are in the Southern Hemisphere, it is a different time of day: they are behind Northern Hemispheric time by about twelve hours and therefore it is early morning. Having emerged from the darkness of Hell, the poets, from the surface of Earth, gaze with joy and relief at the stars, a word that is not only the last word of *Inferno* but also of each of the other two canticles of the *Commedia*.

SELECT BIBLIOGRAPHY

[The following is a list of works I consulted during the preparation of this book. Those marked with an asterisk are recommended for readers who are relatively new to Dante studies and who wish to broaden their knowledge of the great Florentine and his works. Of course, other excellent translations of the Commedia and other critical studies of Dante abound; however, I have not listed them here because I did not consult them for this volume. Interested readers may wish to examine, for example, the fine annotated translations by Allen Mandelbaum and Mark Musa.]

Alighieri, Dante. *La Divina Commedia*. Vol. I, *Inferno*. Edited by Enrico Bianchi. Firenze: Casa Editrice Adriano Salani, 1961. An annotated Italian edition with a very helpful Italian prose version on facing pages.

————. *La Divina Commedia. I Inferno*. Edited by Ernesto Bignami. Milano: Edizioni Bignami (no date). The Italian text of *Inferno* plus a running commentary on the poem and very informative notes.

————. *The Divine Comedy of Dante Alighieri*. The Carlyle-Okey-Wicksteed Translation. New York: Random House, 1932. The translation is quite dated, but the notes are sometimes useful. The Genealogical Tables in the Appendix are well done.

*————. *The Divine Comedy*. Translated by John Ciardi. New York: W. W. Norton & Company, 1961. A version of Dante's poem that uses a modified form of *terza rima*. Ciardi takes liberties with the original, offending purists, but his Dante is an exciting read. The notes are admirably concise.

————. *La Divine Comédie*. Translated into French by Alexandre Cioranescu. Lausanne: Editions Rencontre, 1968. A fine French version of the poem. The notes, though minimal, often contain original observations.

*————. *La Divina Commedia*. Edited and annotated by C. H. Grandgent; revised by Charles S. Singleton. Contains the Italian text of the entire poem. The brief Arguments at the beginning of each canto are mini-essays of a high order.

*————, *The Divine Comedy.* Translated by Henry Wadsworth Longfellow. Boston: Houghton Mifflin and Company, 1865. Although Longfellow's verse translation is quite literal, it is accurate. Those qualities make it particularly useful for the English reader who may struggle with the Italian. Unfortunately, this version is also awkward and unrhythmical. Longfellow's notes, sometimes inaccurate, are nevertheless rich: he often quotes at length from historians, biographers, poets, etc.

————. *La Divina Commedia seconda l'antica vulgata,* a cura di Giorgio Petrocchi. 4 vols. Roma: A. Mondadori: 1966–68. The definitive Italian text of Dante's poem.

————. *La Divina Commedia: Vol. I Inferno.* A cura di Natalino Sapegno. Firenze: La Nuova Italia, 1955. Contains the complete text of *Inferno.* Sapegno is one of the leading Italian commentators on Dante.

*————. *The Divine Comedy: 1: Hell.* Translated by Dorothy Sayers. Middlesex: Penguin Books, 1949. An admirable *terza rima* translation that contains a few too many archaisms. The Introduction and notes by this fine Dante scholar are thorough, stimulating, and often entertaining.

*————. *The Divine Comedy: 1: Inferno.* With translation and comment by John Sinclair. New York: Oxford University Press, 1961. The prose translation is accurate, if unexciting. The short essays that follow each canto are superb.

*————. *The Divine Comedy.* Translated, with a Commentary, by Charles S. Singleton. Princeton, N.J.: Princeton University Press, 1977. The prose translation is very precise, but it is the extensive annotations of this six-volume edition that make the book a scholar's delight. It is the best annotated edition in English, by far.

————. *La Divina Commedia.* Edited by Pietro Vetro. Milano: Edizioni A.P.E., 1993. Italian text of the *Inferno* with an Italian prose version on facing pages and excellent notes in Italian.

*Barbi, Michele. *Life of Dante.* Translated by Paul Ruggiers. Berkeley and Los Angeles: University of California Press, 1954. Perhaps the best brief biography of Dante available in any language.

*Bergin, Thomas. *Dante.* New York: Orion Press, 1965. A short but dense "life and times" book by a fine scholar.

*Carroll, John S. *Exiles of Eternity: An Exposition of Dante's Inferno.* Port Washington, N.Y.: Kennikat Press, 1971 (revision of edition of 1904). This excellent volume, the first of three on the *Comedy,* is an extended commentary on each canto of *Inferno.* A very scholarly work, if somewhat dated.

Enciclopedia Dantesca. Edited by Umberto Bosco. 6 vols. Roma: Istituto dell'Enciclopedia italiana, 1970. A superb reference work (completely in Italian); a "must" for serious students of Dante.

Fergusson, Francis. *Dante.* London: Weidenfeld and Nicolson, 1966. Solid, general introduction to Dante's life, works, and times.

Flora, Francesco. *Storia della Letteratura Italiana.* Verona: Arnoldo Mondadori, 1972. An awesome, five-volume history of Italian literature from the beginnings to the twentieth century. The first volume contains several excellent chapters on Dante. (The book cries out for translation into English.)

*Fowlie, Wallace. *A Reading of Dante's Inferno.* Chicago and London: University of Chicago Press, 1981. One of the best general introductions to the *Inferno* available to English readers. There is a chapter on each canto. Fowlie's deep knowledge of modern French literature leads him to make frequent interesting parallels between Dante and French authors.

*Fox, Ruth Mary. *Dante Lights the Way.* Milwaukee: Bruce Publishing Co., 1958. Intended primarily for the novice, this introduction to Dante's thoughts on the idea of love is clearly written and makes him more accessible without resorting to oversimplification.

Freccero, John. *The Poetics of Conversion.* Edited by Rachel Jacoff. Cambridge, Mass.: Harvard University Press, 1986. A very scholarly work for more advanced students by a leading Dante scholar. It consists of a series of essays on various aspects of the *Commedia.*

Giamatti, A. Bartlett. "Italian," in W.K. Wimsatt's *Versification: Major Language Types.* New York: Modern Language Association, 1972. A brief, informative essay on Italian versification.

*Gilbert, Allan. *Dante and His Comedy.* New York: New York University Press, 1963. An excellent analysis of Dante's poem. The chapter entitled "Outline-Analysis of the *Commedia*" provides a concise overview of the poem.

*Grindrod, Muriel. *Italy.* New York: Frederick A. Praeger, 1968. A compact history of Italy. The chapter "From Rome to the Renaissance" offers a concise and very accurate summary of medieval Italian politics, so necessary to an understanding of the *Commedia.* Ms. Grindrod's succinct outline provided a number of details for the Introduction to the present volume.

*Jacoff, Rachel. *The Cambridge Companion to Dante.* Cambridge: Cambridge University Press, 1993. Outstanding essays on Dante by a number of leading Dante scholars, including Giuseppe Mazzotta, John Freccero, and Robert Hollander.

Kirkpatrick, Robin. *Dante's 'Inferno': Difficulty and Dead Poetry.* Cambridge: Cambridge University Press, 1987. Sparkling and original essays on *Inferno.* Intended strictly for the "cognoscenti."

*Quinones, Ricardo J. *Dante Alighieri*. Boston: Twayne Publishers, 1979. A general introduction to Dante's life and work.

Scartazzini, G.A., and Vandelli, Giuseppe. *La Divina Commedia. Testo critico della Società Dantesca Italiana*. Commentary by Scartazzini. 17th edition, revised by Vandelli. Milano: Ulrico Hoepli, 1958. Scartazzini's insights into Dante are often profound. A brilliant historical, philosophical, textual, and linguistic commentary that is just beginning to show its age.

*Toynbee, Paget. *A Dictionary of Proper Names and Notable Matters in the Works of Dante*. Oxford: The Clarendon Press, 1968. No serious Dante student or scholar can do without Toynbee's superbly researched book. Every character and all other proper nouns in the *Commedia* are accurately defined. Though written early in this century, the book has held up wonderfully over the years.

*Vernon, William Warren. *Readings on the Inferno of Dante*. 2 vols. Chiefly based on the commentary of Benvenuto da Imola. London and New York: Macmillan and Co., 1894. It is always interesting to hear what Benvenuto, one of the very early commentators, has to say about the *Commedia*. Here, he comes to us filtered through the mind of Vernon, who also serves the scholar and general reader alike by his meticulous literal translation; unfortunately, it is sometimes inaccurate, for Vernon wrote before the advent of twentieth-century scholarly editions of the *Commedia*.

Villani, Giovanni. *Cronica*, edited by F. Gherardi-Dragomanni, 7 vols. Firenze: S. Coen, 1844–47. The classic history of Florence, written by a contemporary of Dante's.

LIST OF PAINTINGS

Frontispiece. *Evangelist*, 1995. Oil, pencil, and Xerox transfer on board, 11" x 13¾". Copyright © Forum Gallery, New York. Courtesy of Forum Gallery, New York. Photograph by Stephen Petegorsky.

Page 2. *Small Mandala I*, 1996. Oil on paper, 12½" in diameter. Copyright © Forum Gallery, New York. Courtesy of Forum Gallery, New York. Photograph by Stephen Petegorsky.

Page 20. *Landscape*, 1967. Oil on panel, 15½" x 17½". Private collection. Copyright © Forum Gallery, New York. Courtesy of Forum Gallery, New York. Photograph by eeva-inkeri.

Page 38. *Piazza at Night*, 1963–1964. Oil on panel, 11" x 10". Evansville Museum of Arts and Science, Indiana. Bequest of William A. Gumberts, 1984.30.107. Copyright © Forum Gallery, New York. Courtesy of Forum Gallery, New York. Photograph by Walter Rosenblum.

Page 46. *Bathers in a Landscape*, 1962. Oil on wood, 8¼" x 9⅜". Hirshhorn Museum and Sculpture Garden, Smithsonian Institution, Washington, D.C. Copyright © Forum Gallery, New York. Courtesy of Forum Gallery, New York.

Page 56. *Young Lady and Her Demon*, 1988. Oil and alkyd on panel, 17¼" x 14¼". Private collection. Copyright © Forum Gallery, New York. Courtesy of Forum Gallery, New York.

Page 96. *Allegorical Street Scene*, 1961–1962, repainted in 1963. Oil on paper mounted on wood, 7¾" x 9¼". Hirshhorn Museum and Sculpture Garden, Smithsonian Institution, Washington, D.C. Copyright © Forum Gallery, New York. Courtesy of Forum Gallery, New York. Photograph by Geoffrey Clements.

Page 106. *Hermaphrodite*, 1964. Oil on wood 18" x 24". Private collection. Copyright © Forum Gallery, New York. Courtesy of Forum Gallery, New York.

Page 114. *Assassination of the Lion*, 1994. Pencil, oil, and acrylic on board, 16" x 12½". Copyright © Forum Gallery, New York. Courtesy of Forum Gallery, New York. Photograph by Stephen Petegorsky.

Page 124. *Large Room at Greystone State*, 1995. Oil, pencil, and Xerox transfer on board, 33½" x 31". Copyright © Forum Gallery, New York. Courtesy of Forum Gallery, New York. Photograph by Stephen Petegorsky.

Page 148. *Street in Rome,* 1965. Oil and magazine photographs on wood, 9½" x 7". Collection of Mr. and Mrs. John Wasserman. Copyright © Forum Gallery, New York. Courtesy of Forum Gallery, New York. Photograph by Smithsonian Institution Photographic Services.

Page 164. *Pear and Demons,* 1987–1988. Oil on board, 41" x 27". Copyright © Forum Gallery, New York. Courtesy of Forum Gallery, New York.

Page 172. *Santa Fe Shrine,* 1987–1988. Oil, mixed media on two wood panels, 99" x 96". Collection of Estabrook Foundation. Copyright © Forum Gallery, New York. Courtesy of Forum Gallery, New York.

Page 248. *The Queen,* 1993. Oil on board, 96" x 48". Collection of Janice and Mickey Cartin. Copyright © Forum Gallery, New York. Courtesy of Forum Gallery, New York. Photograph by Stephen Petegorsky.

Page 256. *Manger Scene,* 1987. Oil on board, 20" x 14". Copyright © Forum Gallery, New York. Courtesy of Forum Gallery, New York. Photograph by Stephen Petegorsky.

ABOUT THE TRANSLATOR

Elio Zappulla is the author of several scholarly articles on Dante and Italian literature. He teaches at Dowling College and lives in Stony Brook, New York.